THE PRESIDENT'S HENCHMAN

JOSEPH FLYNN

VARIANCE
ARKANSAS

Library of Congress Control Number: 2008941633

ISBN: 1-935142-02-X
ISBN-13: 978-1-935142-02-7

Cover illustration and design by Jeremy Robinson
Interior design by Stanley Tremblay

Published by Variance LLC (USA).

10 9 8 7 6 5 4 3 2 1

www.variancepublishing.com

Printed in the USA

Visit Joseph Flynn at www.josephflynn.com

For Dad, who introduced me to storytelling,
and in memory of Mom, who taught me all about character.

ACKNOWLEDGEMENTS

My thanks to my wife, Catherine, who is always the first editor of everything I write; to Ellen and Steve Feazell for being gracious hosts while I did research in Washington, DC; to Lissy Peace for bringing the book to the attention of Variance Publishing; to Tim Schulte and Jeremy Robinson for including my book in the growth of their new company; to Bob and Sarah Schwager for their keen and insightful editing and copyediting; to Trish Stevens for her energetic, on-point promotion; and to Stanley Tremblay for his elegant book design.

THE PRESIDENT'S HENCHMAN

CHAPTER 1

WHEN MCGILL was formally introduced to the White House press corps, Helen Thomas asked him how it felt to be the country's first First Gentleman.

He responded, "I prefer to think of myself as the president's henchman."

The line got a good laugh from the newsies; even Press Secretary Aggie Wu grinned. But Chief of Staff Galia Mindel reacted to the remark with a mighty frown. McGill saw the look of disapproval but didn't worry. He didn't work for her.

Just wait until Galia learned he'd gotten his P.I. license.

And his concealed weapons permit.

She'd be about as thrilled as the Secret Service had been. They'd changed his code name from Valentine to Holmes, which McGill had laughed at, and, on the whole, considered an improvement.

Galia wasn't likely to crack wise, though. She'd try to fight him. And lose.

McGill's career choice came with a presidential stamp of approval.

"What exactly does the president's henchman do?" Candy Crowley inquired.

"Things nobody else can," McGill told her with a twinkle in his eye.

Galia didn't like that answer either.

JAMES JACKSON McGill became a minor historical figure when his wife, Congresswoman Patricia Darden Grant (R-IL), became a major historical figure by becoming the first woman to be elected president of the United States. McGill had worked as the de facto head of security for Patti's presidential campaign. Before that, he'd been a Chicago cop for twenty years, and the chief of police for five years in the posh North Shore suburb of Winnetka, Illinois.

It was in this latter capacity that McGill met the future president. He solved the murder of her first husband, philanthropist Andrew Hudson Grant. Cracked the case in twelve hours, which was why the president-elect couldn't argue with McGill when he told her the week before her inauguration that he was going to have to find something to do while she was busy running the country. He wasn't ready to go fishing or spend all his time cutting ribbons.

"You still want to be a cop, don't you?" Patti asked.

"Yeah."

"But I know you don't like any of the federal agencies. So, you don't want me to appoint you to run, say, the FBI."

"No."

"Do you want to stay in Illinois? Have a commuter relationship?"

McGill shook his head. Firmly.

"So what does that leave?"

"Private license," he said.

Patricia Darden Grant was a very smart woman. She processed information like a supercomputer. But that one stopped her cold—long enough to make her laugh, anyway.

"You … you want to be the private eye who lives in the White House?"

McGill said, "Why not? You're the only one who gets to break tradition?"

What could she say to that? Only: "You'll be careful, Jim?"

"Sure," McGill said. "Won't do a thing to embarrass you."

"I wasn't talking about politics. I can always get another job. But I don't want to bury another husband."

McGill kissed the most powerful woman in the world, loving her more than ever, and did his best to reassure her he would be around for a long, long time.

MCGILL ABSOLUTELY refused to have more than one Secret Service agent assigned to guard him. The head of the White House Security Detail was an unsmiling humanoid named Celsus Crogher. Although Crogher was only in his late forties, his gray hair was turning white. His eyes were the color of silicon; his skin was slate. It was as if all pigment had been pruned from his family tree. Crogher wanted McGill's protection closer to platoon strength. The president brokered a compromise: McGill would have one Secret Service bodyguard and an armed driver from the White House Transportation Agency.

McGill interviewed several men and women for each position; and in the end, he picked Secret Service Special Agent Donald "Deke" Ky. The son of a Eurasian Vietnamese American mother and an African American GI father, Deke had tightly waved black hair, blue eyes behind epicanthic folds and skin the color of a new penny. Leo Levy was a self-described good ol' Jewish boy from North Carolina. Long and lanky, with a face out of the Levant and an accent out of Andy Griffith, he'd driven the NASCAR circuit before getting into government work.

Both men had exemplary records, and each took a solemn pledge never to rat out McGill for anything he said or did. Celsus Crogher and Galia Mindel were not to be privy to any of the doings of McGill Investigations, Inc. Beyond that, Deke and Leo were to let McGill know if they detected any government busybodies snooping on him.

STARTING IN February, just after Patti's inauguration, McGill walked all over Washington, D.C., like a rookie cop learning his new beat. Before meeting Patti, he'd visited the city only once, as part of an American Studies course at Saint Ignatius College Prep. Deke Ky walked between McGill and the street. Leo Levy idled along in a supercharged and armored black Chevy sedan a half block behind.

As often as not, McGill went unnoticed. When people did recognize him, they usually just smiled and called out hello. The exceptions were the elderly and the kids. Both groups wanted to talk with him, not infrequently from a distance of a few inches.

The kids' questions were easy to answer.

Did he think the president was pretty? Gorgeous.

What sports teams did he like? The DePaul Blue Demons.

Had Michael Jordan played better in Chicago or Washington? Chicago.

Was he going to be president, too, someday? No. One president per family was enough.

The elderly had more serious matters in mind: war and peace, the economy, the environment, crime, immigration. Almost without exception they would rest a hand lightly on his arm as they spoke.

When an opinion was called for, McGill did not bob and weave. His answers were sincere and plainspoken, but he did preface whatever he had to say with: "Please understand, this is just my opinion, and I'd appreciate it if it stays between us."

Nobody went running to the newspapers with McGill's words of wisdom.

Quite often, the old folks also asked for his help. With Social Security. Medicare. The Veterans Administration. At first, McGill didn't know how to help. So he took people's names and phone numbers and promised to get back to them. Soon, though, Deke carried with him a BlackBerry that stored the names and direct phone numbers of every top administrator in the federal and district governments. McGill passed them along to those in need of assistance.

And added, "Tell them Mr. McGill said you should call."

Hoping he had the clout people imagined he did.

It turned out he did, and that was how his walking tours became news. Someone let it be known how helpful he'd been. Soon it became impossible for him to go out without a media horde at his heels and a throng of supplicants in front of him. No good deed went unpunished.

He had to start traveling in the back of Leo's Chevy.

BY THE time the cherry blossoms appeared, he knew his way around town, at least a little. And he found office space to rent on P Street just above the Rock Creek Parkway. The building was a rehabbed three-story ivory-brick structure. It housed a commercial recording studio, A-Sharp Sound, on the first floor, and a small accounting firm, Wentworth and Willoughby, on the second. W&W actually moved down one floor to accommodate McGill Investigations, Inc. The Secret Service explained that in the event of an emergency Mr. McGill might have to be evacuated from the roof of the building by helicopter.

McGill apologized to the other tenants for all the bother he'd caused—which included the feds investigating every employee of both existing businesses back to infancy to see if he or she might be a threat to McGill's life—and compensated his new neighbors with tickets to a Redskins game or a Kennedy Center performance, per their preference.

ON THE morning in May when McGill arrived for his first day of work, there was a line down the hall. By ten o'clock, the queue ran down the staircase to the ground floor and out the front entrance. The building's owner, an astute Armenian immigrant named Dikran Missirian, quickly rented several café tables complete with Cinzano umbrellas. He provided complimentary sparkling mineral water and gourmet coffee to the waiting crowd.

Business cards were exchanged all around.

Dikki made several valuable business contacts that day.

McGill netted not a single client.

Without exception, the ladies and gentlemen waiting to see him were lobbyists. Sugar, sorghum, and sweet corn were among the foodstuffs they represented. Trucks, trains, and planes were just a few of their preferred modes of transportation. Albania, Algeria, and Angola were but the beginning of the countries whose interests they advanced.

None of them had a criminal matter or even a straying spouse to investigate.

All of them offered retainers, six to seven figures per annum, in the event they might someday need professional investigative services. McGill politely listened to each of them and respectfully turned down all of them.

He explained that he worked cases. Couldn't take money on the mere possibility that something might come up.

Didn't say he'd never sell access to his wife, the president, but everybody seemed to understand. Most of them were gracious about being rejected. They'd given it the old college try and were happy just to meet him and shake his hand.

A couple of type-A personalities, however, wouldn't take no for an answer, until Deke Ky quickly put a whispered word into their ears. Both hard chargers abruptly turned pale and left the office on wobbly legs.

McGill appreciated Deke's concern but didn't feel that prospective clients, no matter how rude, should be threatened with either lengthy in-carceration or swift death. He needed someone to run interference for him—someone who could discourage the jerks with nothing more than a hard stare. So he got on the phone to Chicago.

"Sweetie? It's Jim. If you're not busy, I've got a job for you."

MARGARET "SWEETIE" Sweeney had been McGill's strong right arm on the force in both Chicago and Winnetka. She'd even taken a bullet that rightfully should have been McGill's. A rich suburban punk had kidnapped his ex-girlfriend and locked the two of them in his bedroom. Things got to the point where murder-suicide looked imminent. McGill's plan had been to break down the door on the count of three. Sweetie went on two.

"So I'm gonna be what around here?" Sweetie asked when she arrived the day after McGill called. "The office manager, the dragon lady, the anchor on your more outlandish impulses?"

"My partner," McGill said. "The bad cop to my good cop. Same as al-ways."

Sweetie noticed Deke looking at her. She knew right away McGill had told him about her. Now, the Secret Service hero was wondering: Could *he* really take a bullet for someone?

"Only one way to find out," Sweetie answered the unspoken question.

Deke pretended he didn't know what she was talking about.

"Patti says to come by for dinner tonight," McGill told her.

The president had a special place in her heart for Sweetie after learning what she'd done to spare McGill. And, of course, the grief Sweetie had later saved her from personally.

Sweetie smiled, and McGill thought, as he always did, that she looked like St. Michael the Archangel … or a Valkyrie, if you preferred Norse my-thology.

"Yeah, I'd like to see her, too," Sweetie said. "Did she get my birthday card?"

"Made her day," McGill answered truthfully.

The card had been addressed to Mrs. James J. McGill, 1600 Pennsylva-nia Avenue.

CHAPTER 2

MONDAY

FOR THE next four weeks, with Sweetie stationed in the outer office like a desk sergeant, not a single lobbyist pestered McGill. Neither did anyone else. Word had gotten around official Washington: The president's henchman was not a back door to the Oval Office. And the Metro Police seemed to have a mortal lock on all local criminal investigations.

It was beginning to look like McGill would have plenty of time for ribbon cuttings. Galia Mindel had sent him a request to provide a recipe for his favorite dish—to be included in a new edition of *The First Ladies' Cookbook.*

Things were so slow that first Monday in June that Deke and Sweetie, who'd received her own concealed weapons permit, had gone to a firing range at lunchtime to shoot it out for the office deadeye championship. Leo, parked out front, had been left to hold down the fort.

Apparently, Leo let Chana Lochlan slip past him. More likely, he decided she wasn't a threat and got her autograph.

McGill was eating a turkey sandwich at his desk and reading the *Chicago Tribune's* sports section online when "the most fabulous face on television," as judged by *People* magazine, knocked on his open door. "Mr. McGill, may I come in?"

The first thing that struck McGill was her size. With only moderate heels on her shoes, she had to be six feet tall. She was whipcord lean and even in her business suit gave the impression she was ready to compete in a triathlon. Then there was that fabulous face—a proud nose, a generous mouth, a defiant chin, and shoulder-length black hair framing big hazel eyes.

McGill swallowed the food he'd been chewing and gestured her to a guest chair. He knew who she was, of course. He'd even glimpsed her in person a time or two. Chana Lochlan was the White House reporter for the World Wide News (W²N) cable network. Her job was to cover McGill's wife. In an honest and forthright way, if you believed in ad slogans.

To stick a knife in at every opportunity, as McGill saw it.

"Would you mind if we closed the door?" Ms. Lochlan asked.

McGill studied her as though she were a painting. It was a pretty darn nice face. All the more so for the first few faint lines that TV makeup usually covered. Still, it wasn't quite in Patti's league. But then the president had prepared for a career in politics by working as a model and acting in Hollywood movies. That and graduating from Yale with honors, building houses with Jimmy Carter and Habitat for Humanity, and doing innumerable other hands-on good works.

Chana Lochlan probably had a long list of virtuous deeds on her résumé, too, but McGill knew that wasn't what people would talk about if they learned she'd been in his office with the door closed.

"We're the only ones here, Ms. Lochlan. No need to close the door. If you've come to ask about an interview, there's someone at the White House who handles those requests for me ... I think."

"I didn't come for an interview."

McGill blinked. Chana Lochlan was going to be his first client?

"You know, it's true what they say about you," she said.

"What's that?"

"You do look a little like Harrison Ford before he went gray."

"I used to say more like Rory Calhoun, but nobody seems to remember him anymore. Ms. Lochlan, are you here to talk about hiring me as an investigator?"

She looked over her shoulder at the entrance to the office suite.

McGill glanced at the time on his computer monitor. "We'll have fifteen minutes to ourselves if you have something to say."

"You're not going to close the door?"

McGill shook his head.

"You're a very careful man."

McGill waited. She'd talk or she'd leave.

"A question or two first," she said. "Does what I tell you stay with you? Or does it reach the president? I cover her, as I'm sure you know. I ask her hard questions. Maybe you even think some of them are politically motivated."

McGill kept himself from nodding.

"But doing my job would be very difficult if the president knew what I had to tell you."

McGill hadn't considered the question before, but he thought it fair.

He said, "The president and I don't keep secrets from one another—about our personal lives. But she doesn't tell me if she's going to have the Marines seize Lichtenstein. So it seems reasonable I should keep the details of my investigations from her."

"Then I can expect confidentiality?"

"Yes." A thought occurred to McGill. "I might, however, consult with my colleague in the firm." *Might.* As if Sweetie would stand for his keeping secrets. "She'd be bound by the same obligation to confidentiality I would."

That was agreeable to Chana Lochlan, though she took one more look over her shoulder.

"Two days ago, at my home in Georgetown, I was awakened by a phone call at 4:00 A.M. I picked up the phone and mumbled hello. The caller was a man. His voice sounded white, educated, Midwestern American. At a guess, he was thirty to fifty. He began by asking me a question. He said, 'Do you remember the last time we made love?'"

McGill picked up a pen, opened a notepad. "Is your home phone number unlisted?"

Chana nodded.

"Is it on your business card?"

She shook her head.

"Have you ever given it to a source?"

"I made that mistake once, early in my career. But that was in New York."

"And this man didn't sound like that one?"

"Not at all. If I hadn't been uncertain I'd heard the question right, I'd have hung up before the caller could go on. As it was, I heard him say, 'Come on, Gracie, you remember.'"

McGill understood the significance of the remark.

"Chana is a Hebrew name meaning graceful. Graceful. Gracie."

The newswoman raised her perfect eyebrows.

"My first wife and I have two daughters and a son," McGill said.

"I know. I read your bio before coming here. But your girls are named Abigail and Caitlin. Your son is named Kenneth."

"Abigail is also a Hebrew name. Meaning: gives joy. When Carolyn was pregnant with Abbie, we bought the best naming book we could find. Three kids later, names and their meanings got to be a hobby of mine. Anyway, your caller knew a nickname of yours. A private one?"

"Only my dad and my ex used it. I can't remember anyone else calling me that."

Some questions could be asked and answered without a word being spoken. Had the caller been her father? Chana Lochlan's look said don't even think about it.

"And it wasn't your former husband on the phone?" McGill inquired.

She shook her head. "Michael died on his honeymoon with his second wife. Hang gliding in Hawaii."

"So some unknown male knows your unlisted phone number, calls you at home, also knows a private nickname, and intimates he was once your lover."

"Intimates authoritatively," Chana said. She took yet another look over her shoulder. They were still alone, but when she resumed speaking, her voice dropped to a whisper. "He took me through a reminiscence of love-making. He knows what I like. Knows in such detail that mere guesswork can be ruled out. He also knows ..."

She stopped to look at the notes McGill was making. He tried to alleviate her discomfort. "Tell me only what you need to. If I have questions ... I'll try to be delicate."

Chana Lochlan steeled herself and continued. "He knows my body: moles, freckles, birthmarks. Things I need two mirrors to see."

"Did you get the feeling he was working himself up?"

"No. His voice was very gentle. Loving, even. When he finished, he made this little kissing sound and told me to go back to sleep. Amazingly enough, I did … and I dreamed of the lovemaking he'd just described. I could see his body but not his face."

McGill thought in silence for a moment. He looked at Chana Lochlan's eyes. Fear made flecks of yellow burn bright in the hazel irises.

"You think he's coming for you, whoever he is," McGill said.

"Yes, I do."

"I do investigative work not protection."

"And I work in the public eye, Mr. McGill. The minute I hire a body-guard, *I* become a story, and that's not what I want. I hope you can find this man and stop him from doing …"

"Whatever he has in mind."

"Yes."

McGill took the case. Chana Lochlan was gone before Sweetie and Deke came back. It was only when Sweetie asked if he'd had any calls while they were out that McGill remembered he was now a businessman and no longer a cop. He'd completely forgotten to discuss money with his first client.

Somehow, it had slipped her mind, too.

CHAPTER 3

TUESDAY

THE PRESIDENT'S day began at 4:30 A.M. She leaned over and kissed McGill, who enjoyed the privilege of sleeping in till six o'clock. Her husband also enjoyed his morning kiss, not simply lying there and accepting it but putting his arms around her and kissing back. Sometimes, when McGill held on, and the affairs of state allowed, the president didn't get out of bed until 4:45.

Patti Grant was used to getting up at hours most people would consider ungodly. She'd done it as both a model and an actress. Rising for sunrise shoots on tropical beaches. Appearing on sets for early calls. Even when she'd been married to Andy Grant and could have slept as late as she liked, she was unable to linger in bed. If the weather was fair, she loved to watch the sun rise out of Lake Michigan. If things were gloomy outside, she'd get up early anyway, relishing the feeling that she was getting a jump on everyone else.

Not a bad attitude for a woman in her position to have.

McGill was asleep again by the time she stepped into her bathroom. She examined herself nude in a full-length mirror. The presidency was yet another of her jobs where appearance mattered. Her dark brown hair had yet to show any gray, but it was no longer shoulder length. It had been cut to a bob, short enough to require minimal care, not so short that anyone could accuse her of trying to appear mannish.

Now there was an idea that would make McGill laugh.

She was still slender and well toned, but she was twenty pounds heavier than when she'd made her living appearing before cameras. Back then she thought she'd looked like a pencil with an expensive hairdo. She figured she could add another ten to fifteen pounds over a two-term presidency and still look good.

When she finally left the public eye, she could imagine letting her hair grow long as it turned white. She'd cherish her smile lines and crow's-feet. And she'd kiss her husband's bald spot if he had the grace to have one by then. Life would be good.

She was looking forward to growing old with McGill.

She pulled on a tank-style swimsuit and a terry cloth robe and walked barefoot to the White House swimming pool. She swam laps for twenty minutes, doing neat kick turns, maintaining an aerobic pace, not going so fast she couldn't review the events of the previous day.

Next came twenty minutes of strength training: dumbbells and exercise machines. During her workout, she listened to intelligence briefings from the CIA and FBI through the ear buds of her iPod. The highlights provided by the spooks and G-men were supplemented by briefing books if she thought any item demanded her in-depth attention.

Finally, she did twenty minutes of tai chi to align her energy along the proper paths and give herself flexibility and peace of mind. This was the time when she often had insights about how to address the dangers that the government's watchdogs had alerted her to moments earlier.

For political problems, she had her own shrewd instincts.

And Galia Mindel.

GALIA WAS fifty-six years old. As the president had been, she was a widow. Unlike the president, her husband had been taken by illness not murder. A New Yorker to her roots, Galia had a PhD from Columbia in Modern Political Thought. She was handsome in the fashion of a headmistress at a no-nonsense girls' school. Only five-foot-four, she wore her hennaed hair up and her heels high to give an impression of height. Her girth was all her own. Image-conscious, she worked hard to keep her weight in check; the struggle was ongoing and intense.

Galia looked up from a note she was making on the pad resting on her lap. Her eyes were drawn to the picture of McGill that sat in a silver frame on the president's credenza in the Oval Office. Rory Calhoun, she thought. McGill was right about that. She was old enough to remember the actor. Handsome, smiling, manly ... nothing but trouble when reincarnated as James J. McGill.

The president's henchman, indeed. That was *her* job.

"Galia," the president said, addressing her a second time.

The chief of staff snapped to. "Yes, Madam President."

"The note I received from you at breakfast asked if I could be at my desk ten minutes early." The president gestured: Here I am.

Galia wondered if McGill had informed the president that he'd acquired his first client. Or who that client was. To the president, she said, "You'll remember, ma'am, we agreed that you, more than any previous president, could expect a series of challenges early in your administration."

"I remember," the president said evenly. "And now one has come up?"

"It has."

"Foreign or domestic?"

"Domestic. The Pentagon."

The president waited for the other shoe to drop.

"The Pentagon," Galia repeated, "and Senator Michaelson."

THE ELECTION of Patricia Darden Grant to the presidency had done more than end over two hundred years of the exclusively male hold on the office; it had caused a tectonic shift in American politics. The new president was a Republican, but a *moderate* Republican. Some went so far as to say a RINO. Republican in name only.

She was fiscally conservative, but socially ... hard to pin down.

She believed that the Second Amendment provided for the right to bear arms, but not the right to bear arms *secretly*. As she saw it, the government had a legitimate interest in seeing to it that all firearms were registered, their owners were identified, and a federal database of the distinct markings each weapon left on its projectiles was established.

She believed that every American came with a full menu of legal rights, irrespective of sexual orientation. Gays and lesbians, she said, should be allowed to serve openly in the military. *However,* every American also had the right to be free from unwanted sexual attention. So gays and lesbians would have to serve in capacities that didn't require them to live in communal settings.

She believed in reproductive choice, but insisted that in the absence of a medical emergency or other extraordinary circumstance, a woman who carried a pregnancy past the first trimester had *made* her choice and no termination past that point should be allowed.

The conventional wisdom had it that such political heterodoxy should have made it impossible for Patti Grant to win the Republican primaries in which conservative activists were said to hold all the cards. But then the conventional wisdom also held that a woman never could win because a woman never had won.

Patti trumped the traditional thinkers on three counts.

The first was an outpouring of sympathy and admiration for her. Her first husband, Andy Grant, had been killed by radical antiabortionists who had tried to coerce Patti into voting their way on the Support of Motherhood Act, a piece of legislation that would have provided government-paid medical care and a guaranteed adoption for the children of those victims of rape and incest who chose to carry their pregnancies to term.

Patti's position was that any woman who'd suffered a trauma as horrifying and invasive as rape or incest should not be pressured by anybody, especially not the government, to perpetuate her pain for nine months. Beyond that, the adoption guarantor noted in the bill was the Salvation's Path Church of Richmond, Virginia. The separation of church and state would have to be thrown out the window for the bill to stand.

Even so, Congresswoman Grant suggested that the Salvation's Path Church and other like-minded organizations had conceived a worthwhile alternative to abortion, *if* it was offered privately and in a spirit of compassion to those victims of crime who would find it a comfort rather than a second assault.

That wasn't nearly good enough for the forces pushing the bill. They *wanted* the Support of Motherhood Act to be challenged. Given the cast of characters sitting on the Supreme Court, they thought they could persuade or bully five votes for their side. Demolishing the separation between church and state was *exactly* what they had in mind. Then they could really start in on making their agenda the law of the land.

And they identified Congresswoman Patricia Darden Grant as the linch-pin vote they had to have. A Republican, but a moderate, she'd worked closely with legislators on both sides of the aisle in the House and in the Senate. A politician and a former movie star, who'd never known scandal in either Washington or Hollywood, the two great cesspools of American public life, she was both well-known and widely admired. Put her pretty face at the front of a crowd supporting the bill, and it couldn't lose.

Only Patti wouldn't play ball. So Andy got a threatening message. *Get your wife to vote the right way. Do it, or she'll know what it's like to see the taking of an innocent life.* And in the end that was just what happened.

But Patti hadn't given in, and McGill had caught Andy's killers.

AS A profile in courage, nobody else in the Republican primary field came close. Voters who might have had questions on the issues gave Patti the benefit of the doubt because of her strength of character.

Then there was the strength of her presentation. In the primary debates, she was just plain smarter than anyone else on the stage, and it showed. A trained actor, she delivered her lines with an eloquence, a sense of timing, and a range of emotions that left the other candidates looking like cardboard cutouts.

Finally, a large part of the electorate, male and female, simply fell in love with Patti. It wasn't the kind of thing most voters would ever admit to pollsters, but it warmed their hearts to cast a ballot for her. Here and there, however, an occasional woman would confess that it was wonderfully romantic that the congresswoman had married McGill. You looked at that, they said, and you could believe that good could still triumph over evil.

In the general election, Patti and her running mate, Governor Mather Wyman of Ohio, were the all-but-unanimous choice of Republican voters; the conservatives had nowhere else to go if they hoped to have any influence. She carried independents four to one. Even a third of the Democratic vote went her way.

Given a mandate, she promised to govern from the center and work in a bipartisan fashion whenever possible. Which, of course, pissed off the left and the right no end. Both extremes claimed that the new president would blur party identities.

What really scared them, of course, was that she would start her own centrist party. Make it the first new major political party since the early nineteenth century, leaving them at the margins, consigned to purgatory if not hell.

So the new president, while hugely popular, was not without her share of enemies.

Or challenges.

Like the one from the Pentagon that Galia was telling her about.

"HER NAME is Carina Linberg," Galia informed the president. "She's a colonel in the Air Force. Works in military intelligence at the Pentagon. Until yesterday, it looked like she'd be the youngest woman in that branch of the service ever to become a general."

Patti knew a cue when she heard one. "And now?"

"Now she's being investigated to see if she should be brought before a court-martial." Galia gave it a beat. She had a sense of timing, too. "For adultery."

That stirred the president's memory. "Wasn't there another case like this some years back? Another woman in the Air Force. A bomber pilot, I think."

Galia nodded. As usual, she had the facts at her fingertips. "Lieutenant Allison Neely. In that case, however, Lieutenant Neely had two lovers. One was a married civilian employee of the Air Force and the other was an Air Force enlisted man. Lieutenant Neely was ordered by her base commander to stop seeing both men. She didn't. So the charges against her also included refusal to obey an order and fraternization with enlisted personnel."

The president nodded. "Now, I remember. It was those charges the military said were most important. Lieutenant Neely's conduct was detrimental to the good order and discipline of the service ... and at the time I agreed with them."

"Much to the displeasure of NOW and other feminists," Galia reminded her.

The president shrugged. Any political decision was bound to anger someone.

"So how is this case different?" she asked.

"Colonel Linberg was sleeping with a Navy man. Captain Dexter Cowan. Her naval counterpart in military intelligence. She claims he told her he was divorced. He says he told her he was separated from his wife, but that he and Mrs. Cowan were talking about a possible reconciliation. Both sides agree that Captain Cowan didn't wear a wedding ring to work."

"So there are no other charges against Colonel Linberg? The military can't say the adultery is incidental to more serious infractions?"

"No, Madam President. Adultery is the sole charge."

"How often does that happen?"

Galia flipped a page in her notebook. "There were sixty-six cases in the Air Force last year that included adultery charges. Sixty-five of them also included other serious charges."

The president sat back in her chair. "The exception was another woman? "A man."

"Even so. It looks like this is a handy charge to trot out when you want to ruin someone's career."

"Including yours," Galia said, closing her notebook.

"Hence the mention of Roger Michaelson."

"Exactly. The junior senator from Oregon has an abiding hatred for you."

Patti Grant wasn't about to argue that point.

Galia continued, "There is absolutely no reason why the Air Force couldn't resolve the Colonel Linberg matter administratively; that would be the most common way to dispose of it. If it wasn't dropped entirely as an un-provable he-said, she-said case."

The president's mind leaped ahead. "If I side with Colonel Linberg, the Pentagon will think I'm a meddling woman who never wore a uniform. Someone not fit to be commander in chief."

"And your loose Hollywood morals will finally be revealed."

"But if I side with the military, I'll be fair game for millions of women, and not just movement feminists. I'll be destroying the career of a talented woman for an offense that's based on one man's word. An offense that would never even be prosecuted in a civilian court."

"Yes, but if a court-martial finds Colonel Linberg guilty of adultery, she could end up serving prison time at Fort Leavenworth."

"Either way, my administration could be crippled at the outset." The president nodded to herself. "You're right, Galia. This is worthy of Roger

Michaelson. Is there any proof he's actually involved?"

"Other than his seat on the Senate Armed Services Committee? Not yet."

"And who do you have waiting outside to see me?" The president wasn't just making a good guess; she knew Galia Mindel.

"The Air Force chief of staff, General Altman."

"Fine, I'll have a cup of coffee with him. But who will do the actual investigation on this case?"

Galia bit her lip. "That would be someone from the Air Force's Office of Special Investigations."

"Find out who that someone is," the president instructed. "Have his service record on my desk in an hour; have him ready to see me in ninety minutes."

LIEUTENANT WELBORN Yates was twenty-four years old. He had blonde hair, blue eyes, and pink cheeks. A trim five-ten with good shoulders, he could have been a poster boy for the Air Force, not one of its criminal investigators. His arrival at the Oval Office was punctual to the second. Saluting and standing at attention, he looked so young to the president she felt she must already be wizened and white-haired. It took Galia's clearing her throat to bring Patti out of her reverie.

"At ease, Lieutenant," the president said. "Please take a seat."

"Yes, ma'am," he said with a soft South Carolina drawl.

Lieutenant Yates took the chair next to Galia. Once he was released from his rigid posture, Patti could see how nervous he was. A muscle twitched in a pink cheek. Looking at her only made him more tense. His eyes darted around the room. Then they fastened on McGill's picture, Patti saw. Something about it seemed to tell him everything was okay.

Jim's shit-eating grin, she thought.

Or maybe that she would have such a photo in the Oval Office.

Patti read from Lieutenant Yates's personnel folder. "You trained to be a fighter pilot."

Turning back to her, he said, "Yes, ma'am."

She closed the folder and looked at the young man not as his ultimate superior but as one human being to another. "I'm very sorry for the losses you suffered, Lieutenant. Your friends' deaths and your chance to fly."

"Thank you, ma'am."

"Are you still receiving psychological counseling?"

Welborn blinked, but didn't look away. "Only at such times as I feel the need, ma'am … Not so often anymore." He looked as if that was all he had to say, but then he added, "Mostly, these days, I find comfort in talking with my mother."

"She's a good woman, your mother?"

"The best, ma'am." Welborn then lightened the moment with a grin. "Why, I believe she even voted for you."

The president smiled, too. "Please give her my thanks and tell her I'll do my best to live up to her trust."

"I will, ma'am."

"Lieutenant, in reading your record, I see that you've completed your Criminal Investigator Training Program and your OSI agency-specific coursework. You're now a federally credentialed special agent. But you are in your first-year probationary period. Do I have all that right?"

"Yes, ma'am, you do."

Galia stood up. Welborn started to get to his feet, too, unsure if he was suddenly being dismissed. The chief of staff waved him back into his seat.

"Please excuse me, Madam President, but there's another matter that requires my attention. If that's all right with you."

The president nodded; sure that Galia had scripted her departure, even though she hadn't shared that knowledge with her boss. Before leaving, Galia handed the president a sheet of paper.

"Perhaps this will add to your conversation with the lieutenant," she said, and departed.

Patti took in the contents of the page at a glance. She slipped it into Yates's personnel folder and turned her attention back to him.

"You have an office at Andrews, Lieutenant?" Andrews Air Force Base, in nearby suburban Maryland, was the headquarters of the Office of Special Investigations.

"A desk, ma'am."

"The Colonel Linberg matter is your first investigation?"

"Yes, ma'am."

"Have you done any work on it yet?"

"No, ma'am. The file landed on my desk only an hour before I was ordered to report here. I was reading it and contemplating my first interview with the colonel when I got your call."

She looked at the young man in front of her for a long moment, thinking this was what being president was all about. The power to change people's lives profoundly. Though not necessarily for the better.

"Lieutenant, you'll soon have an office. Here at the White House."

Welborn's eyes went wide.

"And I'll be the one who decides how your probationary period works out," the president added. "Get everything you need from your desk at Andrews. Your new digs will be waiting for you when you get back."

THE PRESIDENT stepped into a briefing in the pressroom, unannounced. The newsies all had the manners to get to their feet without being told, and Patti sat them back down again.

"I just stopped by to make sure you're not abusing my press secretary too badly."

"Just badly enough, ma'am," a voice in the back called out, drawing a laugh.

"Fair enough.   Let Aggie know if you have any suggestions how we might all work better together. Feel free to offer constructive self-criticism, too."

The president was about to leave when David Gregory snagged her with a question, "Madam President, have you seen that some media outlets have started to refer to you by your initials, PDG?"

"Yes, I've noticed that, David."

A mischievous smile lit the reporter's face. "But have you heard that some people say that your initials stand for Pretty Damn Good?"

Keeping a perfectly straight face, she answered, "That's close to what I've heard, but I believe you left out the comma. It should be: Pretty, damn good."

The president dazzled the reporters with her best smile and left with a wave. Knowing the sound bite would be all over the news that night.

MCGILL WAS already home when the president returned to the residence for the night. He hadn't seen his wife the night before; the press of business had kept her away until he was already asleep. Now, he had two bottles, each in a silver ice bucket, waiting for her. Poland Springs Sparkling Mineral Water. Leapfrog California Chardonnay. Patti sat next to her husband on the drawing room sofa and opted for the water.

"I'm gainfully employed again," McGill told her. "My first client."

"I know," Patti said.

"You know?"

"I'm the president. I know everything."

McGill wasn't omniscient, but he was pretty quick. "Galia told you. And no way Sweetie, Deke, or Leo told her. So she's either got my office bugged or somebody on the client's side ratted her out."

"Chana Lochlan. I stopped by the pressroom today to take a good look at her."

Patti wasn't the jealous type, McGill knew, but her curiosity was relentless.

"If Galia has my office bugged, are you going to fire her?"

"I'll slap her wrist. Tell her not to do it again."

"Good to know where I stand in the pecking order."

Patti kissed McGill. As always, he could imagine a thousand violins starting to play as the closing credits of a movie rolled. "You know where you stand," she said. "But I do need Galia."

"Your pacification effort is working, don't stop now."

"Jim, I need a favor."

The nice thing about being married to a trained communicator, it was easy to pick right up on her tone. McGill stopped joking and sat back. He opened his hands wide.

"Whatever I can do."

She told him about Colonel Carina Linberg and Lieutenant Welborn Yates.

"Welborn?" McGill asked.

"A lovely young man. Dedicated to the service of his country."

"Working his first case. Likely susceptible to pressure from above, if I'm reading between the lines right."

Patti nodded. "That's why I moved him to the White House. To shelter him. I've taken quite a liking to him."

McGill only nodded. He wasn't the jealous type either.

"Lieutenant Yates and three friends, all Air Force, were on their way back to California after another buddy got married in Las Vegas. It was the wee small hours of the morning, they were a block away from the freeway entrance when a car ran a red light and broadsided them."

"Welborn was the sole survivor," McGill said, knowing immediately.

"Four fighter jocks. Only one thought himself mortal enough to need a seat belt, and Welborn, despite his seat belt, sustained damage to his right inner ear. Doesn't keep him from doing most things, but he can't take the multi-G forces of flying fighter jets."

McGill poured a glass of wine for each of them.

"Gets worse, doesn't it?" he asked.

"The driver of the other car walked away, was never found, and the car had been stolen the night before. No identification has ever been made."

McGill sipped his wine. "So Welborn stays in the military and learns the skills he figures he'll need to track the SOB down someday."

"I'm told an OSI posting is the second-most-popular career choice in the Air Force, but, yes, that's my assumption, too. Which tells me he has a strong sense of justice."

"Or vengeance."

"You haven't met him."

McGill shrugged and drank some more wine.

"So you think the kid will play it straight on the Linberg case," he asked, "with you giving him political cover?"

"Yes."

"And you'd like me to do what, tutor him? Let him know the kinds of things that don't get covered in the textbooks and the lectures."

"Exactly. Only he'll never see you. I'll be your go-between."

"Our little secret?"

Patti nodded.

"Unless Galia has the residence bugged, too," McGill said.

"That would be cause for termination."

McGill smiled. "Like I said, whatever I can do." He kissed his wife and excused himself to take a shower.

Patti took her wineglass and went to a window looking out on Lafayette Square. Using her free hand, she pulled back a curtain that McGill had closed. A dozen or so protestors walked a tight, relentless circle, as they'd done every day since she'd moved into the White House.   The Peace Vigil people who'd camped out opposite the White House continuously since 1981 had ceded some of their space to the new group.   Each of the protestors carried the same sign: FREE ERNA.

Erna Godfrey.   Current resident of the Federal Death Penalty Facility in Terre Haute, Indiana.   Wife of Reverend Burke Godfrey, pastor of the Salvation's Path Church.

The woman who'd killed Patti's beloved first husband, Andy Grant.

CHAPTER 4

Two Years Earlier

ANDY GRANT was the kind of billionaire who opened his own front door when someone rang the bell. Of course, Andy's doorbell was located outside a gate three hundred feet from his house, and hidden TV cameras revealed just who had come calling. The Grant estate was protected on the north, west, and south by twelve-foot-high ivy-covered walls. Motion detectors and other electronic devices warned against climbers and vaulters. On the east lay a private beach and Lake Michigan.

In the depths of some of the colder winters, it would have been possible to ice-skate onto the grounds, but no one had tried that yet. Nor had any other form of seaborne attack been launched.

But the first thing Chief McGill said after Andy had introduced himself that warm morning in late May was, "You've got to do something about your waterfront exposure."

"What would you suggest, mining the beach?" The question came not from Grant, but from his wife, the congresswoman, who'd heard McGill's comment as she descended the main stairway.

"I don't think you're zoned for that," McGill said evenly, "and it might upset the neighbors if one of their dogs wandered over and got blown up."

Like her husband, Patricia Darden Grant was dressed casually; she wore shorts and a sleeveless top. Unlike her husband, she was barefoot. Unlike her husband, she was hostile.

Something Andy Grant was far too sharp to miss, far too genial to let go un-ameliorated.

"The chief's done his homework, Patti," he said. "He not only knows the neighbors have dogs but where they like to drop their loads." He turned to McGill with a grin. "Maybe we can get a zoning exception."

"MY PROFESSION is giving money away wisely," Andy Grant said. He had curly ginger hair and smart green eyes. Average in height, he looked as if he enjoyed one too many cupcake per day. But he seemed comfortable with his appearance and moved with physical grace.

The discussion had moved to the terrace above the beach at the back of the house. Andy and McGill sipped lemonade from tall tumblers at a round glass-topped table. A third glass awaited the congresswoman's thirst. She worked nearby fussing with potted plants that looked perfectly tended to McGill. But then, gardening wasn't the point. She was close enough to overhear every word without having to look at the bothersome cop.

"Wisely must be the hard part," McGill answered. "Like being a genie and not having the wishes you grant backfire."

Andy laughed. "Very good. I hope you won't mind if I use that line."

McGill nodded his approval. Maybe Andy Grant was stroking him, maybe he wasn't. Either way, for a rich guy, he was very easy to like. Except to the people who had threatened to kill him. Reason enough to over-look his wife's continuing grump, McGill supposed.

As alert to moods as ever, Andy asked, "Chief, just how serious do you think this threat against my life is?"

McGill saw Patti Grant turn to look at him. Intently. She wanted to watch his face as he answered the question. He took out a duplicate of the threat message. The original had been left that morning inside a subscrip-tion copy of the *Wall Street Journal* delivered to Andy Grant's mailbox out-side his gate. When Andy had unfolded the newspaper to read it, the note had fallen into his lap.

Get your wife to vote the right way. Do it, or she'll know what it's like to see the taking of an innocent life.

"The note doesn't specify the vote in question," McGill told the philanthropist. "Nor does it say which way is the right way to vote, but when you read it to your wife, she understood perfectly, or so you told me."

Andy nodded, and said quietly, "Yes, she did."

The congresswoman's rebuttal was a good deal louder. "It could all be a bluff!"

She marched over to the table, stood before McGill, daring him to contradict her. This time Andy Grant didn't intervene. Candor was more important than comity now.

"Congresswoman," McGill said, meeting her eyes, "I won't ask you if you've ever made a death threat because I'd bet you haven't. Never in any serious manner. But this note is serious. It communicates a threat that's real. A threat that resonates. That's why you're so scared."

McGill was sure she wanted to pick up her drink and throw it in his face. But if she did that, she'd let Andy know just how terrified she was. Then how could she cast the vote that would endanger his life?

McGill had no choice but to continue. No way to spare Mrs. Grant's feelings.

"If you vote against these people—"

"You think there's more than one?" Andy asked.

"One is possible. But a group is more likely." He turned back to the congresswoman. "If you vote against them after you've been warned, what do they say to themselves? 'Well, it was worth a try.' If they don't at least *attempt* to kill Mr. Grant and give it their all, they won't be able to believe in themselves anymore. Add in the inevitable religious element, and what they will believe is they're all going to hell. I'm sorry, Congresswoman, but this is real. Defy these people, and they *will* come for your husband."

Patti Grant loathed McGill at that moment.

But Andy agreed to install an underwater barrier to protect his beach.

THE NEXT day, McGill got a courtesy call from the FBI office in Chicago. They'd been advised of the threat on Mr. Grant's life by Congresswoman Grant. The congresswoman wanted the Bureau to take over the case. Only, as far as they could tell, Mr. Grant's being a private citizen and Congresswoman Grant's saying her husband never tried to influence her congressional votes, the threat was a matter for the local police.

Still, the case was being studied by DOJ lawyers in Washington to see if there was any reason federal authorities should take over. Sweetie was in McGill's office when he took the call, and he gave her the gist of the conversation.

"The lady wants some control back in her life," Sweetie said. "She figures she has a better chance of getting it with the feebs than with you."

McGill nodded absently.

"There is a way in for them," he said. "They'll spot it before too long."

Sweetie gave him a look.

McGill told her, "Andy Grant said his copy of the *Journal* wasn't in the newspaper box outside his gate; it was in his mailbox."

"Federal turf," Sweetie said. "Maybe Mr. Grant didn't share that with his wife."

"Maybe." McGill got to his feet. "I'm going to talk with him again. You start asking around. Did anyone see a passerby who didn't look North Shore near the Grant house yesterday morning? Someone who took Andy Grant's newspaper out of its receptacle and put it in the mailbox? Start with the *Journal's* delivery person."

"We should've thought of that right away."

"I know," McGill said.

"Well, aside from getting shot occasionally, we don't get to do much real police work out here in the leafy 'burbs. A cop can get mentally lazy."

"Let's watch out for that."

THERE WERE two armed guards at Andy Grant's gate—a first for Winnetka—and his mailbox had been removed. The *Journal's* plastic bin, too. McGill wondered if the FBI had them. Some sharpie had learned how the threat was transmitted and had carted off the containers to check them for fingerprints and DNA. There had been neither on the threat message itself.

The guys at the gate called for a colleague to meet McGill at Andy's front door.

Andy waited just inside and shook McGill's hand when he entered. The congresswoman, he told McGill, had departed for Washington to tend to the people's business. Just as well. She hadn't been happy about his hiring the new security people, but Andy had thought there was no reason to do things halfway.

"Feds have your mailbox and paper bin?" McGill asked.

Andy shook his head. "The new security guys. When they heard I go out to pick up the paper and the mail myself, they took them away. Said they represented unacceptable risks."

McGill nodded. "Meaning the people who've threatened you could make good by booby-trapping one or both. That was one of the things I was going to talk to you about. That, and things like varying your routine."

"Yeah. They've talked to me about that."

McGill was starting to feel like the slow kid in class.

Ever sensitive to other people, Andy clapped him on the shoulder, and said, "The security guys said you were right on the money about protecting the lakeside of the house."

"Your tax dollars at work," McGill said.

Andy laughed. Then he looked a good deal more sober.

"I told Patti, of course, that she couldn't let any of this affect the way she votes. We start down that path, and it's the end of democracy in this country."

"You're absolutely right."

"But I *am* scared. The new water barrier's going in right now."

Which explained the sounds of heavy machinery McGill heard.

"I'd be scared, too," he said, "and I get to carry a gun."

"Just so you know, Patti's anger at you was nothing personal; she's more frightened than I am."

McGill nodded. He knew all too well what fearing for a husband's safety could do to a woman. His ex had left him when she couldn't take being a cop's wife any longer—after he'd been shot on the job.

"We're looking for whoever left the threat," McGill told Andy. "Let me know if there's anything else I can do."

ONE THING McGill could do occurred to him that evening. He called Andy and got the phone number of the supervisor of the work crew that was putting in the barrier off the Grants' beach. The man's name was Costello, and he had a suspicious nature. He insisted on talking to Andy Grant himself before he said anything. Then he said he'd call McGill at the number listed for the village police in the phone book.

McGill told Costello he appreciated his precautions and would wait for the return call. He wondered if the man was naturally careful or if he'd been briefed by Grant's security team.

In either case, the wait was short. Costello called back in five minutes.

"Mr. Grant says to talk to you, Chief. So whattya want to know?"

"How soon before you finish the job?" McGill asked.

"It's done. Rush job, premium pay."

Money did have its advantages, McGill thought.

"What kind of a barrier did you put in?"

"Structural steel beams. Anchored in the lakebed eighteen inches apart, pointing out and up at forty-five-degree angles. Rip the bottom right outta any boat that tries to land on that beach."

Effective but damn ugly, as McGill envisioned it. He was sure it would offend the community's sensibilities. Too bad if the Grants were in danger. Winnetka had its *aesthetics* to consider.

Costello interpreted the chief's silence perfectly. "The beams don't break the surface. They stop a few inches under the water. But not enough for a boat to get over. Of course, we get a dry year, and the lake level drops..."

"We'll worry about that later," McGill said.

"Hey, rich people don't have worries. They chase 'em away with Franklins."

Andy Grant wasn't going to solve his problems with money, but McGill didn't want to get into a debate. He asked Costello, "Did you notice anyone taking an interest in the job you were doing? Anyone who didn't look North Shore?"

Costello laughed harshly. "You mean rich, white, and to the manor born?"

"Yeah."

"No. A few boaters eyed us for a while. You could tell they were interested in what we were doing. Like maybe this was some new status symbol they had to have, too. But every last one of 'em looked *real* North Shore."

AN HOUR later, just before sunset, McGill took his boat out onto the lake. It was a small aluminum skiff with a ten-horse outboard. His dad had given it to him so the two of them could go fishing on the Chain O' Lakes. He'd never had it out on Lake Michigan. As he chugged along, he made a conscious effort not to venture out any farther from the shore than he thought he could swim—and he scolded himself for not bringing a life jacket. He came to a point just east of where he estimated the Grants' new barrier to be, turned toward the beach, cut the engine and raised the motor out of the water. Momentum eased the little craft forward.

The skiff didn't draw much water, and with only one man in it, McGill wanted to know if it might skim over the newly installed—

A steel beam hit the aluminum hull far sooner than McGill expected. The jolt almost knocked him into the water. He had to grab the sides of the skiff to regain his balance. When he did, he thought he could see Andy Grant in a second-floor window at the left corner of the house. Then a high-intensity spotlight illuminated his boat. McGill squinted and shielded his eyes. He could make out a man on the beach holding a scoped rifle. The guy brought the weapon to his shoulder.

That was when McGill realized *he* didn't look North Shore. Not in his jeans, T-shirt, and humble small watercraft. Be a helluva thing to die in a case of mistaken identity.

McGill did the only thing he could. He pulled out his badge and held it in front of the eyes he now squeezed shut. After the longest three count of his life, he took a look. The marksman had lowered his rifle and moved his spotlight slightly to McGill's right.

McGill could see that the man was yelling at him, but he couldn't hear the words. The distance was too great and the pounding of his heart was too loud. Still, he doubted the man was thanking him for testing the Grants' new defenses.

He turned the skiff around and headed back to the launching ramp.

Believing the lake would not be the avenue of attack.

Just to be safe, though, he called every marine copper he knew from Milwaukee to Gary and let them know of his worries and to ask that they call him if they spotted anyone suspicious.

CONGRESSWOMAN GRANT cast her vote opposing the Support of Motherhood Act. It failed and ... nothing happened. A month went by. Patti came to believe she'd been right. The threat had been a bluff and nothing more. She began to find the presence of a large number of security men in and around her home intrusive.

She spoke to Andy about letting them go.

"I'll talk to the chief, see what he thinks," her husband said.

He did and reported back. The Grants discussed the matter in their kitchen as they prepared a light supper to eat outside.

"Chief McGill thinks we should move. Temporarily. But without notice. Or publicly revealing where we've gone."

"That's preposterous."

"He says it only makes sense for attackers to wait until the defenders relax. But if we take the initiative, change the place we live, we might force them out into the open."

Patti's eyes narrowed. "In other words, he hasn't been able to find *any* evidence that the threat was *ever* real."

"No, and it's eating him up. Because he's positive the threat *is* real."

Congress was in its summer recess. It would be a natural thing for the Grants to take a vacation trip, then … simply not come home. At least not for a while.

"I won't do it, Andy."

Andy sighed and nodded. "I don't like the idea of being run out of my house, either."

"We'll keep the security men."

"Or let them go if they bother you too much."

They carried their food and drinks outside, nibbled for a while without talking.

Finally, Patti asked, "You like him, don't you?"

"The chief?" Andy asked. "Yes, I do. He's smart, honest, has a ton of experience. His professional accomplishments aside, everybody I've talked to about him says he's a good man and a devoted father. He has three kids, two girls and a boy."

That hit home. Both Patti and Andy were infertile. Their shared sense of personal regret was one big reason why the Grant Foundation sent millions of dollars each year to organizations with proven records of bettering the lives of children in need.

"Good for him," Patti said, and left it at that.

AFTER LABOR Day, Congresswoman Grant returned to Washington when the House of Representatives reconvened. She declined Andy's suggestion of having a bodyguard accompany her, and he didn't push it too hard. By that time, he was beginning to have doubts, too, that the threat against his life had been real.

Chief McGill still thought it was, but even the most astute professional made mistakes. Andy dismissed the security force at his house, thinking it would make a nice surprise for Patti, the next time she came home, to have the house to themselves. He didn't notify the chief of his action; he didn't want to debate the matter anymore.

Andy kept the new armored Mercedes and the chauffeur who'd been trained in evasive driving. He varied his routine. He was alert to his surroundings. But that was it. He just wasn't going to be afraid all the time. It took all the joy out of life.

He was killed three days after he let his security people go.

The attack came from the lake. Nobody had to storm the beach. The night was still, the lake was flat, and a cabin cruiser was used as a shooting platform. From a point just outside the barrier, a rocket-propelled grenade was fired through Andy and Patti's bedroom window.

Second floor at the left corner of the house.

WHEN HE got the news of an explosion at the Grant house—a terrified neighbor had called the village police—McGill wanted to kill someone himself. "Goddamnit, goddamnit, *goddamnit!*" he roared, and slammed the phone down without thinking.

Klara, his dispatcher, called back and told McGill that Sweetie was on the way to his house. ETA five minutes. While he got dressed, he told Klara to make sure every one of his thirty-six sworn officers was out on the street. He ordered that the Village of Winnetka be sealed. Absolutely no one was to leave his jurisdiction without his permission.

He also told Klara to make sure that every cop in the country—and Canada—got the word of what had happened. But he was not yet able to tell his brother officers for whom they should be on the lookout. Then the brief *whoop* of a police patrol unit announced Sweetie's arrival.

McGill lived in the northwest corner of Evanston, two gilded suburbs down the social ladder from Winnetka and the Grant estate. Fifteen minutes away in normal traffic. Less at that time of night. Much less at the speed Sweetie was driving.

But there was still plenty of time for Sweetie to tell him.

"The neighbor who phoned in the report said the explosion was in Mr. Grant's bedroom. Apparently, he has a clear view of the Grant's place from his house. He was embarrassed when he had to admit he knew what the room was. But you live next door to a former movie star's boudoir..."

Sweetie shrugged at human foibles.

"Did he see any sign of life after the blast?" McGill asked.

"Klara asked about that. The neighbor said no."

"Had anyone noticed if Mr. Grant was home tonight?"

Sweetie nodded. "The neighbor. Saw him in his bedroom before the light was turned off."

"Shit."

Sweetie asked, "You going to make the call, Jim?"

He nodded and took out his cell phone. He had the number in the 202 area code committed to memory. Andy Grant had given it to him. Just in case.

She answered on the third ring, and McGill said, "Congresswoman Grant? This is Chief of Police James J. McGill. I have some bad news ..."

THE FBI called McGill just as he reached the Grant estate. Sweetie had radioed the company that maintained the property's electronic security system and was given the code to open the gate. She was punching it into the keypad as McGill took the FBI call. The gate rolled open, but she waited at the entrance to the driveway while McGill talked to the feebs.

The Special Agent in Charge of the Chicago office, a guy named Braun, told McGill that Congresswoman Grant had informed them of what had happened. The Bureau was assuming control of the case.

"Like hell," McGill said. "You have no jurisdiction. You said so yourself."

He gave it a moment to see if they'd learned about the mailbox, but they still didn't know. Andy had never told anyone but him. So McGill continued, "You set foot on my crime scene, I'll arrest you for interfering with police officers in the performance of their duty."

Braun laughed bleakly. "You've got some balls, buddy. But you know what? Our lawyers can beat up your lawyers, and we've got more of them."

There was no arguing that, so McGill gave the fed something else to chew on.

"You want something to do? Think about this. Maybe these assholes won't be happy until they kill the congresswoman, too. Protecting her, now that's a federal responsibility."

McGill left Sweetie at the gate with orders to allow no one in except the crime-scene team from the Cook County Sheriff's Department.

"Paramedics?" Sweetie asked.

The nosy neighbor had reported that the explosion had been blinding, deafening, and strong enough to crack his windows next door, over a hundred feet away. How was anyone going to survive that? But McGill said, "Okay, them, too."

Sweetie closed the gate behind them and blocked the driveway with her patrol unit. McGill went to the house on foot.

THE ONLY chance for Andy was if he'd been somewhere else in the house. McGill quickly checked every room, calling out Andy's name. Loudly at first. Softly and with growing despair the closer he got to the blast area. The door to the Grants' bedroom leaned out of its frame like a drunk falling off a curb, providing a view of the carnage within.

Andy Grant had been sundered, and there had been a fire. Put out by a sprinkler system that had survived the blast and was still going. Watering down the stink of the explosion and the charred flesh. The largest piece of Andy that McGill could identify was a blackened lower left leg severed at the knee. McGill had seen dead bodies before, more than a few, but nothing like this. This was a scene from a battlefield.

He raised his eyes and looked out at the lake, made all the easier with half the wall on that side of the room gone. Not a boat in sight. So much water in which to dump the murder weapon. He took out his cell phone and started calling his list of lakefront police departments. He had them on voice dial. Maybe the assholes who had killed Andy would do something stupid.

A minute later, a cop he called in Kenosha said something smart.

"You alert any grouper troopers on the other side of the lake? You know, in Michigan?"

Landlubber that he was, the thought hadn't occurred to McGill. Crossing forty miles or more of open water. He'd thought only of hugging the near shore. Worse, he didn't know any coppers over in Michigan. But his friend in Kenosha did. Said he'd start making calls and get back to McGill if he came up with anything.

McGill had just said thanks and clicked off when Sweetie called up to him from the front door. "Feebs are here. Got a judge's order allowing them onto the property. I told them I'd have to take it inside, read it in a good light. They gave me five minutes."

McGill descended the stairs. If Sweetie was in the right mood, he wouldn't put it past her to shoot it out with the federal government, but he could see she thought this was neither the time nor the place.

"I'll let them in ... but Margaret?"

The use of her proper name between the two of them was reserved for only the most serious of occasions.

"Yes?"

"Don't let Mrs. Grant see what's happened to her husband. I doubt she'll get here before they take him—his remains—away, but just in case, don't let her see."

Sweetie nodded. Now she was in the right mood.

MCGILL FELT more certain than ever of one thing: Andy's death wasn't a lone-wolf killing. Somebody had put the threatening note in his *Journal*. Somebody had scouted his house from the lake. Probably saw Costello's crew putting in the barrier. Maybe even saw Andy in his bedroom the way McGill had from his skiff. Then somebody had figured out a plan to overcome the barrier ... and somebody had pulled the trigger on Andy.

Could have been one *industrious* son of a bitch. But McGill's gut told him it was a group ... *a group with money.*

The thought was an epiphany, one that made McGill shudder. Costello had told him there had been people watching his guys work, but they all looked like they belonged. North Shore. They could have come back at night and watched the house with binoculars, out far enough not to attract the attention of Andy's security team.

McGill groaned at the god-awful mistake he'd made. He'd kept thinking that the killers would look like cornpone crazies. Hicks. Stand out like Ma and Pa Kettle in his designer-label town. But the truth was—had to be—at least one of them blended perfectly because he was homegrown. Provided all the local color the group needed.

Wrote his death threat in perfectly grammatical English.

McGill got behind the wheel of Sweetie's patrol unit, backed it away from the gate of the Grant estate, and called out the key code so the feds could open it.

SAC Braun was the first inside. He double-timed over to McGill's car.

But whatever the fed had intended to say, McGill's look made him think twice. The chief told him, "Mr. Grant is dead, dismembered by the blast. The crime scene is as I found it. Sergeant Sweeney of my department has been ordered not to let Congresswoman Grant see her husband's remains. You and your men will be in peril should you try to countermand that order."

Braun's head jerked as if McGill had given him the back of his hand, but he didn't argue. Some things a judge's order couldn't overrule.

DRIVING TO police headquarters, McGill remembered reading stories of people in Dallas who had celebrated the assassination of JFK. Appalling, but true. When he arrived, he had Klara alert all patrol units to be on the lookout for any home where a party might be going on. He wanted to know if anybody in the village knew of the death of Andy Grant and had reason to cheer about it.

Then he got on the phone and woke up the dean of the Divinity School at Northwestern, the president of Lake Forest College, and the principal of New Trier High School. He informed each of them of what had happened and asked their help in identifying any of their students who had been active in the pro-life movement, especially those who'd been militant in their advocacy.

Normally, the schools would have been reluctant to compromise their students' privacy. But Andy Grant had been well loved locally, a generous contributor to endowment funds, and the spouse of a prominent member of Congress. Assured that McGill would be discreet, they all agreed to cooperate.

Next, McGill started to call the rectories and parsonages of every church from Evanston to Waukegan. Somewhere in the haystack he was amassing, he was sure he would find his needle.

He was between phone calls when Klara poked her head into his office, and, trying not to make too much of it, said, "Chief, that idea of yours about parties, maybe we've got something. In Kenilworth."

Kenilworth lay immediately south of Winnetka. It was more a congregation of old money than an actual town. Too small to have its own police and fire services, Kenilworth contracted them out to Winnetka. Not content to rely on public agencies, however, Kenilworth was also heavily patrolled by private security companies.

Klara had extended the party-watch alert to the private cops.

One of the Kenilworth security patrols had just taken into custody a young man named Lindell Ricker. The private cops had been responding to a silent alarm at a lakefront property. The problem was, they told McGill when he was patched through to them, Mr. Ricker claimed he'd done nothing wrong. He was simply staying at his *parents'* house. He carried a Virginia driver's license identifying who he was, and an old student ID from New Trier giving the correct Kenilworth address.

But he apparently hadn't known that his father had installed a separate alarm on his wine cellar. The private cops had walked in on him as he was drinking champagne and wearing a goofy smile on his face. All alone but acting like he was having his own little party. They asked McGill what they should do.

He said cuff him; he'd be right over to arrest Mr. Ricker.

MCGILL TOLD Lindell Ricker he was under arrest for suspicion of murder and read him his Miranda rights in front of the two private cops, whom he then swore to secrecy. He transported his prisoner back to police headquarters and once again read Ricker his rights in front of Klara and two patrol cops who'd been called in specifically to witness the event. Klara and the uniformed officers were also sworn to secrecy.

Then, as Ricker declined to say a word to anyone much less request a lawyer, McGill put him in a holding cell and waited for Sweetie. McGill was sure there was a religious element to the killing of Andy Grant, and while he was a first-rate interrogator in most situations, he'd never seen anyone better than Sweetie when it came to dealing with suspects who thought they were doing God's work. She arrived three hours later, looking both sad and vengeful.

"The congresswoman come home?" McGill asked.

Sweetie nodded. "The president let her borrow his plane."

"Everything work out okay?"

"Mr. Grant's remains were still on-site when she got there. I had to put her in a bear hug. She struggled and yelled some, and the feds looked like they didn't know whether to spit or go blind. But I kept talking to her quietly ... and finally we just prayed for him. Asked God to gather Mr. Grant's soul into His company. Right there in front of everyone. I think some of the feds even said amen with us."

Sweetie had been a novice in a convent before leaving to become a cop.

"Where'd you take her?"

"I had one fed drive us to St. Francis and another bring my patrol unit along. She's in a private room, sedated, under another name. Father Bernini, the hospital chaplain, is there in case she wakes up. A couple feds are out in the hall standing guard." Sweetie sighed. "I can't remember the last time I saw someone in such pain."

McGill nodded, and said, "We've got one of them."

Sweetie's sadness disappeared. All that was left was vengeful.

"Let's go talk to him," she said.

THIS TIME, McGill turned on the video camera. State law for all interrogations. He asked once more if Lindell Ricker wanted a lawyer.

Having had the time to consider his situation and his buzz to deteriorate into sullen anger, he was willing to answer the question. "I don't need a lawyer. I answer only to God's law. I'm willing, no, eager, to become a martyr."

Lindell Ricker was twenty-two years old. Righteous and full of himself. He was playing to the camera and completely missed the gleam that came into Sweetie's eyes.

"I called your parents while you've been here," McGill said. "The security company had a number for them in Florida. They were really surprised when you came home this summer. Especially after you'd told them the way they live they're sure to go to hell. You scare your parents. That's why they went south out of season."

"They're sinners," Lindell said.

"Maybe so, but you're the one who broke into your father's wine cellar. Didn't know he'd put a separate alarm on it, did you? Had to protect all that expensive, sinful wine. You pick out a nice bottle to guzzle?"

Lindell only frowned.

"Let me see if I've got this right," Sweetie said, joining in. "Your parents are sinners, but you're a would-be martyr?"

Lindell tried to hold her gaze; couldn't. But he managed to say, "Like you've never seen."

"How about like this?" Sweetie asked.

She undid the top two buttons of her uniform shirt and Lindell looked up. Sweetie took out the St. Sebastian medal she wore on a chain around her neck. She also gave Lindell a glimpse of the scar on her upper chest where she'd taken the bullet for McGill. The scar was sizable.

"You know what this is?" Sweetie asked, holding out the medal.

"Papist idolatry."

"Yeah, yeah. But do you know the story of St. Sebastian?"

Lindell didn't answer. Sweetie told him anyway.

"Saint Sebastian was actually a little like you. The son of wealthy parents." Lindell looked up, a hint of interest on his face. "Now Sebastian's parents, they were good Romans. Believed in all the old Olympian gods. Their son, though … he was a secret Christian."

Sweetie had him now.

"Did I mention that Sebastian was also a Roman soldier? A captain of the guard. His family money gave him clout. His military rank gave him status. He was a golden boy. Could have had anything he wanted. But then the emperor, Diocletian, who hated Christians, started a persecution. Sebastian decided if he was truly a man of faith, he would have to reveal himself. So he did."

Sweetie paused and stepped out of the room to get a bottle of water. She came back and drank, not offering any water to Lindell. "You have the conviction to reveal your secrets, Lindell?" she asked. Before he could respond, she held up her hand. "No wait. Let me tell you the rest of the story before you answer.

"Because of his family's high standing, the emperor himself asked Sebastian to renounce his Christian faith. He refused. His faith was strong, and he wanted the world to know it. So the emperor had him taken outside the city gates. Sebastian was tied to a tree and shot full of arrows.

"Only he *didn't* die. That ticked the emperor off good. So the emperor had Sebastian taken down from the tree and beaten to death. Now *that's* my idea of a martyr." Sweetie sat on a corner of the interrogation room table, all but on Lindell's lap. He looked up at her, watched her throat move as she took another drink. Then she asked him in a quiet voice, "You got the stones to match up with St. Sebastian, Lindell?"

Lindell focused on Sweetie's medal while he looked for an answer.

Sweetie inclined her head to the door, and McGill slipped out.

MCGILL WAS on the phone when Sweetie came out of the interrogation room. His face was flushed. "Sonofabitch! That's got to be them. Yeah, grab them and hold them for us while we get the extradition request started. Yeah, thanks. Come to town sometime, dinner's on me."

He hung up and looked at Sweetie as she took a seat.

"A boater at a marina in Holland, Michigan, an army vet, called the cops to report a guy on another boat unloading what he swore was a rocket launcher. Got the make, model, and plate number of the vehicle the rocket man and three other people drove off in. Ten minutes ago."

Sweetie said, "That'd be a green Toyota minivan, Virginia tag number 405 413J. The people are Erna Godfrey, the trigger-*woman,* and Walter Delk, his wife Penny, and their adult son, Winston, the accomplices."

McGill looked at her and smiled. "You got all that on tape?"

Sweetie nodded. "And in Lindell's own hand. It's being typed up right now."

"He signed his Miranda waiver, of course."

"Of course."

"Sonofabitch, we're gonna get all of them. That was great, that story about St. Sebastian."

"The patron saint of police officers."

McGill fell silent for a moment. Then he said quietly, "Of course, with no one in the interrogation room but the two of you, after you turned the camera off, you might have pointed out to Mr. Ricker that our case against him would be much more problematic should he recant his confession. Even with the tape, he might claim duress. He might go free, needn't be a martyr at all." Sweetie waited, she knew McGill wasn't finished. "Which isn't to say that someone might not tie him to a tree and shoot him full of arrows. Beat him to death if necessary. But I won't ask you about that."

"No, don't," Sweetie said.

MCGILL WAS the first person Patti Grant saw when she opened her eyes.

He didn't ask how she was, he just told her the news. "We have five people in custody for killing Andy."

She didn't say a word, only started to cry. McGill brought her a box of tissues.

"I'm so sorry for your loss," he said. "I knew Andy for only a short time; I wish I'd known him longer." He turned to go, but Patti caught his wrist.

"Who ... who are they?" she asked.

McGill told her, and she said, "There are more, at least one."

Patti Grant was sure that Erna Godfrey wouldn't have killed anyone without her husband—the Reverend Burke Godfrey, pastor of the Salvation's Path Church—knowing about it and approving.

That assertion had been voiced flatly, a simple statement of fact. But Patti's voice turned bitter when she mentioned two more possibilities. "Representative Doak Langdon of Georgia and Senator Howard Hurlbert of Mississippi, cosponsors of the Support of Motherhood Act, and members of my own party."

A televangelist, McGill thought he could handle. Two sitting members of Congress ... he was glad of the decision he'd made.

"I turned the case over to the FBI," he said. He told her that Lindell Ricker noted in his amended confession that he'd put Andy's copy of the *Wall Street Journal* into the Grants' mailbox. He'd done so because he thought there'd be less chance of anyone stealing the newspaper, and the threat it contained, that way. McGill had Ricker make that point clear because Illinois moratorium on the death penalty was ongoing and—"I don't really know your position on capital punishment, Congresswoman," he admitted.

"I'm no longer certain myself."

"Well, the feds are pursuing it as a death-penalty case."

Patti only nodded, making McGill wonder if she was thinking a plea bargain would be agreeable to her if it got Erna Godfrey to implicate her husband and the two pols. But that wasn't his problem.

"I really am sorry, Mrs. Grant. Please accept my condolences."

She let McGill's wrist go and nodded.

"Thank you. Thank you for ..." That was as far as she got.

She grabbed a fistful of tissues, and McGill left her to grieve in private.

THE MOURNERS at Andrew Hudson Grant's funeral numbered more than a thousand. The president of the United States was forced to send his condolences, but the First Lady and the vice president were there. As were more than a hundred members of Congress. Winnetka Village President Henry Healy was one of the pallbearers. Friends, both exalted and humble, came to say goodbye. Sergeant Margaret Sweeney, formidable in her dress uniform, and an honor guard of fellow officers, represented the village police department.

Other than the president, the only person of note missing was James J. McGill.

He turned up at the cemetery the next day, after the crowd had gone home. He knelt beside the freshly turned plot of earth, made the sign of the cross, and asked God to grant Andy eternal rest ... and to forgive him for letting a good man die. When tears filled, then overflowed McGill's eyes, he didn't bother to wipe them away.

There was no one around to see him, he thought, and he was almost right.

Only the widow, unable to stay away and watching from a distance, saw him.

THE TRIAL of four of the five conspirators in Andy's death was scheduled quickly and proceeded without delay. Lindell Ricker, per his plea bargain, testified against the others. The defense did not contest the facts of the case. Rather it argued that the defendants had acted out of a moral imperative. To save the lives of countless unborn children it was necessary that Andrew Grant lose his life. Only such an extreme lesson would finally make it clear to *all* politicians that the law must be changed to allow *no* abortions.

Erna Godfrey was far more blunt. "Once his wife refused to save him, God wanted that man dead."

The jury took only sixty-five minutes to disagree and return a verdict of guilty.

Erna Godfrey, spurning the offer of a lesser sentence if she would implicate her husband, was condemned to death. Walter, Penny, and Winston Delk were sentenced to life without parole. Lindell Ricker was sentenced to ten years, a long time but hardly the stuff of martyrs. Representative Doak Langdon and Senator Howard Hurlbert, cosponsors of the Support of Motherhood Act, would run for reelection unopposed.

The reporters covering the trial asked Congresswoman Grant if she thought the sentences were fair. McGill was standing nearby and could have tried to run interference, but he didn't think Patti Grant would have wanted that. And he was curious, too.

She said, "There's nothing fair about having someone you love getting killed. There's no undoing it. There's no forgetting it. There's only the hard work of trying to find peace. What happened here today is the first step down that path. Ask me ten or twenty years from now if the sentences were fair; maybe I'll have a better answer."

The media mob turned to McGill and asked him the same question.

"I think they should all be strapped to gurneys," he said.

TWO WEEKS later McGill was cooking Italian for his three kids and a soon-to-arrive friend when the doorbell rang. A moment later, McGill's youngest, Caitie, appeared in the kitchen, leading Patti Grant by the hand.

"Dad, company," Caitie announced.

The McGill children were no slouches. They read the papers, knew who Patti was, what had happened, and their father's role in the matter. They were also smart enough not to let their favorite meal with their dad, angel-hair pasta with tomatoes and basil, descend into a somber occasion.

"Invite her to dinner, Dad," Kenny said, mischief in his eye. "It's about time we had a good-looking woman around here."

His sisters blew raspberries at him. Patti suddenly looked uncertain of herself, but before she could say anything, Caitie added, "The congresswoman brought some men with her. Four, I think. They're outside."

McGill raised his eyebrows.

"Protection," Patti said. "The president insisted. For a while anyway. I … I'm sorry. I should have called first. I just wanted to properly express my appreciation for … for … I don't want to interrupt your dinner."

She was backing out of the room when McGill asked, "You know how to slice tomatoes?"

"Pardon?"

"We're having one guest for dinner, but we can set another extra plate.

I'm making pasta and my famous focaccia. You will have to earn your keep however." He held up a knife.

While she was trying to decide, Caitie piped up, "You won't mind eating with Democrats, will you? We're all Democrats here. Every McGill is."

The elder McGill rolled his eyes. "I'm an independent."

Older and more sensitive, McGill's eldest child, Abbie, said, "It would be an honor to have you join us for dinner, Congresswoman Grant."

Kenny just waggled his eyebrows. Patti couldn't help but laugh.

"Thank you. I think I will join you. After all, some of my best friends are Democrats. Not to mention an independent or two." She took the knife from McGill.

They worked next to each other at the kitchen counter. McGill kneaded the dough for the focaccia. Patti sliced the tomatoes. The McGill children kept the conversation light but shared furtive glances. They could tell already. Something was happening here.

They were right. That night was the beginning of something lasting, even after Patti told McGill that to honor Andy's memory she was going to run for president as he'd urged her to do.

"Who better?" McGill said.

CHAPTER 5

WEDNESDAY

GALIA MINDEL typically arrived at her West Wing office, a few steps from the Oval Office, before her secretary or any other staffer, but that morning someone else got there first. McGill sat at her desk, his feet up on her polished mahogany, reading from a file folder on his lap. The folder was stamped in red: TOP SECRET. A stack of other files rested on the desk. At McGill's elbow was an open box of donuts, crumbs and flecks of sugar further marring Galia's beautiful work surface.

McGill looked up when she appeared and smiled.

"Morning, Galia," he said. "Care for a donut?"

The chief of staff was dumbstruck. McGill never set foot in the West Wing unless the president sent for him. That was one of the man's saving graces. He was publicly apolitical. He'd even declined the opportunity to throw out the first pitch of the baseball season. But here he was, his big feet up on her desk, grinning and reading—

Newsweek? That was what Galia saw when McGill let the TOP SECRET folder fall open on her desk.

McGill stopped smiling, and said, "Close the door and have a seat. We need to talk."

Galia thought briefly of telling McGill to close the door and not let it hit him in the ass on his way out. But, damnit, you just couldn't bully the president's hench—the president's *husband*. She closed the door and, choking on her pride, sat in one of her own visitors' chairs.

"I saw the look on your face, Galia," McGill said. "You thought I'd broken into your desk and was reading through files that were none of my business. Not a very pleasant feeling, is it?"

Galia was able to speak now but couldn't bring herself to answer.

McGill sighed. "You're a real piece of work, lady. My problem is the president told me she needs you."

Galia allowed herself a tight smile.

McGill took his feet off the desk and leaned forward.

"She also said there's a line: Cross it, and you're gone."

Galia's smile disappeared.

"So really it's up to you," he told her. "If you like your job, if you want to keep it, you'll learn to play nice. Meaning you'll never snoop on McGill Investigations again. My business and my clients are off-limits to you. If you resent that, if it thwarts your sense of prerogative, too bad. Content yourself with being helpful to the president."

McGill got to his feet and gave Galia his best cop stare until she looked away. He crossed the office. Galia didn't turn to watch him go. He left the door open as he departed.

And called back, "Enjoy the donuts, Galia."

He knew as well as anyone else in the White House that the chief of staff was perpetually on a diet and how much trouble she had sticking to it.

CELSUS CROGHER, the SAC of the White House Security Detail, was waiting for McGill just down the hall from Galia's office. McGill had been a resident of what Bill Clinton had called "the crown jewel of the federal prison system" long enough not to wonder how the White House Secret Service boss knew where he was. It was Crogher's job to know where the president and McGill were at all times—and the man was nothing if not serious about doing his job.

But this was the first time he'd approached McGill personally since he'd lost the battle over how many of his minions would ensure that McGill didn't go toes up.

"Morning, Celsus," McGill said. "Galia's got donuts if you're hungry."

Not that McGill thought Crogher ate. He suspected that somewhere beneath the SAC's clothing, there was a pair of electrodes he used to recharge his batteries for an hour or two each night. Eyes wide open, of course.

Crogher, as he always did, got straight to the point. "Mr. McGill, I'm not getting the cooperation I need."

"From whom?" McGill asked.

"From Captain Sullivan of the Evanston PD." Barbara Sullivan was the Evanston copper who coordinated the protection of McGill's children.

Normally, the president's children were provided with Secret Service protection. But McGill's children were the president's stepchildren, who also had a mother and a stepfather. Such a blended family was new to the presidential scheme of things.

Everybody agreed that Abbie, Kenny, and Caitie had to be protected. Andy Grant's tragic death was an example of the jeopardy that could attach to anyone the president loved, and Patti Grant had come to love McGill's children dearly. So the federal government thought to extend Secret Service protection to them.

But not to their mother and stepfather.

Then the kids had met Celsus Crogher and said no way.

The president settled the matter. Patti insisted that since she was the reason the children needed protection in the first place she would be the one to pick up the tab. She was the only one, other than the government, who had the means to afford around-the-clock security for the children, their mother, and their stepfather, who, like McGill, were Evanston residents.

Barbara Sullivan, who might have been Sweetie's older, kinder, no-less-tough sister, ran the security detail, using off-duty Evanston patrol and detective personnel. Strictly as a courtesy, Barbara had agreed to keep Celsus Crogher informed with semimonthly reports.

Now Crogher told McGill, "I asked Captain Sullivan to switch to a weekly reporting basis."

McGill frowned. "Why?"

Crogher was silent, and that was all the answer McGill needed.

"Are my children at increased risk, Crogher? Sonofabitch, did you tell Barbara?"

Of course, he hadn't. Feds never told local cops anything. And a local cop was how Crogher would always see McGill. No, now he was even worse in the SAC's eyes. He was a *private* cop. Holmes.

McGill didn't know if he could cold-cock Crogher, but he was sorely tempted to try. It wasn't the uncertainty that stopped him; it was his promise to Patti not to do anything to embarrass her. But Crogher must have recognized the threat of violence in McGill's eyes because he took a sudden step backward. Even that gave McGill no satisfaction.

He strode back through Galia's doorway, and told Crogher, "Get in here."

Galia had left by the back door, the one to the Oval Office, leaving the donuts behind. McGill picked up her phone, got an outside line, and called Barbara Sullivan.

"Barbara? Jim McGill. I'm going to put SAC Celsus Crogher on the line." McGill handed the phone to Crogher. "Every last thing you know. Don't hold back a word."

Crogher began a terse recitation, never acknowledging Barbara Sullivan. A machine who'd had his PLAY button pushed, he was nevertheless effective in bringing McGill to a cold sweat.

Federal government monitoring of right-wing Web sites and chat rooms, as well as classified intercepts of other communications, had picked up increased and increasingly threatening mentions of the president's *illegitimate bastard offspring*. Stories were circulating that the president and her current husband had been longtime secret lovers. Abbie, Kenny, and Caitie were really the president's out-of-wedlock whelps. She'd gone to a private clinic in Switzerland to birth them. When sad sack Andy Grant finally wised up, the president and McGill had him killed so the faithless wife wouldn't lose all those billions in a divorce. Then they blamed the killing on poor God-fearing Erna Godfrey, who was sitting in jail right then waiting to die. Well, if the goddamn government killed Erna … maybe the thing to do was go after those kids.

Crogher handed the phone back to McGill.

Barbara promised to alert her people and call McGill nightly for as long as necessary.

McGill didn't know if Crogher had come completely clean with him, but he'd certainly heard enough for now.

McGill was leaving the West Wing when he felt a hand catch his left arm. He'd been too preoccupied to notice anyone approach, but when he looked around, he saw the White House physician, Artemus Nicolaides. Nick to all who knew him.

Nick was sixty or so, McGill had heard, but looked to be in his late forties, even with his shaven scalp. His Mediterranean complexion tanned on exposure to a sunny smile, and he was lean and fit, which he attributed to the daily consumption of olive oil and power walks up and down the National Mall.

"You don't look so good, my friend," Nick told McGill. "Pale, even for an Irishman. Fall sick, then what kind of henchman will you be for the president?"

"Patti called you again," McGill said.

"The president loves you, a gift as rare as a man might know. She asked me to remind you once more that you are overdue for your annual physical examination. Several weeks overdue. Also, you are pale."

"Even for an Irishman," McGill added. He gently disengaged his arm from Nick's grasp. "Soon, Nick, I'll have my checkup soon. I'll come to your office."

Nick smiled with perfect white teeth. "For you, I even make house calls."

MCGILL GOT into the backseat of his black Chevy. Leo and Deke sat up front. Leo went to put the car in gear, but McGill told him to wait. Leo waited, looked at the boss in his rearview mirror. Deke looked over his shoulder at McGill.

He told them of Galia's snooping. "I know neither of you blabbed."

"Not one little peep," Leo agreed.

Deke nodded.

"I'm going to have the office swept for bugs. I'll find a private firm. Just so you know, there will be an unfamiliar face or two around soon."

"We should do a background check first," Deke said, "on whoever you hire."

"I'll check them out. I can't ask you guys to be involved because then your bosses will be involved, and pretty soon the whole federal government would know. I just wanted to alert you so some electronics guy doesn't find himself looking up the barrel of an Uzi."

McGill sat back, thinking Leo would drive off.

But the driver didn't drive, and the bodyguard didn't look for threats.

"What?" McGill asked.

"You tell us," Deke said.

They could see something else was wrong, McGill thought, and they were right to want to know about it. Anything that put him off his game increased the risk to them. He shared the news about the threat to his children that he'd pried out of Crogher.

"You ought to let us put another ring around them," Deke said. "The Service could work things out with the local police so we're not stepping on each other's toes."

"That's what I'd do if they were my kids," Leo agreed.

"I'm thinking about it," McGill said. Then he realized he'd have to let Carolyn know what Crogher had told him. Poor Carolyn. His ex-wife had been terrified about the dangers he'd faced as a cop. Now, when she heard the kids were the subjects of threats … he decided to call her when Lars was home. Carolyn's new husband, a pharmacist, was a steady guy. A *safe* guy.

Hell, maybe he'd ask Patti to buy them a sheep ranch in New Zealand.

Let the kids grow up to be Kiwis.

"Let's go," McGill said. "I'm not the only one with problems."

CHAPTER 6

LIEUTENANT WELBORN Yates had never been to the Pentagon before the morning he showed up to interview Colonel Carina Linberg, but he wouldn't have been surprised if a body-cavity search were required to gain entrance. Not after the terrorist attack on the building. After all, he might be an Air Force officer with a legitimate reason to be on the premises, or he might be an SOB with a great disguise and a credible cover story.

If protecting the building were his job, he'd check out everyone down to their corn pads.

So when he arrived at the security checkpoint and an Air Force major on the far side of the metal detector nodded to the chief of the detail, who then waved Welborn through, he was sure somebody must have made a mistake. He started to open his briefcase for inspection.

But the major, whose name tag read SEYMOUR, told him curtly, "Don't bother with that, Yates. General Altman is waiting to see you."

"Sir?"

"General Warren Altman. The Air Force chief of staff. You've heard of him, Lieutenant?"

Welborn had. Four stars on each shoulder. That General Altman.

"Yes, sir. But he's not who I came here to see."

Major Seymour smiled, his teeth a brilliant white against his dark skin. "But that's who you're going to see, Lieutenant. If for no other reason than the general sent me to fetch you."

"Yes, sir," Welborn said.

THE FIRST thing Welborn noticed was that the general's office was bigger than the Oval Office. The second was that Major Seymour was literally breathing down his neck. Nothing he could do about that. He was standing at attention, holding his salute.

General Altman was seated behind his desk, speaking on the phone. Seeing the man up close, Welborn thought he looked too young to have all those stars. His hair was still dark, his jaw was still firm, and the lines around his eyes only made him look like someone you didn't want to rile. Someone Hollywood would put in a movie.

The general looked at Welborn now as he continued to speak. He had his right hand cupped around the receiver's mouthpiece, and his voice was too low to hear, but Welborn had the uneasy feeling he was the topic of conversation.

The general put the phone down and returned Welborn's salute. But he did not put him at ease. And Major Seymour's breath, hotter if anything, continued to take the starch out of his collar.

"Good morning, Lieutenant."

"Good morning, sir."

"I hope you don't mind if I take a few minutes of your time."

"No, sir. I'll apologize to Colonel Linberg for my tardiness."

The general smiled, but it only confirmed Welborn's earlier impression: Here was a man you didn't want to cross. "Don't worry about the colonel," he said. "She'll keep."

The general picked up a pen and began to make a note on a pad of paper. With his pilot's eyesight, Welborn could see the precision of the general's handwriting. And even a name, written upside down from Welborn's point of view: *Merriman*.

He decided it was better not to snoop on the general and looked away.

"How do you like your office at the White House, Lieutenant?" the general asked.

When Welborn looked back, he saw General Altman was staring directly at him, and he immediately felt there was no good answer to the question. But he said, "It's more than I ever expected, sir."

The general smiled again, giving Welborn the feeling that he had already crossed this man.

"More than any of us expected. A nice temporary billet for you, but a problem for me."

"Sir?"

"Having you outside your normal post at Andrews adds one more step to the process. Reporting the progress you make on your investigation becomes more time-consuming, if nothing else. And if someone, say the president's chief of staff, tries to manage the outcome of your investigation for political reasons, it could conceivably hurt the Air Force. Possibly even your career, should the politicians decide they need a scapegoat."

Welborn made an effort to keep his face impassive.

"We wouldn't want that to happen, would we, Lieutenant?"

Major Seymour's breath felt like a draft from a blast furnace now.

"No, sir."

Altman's voice changed tone, became almost paternal.

"I think a mistake was made assigning a new man to this investigation, Lieutenant. I'm taking you off the case. You will return to your desk at Andrews. I'll inform the president that a senior investigator will be taking over, and he will need to work out of OSI headquarters."

Welborn closed his eyes briefly, a silent comment the general did not miss.

"Something wrong, Lieutenant?"

"If I may, sir?" Welborn raised his briefcase by a millimeter.

The general looked past Welborn to Major Seymour, who looked at the briefcase and suddenly wished he had allowed the lieutenant to open it.

"You have something to show me?" the general asked Welborn.

"Yes, sir."

Altman nodded and Welborn opened his briefcase, withdrew an envelope, and handed it to the general. The envelope was White House stationery; so was the sheet of paper it held. As the general read the message from the Executive Mansion, his face grew red. When he finished, he carefully folded the sheet of paper, placed it back in its envelope, and returned it to Welborn.

"Do you know what that message says, Lieutenant?"

"Yes, sir."

"Do you agree with it?"

"It's not my place to agree or disagree, sir."

"You're right about that. Tell Major Seymour what the message is."

"Major, the message General Altman just read is from the president. It states that I am not to be relieved of my duties in the investigation of the charge of adultery against Colonel Linberg. Nor is any other investigator from OSI to be assigned to work with me. Furthermore, I am to report my progress to no one other than the president. If any superior officer tries to countermand these orders, I am respectfully to refuse such a countermanding order and immediately refer that superior officer to the White House."

After a moment of disbelieving silence, General Altman said in a dead-pan voice, "So there you have it, Major. The chain of command on this matter now consists of only two people: the president and the lieutenant. Quite an extraordinary concept. Over-throws more than two hundred years of military tradition in this country. For purposes of his investigation, Lieutenant Yates now outranks every general in the Pentagon."

Those words had no sooner been spoken than Welborn felt Major Seymour's fiery breath withdraw from his neck.

"What do you think of that, Lieutenant?"

Welborn felt a chill, and not just from Major Seymour's sudden distance.

"It's not my place to have an opinion, sir."

"No, it's not. For that matter, it's not the major's place, nor mine, to have an opinion of any order we receive from the president."

The general's statement was entirely appropriate. Would look irreproachable if printed in a newspaper. But it didn't come close to matching the look on his face.

"I think we've taken up enough of the lieutenant's time, Clarence," the general told the major. "I don't want to speculate about what else he might have in his briefcase."

Welborn could almost hear the major wince, and the cold settling into Welborn's bones deepened. The world was turning upside down. He tried to restore a semblance of normalcy by snapping off a picture-perfect salute. But the general's response was only halfhearted.

Even so, Welborn executed a parade-ground about-face. Major Seymour held the door open for him. As he started for it, the general had one more question.

"Lieutenant?"

Welborn turned crisply once more.

"Yes, sir."

"You don't have to answer, but I'm curious: Did you vote for her, the president?"

Welborn took a deep breath. Refusing to answer would be giving his answer, only in a cowardly silence. He let the breath out.

"Yes, sir, I did."

MAJOR SEYMOUR closed the door behind Welborn as he stepped out of the general's office. Then he grabbed Welborn's upper right arm, and treated him to another round of his preternaturally hot breath. This time on Welborn's ear.

"Four years or eight, administrations come and go," the major said quietly. "You want to make the Air Force your career, Lieutenant, you better remember that."

Welborn turned to look the major in the eye. And he flexed his arm. At the Air Force Academy, he'd developed a passion for free climbing in the nearby Rocky Mountains. He was told going in that if you took up a hobby where your life could literally hang by your fingertips, you'd better have some serious upper body strength. Being able to do a set of a hundred pull-ups, it was suggested, was reasonable preparation. Which had seemed like something not even Special Ops crazies would demand of themselves. Now it was part of his daily routine.

Major Seymour was no office commando, but his grip on Welborn's arm started to slip and when the futility of trying to hang on became obvious, the major let go.

Welborn saluted him and went to find Colonel Linberg.

He needed an MP to help him. He got lost on his second turn. Rather than wander around and waste time, he knocked on a door, went inside, and asked for help. His mother had taught him there was nothing wrong with a man asking for directions. Women appreciated men with common sense. The MP was dispatched to make sure Welborn didn't have to ask for directions at any door where he wouldn't be welcome.

Colonel Linberg's tone was hardly welcoming, but when he knocked, she said, "Enter."

Welborn stepped into an office that was a tenth the size of General Altman's. The only furnishings in the room were the desk Colonel Linberg sat behind and the chair she sat upon. Both looked old enough to be on exhibit at the Smithsonian. On the desk in front of the colonel was an open copy of the Uniform Code of Military Justice. Next to it was a pad of lined paper.

The colonel, apparently, had been assigned the duty of copying the UCMJ in longhand. She was far from finished with her task. Her career, however, appeared to be over. Nonetheless, Welborn saluted her as smartly as he had the Air Force chief of staff.

"Lieutenant Yates, OSI, to speak with the colonel, ma'am."

His sense of punctilio seemed to lift her spirits, and she returned his salute sharply.

"I'd offer you a chair, Lieutenant," Colonel Linberg said, "only I don't have one to spare."

"Yes, ma'am."

She gave him a long look. "Are you here to ask me all sorts of embarrassing questions, Lieutenant?"

"Embarrassment is not my purpose, ma'am."

"But if it happens anyway ..." Colonel Linberg held up a hand. The one holding her pen. "I'm sorry, Lieutenant. Your conduct has been entirely professional. I'll see if I can comport myself on the same level."

She put her pen down and folded her hands on the desk. Like a schoolgirl about to pray, Welborn thought. Or a defendant awaiting the reading of a jury's verdict. In either case, she seemed determined to meet her fate without flinching.

Which only added to her attractiveness. Light brown hair cut short, but stylish, for military utility. Clear blue eyes. Strong straight nose. Expressive mouth. The colonel was a looker.

"Are you trying to peer into my soul, Lieutenant?" she asked Welborn.

"Yes, ma'am," he answered evenly. "That's a class they make us take at Glynco these days." Glynco, Georgia, was the site of the Federal Law Enforcement Training Center.

He had her there for a moment. Then she smiled. As much as she was able.

"You're joking."

"About Glynco, yes, ma'am."

"But not about something else?"

"Outside of class, I was told it's a good idea to pay attention to a face in repose, like yours was just now. That'll give you a baseline, make it easier to know when someone's telling you the truth."

"Or lying."

"Yes, ma'am. Have you had breakfast?"

"I beg your pardon."

"I'd like to conduct this interview ..." Welborn looked around the tiny office. "... somewhere else. Outside the building. Where we can speak freely. I thought you might be hungry."

Colonel Linberg frowned and pulled a brown paper bag out of her desk.

"I'm tasked to stay in this office until 1700 hours, including lunch."

"I understand, but my investigation takes precedence over any other duties you may have. If anyone questions your absence, you may refer them to me."

This time Colonel Linberg smiled broadly.

"Refer them to *you*? And who cuts your marching orders, Lieutenant?"

"The president, ma'am."

WELBORN DROVE Colonel Linberg to a place he knew in Alexandria where they offered a selection of gourmet coffees and fresh pastries. It would be the second time that day he would be eating and conversing with a good-looking older woman. The first time had been breakfast with the president at the White House.

That was when she'd given him the letter he'd shown to General Altman.

Pretty damn smart to look ahead and see that the brass might try to replace him.

The president had also been the one to tell him to conduct his interview with Colonel Linberg outside the Pentagon. To tell him to use a face at rest as a point of comparison for the expressions a person might later reveal. To use carefully chosen humor to establish a rapport with his subject.

Welborn had listened carefully, another of the virtues his mother had taught him, and was pleased that he'd been able to put all of those instructions to good use.

He'd wondered, at the breakfast table, how the president had come by all of her advice. Then he remembered that whatever else she was, the president was also a cop's wife.

CHAPTER 7

LEO WAS driving McGill to a high-end health club on New York Avenue called Corporate Muscle. It was close enough to the White House to be an easy walk. On a gorgeous day like that Wednesday, McGill would have preferred to walk. It had been several weeks since he'd been out and about on foot; the media was no longer stalking him. He told Deke Ky they would have to stretch their legs later on.

"You know the president talked to me personally, before SAC Crogher approved me for this duty," the special agent said.

That was the first McGill had heard of it.

"She wanted to be sure I was ready to sacrifice my life to save yours."

"I thought all you guys were."

"We are. But she wanted to hear it from me directly."

"And you convinced her?"

"I asked the president to call my mother. She did. My mother told the president that she'd given me orders to protect the president's henchman at all costs. *All* costs. The president thanked my mother and has never doubted me from that moment on."

"Your *mother* told you to sacrifice yourself for me?" McGill asked.

Deke nodded.

McGill's own mother, a voice teacher, had taught him to be honest, respectful, and how to sing on key. He'd always thought that had been enough.

"So, you're telling me you don't want me to take any more walks?"

"I can't tell you anything except when to duck."

Deke almost added a "sir" to the end of his statement, but McGill had asked his bodyguard to speak informally—and frankly—unless Crogher, the media, or some other potential troublemaker was around.

"But you're getting at something," McGill said. "What is it?"

"You carry a gun. I'd like to know how well you shoot."

Entirely reasonable, McGill thought.

"We'll go to the firing range, and you can see for yourself."

"Thanks."

McGill thought of his children. "You think my threat level is elevated, too."

"You're working now."

"You didn't anticipate that?"

"For a while, it didn't look like it was going to happen."

Leo pulled the Chevy to the curb outside the building that housed Corporate Muscle. McGill caught his eye in the rearview mirror.

"Leo?"

"My mother's Jewish. I had to quit racing NASCAR for her."

"So you won't die for me?"

"No, but I'll shoot someone if I have to."

THE MANAGER of Corporate Muscle was absolutely delighted to see McGill walk through the door and struggled bravely not to shed a tear when he told her he was there to meet someone, not sign up for a membership. She cheered up when he let her buy him a freshly made cup of veggie juice and autographed a napkin for her.

The juice bar was separated from the workout area by clear plastic walls, and Deke's stoic mien and head-on-a-swivel wariness kept anyone else from approaching their table.

McGill unabashedly watched Chana Lochlan go through her workout. She had a female personal trainer to guide her, but Chana looked like a natural athlete who knew exactly what she was doing. Didn't need fancy workout togs either. Plain white sneakers, anklet socks, gym shorts, and a UCLA softball team T-shirt. She was pushing 160 pounds on the chest-press machine—at least 20 pounds more than her body weight, McGill estimated.

"Didn't think she was that strong," he said.

Deke glanced Chana's way.

"These places attract really competitive people. There's an affiliated club called Political Muscle. You should see them bust a gut in there."

McGill grinned.

"What about you federal law enforcement types? You have your own gym?"

Deke looked at McGill, and said with a straight face, "Yeah, we call it Killer Muscle."

Chana finished her workout just when she'd told McGill she would, spotted him, and came over to his table wearing a towel around her neck. Deke vacated his seat for her and took up a position that guaranteed McGill's privacy.

The newswoman sat down and wiped the sweat from her brow. She was flushed from her workout, and McGill thought she came closer to Patti's level of beauty than he'd first believed. It wasn't hard to imagine someone becoming obsessed with her.

"We didn't talk about money," Chana told McGill.

He shrugged. "I'm new to the business world."

"How's five hundred a day plus expenses sound?"

McGill knew Washington lawyers, the fancy ones, made five hundred dollars, or more, per hour, but he still hadn't checked out the local rates for PIs.

"Okay. If that's too much, I'll give you a rebate. If it's too little, we'll call it an introductory discount."

She smiled. "No offense, but I hope I won't be needing your services again."

"I suppose I shouldn't depend on repeat business."

"I have the information you asked for: The list and the bio are in my locker."

"Which is locked, not just watched over by an attendant, right?"

"Right. You really are careful, aren't you?"

McGill sighed. "Maybe not as careful as I should be. Or possibly you're not. In either case, a word of disclosure is in order."

He told her that Galia Mindel knew he was working for her. Which meant the White House chief of staff had either bugged his office, or she'd heard about it from someone at World Wide News. The latter possibility justified Chana's precaution of meeting with McGill at her gym instead of her workplace.

In either case, McGill related, he'd spoken personally with Ms. Mindel and left no doubt that McGill Investigations lay outside her professional purview.

A tight smile graced Chana Lochlan's face. "Tore her a new one, did you?" And when McGill didn't respond, she added, "Good. Wish I'd been there."

"The point is, the confidentiality I promised has been compromised, at least to some degree. You might want to find another investigator."

Chana shook her head.

"You don't know how hard it was for me to come to you. The only reason I did … well, I thought …" She wiped her forehead again with the towel. "It's hard to be the objective journalist here, but I thought it was great, what you did for the president."

"What I did," McGill said in a quiet voice, "was fail her terribly."

"I'm not overlooking that. But you didn't let that stop you; that's what impresses me. You set things right in the end."

Tell that to Andy Grant, McGill thought, but he didn't say anything.

He jumped, though, when Chana Lochlan put her hand on his.

"Sorry, I didn't mean to startle you," she said with a grin. Then her face became sober, and she added, "I didn't mean to bum you out, either. I just wanted to say I thought you'd be the one to get the job done for me. I still do."

McGill gently withdrew his hand. "Thank you."

She stood up. "I'll go get the list and the bio for you now. We'll both be more careful from now on. Especially about the list, okay?"

McGill agreed and watched her go.

The bio would be a standard capsulization of Chana Lochlan's life, suitable for family reading, PR-department-approved. The list, though, would give the names of all of Chana Lochlan's lovers. She and McGill had discussed the subject at his office. If a stranger knew her body and her sexual partialities, then he must have learned them from someone with firsthand knowledge. Someone who'd been there and done that.

McGill took his reading material back to the office, where he could lock it in his wall safe. First, though, he and Sweetie pored over the life and times of a media celebrity, scanned the lovers' list, and shared their first impressions.

"Ms. Lochlan became sexually active at eighteen," McGill recapitulated, "and by her present age of thirty-five, she's had fourteen lovers."

"Take out the three years she was married, and it works out to about one new man per year," Sweetie said.

"Not willing or able to make a long-term commitment. One of the two."

Sweetie looked pensive.

"What?" McGill asked.

"It's too neat. A straight-line progression: new year, new man. No repeat customers. We have a good-looking, successful, well-paid woman here. She didn't impress any of these Romeos enough to make him clamor for a second chance? None of them meant enough to her to call him some night when she was lonely?"

McGill said, "Does seem strange."

He hadn't thought of it, he guessed, because he'd had only three lovers in his forty-six years. Might not seem like a lot, certainly not a number to brag about, but he liked to think it was because each time he'd made a terrific choice, been lucky enough to find a woman with whom he might have gone the distance.

He certainly intended to go the distance with Patti.

"You're thinking maybe Ms. Lochlan left a name or two off her list," McGill said to Sweetie. "Someone who means more to her than just a new calendar boy."

"Yeah … or we're a couple of fuddy-duddies completely out of touch with the sexual cravings of the modern career woman."

Unable to reach a conclusion on that point, McGill told Sweetie about Galia knowing who his first client was.

"The more I think about it, the more I think she got the scoop from someone at World Wide News. I don't see her having a crew break in here and wire us for sound. Too Nixonian."

"Let's hope so, or the 'Chana Lochlan's Lovers' story could be all over the *Enquirer.*"

"I'm going to have someone come in to check for bugs, just to be sure."

"No, I'll do it. We'll keep a lower profile that way."

McGill said thanks, then told Sweetie about his conversation with Celsus Crogher that morning. Sweetie's face got very hard.

"What are you going to do?" she asked.

"Deke suggested reinforcing Barbara Sullivan's people with Secret Service personnel."

"Yeah, that'd be the first thing he'd think of."

"I was thinking of asking you to go see how things look. The kids love you."

Sweetie nodded. She felt the same way about McGill's children.

"You want me to go now?"

"Barb's going to call me tonight. I'll let you know tomorrow."

"No, I'll go as soon as I can get a flight. I'm supposed to see an apartment at lunchtime, but I'll blow that off." Sweetie had been living in a hotel for months.

"Go look at the apartment. I'll get you on a mid-afternoon flight. People are happy to do me favors. You'd think I was someone special."

MCGILL AND Deke had lunch on a bench at the National Mall. Leo ate in the car. It was McGill's treat, kosher dogs, fries, and soft drinks all around. The Mall was McGill's favorite place in town, but then it was easy to like a national treasure. Some critics complained that too many monuments were forcing their way onto the Mall, and McGill could see the time coming when the word would have to be given: Sorry, full up.

Maybe it would even fall to Patti to be the hard nose who had to do it.

For all its museums and memorials, the Mall was also a place simply to enjoy being outside on a sunny day. People tossed Frisbees on the grass or played lunchtime soccer. Mothers pushed children in strollers, guides gave bicycle tours, and everybody from tourists to office workers to formations of Marines chanting in cadence, jogged along the pathways.

And the parking on adjacent Jefferson and Madison Drives was free.

McGill said to Deke, "Great place."

The special agent nodded, as he ceaselessly scanned their surroundings. He said, "Some people come here and just smile. Others cry. But for the same reason."

"It reaffirms their faith that we can accomplish great things?" McGill asked.

Deke was about to answer when he suddenly looked toward Third Street, just west of the Capitol. Something had caught his eye, and he reached under his suit coat for his Uzi. McGill quickly got to his feet and turned to see what was the matter.

What he saw was a naked woman with long blond hair astride a white horse. The woman had the horse moving in their general direction at a trot. Deke had his weapon out now, but his finger was not yet on the trigger. Off target, off trigger.

McGill said, "I don't think she's carrying any concealed weapons."

Deke didn't respond. He just kept watching. As did everyone else on the Mall. Reminded McGill of a scene from the old science-fiction movie, *The Day the Earth Stood Still,* when a flying saucer landed on the Mall. A spaceman with a giant robot or a naked woman on a horse, they were both showstoppers.

Then a scrum of rugby players wearing Georgetown T-shirts decided that the *au naturelle equestrienne* was a prize worth capturing. They ran after her, but the rider saw them coming and urged her mount to a gallop. McGill and Deke watched as she charged by.

Then Deke looked around, suspecting that the woman might have been a diversion for other malefactors. But none was to be found. And now people were looking at the man with the automatic weapon in his hands. He tucked it back under his coat before anyone got too alarmed.

"You had enough excitement?" he asked McGill.

"You think she'll do an encore?"

"I can't believe she did it at all."

Both men looked to the west. As the rider reached Seventh Street, she brought her mount smartly about and rode it into a waiting horse trailer. A man wearing a baseball cap and sunglasses closed the doors behind the woman and the horse and quickly drove off.

"You don't know her, do you?" McGill asked Deke.

He nodded. "Yeah, I do. Never saw her like that, but she used to date a guy I know."

"What does she do? Some kind of exotic entertainment?"

Deke looked at McGill. "She's the chief legislative aide to the Minority Leader of the House of Representatives."

"Oh," McGill said. Then he added, "Glad she's not a member of the president's party."

CHAPTER 8

DAMON TODD was drawing stares. Not that there was anything special about his size: five-foot-ten, 180. His dark brown hair was cut short and brushed forward. His eyes were gray-blue and restless. His nose was strong and straight. His lips were full but masculine. A good-looking guy, but no more compelling than the new faces found on magazine covers every week.

What set Todd apart was his muscular definition. It started at his hairline. Every muscle in his body was exquisitely delineated. His body-fat composition was 1.75 percent, and he was thinking the .75 might be more than he needed. His skin was a canvas stretched tight over every sinew. Veins and arteries stood out in sharp relief. Great vascularity as muscle-heads liked to say. The complete package was almost overwhelming.

Which was why people just had to look at him.

Then look away quickly before he caught them.

Because you wouldn't want a guy like him mad at you.

Todd's attention was on the man seated across the table from him at the Potbelly's Sandwich Works shop on L Street. He was wondering if the CIA hired Indians. Not Hindus, Native Americans. The guy had a coppery cast to his skin, straight black hair, and an aquiline nose. Pretty distinctive looking for a profession where you were supposed to blend in. But maybe all that stuff about being able to lose yourself in a crowd was just TV crap. Get a guy who made people look twice, play against expectations, and maybe nobody would ever suspect him.

Or the fucking guy could be a cop. But then Todd had never heard of an Indian cop either. Not outside of someplace like Arizona or New Mexico.

"Something wrong?" the guy asked. He'd shown Todd an ID in his car. It said he was a CIA field officer, and his name was Daryl Cheveyo.

"Never met anyone in your line of work before," Todd said. "Just trying to match reality with preconception."

That seemed to satisfy him. But Todd started to wonder if Cheveyo had backup. He might not *be* a cop, but the Agency could have called the cops.

Todd looked around, trying not to be obvious about it. The shop was packed. All the tightly spaced tables around them were full. A line of people going out the door was waiting to place orders. There was even a black man with gray hair playing blues guitar on a tiny elevated stage—had to reach it with a ladder—opposite the cashier.

It wasn't the kind of place Todd would've picked for their meeting.

"Why'd we meet here?" he asked.

Cheveyo swallowed the bite of his tuna sandwich and chased it with a drink of orange soda. "Lunch was the only time I had to meet you today. Your sandwich okay?"

Todd hadn't touched his turkey breast with sprouts on wheat. Not that he wasn't hungry. He could have polished off a dozen sandwiches. But he had a midday workout scheduled before he could eat, and discipline was everything.

"I'm saving it for later."

"Okay."

Todd began to drum his fingers on the table. What he felt like doing was hurling it through the window. And the Indian spook right with it. But he didn't think that kind of volatility would help his cause. He saw that Cheveyo was looking at him and stilled his fingers.

"Your people are studying my data?" Todd asked.

He'd made a cold call to the CIA and sent copies of all his research papers to Langley. Trusting that the Company would see the value in what he was proposing, he hoped they would overlook the liberties he'd taken with his test subjects and not turn him in to the cops.

Lately, though, he'd begun to worry that the CIA would simply steal his work. No way *he* could complain to the cops. Of course, if they wanted to rob him, they'd better kill him, too.

"They're looking at it in great detail."

"And great interest?"

"That's not for me to say." Cheveyo returned his attention to his sandwich.

Summoning all his self-control, Todd said in an even tone, "I hope you can understand why I'm on edge here. You people are my last chance for validation."

"We appreciate that, Doctor. Try to be patient a little longer."

Todd wasn't sure Cheveyo should have used his professional title. Felt like the spook was giving away his secrets. But hearing it also reminded him who he was, calmed him down.

Didn't make him any less hungry, though. He was always hungry these days. Holding off on the sandwich until later was pure torture. Thing was, he'd gotten to the point of *liking* the pain. He said, "You don't mind me asking, are you Native American?"

Cheveyo looked at him. "Half. My dad's Hopi; my mom's Anglo."

"Your family name, does it have any special meaning?"

The CIA man nodded. "Cheveyo means spirit warrior."

Todd liked that. "You bring any special talents to your job?"

"I'm just a nose-to-the-grindstone guy … but I speak Navajo."

A Wind Talker?

Would Cheveyo have shared that with him if things weren't looking up? Or if the CIA hadn't already decided to kill him. Hard to say which it was.

If they gave him a chance, though, they'd invite him to join up.

THE LANDLORD was a lawyer named Putnam Shady. He owned a two-story brick town house on Florida Avenue and said it was worth $950,000. There was no mortgage; he owned it outright. He wanted $850 per month for the one-and-a-half-room-plus-bath apartment in his basement. He'd set the rent at the amount necessary to pay for one-half of his monthly business lunches. As long as restaurant prices held stable, he said, the rent would be, too.

He was trying to be funny, but Sweetie didn't laugh. She went into the bathroom, found it small—shower stall, no tub—but clean. The appliances in the kitchenette were also small but new and a good brand. The main room was reasonably big, maybe fifteen by fifteen, and the closet was more than adequate to hold all the clothes she owned. The whole place was painted white, the floor was polished hardwood, a decent amount of light came in through the front windows, and there was no smell of water seepage or sewer gas.

For a woman who'd felt comfortable in a cubbyhole at a convent, it was great.

"Any problem if I put a floor safe in the closet?" Sweetie asked.

"For ma'amselle's jewelry?"

Sweetie pulled back her sport coat and revealed her gun.

Some people saw a lethal weapon and got scared. Others were immediately fascinated. Putnam Shady was the first guy Sweetie ever saw who got hot. He'd given her the eye as soon as he'd seen her and had been taking discreet peeks ever since, but seeing the hip-holstered Beretta put his inhibitions down for the count. Now he stared and didn't care if she noticed.

"Problem about the gun?" Sweetie asked.

"You're a police officer?" he inquired in return.

The notion seemed to excite him further.

"Used to be. I retired. I work private investigations now."

Sweetie's age and occupation were entered into whatever fantasy matrix the lawyer was constructing. He was about ten years younger than she was, Sweetie figured, and not a bad-looking guy, but if he got too flaky, she'd look elsewhere.

As it was, she looked at her watch. She had to get to the airport. The McGill kids needed her. She didn't have any more time to—

Putnam Shady interpreted her gesture and expression correctly. He put his eyes back in his head and cleared his throat.

"A safe is actually a very good idea. For your, um, weapon and any other valuables you might have. I'll have it put in at my expense so the work will be up to my standards. Think I'll get one for myself while I'm at it. A safe, that is."

He straightened his lapels and extended his hand to Sweetie. The perfect gentleman now.

"The place is yours if you want it."

Sweetie's doubts lingered, but she had a plane to catch, and she didn't like having to say her rosary every night in a room where the TV and the paintings were bolted down. She took Shady's hand. Being a lawyer, he thought to add, "You do have references, of course."

"One or two," Sweetie answered.

WELBORN YATES sat in his White House office transcribing his audio taped interview with Colonel Carina Linberg into a cryptic shorthand a rocket-scientist friend at the Air Force Academy had taught him. Later, he'd enter it into a password-protected file on his personal laptop. Only when the president asked to see it would he decrypt and print out the file.

He wasn't sure that he would include the fact that he was trying very hard not to fall for Colonel Linberg. Honesty on that point might call his objectivity into question.

The colonel hadn't come on to him, not in any obvious way. That would have raised his suspicions immediately. It was just that she'd been decent enough to talk to him like he was a human being and not just a wet-behind-the-ears junior officer. Or an antagonist who was out to get her.

"At first, I just liked Dex's looks," she told Welborn over coffee and a raspberry croissant. "He's a handsome man, gorgeous, really, in his Navy blues."

Welborn sipped his own coffee without interrupting. He'd asked her how she came to be other than professionally involved with Captain Dexter Cowan.

"I've felt that way a time or two before," she said. "I guess it's only natural for a woman in my profession to like men in uniform. Some of them are so damn handsome."

She paused to look at Welborn, as if really seeing him for the first time. Her eyes seemed to say, "You should know, you're one of them."

The conversational opening was there, but Welborn declined to take it.

Colonel Linberg continued. "But nobody ever sent me head over heels before until Dex. All the more as I came to learn he was more than just a pretty face. He's knowing, funny, considerate … and, sorry to say, a damn liar."

"He told you he was single?" Welborn asked.

"He did."

"And by his own admission he didn't wear a wedding ring."

"No, he didn't. And not for a very long time, if ever. Women know what to look for: skin that's pale because a ring has shielded it from the sun. Or simply an indentation where the flesh has been compressed as it continues to expand elsewhere."

She glanced at Welborn's left hand as it held his coffee cup.

"You don't wear a ring, probably never have."

"No, ma'am."

"Dex's hand is just like yours."

Welborn tried not to read anything into that.

"At some point," he said, "you and the captain began to see each other outside of work."

"Six weeks after we began working together. Physical tension had been present from the start, and by that point it was pretty unbearable for both of us. We both had to be careful at work, of course. Our jobs call for a high degree of focus and sober judgment."

The colonel laughed again.

"That was the rationalization we used for going out the first time. We needed to dispel the tension so we could do our jobs better. We'd learned by then that we're both very ambitious people, and our joke was that if he was going to make admiral, and I was going to make general, we'd have to get all this unspoken personal stuff sorted out pretty soon."

Colonel Linberg sipped her coffee.

"Dex said we wouldn't have to worry about talking out of turn because we both knew all the same secrets. So I said why didn't we go out for a drink?"

"You extended the first invitation?"

"Yes … Hasn't any young woman ever asked you out, Lieutenant?"

There was an undertone of challenge in her voice.

"Yes, ma'am."

"Then you know there's nothing improper about it."

"No, ma'am. Nothing at all."

"Dex told me that first night that he was divorced. Not separated, divorced. He told me before we left the bar where we'd had drinks, before we went to the hotel."

"Do you remember how many drinks you had that night?"

"Two," Colonel Linberg said with certainty. "I never have more than two. I learned long ago that if I do, I'm not good for anything. And that night I wanted to be very, very good."

"Yes, ma'am," Welborn said as dispassionately as he could. "At any other time during your relationship with Captain Cowan, did he inform you, or did you hear from anyone else, that he was married?"

"No." Carina Linberg started to say something else but she stopped.

"Ma'am?"

The colonel began to strangle her napkin. "During the time we were ... sexually involved, I noticed some male officers glancing at me, snickering in an adolescent way. They tried not to be obvious about it, and they always looked away when I looked at them. I thought maybe my body language and Dex's had given us away, even though we tried to be very proper while at work."

"You never thought Captain Cowan might have—"

"Boasted of his conquest? Not then. But now I wonder if they not only knew about us but also knew that Dex was still married."

"Can you give me these officers' names, ma'am?"

Colonel Linberg provided them without hesitation.

"And when did you finally learn that the captain was married?"

"The day I was assigned to my new office and duties." She finished her coffee. "Thank you for the reprieve, Lieutenant, but unless you have more questions, I probably should be getting back."

"Yes, ma'am." There was a time to push and a time to back off, he'd been taught.

Welborn drove Colonel Linberg back to the Pentagon. He opened the car door for her, and they exchanged salutes. He watched her walk toward the building with her back straight and her head held high. But by the time she entered the massive building she looked very small. That was when he first thought she was a woman in need of rescue.

And he would be what ... her hero?

That wasn't what they'd taught him at Glynco. General Altman had been right. The case called for a more seasoned investigator. But there he was and—

THE PRESIDENT knocked on his door and stepped into his office. In a heartbeat, Welborn was standing at attention.

"At ease, Lieutenant. Please."

Welborn assumed the at-ease position, but still found it hard to relax around the president, especially when she had someone with her. In this case a beautiful young woman with red hair. She looked familiar, but he couldn't quite place her.

"Lieutenant Yates," the president said, "please meet Kira Fahey. Ms. Fahey is a summa cum laude graduate of Ohio State University and Vice President Wyman's niece."

Now Welborn remembered. He'd seen the girl sitting on the stage when the president and vice president had been inaugurated. Vice President Wyman was a widower and childless, and he'd been accompanied by his sister and his niece.

"Pleased to meet you, Ms. Fahey," Welborn said.

"Likewise, Lieutenant," Kira said, a look of mischief in her eyes.

"The lieutenant has lovely manners," the president assured the young woman. "I think the two of you should get along nicely."

"Ma'am?" Welborn asked the president.

"Ms. Fahey is also newly employed at the White House, Lieutenant. As of now, she is your liaison to me. If you need to see me, bring your request to her."

Welborn snapped back to attention and saluted.

"THAT TUXEDO makes you look like a movie star," the president told McGill.

They were in the presidential limo on their way to the Kennedy Center. The occasion was a night of comedy: *232 Years of Laughing at the President.* Historians, actors, and stand-up comics would recount the history of how Americans loved to laugh at the men, and now the woman, who governed them. Tonight was the show's premiere. Patti and the rest of the world would get their first look at the material that was targeted specifically at her.

McGill had promised to shoot anybody who went too far.

"Which movie star?" he asked his wife.

"George Raft," she said. Delivered the line with a straight face and innocent eyes. The woman could still act.

"Is that payback for abusing Galia?" McGill asked.

Patti nodded. "I can understand why you wanted to lay down the law yourself, but the donuts, that was mean."

"I didn't think anyone would take it right if I spanked her."

The very thought made the president laugh.

"Did you find someone to distract the boy detective?" McGill asked.

It had been his idea to make sure there was a fetching young woman in the lieutenant's life. If this Colonel Linberg did turn out to be a *femme fatale,* he didn't want to have Patti's personal investigator misplacing his affections. Leaving egg all over everyone's faces.

"Kira Fahey," Patti told him.

McGill grinned. "Now there's a man-eater chomping her way up the food chain."

"Lieutenant Yates has been trained for combat. I thought they'd make an interesting couple. Certainly they'll occupy each other's thoughts for the next several months."

No arguing that, McGill thought. Well, the poor sap was Patti's pet to abuse as she saw fit. It was time to turn to more serious matters, anyway.

"You heard from Celsus Crogher today?"

The president nodded and seemed relieved when McGill told her that he'd sent Sweetie to assess the situation and to reassure—

"Oh, God," McGill groaned, "I forgot to call Carolyn."

Patti handed him the limo's phone. Secure communications to anyone in the world.

"Go ahead. I won't listen."

"Please do. I often need sensitivity lessons." He tapped in his ex-wife's number, and his youngest child, Caitie, soon answered the phone. McGill said, "Hi, honey. It's Dad."

"Daddy," his daughter said, "is somebody really trying to kill us?"

Ever blunt, Caitie didn't sound frightened, just curious.

"Who told you that?"

"Nobody. I was on my way to the kitchen to get a snack. The door was closed, but I heard Sweetie's voice in there. I listened in and heard her talking to Mom and Captain Sullivan."

"Did you tell Abbie and Kenny what you heard?"

"Yeah. They didn't believe it either. Who'd want to kill us? We're just kids."

McGill winced. Patti saw his pain and took his hand.

"Nobody wants to kill you, honey. Even if they did, no way would Sweetie, Captain Sullivan, or I let them."

"That's what I thought," his daughter said, unconcerned.

"Is your mom there?"

"She's upstairs lying down. Lars is with her."

"Okay. Please tell her I called, and I'll call back tomorrow. I love you, honey."

"I love you, too, Daddy. Is Patti there?"

McGill handed the phone over. His wife and his daughter talked briefly. Patti laughed and said she'd see what she could do. Then she added that she loved Caitie, too.

The president told her husband, "Miss McGill would like you to intercede with the White House chef when the family gathers for Thanksgiving dinner. She'd like you to make your own personal stuffing for the turkey because all others are yucky. And if you can't persuade the chef on your own, she asked if I could help."

McGill smiled, but hearing his daughter's voice had driven home how vast his pain would be if he lost any of his children.

"We don't know that they'll try, Jim. And we won't let them get close if they do."

"Bring in the Secret Service?" he asked.

"We have to."

"Not Crogher."

"I'll talk to the director and find the right person."

"Thank you." He squeezed his wife's hand. "So how was your day, dear?"

McGill's question was asked in jest. He never stuck his nose into presidential business. Never offered an unsolicited opinion. He'd told Patti at the start his support was unconditional. The only time he ever needed to hear anything was if she needed to talk.

Which just then she did.

"The CIA thinks Raul Castro is dying. The end could be soon."

For years it had been Fidel that so many people had wanted dead. Out of power. But then the wily old revolutionary fooled everyone by handing over the reins to his younger brother, Raul. The previous U.S. administration's propensity for regime change had not been lost on Fidel. First, he came down with an illness described as life-threatening by some and not serious by others. Photos of the Cuban leader in a hospital bed appeared, and, to the layman's eye, his condition didn't look good. Then came assertions by the state propaganda organs that Castro would be back on the job soon. But he wasn't. And there were no more photos to show whether he was rallying, failing, or even dead.

Fidel's brother, Raul, assumed day-to-day control.

But now Raul was on the brink, according to the spooks.

"If Raul goes," Patti told McGill, "the CIA thinks there could be a power struggle to claim the Castro brothers' mantle. Perhaps even outbreaks of fighting between factions. And the Cuban exile community is making plans to invade. They have a secret base in Central America, Costa Gorda, funded and organized by my predecessor."

McGill said, "An invasion, of course, would unite the factions on the island, and, what, you're worried Havana will strike back at us? You really think they'll test you?"

During the previous year's first presidential debate, a conservative columnist had questioned whether Patti had the resolve—he meant the balls, but didn't want to be indelicate—either to deter, or if necessary, strike back meaningfully against any terrorists who had a 9/11-scale atrocity in mind.

Patti stared hard at the curmudgeon for a beat, then said, "If another assault is launched against the United States by any foe, we will determine the countries that supported the attackers and destroy their capital cities completely, without warning or mercy. If the United States is attacked with a weapon of mass destruction, that attack will trigger a nuclear response. Any aggressor nation involved in any way will be obliterated."

Some moments later, after the audience at the University of Chicago, the site of the debate and, by no coincidence, the world's first controlled nuclear chain reaction, caught its breath, Patti's opponent used a hundred or so words to say, "Me, too."

But she'd been the one to articulate what came to be known as the Grant Doctrine. And to that day, nobody had dared to cross the line she'd drawn. Or wonder about her resolve.

Now she told McGill, "Revolutionary Cuba has always placed a strong emphasis on medical training and health sciences. Langley's pretty sure they've put that expertise into creating biological toxins."

"Jesus. That crosses the threshold, doesn't it? For weapons of mass destruction."

Patti nodded. "But the thinking is the Cubans won't try to use those weapons against us."

"Then what?" McGill asked.

"Another scenario. In the event a credible threat against Cuba appears ready to launch from the capitalist side of the water, it's *socialismo o muerte* time."

"Socialism or death?" McGill asked.

"Fidel's legacy. His ultimate plan against having his revolution destroyed is to use his biological weapons against his own people. Genocide. Jonestown writ large. Leaving millions dead, the island despoiled, and the Yankee imperialists to blame."

"My God."

"The other possibility is that the whole notion is one big Cuban scam to get me to disarm the exiles in Costa Gorda. Make a fool of the new *mujer* in the Oval Office."

The motorcade glided to a stop in front of the Kennedy Center. A Secret Service agent opened the limo's door, and the First Couple emerged, public smiles fixed firmly in place. Ready to enjoy a night of comedy.

CHAPTER 9

THURSDAY

CHANA LOCHLAN was waiting outside McGill's P Street office. The building's landlord, Dikki Missirian, had kept one of the café tables he'd obtained for the initial rush of McGill's prospective clients and was filling a cup with coffee for Chana.

Dikki saw McGill's Chevy pull up to the curb and quickly produced a second cup for his famous tenant. "Coffee, Mr. McGill?"

It was another beautiful day—the sun was shining, and the temperature was mild for summer in Washington. A cup of coffee outdoors sounded good to McGill. Last night's show had gone well. Patti had come in for her share of kidding, but the humor directed her way had been witty for the most part, with only one mean-spirited joke. His wife had made him promise not to kill the perpetrator. Sweetie had called in that morning. The McGill children had slept safely and soundly, as had their mother and stepfather. The situation with Cuba was still hanging fire, but not getting worse.

From the look on Chana Lochlan's face, though, McGill's run of glad tidings had just come to an end. He told Dikki, "Coffee would be great. Can you bring it upstairs? Ms. Lochlan and I will be in my office."

Then he took Chana upstairs, waited for Dikki to bring the coffee, and this time he closed his office door before she could even ask.

He sat down and said, "How bad is it?"

"Very." She opened the soft black-leather attaché case she carried with her and pulled out a jade green thong. Looked like silk to McGill. But he wasn't sure why she was showing him the skimpy undergarment, and he reconsidered the wisdom of closing his office door.

"I found this in my dresser drawer this morning."

McGill arched an eyebrow.

"It's not mine. I don't wear things like this."

Begging the question of how it got there.

"The caller?" McGill asked. "Was there any sign of a break-in?"

"No."

"Did you call the police?"

"And tell them what, someone's donating lingerie to my wardrobe?"

"No, that someone trespassed on your premises and is sexually harassing you."

"You were a cop," Chana said. "Would they do anything more than take a report?"

McGill shook his head. In a small, affluent town like Winnetka, the PD could increase the number of drive-bys a patrol unit would do. Keep a watchful eye out for an intruder. But in a big city like Washington, the cops were too busy with actual mayhem and the budgets were too limited for such personalized service.

"He's coming for me," Chana said, "and you don't do protection."

Her tone wasn't accusatory, but it stung McGill nevertheless.

"If I did, are you now willing to accept the publicity that would come with it?"

"No."

"I can call in someone with expertise in evidence collection. We can go over your residence, look for fingerprints, DNA remnants."

"Search my house?"

The question was rhetorical, McGill could see. She'd already had one stranger invade her personal space. The thought of having others poke around did not appeal.

So she rationalized. "I have my confidential-source information there. My story notes. Ideas for projects."

"Which you probably keep all in one place."

"A locked, fireproof filing cabinet, yes."

"Did you think to check it? If someone got into your house …"

Chana Lochlan looked horrified.

"I'll call my producer and tell him I'll be late. Can you come home with me right now?"

"We'll take my car," McGill said. He went to the door and opened it for her.

Chana extended the thong to him. "May I leave this with you?"

"Is there a store label in it?"

"No, it's been removed."

McGill took it anyway. "I'll see what I can find out." Then he thought to ask, "Is the size right?"

Chana looked him in the eye. "I *didn't* try it on … but it appears to be."

"May I ask how much your clothing sizes have changed in, say, the last five years?"

"They haven't. What are you getting at?"

"We're working on the assumption that the caller, now the intruder, is someone who knows about you from a former lover. Someone who was a long-ago lover might think of you … well, as a smaller size."

For the life of him, though, McGill didn't see how she could be any trimmer.

"I haven't added an inch to my waist, hips, or thighs since college," she told him curtly.

"Commendable," McGill said. "Unfortunately, it doesn't narrow the field for us."

McGill gestured Chana out ahead of him. Without her seeing it, he handed the green thong to Deke, and murmured, "Stick that in your pocket and don't lose it."

Should some mad assassin be lying in wait, McGill thought, better that the thong be found on Deke than on him.

LEO HAD a call waiting for McGill when he, Chana, and Deke got into the Chevy.

"Forwarded from the White House," Leo said. "You just missed it ups-tairs, so it came here. The first Mrs. McGill."

McGill gave Leo the address for Chana Lochlan's Georgetown home, then looked at the reporter. "I'd like to take this phone call and keep it private."

She nodded absently, lost in her own thoughts.

McGill picked up the phone, "Carolyn, is everything all right?"

"We're all ... fine. I guess. Thanks ... for sending Sweetie. That meant ... a lot."

The message was reassuring. But his ex-wife's delivery was not. Her pace was so plodding she seemed to be searching for words in a foreign language.

"Carolyn, what's wrong?"

"Huh? Nothing. Just a little groggy. I needed a sleeping pill last night ... and after Lars went to sleep, I took another one."

"Just one?" McGill asked uneasily.

"Just one. I woke this morning with a ... a revelation. I wanted to tell Lars, but he'd left for work. Then I realized you're the one I should talk to, anyway."

"This is about the kids?" McGill asked.

"Of course."

"Carolyn, I'm so sorry all this is happening."

He saw Chana start to emerge from her self-preoccupation, but when he shook his head at her, she turned her gaze out the window.

"It's not your fault, Jim ... Hell, I voted for Patti myself."

"And if you had it to do over?"

Carolyn's voice grew heated and with the anger came clarity. "I'd do it again, damnit. What you and I did isn't the problem. It's what these other damn people are doing. Okay, I'm going to tell you my idea now."

McGill said, "Go ahead."

"Why I couldn't get to sleep last night: I kept thinking what if these people come, and they get past all the cops."

McGill told her Secret Service reinforcements would be arriving soon.

"No matter how many *bodyguards* there are, what if these bastards get past all of them? And I'm the last one left, the only person between them and Abbie and Kenny and Caitie. How can *I* stop them?"

He heard Carolyn start to cry, but then she caught herself, and the hard edge came back into her voice. "Jim, I want you to make me a promise."

McGill said, "Anything I can do."

"Good. Because I'm not letting anyone kill our kids." Then she said something that he never could have imagined hearing from sweet peaceful Carolyn. "I want you to find someone who will teach me to shoot a gun."

"Talk to Sweetie. Tell her I said it's okay."

He went along just like that. No objections. No arguments that she might be more of a danger than a help. Sweetie would teach Carolyn not only the mechanics but also the morals of shooting a gun. Not that there was any room for moral debate in his mind. Not this time.

There was just one problem.

"Keep it hidden, Carolyn." A former cop's wife, she knew about gun safety around the house, but there was something more on McGill's mind. "Because knowing Mom has a gun? That'd be the one thing to tell the kids the threat is real."

WELBORN YATES was leaning against a tree in the Chesapeake & Ohio Canal National Historic Park outside of Washington stretching his hamstrings, calves, and Achilles tendons when Captain Dexter Cowan pulled into the adjacent parking lot. The captain drove a navy blue Dodge Viper. He parked it on the far side of Welborn's tan Honda Civic.

The captain's car looked like its namesake. Next to it, Welborn's car looked like a field mouse about to be devoured.

Welborn had called Captain Cowan the day before to set up an interview, to get his side of the *Linberg v. Cowan* story. The captain had asked if Welborn was a runner; if so, was he up to running and talking at the same time? A charitable interpretation would be ... well, there was no charitable interpretation. The captain was asking how tough he was. How *manly*.

Which was perfectly okay with Welborn.

Welborn's favorite instructor at Glynco had told him: If some smart-ass wants to underestimate you, encourage the SOB. He wondered if the president knew that bit of lore; he'd bet serious money her henchman did.

Captain Cowan unfolded himself from his car. Had to be six-three, Welborn figured. He had black hair and eyes that were just about as dark. His face was all chiseled planes but asymmetrical, the product of a sculptor with a vision problem. Or a sense of humor.

Cowan wore crisp new running clothes: a white T-shirt that said NAVY where it stretched tightly across his chest, navy blue shorts circling a trim waist, and un-scuffed white running shoes.

Welborn wore old baggy sweats and run-down cross-trainers with paint drippings on them. His shirt did identify his branch of the service, however. USAF. But the lower horizontal bar of the F had worn away.

Encourage the SOB.

Welborn properly saluted his superior officer as Cowan approached.

"Lieutenant Yates, Air Force OSI, sir."

Captain Cowan returned the salute and smiled. Nothing asymmetrical there. His teeth were perfect. He extended his hand to Welborn, who took it.

"Nice to meet you, Lieutenant. You ready to go?"

"You're not going to stretch first, sir?"

Cowan laughed, a deep rich sound.

"No need. With my car's suspension you can feel every crack in the asphalt. It's like getting a rolling massage. A vigorous one."

The captain gave Welborn a nod and took off down the running path.

Welborn caught up, making it look like he was laboring already.

"Five miles okay, Lieutenant?"

"I'll do my best, sir."

They passed a couple of middle-aged jocks, civilians, jogging in the same direction. Cowan gave a polite nod as they went by. Welborn picked up on the cue and waved.

Once they were out of earshot, Cowan glanced over at Welborn, and asked, "So did Carina tell you I was a liar?"

"Yes, sir. That was the colonel's word exactly."

Captain Cowan smiled. Ruefully, Welborn thought.

"And you're a sworn federal agent. Lying to you is like lying to the FBI: a crime."

"That's also correct, sir."

"Well, Lieutenant, then I'll have to tell you the truth. I did lie to Carina that first night we went out. I told her I was divorced. I wanted her so badly my balls ached, and I said what I thought was most likely to get her into bed with me."

Welborn did his best to keep his face impassive, but he was astounded. The last thing he'd expected was a confession. The man was admitting that his preliminary statement had been a lie.

"I also told her the truth," Captain Cowan continued.

This time, Welborn couldn't keep his face from turning red. This guy was jerking him around. But he couldn't ask the bastard just what he was trying to pull because they were approaching the Great Falls of the Potomac where a large number of tourists, foreign and domestic, were snapping pictures of each other against the scenic background.

They crossed a footbridge to the Virginia side of the river before Welborn spoke.

"I'm sorry, sir. But you'll have to explain that one to me."

Cowan nodded. "The first time with Carina was all about sex. For both of us, I think. But the more I was with her, at work I mean, the more I felt for her. Surprised the hell out of me. So I decided I didn't want her to hate me for lying to her—any more than I already had. Which meant I had to tell her the truth, and I did. *Before* we went to bed a second time."

The captain picked up the pace, forcing Welborn to match it.

"Are you saying, sir, that Colonel Linberg listened to your confession, forgave you for what you did, and continued your affair with the knowledge that you were married?"

"That's exactly what I'm saying, Lieutenant."

Welborn looked at the other man, but all he could see was his profile. Not the best angle to determine someone's sincerity ... which might have been what the captain had in mind when he proposed they go for a run.

"Why would she do that, sir?" Welborn asked.

"Because she understood me."

"Sir?"

"We both wanted the same things: sex with each other and stars on our shoulders. She understood that reconciling with my wife would help my military career. Put a better face on my image. She said, in my place, she'd do the same thing. That was after she got over being angry about being lied to, of course. By then she realized the reason for my confession: I was falling in love with her."

"She didn't think, maybe, you had simply confessed because you'd already gotten what you wanted."

"I wanted more of it. I wanted it all the time." Cowan turned his head to look at Welborn. "Come on, Lieutenant. You've met Carina. Is it so hard to believe I'd fall in love with her? Want to be honest with her?"

Cowan turned his gaze back to the trail ahead. For which Welborn was glad. He didn't see Welborn turn red once more. It wasn't hard to for Welborn to imagine how *he* would feel about the colonel had he actually slept with her.

He tried to think of something else, and was surprised when Kira Fahey popped into his head. Then he cleared his mind of all thoughts of carnality and got back to business.

"If you love Colonel Linberg, sir, why did you admit to your affair with her? Why didn't you deny it? Lie to protect her?"

Cowan sighed. "My wife had the goods. A note from Carina about an upcoming tryst. I'd left it in my uniform when I took it to the dry cleaner. Mr. Lo, my very conscientious laundryman, found the note before he cleaned the uniform. He pinned it to the plastic bag covering my uniform. My wife picked up the cleaning that day."

"Your wife turned you in?"

"Not directly. She swears she never went to my C.O. Instead, she complained to a group of other officers' wives. That's all it took. The Pentagon has a broadband grapevine, Lieutenant."

Which would also explain how the other officers knew, the ones Colonel Linberg had mentioned looking at her like gleeful adolescents.

"You know, Captain, that what you've told me today is likely to—"

"Put an end to my military ambitions? Yeah, I've thought about that. But the shit would only get deeper if I lied. So far I've only fudged the truth a little. And if the Navy has no further use for me…" He shrugged. "Maybe it's time to rethink my future, anyway."

"Why is it you're not being court-martialed, sir? Colonel Linberg wasn't the only party to the adultery."

"I'm the prosecution's witness, Lieutenant. Without me there's no case."

"Colonel Linberg's note. What about that?"

"A joke. A prank from a colleague at work."

Welborn thought for a moment. "You could have gotten away with it, the two of you."

"If we'd both been sure the other wouldn't talk."

"So you love the colonel, but you don't trust her."

Captain Cowan found that one harder to answer. When he did, his voice was quiet. "I was afraid she was *too* much like me. And look what I've done. Will that be all, Lieutenant?"

"One last thing, sir: Have you been reassigned to new duties, does anyone have you hand-copying the UCMJ?"

"No." The captain hadn't liked that question at all. "I've been loafing along so far, Lieutenant. I'm going to run at my normal pace now."

"Yes, sir," Welborn said, keeping up even as the captain increased his speed.

The race was on, but it wasn't competitive for long. Cowan had the longer stride, but Welborn was just as fit and fifteen years younger, and when it came to running, youth prevailed.

So much for letting yourself be underestimated, Welborn thought.

He got back to the parking lot a good quarter mile ahead of the captain, and being male and a professional snoop, he had to take a peek inside the Viper. It wasn't the car's interior that caught his attention, however. It was a note on the passenger seat. An appointment for later that morning. Captain Cowan was going to see someone named Merriman.

Merriman. The same name General Altman had made a note of in his office. Welborn got into his Civic and headed home to shower and change before going to his office at the White House.

As he made his way back to Washington, Captain Cowan roared past in his Viper.

There'd be no outrunning him this time.

CHANA LOCHLAN had a two-story redbrick town house off Wisconsin Avenue, just above Georgetown University. McGill had learned enough about Washington real estate prices to infer the kind of money his client must be earning to live there: substantial. She ran up the steps to her front door, key in one hand, cell phone in the other. She was talking with her producer, telling him she'd be late to work, but not so late as to cause any problems.

Chana threw open the door and ran inside. Deke went in next. He never let McGill be the first one through a strange door; he was like Sweetie in that regard. Chana didn't count. If she plunged headfirst into trouble, that was her worry, not Deke's.

McGill stopped at the front door. He looked for scratches on the surface of the lock, signs that it had been picked. The lock was a Medeco dead bolt, a serious means of keeping a door barred. There were no scratches on it.

Deke appeared from within the town house. "All clear."

"And Ms. Lochlan?"

"She closed herself in her office."

McGill nodded and went inside.

His first impression was that he'd stepped into a contemporary art gallery: white walls, abstract paintings, and track lighting. Everything but price tags and signs indicating which pieces had already been sold.

The furniture was all clean lines and sharp angles. Scandinavian with maybe an Italian accent here and there. Area rugs in white, pewter, and charcoal provided visual texture and a measure of relief from all the unyielding hard surfaces.

The most striking feature of Chana Lochlan's home, however, was how damn *clean* it was. There was not a speck of dust to be seen anywhere. Not even a mote dancing in the sunlight that flooded through crystalline windows.

Deke had also noticed how immaculate their surroundings were. "You could fabricate microchips in here."

"Very close to godliness," McGill agreed.

At the moment, he didn't hold out much hope of finding any physical evidence left by the intruder. Then Chana slid open two pocket doors to what McGill had assumed was the dining room but was in fact her office.

McGill asked, "Everything present and accounted for?"

"Yes. Thank God."

"Nothing there that shouldn't be?" The question sparked a thought for McGill. He decided to keep it to himself for the moment.

"No. Did you think I'd find something?"

McGill shrugged. "Let's go see where you found the thong."

Being reminded of that brought back the realization that she had let relative strangers into her home, but she firmed her shoulders and led McGill upstairs. On the second floor were two bedrooms opposite each other at the front of the house. Chana opened the door to hers and waved McGill in.

Ms. Lochlan slept on a sleek platform bed. The rest of the room continued the modern minimalist theme. Except for the wall of bookshelves opposite the bed. It all but groaned under the weight of the volumes it held. Politics, journalism, and … recovering from grief.

McGill checked each shelf closely.

Then he turned, and said, "The dresser where the thong was left?"

Chana opened the door to a walk-in closet next to the bed.

The space was larger than the bedroom McGill had slept in as a boy. Smelled better, too. And like everything else he'd seen in Chana Lochlan's home, except for the glimpse he'd gotten of her office, it was spotless.

The dresser had been built into one side of the closet.

"Which drawer?" he asked.

"The top."

"Do you mind if I look?"

"I'll be downstairs in my office."

"Fine." He waited for her to leave and gave it a few more seconds. Tried to feel if there was any residue of illicit excitement in the air. Peeking through someone's intimate garments was intrusive enough, but planting such an item, one designed to fire the imagination … McGill thought Chana had every reason to be scared.

The intruder, he was sure, already felt he had a relationship with Chana.

McGill looked at the drawer closely, but he didn't see the slightest blur in its polished surface that might have been a fingerprint. Still, he opened the drawer from the lower left hand corner, using a handkerchief so he wouldn't leave his own prints behind.

The drawer held an assortment of panties, brassieres, and unopened packages of hosiery. Each type of garment had its own neat row; each matched up by color and style with the corresponding items in the other two rows. Some of the panties and bras were fairly utilitarian, others were racier. But there were no thongs. No peek-a-boo bras. No fishnet stockings. Nothing that would have embarrassed Ms. Lochlan should she have to be rushed to the hospital.

Being careful not to disturb either the precise arrangements of the undergarments or his client's sensibilities, McGill checked for store labels and sizes. It occurred to him that the intruder might also have done so. Perhaps even before he'd bought the thong he left for Chana. That way he'd get the size right, and he'd have the thrill of knowing he'd shopped where she did.

It was a place to start.

When he finished, he went downstairs to Chana's office, found her sitting at her desk, and closed the sliding doors.

McGill took the comfortably worn leather reading chair that Chana directed him to; she sat on a black, upholstered, ergonomically correct secretary's chair in front of her workstation. A late-model Wintel computer sat on the desktop behind her. A ceramic mustachioed bandito pointed his *pistola* at the machine. Appended to the bandito's sombrero was a homemade dialogue bubble: *Crash even once, and I keel you!*

On the wall over her work area were four framed photos. A gray-haired man whose intelligent eyes and engaging smile showed a clear resemblance to his daughter. Two portraits of toddlers, maybe eighteen months old. At first McGill thought they were both of Chana, but then he realized the child on the left had blue eyes. A fraternal, near-identical twin? Last was a team picture, the UCLA women's softball squad. A banner placed before the smiling group of athletes said NCAA National Champions.

"What position did you play?" McGill asked.

"I pitched, played first when my arm needed a rest."

McGill nodded, looked around again.

"You don't give dinner parties?"

"Hardly even go to any."

McGill could identify with that.

He smiled, and told her, "We've had only one state dinner at the White House since the president took office. If the next one's not for a long time, that's fine with me."

"But you'd never let the president host one without you."

McGill shook his head. "That's covered by the 'For Better or Worse' clause of our vows."

Chana picked up a pen and pad of paper from her desk and scribbled a note.

"Something I should know," McGill asked, "or just an item on your grocery list?"

"Idea for a project some years from now: Ask you and the president how you made it through your White House years. Looking back. After politics are no longer a consideration."

"That's the kind of thing you want to do?"

"What I want, just between us, is to be Bill Moyers. And by the time the president leaves office, especially if it's two terms, it's what I'll need to do."

"Why?"

She looked at him like he was pulling her leg. "You really don't know?"

McGill shook his head.

"Because the next 'Most Fabulous Face on TV' is in journalism school right now," Chana said. "Or high school. And I'll be over the line by then."

"What line is that?"

"The 'Gray-and-Gone' line. As in, if you're gray, you're gone."

McGill thought about it. He couldn't recall seeing a single female broadcaster, at least on a national level, who appeared on camera with gray hair. Men, sure. Lots of them. Women, not a one. But the thought of Chana's being in front of a camera turned his thoughts back to the intruder.

It was a delicate subject to raise, the idea that had occurred to him earlier, but he did his best. "When I asked you before if you'd found anything in this room that didn't belong here, I'd thought of an alternative theory of how someone might know of your private life."

"My sex life, you mean."

"Yes. The idea's fairly disturbing, but it'll have to be checked out."

She folded her arms across her chest. "What is it?"

"Maybe it wasn't a former lover who betrayed your confidence," McGill said.

Chana looked puzzled.

"Maybe," McGill said, "someone planted a tiny video camera in your bedroom. I looked and didn't find one, but that doesn't mean there isn't one somewhere in the room."

Far from being upset, Chana relaxed visibly and shook her head.

"That's not it," she told McGill.

"How can you be sure?"

"I know," she said, "because I don't do *any* entertaining at home."

McGill gave her a look. She didn't make love at home? Why not? *Too messy?* McGill knew his curiosity was obvious even if it remained unspoken. But this time it was the reporter who had no comment.

FRESHMAN REPRESENTATIVE Brun Fleming (R-OH) was in the well

of the House playing to the C-SPAN camera. The only other member present was the chair, Aeneas Papandreou, (R-FL), eighty-two, who'd fallen asleep as the young fool in front of him droned on about the crisis facing the nation's millet farmers, and how if price supports were not increased for these stalwart Americans, the republic's very food supply might soon be imperiled.

"Millet is not a glamour crop like wheat, corn, or soybeans," Brun said. "After all, what is millet but a small, edible seed? I'll tell you what: It's the foodstuff for the livestock that end up on family dinner tables as steaks, chops, and roasts across this country and around the world. Its nutritional content will become essential once the FDA bans all these awful antibiotics from

animal feed that are giving everybody cancer."

Brun wasn't sure he had the science behind that last claim exactly right, but there were plenty of millet farmers in his district and not a single chemical company. He glanced at that old cracker from Florida asleep on the podium. It'd wake that doddering SOB right up if he suggested they divert some of his sugar-subsidy money to the millet folks.   A wave of frustration and anger suddenly swept over the young congressman. It would take years for him to gather enough power to pluck the money tree for his constituents, and who knew if they'd return him to office often enough to grab that power. It just wasn't fair.

It was enough to ... make him sing opera.

Brun broke into "Fin ch'han dal vino" from Mozart's *Don Giovanni.* Right there in the well of the House. On C-SPAN. He sang in a rich baritone the likes of which no one, including Brun himself, ever suspected he possessed. He didn't miss a note. He sang with the power and projection he'd only dreamed of as a younger man ... of Pavarotti in his prime. But where Maestro Mozart directed that the part be sung *fortissimo,* Brun, aided by the microphone on his lapel, rendered it *molto fortissimo.*

Old Aeneas Papandreou levitated right out of his chair, not only waking up but experiencing a fatal heart attack as his backside plummeted back onto its red-leather seat.

The poor freshman representative later claimed to have no recall of his performance. But C-SPAN had it on a digital file. And the whole world marveled at it.

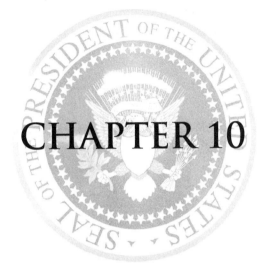

CHAPTER 10

GALIA MINDEL received an invitation from Senator Roger Michaelson (D-OR) to a private lunch in his office in the Richard Russell Senate Office Building. She was assured that the meal would be kosher. In terms of the food, anyway.

Galia arrived punctually and was met at the door to Michaelson's suite by the senator himself. He ushered her in, and she saw that not a single staffer was present. Lunch already awaited them on a serving table, so no one from food services would bother them either. Michaelson closed the door behind her as she stepped into his personal office.

Had Galia been twenty years younger, she would have worried that the senator had designs upon her person. Things being what they were, she knew it was the president he wanted to screw.

Roger Michaelson had been the candidate Patricia Darden Grant had defeated in her first run for the House from Illinois. Worse for him, he'd been the heavy favorite before she got into the race. A schoolboy all-American in basketball from Oregon, he'd been recruited to play point guard at Northwestern. On the court, his physical gifts were only average, but his competitive zeal was unexcelled. He lifted his team, often the conference doormat, to fourth-place, third-place, and second-place finishes in successive years. As a junior, he was named to the All–Big Ten Team. He was an academic all-American in each of his first three years. It was thought—dreamed—that he'd lead Northwestern to a conference championship in his senior year.

In the month before the season began, however, he suffered a serious motorcycle accident. He hadn't been foolish enough to get on a Harley; he'd been struck by one as he crossed a downtown Evanston intersection. He'd crossed with the green light; the cycle had come racing around the corner, running a red.

The impact slammed Michaelson to the ground, fracturing his right femur and his left hip. The kid on the cycle had been drinking and wasn't wearing a helmet. After a flight of forty-five linear feet with an apogee of more than two stories, according to witnesses, the biker landed on his head, fracturing his skull and turning all seven cervical vertebrae to mush. Death was judged to be instantaneous.

It was also judged by many to be too kind a fate for the fool who had put the university's star player in a wheelchair, albeit temporarily. What was permanent was Michaelson's retirement from high-level competitive sports.

For his part, the injured hero showed uncommon grace. He was rolled into the funeral home for the wake of the young man who'd struck him, expressed his sorrow to the bereaved mother on her terrible loss, asked everybody to think twice before ever operating a motor vehicle after drinking, and suggested that all his fans turn their anger into support for the players who would be on the court for Northwestern that year.

All very touching. Except Galia had heard the whispers of how Michaelson had told his best friend on the team that since he wouldn't have the pleasure of stomping that lump of shit to death himself, he was determined to get something out of the accident that had robbed him of his basketball career.

What Roger Michaelson got was a ton of good publicity. His gesture of forgiveness was covered widely and editorialized glowingly. His beginning the school year from his wheelchair and graduating with honors were also news. Acceptance to the university's law school passed without notice, but taking a job with the Cook County State's Attorney's Office instead of taking a lucrative job in private practice received public notice.

So did the high-profile cases the young prosecutor handled in the coming years. Roger Michaelson was as aggressive at putting criminals behind

bars as he was at feeding the ball to the open shooter. It was only natural, some years later, that the county Democrats put his name on the ballot when the North Shore congressional seat came open. A local sports hero, forgiving
victim, and crime-fighting prosecutor, Michaelson was considered a mortal lock.

Until the Republicans, at the last minute, came up with a name that had even bigger marquee value: Patti Darden, onetime supermodel and movie star, matured to be Patricia Darden Grant, wife of philanthropist Andrew Hudson Grant, and a champion in her own right for society's less fortunate.

Politically, there wasn't much daylight between the two candidates. There couldn't be. The North Shore's political views ranged from moderately liberal to liberally moderate. People in the district already had theirs and believed that everyone else should have at least a few of life's amenities. Hondas if not BMWs.

The race would be decided on personal impressions. And there Roger Michaelson was at a twofold disadvantage. From puberty onward, by inclination and coaching, he had been someone who believed in drawing first blood. He was called a slasher in his hoop days. Such a temperament played well in both sports and the courts, but it looked like bullying when a man displayed aggression against a woman. That made things hard for him because Patti Grant pissed him off. She was trying to deprive him of a big prize after the damn accident had already cost him one.

Did anyone really think he'd gone into public service for altruistic reasons? Well, of course, they did. That was what he wanted them to think. But anyone who was the least bit wised up knew what the score was. He'd been paying his dues. And he expected a payoff for himself. But here came this rich broad, a dilettante, never had to do a real day's work in her life.

Every time Michaelson saw her, he could hear a Harley coming around the corner.

As a result, it took all of his self-control not to snap at her when they had their debates, not to vilify her when a reporter asked him to characterize his opponent. He never actually stuck his foot in his mouth, but his body language was enough. In the arenas where he'd competed, it was necessary to show the opposition they had reason to fear you. In his campaign against Patti Grant, all his advisors told him, he was turning off women voters right and left.

He was losing men almost as fast. If most of them didn't actually want to jump his opponent's bones, they wanted to hear her tell them how wonderful they were. Roger Michaelson was certain he was every bit as smart as Patti Grant, but even he had to admit she was more verbal. More glib. As if she'd internalized all that smart dialogue she'd spoken in the movies and could conjure it at will. Meanwhile, he had to watch his every word to make sure he didn't offend anyone and come off like an ogre. What he came off like was a stiff.

God, he hated that woman.

He hated her enough to consider using a smear attack against her. In the desperate final days of the campaign, somebody suggested, gee, it'd be too bad if everyone found out that Miss Prim-and-Proper had gotten knocked up out there in Hollywood—by a guy who had VD and probably used drugs, too—and had gotten rid of the baby with an abortion. Wouldn't that be a shame?

What it wouldn't be was the truth. Michaelson's people had dug into every corner of Patti Grant's life, and there was no dirt to be found. That didn't mean, of course, that some couldn't be manufactured. Lying about your opponent was hardly new to Illinois politics.

Before the dire plan could be put into effect, however, the other side found out. A spy had betrayed Michaelson, and a consultant from the opposition passed the word that if lies were spread about Patricia Grant, the truth would be told about Roger Michaelson.

Namely, that in at least three of his big headline-grabbing convictions as state's attorney, he had suppressed exculpatory evidence, sending three innocent men to jail, one of them to death row. Not only was Michaelson not going to smear Patti Grant, he was told, after she beat him senseless in the election, he was going to announce that he'd "discovered" the exculpatory evidence in those cases. Or the facts would be forwarded to the U.S. Attorney for consideration.

Consideration such as making Roger Michaelson the subject of his own criminal investigation.

Michaelson killed the smear plan, lost the election, and got out of town.

He left it to underlings to clear the three men. He went back home to Oregon. Ever combative, though, he got himself elected to the U.S. Senate two years later.

It wasn't direct revenge, but he felt pleased that he was in the Senate, "the world's most exclusive club," while Patti Grant was one of 435 drones who called themselves representatives.

That sense of superiority turned to ashes in his mouth when his old nemesis became president, an eventuality Roger Michaelson couldn't have imagined. Not until she was nominated by her party, anyway. Then he knew better than anyone she would win the White House.

That was when he began to plot against her.

And now he was meeting with the hired gun who had planted the spy in his congressional campaign ten years ago. Galia Mindel.

"Galia, how nice to see you again," he said, shaking her hand. "It's been a long time."

"Senator," Galia said with a smile phonier than her eyelashes.

"Wait until you see the feast I've laid on for you," he said. He removed the cover from the serving tray with a flourish. A mélange of childhood aromas all but lifted Galia off her feet. Brisket of beef. New potatoes. Pickled beets. Applesauce. Mouthwatering, all of it.

The very meal she would beg her mother to make every week.

She'd sooner eat McGill's donuts than take any of it from Roger Michaelson.

"Senator, how very thoughtful of you. But I'm sorry to say I just can't eat that way anymore. My stomach, you know. All the pressure of working in the White House. I'm afraid this is about all I can handle these days."

She took a plastic cup of plain yogurt from her purse.

Michaelson silently replaced the cover of the serving tray. He offered Galia a silver spoon for her yogurt.

"I'll give the food to my people when they return," he said.

"Where *are* your people?" Galia asked.

"Donating blood. We're having a drive here on the Hill."

He waved Galia to a chair and sat opposite her. "Please. Enjoy your yogurt."

Galia took the senator at his word and ate her yogurt at a leisurely pace. She seemed to delight in every spoonful. In fact, she was taking pleasure in testing Roger Michaelson's patience. He didn't say a word and kept his face impassive, but he couldn't keep his eyes from burning brighter as his anger mounted.

She put the empty cup back in her purse, dabbed the corners of her mouth with a tissue, and returned Michaelson's spoon to him. He twiddled it through the fingers of his right hand like a magician doing a trick with a coin, and just like magic the spoon was bent in half when he finished. Without looking, he tossed it over his shoulder. It landed cleanly in a wastebasket in a corner of the room.

Galia was tempted to applaud, but instead she asked, "Are we ready to talk now?"

"I had occasion to speak with General Altman, the Air Force chief of staff, recently," Senator Michaelson said.

"He came to you, or you went to him?"

"I meet as a matter of course with any number of our nation's top military officers."

"In your capacity as a member of the Senate Armed Services Committee."

"Exactly. In my conversation with General Altman, I learned of a very unusual situation."

"The matter of Colonel Carina Linberg facing charges of adultery."

"Yes." Michaelson didn't like the way Galia anticipated what he was going to say, but he wasn't about to give her the satisfaction of telling her so. "More specifically, the general was disturbed, and rightly so in my view, that the president had drastically abridged the chain of command in this serious matter."

Galia sat mute. Forcing Michaelson to pull a response out of her. Further disrupting his rhythm.

"Do you have anything to say about that, Ms. Mindel?"

"The president is the commander in chief. It's her prerogative to act as she sees fit in this matter or any other involving the armed forces of the United States." Michaelson started to speak, but Galia overrode him. "That is the Constitutional order of things, don't you agree, Senator?"

"Of course, I do." Michaelson was openly angry now, but he kept his volume down. "But just because the president can do something doesn't mean he should."

"She, Senator," Galia corrected. "Doesn't mean *she* should."

"I was speaking grammatically."

"And I was speaking factually."

Michaelson looked like he wanted to throw Galia in his wastebasket. But his self-control was too good to let him go over the edge.

"I'm trying to be helpful here," he said. "The president has no military experience and—"

"I don't believe you've served in the military, either, Senator."

"I've been on the Armed Services Committee for six years," he said through clenched teeth.

"And the president was in Congress two years longer than you've been and now she's in the Oval Office. You really don't want to compare résumés, Senator."

Michaelson took a deep breath, seemed to settle within himself. As if he were preparing to shoot a game-winning free throw in front of a hostile crowd.

"Very well," he said softly. "You leave me no choice. Please inform the president that the committee will be holding public hearings into what we consider an abuse of *her* discretion in this matter and the implications it holds for lowering morale among the armed forces."

"Don't you mean among the four-stars at the Pentagon? But never mind that. In order to hold hearings, you'll need the approval of the committee chairman."

"Senator Dixon has given his approval. He simply allowed me the opportunity of trying to do this the easy way. I guess I should have known better."

Galia thought she should have known better, too. Cutler Dixon, Republican, was the senior senator from Georgia. He'd won his seat by accusing his Democratic predecessor, a Vietnam vet who'd won a Silver Star and lost an eye in combat, of not being patriotic. A social primitive, Dixon was no friend of the president's, but Galia hadn't thought he'd betray her so quickly. A mistake on her part. But Galia was one of American politics' great counter-punchers.

"Okay, Senator, you hold your hearings, but keep one thing in mind."

"What's that, Ms. Mindel?"

"Remember that Congress is the body that wrote the Uniform Code of

Military Justice. Not too many Americans know that. But in the coming weeks, I'm going to educate them. Especially the good women of this country. I'm going to point out how archaic many of the provisions in the UCMJ are, and how they pertain to the fate of Colonel Carina Linberg. And, who knows, maybe some of the president's friends on the Hill will start calling for a review of the whole damn thing to see how much of it should be rewritten. You think your four-stars will like that? And what about all those women whose eyes I'm going to open? You think they're going to be happy with any good-old-boy politicians who stand in the way of reform?"

Galia stood up. "So you go ahead, Senator. Hold your hearings. Open your can of worms."

When Galia strode out of Michaelson's office, she saw that all of his support people had returned to their desks, from the senator's chief of staff on down to the mail boy. She also noticed that not one of them had a Band-Aid in the crook of his arm, the way a blood donor would after being tapped for a pint.

But with Michaelson's crew, she considered it more likely they'd be out sinking their fangs into people's jugulars than giving up their own corpuscles.

The one thing that really bothered her, though, was how the bastard had found out what her favorite childhood meal was. That had been the whole point of that bit of theater. He was telling her that he'd been studying her. Worse, he'd found someone who had betrayed her.

Just as she had done to him ten years ago.

CHAPTER 11

MCGILL TALKED to all his children that night. He spoke to Carolyn, too. And, of course, to Sweetie.

"Dad," Abbie asked, "do you think maybe you could come home for a visit soon? We'd really like to see you."

"Honey, I'm on the next plane if you need me."

"No, I don't ... well, maybe I do. There's need, and then there's *need*. It's not like, 'Help, Daddy, save me!' you know. But I really would like to see you. It'd make me feel better."

Abbie was the most sensitive and perceptive of his children. If anyone was reading between the lines of the current situation, seeing it for what it was, it would be Abbie.

"I'm working my first case, for my first private client right now," he told her, feeling like a jerk even as the words left his mouth.

"Is it important?"

"I'm not supposed to talk about it, but if you can keep a secret ..."

"I can."

"Then I'll give you the outline. There's this lady. She thinks there's a man who's after her. She doesn't know who he is or what he wants, but she's afraid it's something bad."

"That's scary."

"Yeah. I'm trying to find out who the man is and stop him."

"You know what that reminds me of?"

McGill knew. "Andy Grant."

"Yeah. He had someone after him, too."

Neither of them felt the need to mention how that had turned out.

But Abbie said, "You'll get this guy, Dad. I know it."

"I sure hope so, honey."

McGill promised he'd be home for a visit just as soon as he possibly could. Then Abbie turned the phone over to her brother and sister.

Kenny told him he thought it was cool that he now had Secret Service protection and cops watching out for him. He told McGill that he'd extended his cordon—Kenny's words—to include his two closest friends. Now, nobody at school messed with any of them.

"Hey, Dad," his son said. "You know I promised Mom I'd never be a cop, right?"

"Right."

"But I never said anything about not being a Secret Service agent."

"I'm sure your mother never anticipated that."

"Still. You think Patti could set it up for me to get into Secret Service school?"

McGill said they'd discuss it when he was older. If he kept his grades up.

Caitie was still focused on her presidential favor, and McGill told her that her wish was closer to being granted.

"Patti has fixed it so you and I can show the White House chef how we make our stuffing, teach him how to do it."

"In the White House kitchen?"

"Yes."

"*Cool.*"

"But he has to do the actual cooking."

"Is that the law?" Caitie asked.

"Absolutely."

Carolyn came on and told him, "You should have seen the way they lit up when they heard it was you on the phone."

"No father could ask for more. How are you doing? Did you talk to Sweetie?"

"I talked and ..." McGill heard a door closing. "And I did it."

"How did you do?"

"Much better than I ever would have thought. I have a good eye and steady hands, Sweetie says."

"Does that make you feel any better?"

"I feel better and worse all at the same time," Carolyn said. "I'm glad that I don't feel as helpless; I'm depressed that we live in such a violent world."

"Cops feel that way all the time," McGill told her.

"I'm sure they do. I'm sure you do, Jim. And now I understand you a little better, and I'm sorry for some of the things I've said to you."

"Not all of them?"

Carolyn laughed. "Don't push your luck. Sweetie also told me the prayer of supplication she says before she picks up her gun and the prayer of thanks she says when she puts it down without having used it."

"We should all be so mindful," McGill said.

Carolyn handed off the phone to Sweetie. She told him that unless he needed her in a hurry, she was going to drive her car back to D.C. Now that she had her own place, she'd have somewhere to park it.

"Actually, that'll work out fine," McGill told her. "I'd like you to make a stop in Gambier, Ohio."

The town name clicked into place for Sweetie. "Chana Lochlan's home sweet home."

"Yeah." McGill told her about the thong Chana had found.

"Guy's getting creepy," Sweetie said. "He's going to make his move soon."

"That's what worries me," McGill agreed. He told Sweetie about his visit to Chana's town house, the sterility of most of the rooms, and the comfortable clutter of her office.

"We all want to put on the best front, and we all need a place where we can let down," Sweetie said.

"She said she never makes love at home," McGill told her.

There was a lengthy silence before Sweetie responded. "Fourteen lovers and she never brought *one* of them home? That's not natural. People let themselves be vulnerable—intimate—where they feel most secure. Where could she feel safer than at home?"

"That's what I hope you can find out. Visit her father. Talk to him."

"Yeah."

McGill told her of the photos he saw on Chana's office wall.

"Her bio didn't say anything about a sister," Sweetie replied. "Especially not a twin."

"And the one picture that's conspicuous by its absence is Mom's. How come Chana's mother doesn't deserve a place on her wall?"

"You think her father will talk to me?" Sweetie asked.

"I've never known anyone who wouldn't," McGill said.

DAMON TODD saw CIA agent Daryl Cheveyo waiting for him on a bench in Rock Creek Park. Like any American big-city park after dark, Rock Creek could be a dangerous place. People got mugged, raped, and killed there. But Todd assumed that a spy carried a gun and knew how to use it. As for himself, he'd welcome some thug trying to give him grief.

He looked around carefully as he drew near to Cheveyo. Not for miscreants but for cops. He didn't think the CIA would turn him in at this point, but he couldn't be sure. He took a seat four feet from the field officer. Close enough to speak quietly, far enough to take countermeasures if he'd misjudged the situation.

"How are you doing, Doctor?" Cheveyo asked.

"I'm exercising patience. As you suggested."

Todd saw the spook look him over closely. He didn't seem such a nose-to-the-grindstone kind of guy that night. There was an air of clinical detachment about the CIA man. As if he was mentally ticking off a symptomology checklist.

"Is this a better place for a meeting?" Cheveyo wanted to know.

"Not exactly original, but it'll do."

Cheveyo looked as if he expected to hear more, but Todd waited him out.

"I thought you'd like to know that the preliminary evaluation of your work is very positive."

Todd felt a rush of endorphins. His whole body felt pumped. But all he said was, "Yeah?"

Cheveyo nodded. "You've got some people very excited."

"I'm happy to hear that."

"There are doubters, too, of course. But that's only natural."

"What's there to doubt?" Todd asked, trying to keep the irritation out of his voice.

"Well, so far, your data are just words and figures on paper. Interesting but unproven."

Todd started to speak, but bit his tongue. He realized in that moment that Cheveyo was continuing to take a survey of Todd's personality.

Cheveyo continued, "Some of us have noticed, however, certain coincidences between your data and recent—what shall we call it—aberrant behavior by prominent individuals."

Todd said nothing.

"For example, the recent bareback ride on the Mall by the young woman who strongly resembles Nina Barkley, the chief legislative aide to the House Minority Leader. Your data mention a test subject with the initials NB, whose description quite closely resembles our latter-day Lady Godiva. Only we know that Ms. Barkley recently passed a polygraph test, proving more or less that she doesn't engage in public nudity. We find that very interesting."

Todd remained mute.

"Then, of course, there was the startling performance given today by Representative Brun Fleming of Ohio. Who would ever have thought he could sing opera? Who would have thought Congressman Papandreou would die as result?"

Cheveyo leaned in toward Todd.

"You didn't have anything to do with that, did you, Doctor? Because another of your test subjects has the initials BF."

"You certainly can't expect me to admit I did."

"No, I don't suppose I can. The lady on the horse was good, clean fun. The congressman dying, that was unfortunate. Not readily foreseeable, but someone with a bit more experience in these things would have picked a more *pianissimo* piece for Congressman Fleming to sing. So his microphone wouldn't have produced such a booming and unfortunate result."

Todd felt the sting of Cheveyo's words.

"Congressman Fleming has absolutely no recall of his performance. Or how he came to give it. Another intriguing development. But, Doctor ..."

Todd met Cheveyo's eyes.

"We hope there won't be any more of these ... demonstrations. They would only undercut your cause. Continue to be patient with us, all right?"

Todd nodded. "May I ask a question or two?"

"You can ask."

"Your first name, Daryl, it means dearly loved. Were you? By your parents, I mean."

Cheveyo gave it a beat. "Yes, I was."

"And you have some training in psychology?"

"An MD in psychiatry from the University of New Mexico."

"*Doctor* Cheveyo. And you speak Navajo. Any other unusual talents?"

"One or two. Would you like me to walk you out of the park? For safety's sake."

Todd shook his head. He'd heard enough. He got up and walked away. He had someone he wanted to call.

AS HE lay in bed with Patti that night, his arms around her, the two of them taking simple comfort from the warmth and weight of each other's bodies, McGill started to drift off.

Until Patti nudged him gently.

"What?" he asked.

"I've been thinking," his wife said. "About you."

"That's nice."

"Yes, it is." Patti started to say something, but then she kissed him. "Good night."

She rolled to her side of the bed, and McGill's eyes popped open.

"Sorry to be slow on the uptake here," he said, "but *what* were you thinking about me?"

She told him of Galia's meeting with Roger Michaelson.

"Galia was fast on her feet thinking of that review of the Uniform Code of Military Justice. It *is* a good idea, and I might actually push it."

"Three cheers for Galia," McGill said, conceding to himself the woman actually did have her uses. "Meanwhile, back to me."

"That's what I'm getting at. If Galia has thwarted one avenue of attack by Michaelson, and I think she has, he's going to look for another one."

Two seconds later, McGill got it. "Me?" He sat up in bed outraged. "*Me?*"

"I'm sorry," Patti told him. "I should have waited until tomorrow to tell you, but I wanted to make sure you were forewarned."

"I haven't *done* anything. I'm a private citizen. I don't meddle in government at all."

"But you are in an unusual line of work for a presidential spouse. And sometimes in Washington you have to *prove* you haven't done anything. I think you should retain a personal lawyer. Someone ready to be called on if ... when you need him."

McGill lay back down with a thump. "Fine, I'll get a lawyer. Sweetie told me tonight her new landlord is one. I'll talk to him."

"What's his name?" Patti asked.

"Putnam Shady."

"A lawyer named *Shady?*"

"Apt for the likes of Senator Michaelson," McGill told her.

AFTER PATTI dropped her bombshell, McGill got out of bed, unable to get to sleep.

Fucking Michaelson. He ought to punch that guy's lights out.

McGill entered the room that Patti had dubbed McGill's Hideaway and settled into his favorite reading chair. He listened for any sounds the household staff might be making as they went about their twenty-four-hour rounds. As usual, he couldn't hear them. The people who served the First Family's personal needs made Swiss bankers seem boisterous.

Hearing no human sounds, McGill listened for one or more of the White House ghosts; the place was reputed to have several, many of them distinguished characters. Abraham Lincoln was said to have been seen in and around the bedroom that bore his name.

The ghost of William Henry Harrison, who lasted as president for all of a month, hung out, appropriately, in the mansion's attic. Andrew Jackson was another bedroom shade. Abigail Adams walked the halls. Dolley Madison preferred the Rose Garden. The spirit of a black cat lived in the basement and was said to time its appearances to political assassinations and stock market crashes.

There were no apparitions that night, but McGill couldn't wait until his kids came for the holidays and he got to tell them White House ghost stories. Thinking of his children brought him abruptly to his feet. He walked to a window looking out on Lafayette Square.

Now he saw ghouls. With their FREE ERNA signs. Marching in their infernal circle, like foot soldiers of the damned.

"*Fry* Erna," McGill whispered. "And if you fuck with my kids, God help you, too."

CHAPTER 12

FRIDAY

MCGILL RAPPED gently on the front door of A-Sharp Sound, the commercial recording studio on the ground floor of the P Street building where McGill Investigations, Inc. was located. It was early morning, not yet business hours, but there was a light on in the back.

"Might have to give it a little more than that if you want them to hear you," Deke said, looking over McGill's shoulder.

"Or you could let off a burst with your Uzi," McGill replied.

Deke rolled his eyes.

"That reminds me," he said. "We haven't gotten you out to the range to shoot yet."

"Lunchtime today if they have an open firing lane."

"I think they might squeeze you in, considering who you are."

McGill still wasn't used to perks of his position; didn't want to get to the point where he took special privileges for granted. He nodded to the interior of A-Sharp.

"Someone's coming."

It was Maxwell Lucey, the owner and chief recording engineer. He was tall and slim. His shaggy brown hair was streaked with gray. But he had a baby face, looked like he didn't need to shave more than once a week. He unlocked the door.

"Mr. McGill," he said, extending his hand. He nodded at Deke. "Special Agent."

McGill shook hands, Deke nodded back.

"Hi, Max. We're not interrupting an early start on something, are we?"

"Uh-uh. Just winding up an all-nighter." He waved his visitors inside and relocked the door. "Something I can do for you gents?"

"Did you hear us knock?" Deke asked.

Max grinned and shook his head. "There's a pressure plate under the doormat. Step on it, and it makes a light blink back in the studio. So what can I do for you, Mr. McGill, and are there any Redskins tickets in it for me?"

McGill asked if Sweetie had talked with him: she hadn't. McGill explained what he needed. Asked if Max could do it; said Redskins tickets would be forthcoming if he could. Max said he'd be up in fifteen minutes.

MAX CHECKED McGill's phone lines for taps and his office for bugs. He told McGill he'd traded the Army three years of his time in return for tuition to music school. Along the way, Uncle Sam had taught him some useful electronics skills. He pronounced McGill's offices snoop-free and said four tickets to see the Skins play the shit-heel Dallas Cowboys would compensate him nicely.

Confident that he could speak freely now, McGill called Chana Lochlan at home.

"Any more problems?" he asked.

"There was a hang-up on my phone machine last night."

They'd agreed Chana should screen all of her calls.

"Could have been a wrong number. Or did you get a bad vibe from it?"

McGill heard Chana laugh but didn't detect any humor.

"You mean, am I feeling paranoid?"

"I mean, a smart cop respects intuition."

There was a drawn-out silence. "I'm not sure how much you should trust mine. I'm jumping at shadows right now."

"I've had an idea about that. Protecting you, I mean. My associate, Margaret Sweeney, will be back in town tomorrow. She could safeguard you inconspicuously."

"Is she any good?"

"She stopped a bullet for me."

"Jesus … but does she look like a cop?"

"She looks like an angel. An archangel."

"That's the kind with a sword?"

"Exactly."

"Let me think about it, okay?"

"Your decision," McGill said. "In the meantime, I'd like to speak with your bureau chief."

"Why?"

McGill told her that his office had been declared free of eaves-dropping devices. That meant Galia Mindel must have learned about his working for Chana from her end of things.

"And you think Monty would be able to pinpoint the leak?" she asked.

"That's my hope."

"But how is that relevant to my problem?"

"It's a good idea to know about anybody who's poking his nose into your business."

"All right, but not at my office."

McGill said, "Ask your boss if he'd like to see me shoot."

"He'll cream himself."

"We'll try to keep that out of the news."

MCGILL GOT up from his desk and went to the outer office, where Deke waited.

"Let's go," he said.

"Where are we going?"

"Bloomingdale's. In McLean, VA. You still got that thong I gave you?"

"Yeah."

"You know if the store's open yet?"

"No idea," Deke said.

"Well, if it's not, maybe they'll let us in early. Me being such a big shot."

Deke suppressed a laugh. "Yeah."

Then he called down to Leo to get the Chevy ready.

WELBORN SAT in his White House office studying a four-color brochure for the Dodge Viper. Resting on his desk were folders containing the service records of the two principals in his case. The colonel's folder was open, revealing a headshot of Carina Linberg. Even unsmiling for a service photo she was an eyeful. Captain Dexter Cowan's folder was closed.

Welborn's first hint that he had company was the smell of perfume. The scent almost made him leap to his feet until he discerned that it wasn't the president's fragrance. Funny to think that the commander in chief of the world's only superpower wore perfume.

Welborn looked up and saw Kira Fahey. She was staring at the Viper brochure. She lifted her eyes to meet his. "You have family money, Lieutenant Yates?"

The question was impertinent, but Welborn answered anyway.

"My mother is comfortable, Ms. Fahey, but not wealthy."

She ignored his frosty tone and moved around the desk to stand at his right shoulder.

"And the Air Force doesn't let you moonlight?"

"No, Ms. Fahey, it doesn't."

"Then you might want to set your sights a little lower, Lieutenant."

"Is that right?"

"Well, a Viper starts around $81,895, I believe, and goes up from there."

Welborn gave her a look. She had the starting price for the base model exactly right. But that was using one of the standard exterior colors. Captain Cowan's navy blue model was a custom paint job. With that and the gas guzzler tax and sales tax, it had to push the cost over 90K. Navy captains earned more than Air Force lieutenants, Welborn knew, but they didn't make enough money to buy Vipers.

Not when the captain's father and mother were a housepainter and a secretary. Welborn, too, had wondered about family money. Cowan didn't have any. Nor did his wife.

"A boy I knew in Columbus had a Viper," Kira told Welborn, which explained her knowledge of the car's price. "His was red. He said he liked the way it went with my hair. But I think my hair would look more striking in a black Viper, don't you?"

Welborn declined to offer an opinion. Kira turned her attention to Colonel Linberg. "The *Post* used that picture this morning. That's what I came to tell you, if you hadn't already heard: Your case has made the news.

She's an attractive woman. I hope I age as nicely."

He wasn't going anywhere near that one, either. Kira pointed a delicate finger at the closed folder.

"Is Captain Cowan lurking under there? His picture was in the paper, too."

Welborn flipped open Cowan's folder. Kira moved his photo next to Carina Linberg's.

"Handsome couple," she said.

"But which one of them is lying?"

"Could be either one," she said. "Could be *both*."

Kira walked around Welborn's desk and headed for the door. "Come on, I'll show you the story in the paper."

Welborn watched her slim hips swivel around the doorframe; then she unexpectedly leaned back and caught him looking. Smiled like she knew he'd have his eyes on her.

"Oh, yes, I forgot. Ms. Mindel wants to talk with you. About the newspaper story."

BLOOMINGDALE'S DID, in fact, let McGill and Deke inside before the public had access to its wares. The general manager introduced herself as Lida Dalman.

"It's a pleasure to meet you, Mr. McGill," she said.

Ms. Dalman was a handsome woman, smartly turned out.

"I'm sorry to put you to any trouble," he said.

"We understand that some of our customers have special needs."

McGill had never shopped at Bloomingdale's in his life.

"How may I help you?"

He decided maybe he should start shopping there. After the case was over.

"May I count on your discretion?" he asked.

"Of course."

"I'm working on a case. Perhaps you've heard that I do private investigations."

"I believe I've read that, yes."

McGill turned to Deke. "Special Agent."

Deke handed Ms. Dalman the green thong Chana Lochlan had found in her unmentionables drawer. He'd taken the trouble to put it into a plastic evidence bag.

"By any chance," McGill asked, "does your store carry that item? I ask because it was found in the company of similar garments that bear Bloomingdale's labels."

Lida Dalman gave him a smile so subtle Da Vinci should have painted it.

"Very delicately phrased, Mr. McGill. But I believe it's still acceptable to call a thong a thong. I also believe this is one of ours." She held the plastic bag up to the light and turned it any number of angles. "May I remove it from the bag?"

"Go right ahead."

She did. Searched for a label, came up empty.

"Come with me, please."

McGill and Deke followed, Deke leading the way in case an assassin lurked behind a mannequin. They entered the lingerie department. Ms. Dalman stopped at a display table where an array of thongs in an assortment of sizes and colors rested. She plucked one from their midst without disturbing any of the others. She held up the garment she'd selected behind the one she'd been provided. The match was perfect for both color and size. Ms. Dalman smiled again.

"French design, Chinese silk, natural dye, all for the *very* reasonable price of $14.99," she said. "Does that help?"

McGill nodded, then paused as he sought additional delicate phrasing.

"You have another question?" Ms. Dalman asked.

"I do, I'm just not sure how to put it."

"Simply is usually best."

"All right. How does someone know if a thong is the right fit?"

Ms. Dalman's smile grew a touch more impish.

"She tries it on. Over the undergarment she wears to the store."

"And if a gentleman is buying for a lady?"

"Well, with something this personal, you suspect he'd have knowledge of the size in advance. Or access to that information."

McGill considered that. Then he returned to a point Ms. Dalman had raised earlier.

"Would a man buying a thong for a woman be interested in value-pricing?"

Ms. Dalman shook her head. "Romance dictates otherwise."

"But the ladies?"

"Always appreciate value. She knows a man who sees her in something like this is unlikely to say, 'Honey, how much did you pay for that thing?'"

McGill laughed; even Deke cracked a smile.

"So a woman who spots a good buy can feel smart and sexy at the same time."

"And her man," McGill said, "will never be the wiser."

"Never," Ms. Dalman agreed.

McGill thanked her for her gracious help.

There was one more question he could have asked, but it would have put Ms. Dalman in an awkward spot. Which would have been a rude way to treat someone so cooperative.

Instead, he asked for an application for a Bloomingdale's credit card.

AS MCGILL'S government-issue Chevy approached the unmarked building that housed the federal firing range, also in suburban Virginia, Leo asked him, "All right if I watch, boss?"

"Long as you make sure none of these feds steals our ride."

Leo grinned.

"SAC Crogher's likely to be on hand," Deke told McGill.

"Why?" McGill asked.

"Today's the day he shoots each week."

"Lucky me."

Leo pulled into the parking lot and McGill saw a pearl gray Jaguar XJR parked near the entrance to the range. Leaning against it, communing with his BlackBerry, was Monty Kipp, Washington bureau chief for World Wide News.

Kipp was an ex-pat Brit, now a naturalized American citizen. He'd once been editor in chief of a London tabloid. Now, he styled himself as a responsible television journalist. He admitted to conservative leanings but swore he never let them affect his news judgments.

Uh-huh.

Kipp had come to McGill's attention after the newsman, in a drunken moment, had whispered into Press Secretary Aggie Wu's ear that his last great journalistic ambition was to get a current photo of Patti Grant topless.

Sell it for a bloody fortune. Page three, all over the world.

Once a tabloid guy, always a tabloid guy.

Kipp had really upset Aggie with that little gem, but what could she do about it? Nobody else had heard a word. What she'd done was tell McGill.

Who'd thought earlier that day it wouldn't be a bad idea to show Kipp how he handled a gun. Plant the seed that realizing his ambition could come at a very high cost. Then he'd talk to the SOB about Chana Lochlan.

"Pull in next to our friend from the media," McGill told Leo.

MCGILL DIDN'T have to worry about finding space at the range; he had the whole firing line to himself. The range manager had done him the courtesy of hanging his first target for him. Set it up in the center lane. McGill nodded his appreciation. He took off his sport coat and handed it to Deke.

"You knew it was going to be like this, didn't you?" he asked.

Deke shrugged. "You lock onto the target, doesn't matter who's watching."

He was right about that, but McGill had not only Deke, Leo, and Monty Kipp for an audience, he also had Celsus Crogher and a couple of dozen other feds who'd normally be honing their own lethal skills at that moment.

"Everybody's here except SportsCenter," McGill said.

"They're on their way."

It was the first joke Deke had ever cracked in his presence.

Well, at least McGill had set the ground rules. He would shoot CPD qualifying numbers: one hundred rounds at distances of seven, fifteen, and twenty-five yards. He put on the shooting goggles that had been left in the booth and was glad someone—probably at Deke's insistence—had made sure they were clean. As often as not, you'd find fingerprints on the lenses, blurring your field of vision.

Cop humor.

He donned his ear protectors, undid his holster restraint, and toed the line. He drew his Beretta, checked and reseated the magazine, racked a round into the chamber, and took the safety off. He assumed a Modified Weaver position—strong side of the body away from the target about thirty degrees, arms thrust forward slightly bent—and held the weapon in the ready-pistol position—pointed downrange at a forty-five-degree angle.

"Fire when ready," came the amplified voice of the range manager from the control booth.

McGill began shooting before the words stopped echoing. He shot, reloaded, changed targets and distances, shot and reloaded again, all at rapid but rhythmic pace. Technique was essential to good marksmanship, but so was consistency. Following the same motions, just so, over and over again. Practice became muscle memory. Everything kept pace with the timepiece within the shooter's body. Some guys said they shot in sync with their heartbeats, and while McGill believed them, that seemed impossibly slow to him.

He shot in time with the strobe light that went off inside his head anytime he had to fire his weapon, the muzzle blast following the internal flash by a nanosecond. He'd had several instructors and colleagues tell him he'd improve his scores if he slowed down. Just a little.

He couldn't do it. Anytime he held a gun in his hands, his survival instinct *screamed* at him to get off the first shot before the other guy did. He fired, and fired, and fired.

It always took him by surprise when a range manager ordered, "Cease fire!"

It couldn't be over already, could it?

But it was and he had scored ninety-two lethal hits out of a hundred rounds fired.

In Chicago, seventy was passing. Eighty-five to ninety-five was considered good. Ninety-six to one hundred was considered great.

"Better than I expected," Deke said. Praise as high as the special agent's stoicism would allow.

McGill wasn't satisfied, though. "But not as good as you or Sweetie, right?" Then he added, "A hundred more rounds. This time from the holster."

A CHICAGO cop was expected to be able to draw his weapon, bring it to bear, and fire two shots accurately within six seconds; fire two rounds, tactical reload, and fire two more rounds within eighteen seconds. Three-round strings of fire got slightly more time. All that was with the target seven yards away. Longer strings at greater distances got proportionately more time.

Everything depended on a fast, clean draw. No wasted motion. The arm drawing the weapon was kept close to the body and moved backward in a straight line. The weapon was withdrawn only far enough to clear the holster. The weapon was thrust forward to meet the supporting hand. The movement to eye level was a straight line.

McGill's draw was textbook.

His reaction time, however, was far quicker than departmental standards. The men watching him marveled at his hand speed. His Beretta was in his hip holster, then he was shooting. If you blinked, you missed the draw.

Deke muttered, "Jesus."

Kipp uttered, "Crikey."

Celsus Crogher shook his head and left the range.

When McGill finished, he received a round of applause.

He'd shot a ninety-four. Two better than before but still not in the "great" category. He always comforted himself with the thought that he could get off two rounds before most guys could fire their first, and he was almost certain to hit his man with one of his shots.

After that … well, seriously wounded men shot back only in the movies.

He holstered his weapon, left his goggles and ear protectors in the booth, and walked over to Deke, Leo, and Kipp. Deke handed him his coat, and he put it over his arm.

"Nice shooting, boss," Leo told him. He waved and left to get back to his Chevy.

"Feel better now?" McGill asked Deke.

"Yeah," Deke admitted, conceding nothing more.

"Enjoy the show, Mr. Kipp?"

"It was brilliant, Mr. McGill. With that amazing quickness of yours, sir, I wonder if you've ever studied a martial art."

"I've been trained in Dark Alley," McGill said.

Kipp looked puzzled. "Sorry, don't believe I've heard of that one."

"Think street fighting, only organized," McGill told him. "Can you spare me a few minutes, Mr. Kipp? I'd like to talk with you while I clean my weapon."

DEKE SHOWED them to the gun-cleaning room. For the number of shooters the range could accommodate, the cleaning area was very small. Government planning. But they had the place to themselves. Deke waited outside at the door so there would be no intrusions.

McGill rolled up his sleeves and sat at the workbench. He'd fired his weapon dry on the range, but he released the magazine and made sure the chamber was clear. There was *no* excuse for shooting yourself with a weapon you were cleaning.

The safety check accomplished, McGill field stripped the Beretta. He didn't need to look to do it. He turned his gaze to Kipp, who was watching him work.

"Care for a seat, Mr. Kipp?"

The only ones available were on the bench to either side of McGill.

"No, thank you. I'm quite comfortable where I am."

"Do any shooting yourself?" McGill asked.

"No, no. I wasn't in military service when I was young. Bad back, you know. And firearms aren't nearly as common in the U.K. as they are here."

"Even your police don't carry them routinely."

"More so than before. But again, not like this country."

McGill had the Beretta broken down to its component parts. Kipp seemed fascinated by the deconstruction.

"Doesn't look like much, does it?" McGill asked. "Certainly nothing to fear."

"Just odd bits of ironmongery," Kipp agreed.

McGill began to swab out the bore with a solvent-soaked patch pushed by a cleaning rod. Kipp smiled dreamily. Perhaps the male-female symbolism.

"I hear you've expressed an interest in my wife, Mr. Kipp." McGill met the Englishman's suddenly wary eyes. "One that would expose her to great humiliation. All for your base amusement and personal gain."

McGill hadn't planned to bring the matter up so directly, but a few things had come together for him as he shot. Zen marksmanship. His revelations had made him mad.

For his part, Kipp was at a loss for words. Didn't even look like he was breathing. He was probably working out his chances of making a successful break for the door. But he didn't seem to like the odds. So he stood there mute and unmoving.

McGill continued to clean his gun, finished that, and began to lubricate it.

Kipp watched his every move intently.

"You also found out Chana Lochlan hired me, didn't you?"

Kipp nodded reluctantly, as if he couldn't help himself.

"You like beautiful women, so you keep tabs on them. Especially the ones who work for you. You heard Ms. Lochlan hired me, a private investigator, and figured it had to be something juicy. And I'd be doing the heavy lifting. All you'd have to do would be swoop in at the finish, make off with the dirty laundry, and shame your own employee. Or perhaps blackmail her."

McGill began to reassemble the Beretta. He didn't need to look to do this work either.

"Do you have any plans for a page-three photo of Ms. Lochlan?"

Guilt was written all over Kipp's face.

"Do you know *why* she hired me?" McGill asked.

He held the barrel up to the light to check for residue.

"No, no, I don't. As God is my witness."

"But you leaked the fact of who my client was to Galia Mindel. Probably hoping to stir up a hornet's nest in the White House. Just for good clean fun. To be covered in your network's honest and forthright way."

McGill fitted the barrel into the frame rails.

"Yes, that's what I hoped."

"How did you find out Ms. Lochlan had hired me?"

Plainly, Kipp did not want to tell. But McGill soon had the gun back together, and he started to feed cartridges into the magazine.

"I … I bugged her office."

"Not her phones?"

"No, that's too dicey legally. But company property, the courts are allowing employers more liberties than ever before."

"So there are limits on your invasions of privacy. You know that I'm working for Ms. Lochlan but maybe you don't know why."

"No, no, I don't."

McGill slapped the magazine into the Beretta. Kipp squeezed his eyes shut.

"Mr. Kipp?"

He opened one eye.

"I advise you to debug Ms. Lochlan's office."

"Yes, I'll do that immediately. Will that be all?"

McGill shook his head.

"My wife is *never* going to appear on page three, *anywhere* in the world, is she?"

"No, never."

"Because I'd hate to think what might happen if ..."

McGill was tempted to point the Beretta at Kipp, but he didn't.

"Well, it would be very bad for everyone involved."

Kipp laughed nervously, and when McGill gestured to the door, he fled.

CHAPTER 13

DAMON TODD sat on a bench on the campus of Georgetown University. It was a perfect place for a bit of reflection, he thought, tucked into the curve of a walkway, shielded from nearby halls of higher learning by mature trees and other plantings. He'd been a professor once and liked university settings. He especially liked college students. They were so ... *malleable*.

As the sky turned dark and the air became heavy with the imminent arrival of a storm front, he began to sweat. His body core was still warm from his fourth workout of the day. Nothing too strenuous, a three-mile run preceded by a hundred jumping jacks and fifty push-ups. He'd hoped his physical exertion would relieve some of his tension.

He'd dearly hoped for the release an old friend who lived close by might provide, but she hadn't been home when he'd gone to see her.

Daryl—*Doctor*—Cheveyo had counseled him to be patient, and for the better part of the past twenty-four hours, he'd contented himself with thinking about the intriguing nature of his Native American liaison. He knew, of course, that the CIA had pioneered the study of using LSD as a tool in interrogations. There had to be battalions of psychiatrists involved in that work. But that was lab-coat research. Cheveyo seemed to be something more compelling. A spirit warrior psychiatrist. *A shrink-op.*

Something he hadn't known existed. As a concept, though, it held great personal appeal. A man of the mind *and* a man of action. Maybe he could be one, too, after he got his program up and running.

A drop of rain fell from the sky and struck him on the bridge of the nose. He stuck his tongue out and caught it as it ran off the tip of his beak. His first taste of Washington's storied steam-bath summer weather. He liked the metaphor, tasting weather. It amused him.

As more drops began to fall, he stuck out his tongue again and again, taking in the rainwater as if it were fuel. He stripped off his T-shirt, sat there clad in only his gym shorts and sneakers. He glistened in the rain. His every sinew was as defined as an anatomical drawing. He sometimes thought it a shame that skin was a vital organ. He'd have liked to see himself *fully* revealed. Naked muscle and raw willpower. He flicked his tongue out again.

What he'd really like to do was run nude through the storm. Good clean fun as Cheveyo might put it. But he was a little old to go streaking around a college campus. Someone might not see the humor in it. Some of the doubters at the CIA might start doubting him personally.

But if they didn't find out. It was dark. Raining steadily. Who would know?

Only the guy pointing the gun at him. He'd just stepped out from behind a bush. Couldn't have appeared more magically than if he'd emerged from a puff of smoke. Except the gun looked real, and so did the glare in the mugger's eyes.

He wore a red handkerchief knotted around his head and a sleeveless top. His shoulders and arms were muscled, but they didn't have a tenth the definition of Todd's body. Wouldn't be nearly as efficient. Or as strong.

"The fuck you doin' wit' yo' tongue?" the mugger said.

Todd hadn't realized he was still flicking his tongue out to catch raindrops. It seemed to disturb his assailant. Most people experienced discomfort when they saw erratic behavior. So Todd kept it up, consciously now.

"Stop dat shit, an' gimme all yo' money."

Todd raised his backside just enough to slip his shorts off.

The mugger took a step backward.

"Yo' johnson comes up, I shoot it right off."

Todd flipped his shorts to the mugger. He caught them by reflex, held them at arm's length as if they might carry some dread disease. But then he saw the small pocket inside the waistband and understood. That was where this insane motherfucker kept his coin. What little of it he had. The mugger's gun hand moved to raise the pocket's flap.

When it did, Todd was on him. He ripped the gun away from the mugger and threw it over his shoulder. Both of his hands then locked on to the would-be robber's throat. He began to squeeze. The mugger desperately tried to pull Todd's arms apart. His bigger, rounder muscles bulged with the effort. Todd's musculature became striated with blood flow. He not only resisted the effort to break his grip, he continued to increase the pressure.

All the while, he flicked his tongue out.

The mugger's only chance came as he began to black out. His knees buckled, taking Todd by surprise. For a second, as he fell, the stranglehold was broken. But the mugger didn't have the strength to flee or to continue the fight. Todd pounced on him and crushed his windpipe.

As he stood up, he saw that his knees were bleeding from hitting the flagstones. But the rain was already washing the blood from his legs, as it would wash it from the walkway, as it would wash his fingerprints from the robber's gun. There would be no usable evidence left for anyone to find.

Even if there was, he'd only been defending himself.

His actions were entirely justifiable. He put his shorts back on.

Shrink-op.

WELBORN SHOOK Patrick Quinn's hand and hugged Tara Quinn. She held on far harder and longer than he would have. Sobbed on Welborn's shoulder as her husband patted her back, then gently pulled her away.

"Thanks for coming, Yatesy," Patrick said. "We'll go out to eat next time."

"Yes, sir," Welborn said.

He watched as Mr. Quinn took his wife inside and closed the front door of his home. The Quinns were the parents of his late friend, Keith, who along with Joe Eddy and Tommy Bauer, had perished on that awful night in Las Vegas. The parents of the lost sons had formed their own little support group. After the funerals, they'd all come to see him in the hospital. Encouraged him in his recovery and called him Yatesy. Not Highborn,

Lowborn, or Stillborn as their sons often had.

They'd all met Welborn's mother and stayed in touch with her, too. She'd been the one who'd shared the news that her son had been posted to Washington. That had occasioned an invitation to dinner from the Quinns, who lived in nearby Annapolis. After Welborn had arrived, they'd started with a pre-prandial toast to departed comrades and much brave humor. But laughter soon gave way to tears, and they never made it to the dinner table.

Welborn got into his Civic and drove to Ruggers, a joint for military yuppies near the Naval Academy. Keith had introduced him to the place. Said it had two advantages. You got to make fun of the swabbies, and it served a terrific beer called Aviator Lager.

Once you peeled off the label—a *Navy* flyboy—it tasted even better.

The place was packed on a Friday night, and Welborn was lucky to find a seat at the bar. He ordered a burger and a beer. When the comely forty-something behind the bar brought his order, he laid down a General Grant and his car keys. He picked up his bottle of Aviator.

"I'll probably have a few more of these," he said. "If I have more than a few, I'd appreciate it if you'd call a cab for me. And whatever I do, don't let me get into your tip money."

She watched him peel the label off his beer. Assessed him and his civilian clothes.

"You look too sweet to be a Marine. Air Force?"

"Yes, ma'am."

She hung his keys from a hook on the back bar.

"We'll have little chats as the night goes on," she said.

Welborn nodded his thanks and wondered if he wasn't getting a thing for older women.

THE NOTABLE exception was Galia Mindel. She was all business, and Welborn wouldn't have wanted it any other way. Going to see her he'd felt like a schoolboy standing in the principal's office, wondering which of his youthful sins had come to light.

"Have you seen this morning's *Post,* Lieutenant?"

Before he could answer, she flipped a copy of the newspaper open on her desk. It was immediately evident that Kira Fahey had neglected to mention one significant detail. His service photo was right there on the front page with Colonel Linberg's and Captain Cowan's.

"May I sit, ma'am?" Welborn asked.

"Please do. Take a moment to read about yourself."

Welborn sat and read. The story objectively set forth the basic details of the Linberg-Cowan case. But it said eyebrows had been raised at the Pentagon and in Congress by the fact that the case rested in the hands of a first-time investigator still in his probationary year. Beyond that, the president's decision to oversee the investigation directly was also a matter of debate.

When Welborn looked up, Galia informed him, "I just spoke to the Chairman of the Joint Chiefs." The highest-ranking uniformed officer in the military.

"Ma'am?" Welborn asked uneasily.

"And the president had a conversation with the secretary of defense."

"Ma'am?" Welborn felt as if he was sinking rapidly into very deep water.

"My point, Lieutenant, is that while Congress is America's preeminent debating society, we reminded the military that it will follow the president's orders without demurral or comment."

"Yes, ma'am," Welborn said smartly.

"I asked the president to relieve you of the case, Lieutenant. I suggested that she ask the attorney general to appoint an impartial civilian investigator to take over."

Welborn sat in stunned silence, his heart grown suddenly cold.

"She rejected my suggestion. Said the military had to clean its own house."

Damn right, Welborn thought, liking the president more than ever.

"So you're it, Lieutenant. The tip of the spear, as your comrades might say. Only now you've been outed. The military establishment will distrust you. The media establishment will vivisect you. And the people you'll need to talk to will be wary, to say the least. So you'll have to be very smart and even more careful."

The chief of staff's expression said she doubted he was up to the job.

"Yes, ma'am. But what if these people, whoever they are, get in my way?"

"While you're here at the White House, Ms. Fahey will take your phone calls. When you're out on your rounds, refer any reporters who approach you to the White House press secretary, Ms. Wu. If any senators or representatives try to corner you, shoot them."

Welborn's eyes widened.

"A joke, Lieutenant," Galia told him. "One you will never repeat. Because God help you if you fail in any way to justify the president's faith in you."

Welborn left the chief of staff's office feeling shaky.

He was scheduled to leave the White House at 10:00 A.M. to go to the Pentagon for a round of interviews with Colonel Linberg's and Captain Cowan's coworkers. Before he did, Kira Fahey stopped him.

"More people called this morning to talk with you than with the president," she told him. "So far fourteen news organizations have wanted to speak with you, and twenty-three young ladies are proposing marriage."

"Refer the reporters to Ms. Wu, please."

"Already done. And the young ladies?"

"Tell them my photo flatters me too much."

She studied him a moment.

"All right, if that's what you want. But I'd have said it doesn't do you justice."

THE BARTENDER, who told him her name was Carleen, put another bottle of Aviator in front of him. By then the crowd had thinned a bit, and he had some elbow room. Enough so Carleen's quiet voice didn't carry to other ears.

"That's it for you, sugar." She pushed Welborn's change at him. "Leave what you want for the tip."

Welborn frowned. Sensed something wrong. It was only his second beer.

"You're famous, darling, and about to get more so."

Welborn winced.

"Guy at the end of the bar has a newspaper with your picture on page one. Started showing it around. Somebody got on his cell phone, called the local TV station. Sounded like they thought you eating a burger and having a few brews is news. Might be a camera crew coming through the door any minute."

Welborn pushed all the change back to Carleen. She'd earned it.

"All right if I buy you a beer, too?"

"Sure," she said.

Welborn slid the bottle over to her. She returned his car keys.

Without looking around, he asked, "Is the time right to make a break for it?"

"Sure is. Your ride's waiting for you."

Welborn looked around, expecting to see a cab driver, thinking Carleen hadn't wanted him to be seen driving with *any* alcohol in his system.

Instead, he saw Kira Fahey.

Giving him her wicked little grin. Waggling her fingers at him.

THEY GOT into Kira's black Audi TT with her behind the wheel just as the rain moving in from the west started.

"What're we going to do about my car?" Welborn asked.

Kira followed his gaze to the Civic as she pulled out of her parking space.

"If you're lucky, someone will steal it, and you'll get the insurance money."

Welborn frowned, but he was jerked back into his seat by the sportster's acceleration before he could reply. He decided to move past his pique and get straight to the point.

"How did you find me?"

"You noted your dinner with the Quinns on your appointment calendar. Mr. Quinn told me you'd left without eating and suggested a place where I might look for you. *Voilà!*"

Welborn thought that even for a beautiful, affluent, supremely well-connected girl, Kira Fahey was far too pleased with herself.

"All right. *Why* did you find me?"

"Colonel Linberg called the White House and asked for you."

"She did? What did she want?"

"Well, I'm not up on all your military jargon, but she spelled it out for me. She wanted you to know she intends to ask for a RILO. That's all uppercase, I was told."

There was silence in the little German coupe as Kira took the on-ramp onto Route 50 West and merged smoothly into the rain-snarled traffic heading toward Washington. Making sure no one was about to cut her off in the next second or two, she spared a glance at Welborn, who wore a look of disbelief.

"Since I came all this way to fetch you, would you care to enlighten me as to just what that means?"

"RILO means resignation in lieu of."

"In lieu of what?"

"Court-martial. Colonel Linberg wants to give up the fight."

"Maybe she doesn't like the odds."

Welborn nodded, more to himself than Kira.

"Maybe the other side's fighting dirty," she said.

"You think?"

"It's possible. Look what they're doing to you."

Welborn said, "You mean the newspaper story?"

"That and the fact that somebody's following us. Has been since we left that bar."

Welborn wanted to look. At least flip down the passenger-side visor and use the vanity mirror. But he didn't want to give himself away.

"Can you describe him?" he asked. "It is a him, right?"

"Yes." Kira checked her mirror. "The visibility's only so-so, but I'd say he's ... a black man, medium dark, solid ... maybe angry, if I'm seeing him right. Could be military. No uniform, but he has that severely groomed look, you know."

Welborn could think of only one angry black military man who'd have any interest in him. Major Clarence Seymour. General Altman's aide.

Kira asked, "Want me to lose him? I took a high-performance driving course."

So had Joe Eddy, Welborn remembered. And it hadn't been raining in Las Vegas.

"Stay in your lane," he told Kira. "Drive defensively."

THE PRESIDENT was working late in the Oval Office when Special Agent Eb Jenkins, Celsus Crogher's right-hand night-shift man, opened the door.

"Mr. McGill, ma'am," he said.

The president looked up from the document she was reading.

"You're sure it's not Rory Calhoun?"

Special Agent Jenkins, no movie buff, offered a blank look.

"Probably not," the president said. "I believe Mr. Calhoun left us some time ago."

"Yes, ma'am." He let McGill into the room.

He took a seat opposite his wife.

"You're working all by yourself?"

"Me and the guys." The Secret Service and the Marines guarding all interior and exterior approaches. Patti saw the tense look on McGill's face.

"You have news," she said. "Something you think shouldn't wait. Please tell me it's not the kids."

McGill shook his head. Liked the way Patti had said *the* kids, not *your* kids. He hoped someday she'd feel comfortable saying our kids. He'd bet Lars referred to them that way.

"The kids are fine, but there are a couple of other things. One I think maybe I was a little impetuous about. The other ties into the first … but I'd have to violate a confidence to tell you."

"A dilemma." Patti pushed away the paper she'd been reading, sat back, and opened her arms wide. She'd listen, but only if McGill felt he could talk.

He told her about the secret Aggie Wu had shared with him and his little chat with Monty Kipp at the firing range. The ghost of a smile flitted across Patti's face.

"I wish I had seen you shoot," she said. "Will you show me sometime?"

McGill nodded. "You're not upset? You don't think I went too far?"

"From what you told me you were just cleaning your gun. You didn't point it at Mr. Kipp or make any direct threat."

"No, I didn't. You're not bothered by what he had in mind for you?"

Patti laughed. "I don't sunbathe topless. Never have. And I don't think anyone's about to sneak up on me in my shower."

"Just the thought then."

"Some people think that way. I got used to it a long time ago. But it's still new to you."

"New and unwelcome."

Patti came around her desk and sat next to her husband. Took his hand.

"I think you handled matters very well."

"Maybe."

She studied McGill as he wrestled with the other matter that had
brought him to the Oval Office. "Jim, I'm pretty good at keeping secrets.
It's part of my job. I haven't blabbed anything in my sleep, have I?"

"One or two things."

"I'm sorry to hear that. We'll have to sleep in separate bedrooms from
now on."

"Or I could wear earplugs."

She smiled and gave him a quick kiss.

"Okay, let me start," Patti said. "You've told me about Monty Kipp,
you've said the other thing on your mind ties into that, and you're concerned about violating a confidence. Your only client, as far as I know, is
Chana Lochlan. So she's the one whose confidence you don't want to violate. And she works for Kipp. Who talked about getting some illicit
cheesecake shots of yours truly. So ... you're worried Kipp and Ms. Lochlan might be conniving to embarrass you, or me, in some other way?"

"I am."

"Why? Despite the editorial slant of her employer, I believe Ms. Lochlan is a serious reporter."

"You do?"

Patti nodded.

"And what I tell you stays between us?" McGill asked.

"We're husband and wife. You know what that means."

So McGill told her what Chana Lochlan's problem was. Allegedly.

"That's terrible."

"You never had any stalkers while you were modeling or acting?"

"Nothing like that," Patti said.

"Maybe Ms. Lochlan doesn't either."

"What do you mean?"

McGill told her about the appearance of the mysterious thong.

"It had no label, but I tracked it down to Bloomingdale's. The general
manager there was very helpful. From what she told me, I concluded that it
was more likely a woman bought the thong than a man. A man, I was told,
would have spent more on lingerie for his lady."

"How much was the thong?"

"Fourteen ninety-nine."

Patti nodded. "I think you're right. A woman. And so?"

"So this afternoon I did a little data mining."

"Private individuals can do that?"

"There are services on the Internet," McGill told her. "Anytime you pay for something with a credit card, whether it's groceries or thongs, a record is created of your purchase, and it becomes available to other merchants who want to pitch you their merchandise."

"You're not a merchant."

"It's also available to spouses or parents who want to know how spouses or offspring are spending somebody's hard-earned money."

"You're not a spouse or a parent, in this case, either."

"I lied. It's why I go to confession every week."

Patti knew where else McGill was going.

"Chana Lochlan bought the thong herself. The one she claims appeared so mysteriously."

"Her Bloomingdale's credit card did," McGill said.

"Did she mention having lost the card?"

"No."

"Then?"

"Then I wonder if this whole case isn't a Monty Kipp production."

"Me, too," Patti said. "I'm glad you told me."

The phone on the president's desk rang. She picked it up.

"Yes ... please escort her to the residence." She hung up and looked at McGill. "Sweetie's here to see you. Say hello for me, will you?"

CHANA WAS in her home office working when the doorbell rang. She wasn't expecting anyone. People from work didn't drop in unannounced. Nobody did. Looking out the window, she saw it was raining harder than ever. Not likely to be a kid selling band candy out there.

She waited.

The doorbell rang again. She thought to call the cops ... and tell them what?

McGill. She had his private number at the White House. He could get there fast.

But fast enough?

And what if it *was* some innocuous visitor? She'd feel like a fool.

She put her eye to the peephole in the front door just as the bell sounded a third time. She saw a familiar face standing outside getting drenched, not seeming to mind at all. But she didn't move until he realized she was there on the other side of the door.

And he said, "Hey, Gracie, it's me!"

She opened the door, and Damon Todd stepped in. He picked her up in his arms, swung her around, and gave her a big kiss. He kicked the door shut.

Her heart was racing; her head was spinning. She couldn't work out whether she was scared of this man or thrilled to see him again. She even had a hard time remembering just who she was.

Todd saw the confusion and anxiety in her eyes. He felt a momentary flicker of annoyance. A strobe flash across the brain. But it passed quickly. He smiled at her.

"Oh, Gracie, it's only me. Sorry to show up half-naked and soaking wet, but I couldn't wait to see you again. Don't worry, I know just what you need to feel right again."

He led her to her office. He knew the way. He put an arm around her shoulders, felt the firm muscle there.

"You've been working out, Gracie. Getting ready for me?"

"Yes."

"You buy a new thong?"

And now she remembered. *She* had bought the thong. She always bought one before he came. This year it was time to buy a green one.

"Well, I certainly hope you'll model it for me," he said.

She nodded her acquiescence, but her face clouded.

"What's wrong?" Todd asked.

Maybe she shouldn't have gone to see McGill, she thought.

"Gracie?"

No, she *definitely* shouldn't have gone to him. She knew that now.

She looked at Todd like a penitent little girl.

"There's something I have to tell you," she said.

CHAPTER 14

"PATTI SAYS hello," McGill told Sweetie.

"Back at her. How's she doing? Holding up okay?"

"Pretty well. I wouldn't want the job, but she seems to like it."

They had settled themselves in McGill's Hideaway. Every First Family was afforded the privilege of furnishing and decorating the residence to their own tastes. Patti had asked McGill for his input on the matter during the run-up to her inauguration.

He'd said, "I'm a man of simple needs. All I want is a comfortable chair, a sofa where we can snuggle, and plenty of reading light." A genie couldn't have done a better job of wish fulfillment.

McGill sat in his huge, dark brown leather chair. It was so ensuously comfortable the nuns from his parochial school days would have considered it sinful. Sweetie sat on the equally luxurious sofa where McGill and Patti liked to hold each other close, but the fireplace they spent hours gazing at was cold. The lighting was fine for either reading or conversation.

The president had given McGill's Hideaway its name. McGill liked the room so much he thought he might come back someday as a ghost and take up permanent residence.

There was a soft knock at the door, and Gawayne Blessing, the White House head butler, one of the six butlers the place had, entered carrying a silver tray bearing two tall frosted glasses of ice tea. Best ice tea in the world, as far as McGill was concerned.

He'd called the order in barely two minutes ago.

"Ms. Sweeney," Blessing said, serving her, "how nice to see you again."

"Thanks, Gawayne. I spoke to Bishop Dempsey. He's saying a novena for your sister."

Sweetie's words almost pierced the butler's professional demeanor. His eyes flickered with anxiety, but the moment of personal eeling was so brief McGill wondered if he hadn't imagined it. He also wondered how Sweetie had learned anything of Blessng's family and why the butler's sister needed the prayers of a bishop.

"Thank you, Ms. Sweeney." He turned to McGill. "Your ice tea, sir."

"Thank you, Blessing." McGill always had to be careful when addressing the head butler that he didn't lapse into a faux-British accent. His life and times had prepared him for many things, but properly relating to one's butler wasn't one of them.

"Will there be anything else, sir?"

"Sweetie?"

"I'm fine."

"Me, too."

"Very well, sir." Blessing took his leave.

And McGill gave Sweetie a questioning look.

"Gawayne's sister is undergoing a kidney transplant soon. His younger brother is the donor. He's torn up that it can't be him, but his blood and tissue are incompatible."

"Is there anything I can do?"

"You already have."

"How's that?"

"Well, Bishop D's a good guy, and he likes me well enough, but adding your name to the request for the novena put it over the top."

McGill grinned and shook his head.

"Gawayne and his family are all Baptists, but he said anyone asking Jesus to lend a hand would be fine with him."

"And just when did you meet?" McGill wanted to know.

"That first time you and Patti had me over to dinner. I got here early. Gawayne made me feel welcome, and we got to talking."

McGill nodded, unsurprised. He sipped his ice tea. It was flavored with a hint of strawberry that night. The elves in the kitchen always managed to surprise him in some pleasant way. Fighting the battle against being spoiled under the White House roof was an uphill proposition.

"How did things go in Gambier, Ohio?" he asked.

"Eamon Lochlan was out of town. I didn't miss him by much. He's due back on Monday. I can go back if you want me to."

"Tell me what you learned."

"You mean, do I have you sponsoring a novena for anyone else?"

"Exactly."

"No, but I did talk to a neighbor." Sweetie sipped her ice tea and smiled. "They ought to bottle this stuff."

"I suggested that. I got a polite note back from the kitchen, basically said thanks for the idea but don't hold your breath. So what did the neighbor have to say?"

"Her name is Harriet Greenlea. She's eighty-four years old. Reads without glasses. Can hear her cat walking across her carpet. Very little escapes her notice."

McGill grinned. "Does she keep dossiers?"

"Yeah. All in her head."

"Let's start with the missing mom."

"Marianne. Like dad, a full professor at the university. Onetime professor, anyway. Left the school, the town, and her family when she was passed over for the chair of the Women's Studies Department. She'd taught a course called Theories on the Construction of the Liberated Woman."

"How old was Chana when Mom left?"

"Nineteen. Just back from her freshman year at UCLA. A choice of schools that didn't sit well with Mom. Marianne wanted her daughter to go to the Ivy League. Or better yet, the Sorbonne. Somewhere she could be on the ramparts of the feminist struggle. Instead, she went to L.A. and played softball."

"Sounds liberated to me. Like she had her own theory."

Sweetie grinned.

"How about Dad?" McGill asked.

"'The good guy,' Harriet said. Tolerated his wife's 'foolishness' for far too long. The class he teaches falls under the rubric of World Literature.

He wrote a book called *The Pen and the Hangman: The Voices of Oppressed Peoples*. It's a collection of short biographies, writers from around the world who risked their freedom and sometimes their lives to tell their stories."

McGill connected a couple of dots, which Sweetie took for looking thoughtful.

"What?" she asked.

"Chana Lochlan told me she wants to be another Bill Moyers someday. Said she has a list of projects she wants to do. I bet one of them is bringing her father's book to television. Maybe even have him narrate. I'd also bet Chana was Daddy's girl right from the start. Which would have made it easier for Mom to leave."

Sweetie nodded.

"What about her sister?" McGill asked. "What's she doing?"

"She died at age three, childhood leukemia, before Chana was born."

McGill winced. Stories like that always hit him hard. They conjured fears of some god-awful fate overtaking one of his kids. The same beseeching prayer always leaped to mind: *Me first, Lord. Take me and spare my children. Please.*

"How soon afterward was Chana born?" he asked.

"Ten months."

"Replacement child." A thought occurred to McGill. "What was the sister's first name?"

"Nanette."

"I'll have to look that up."

"I already did," Sweetie told him. "It means grace."

"Nan and Chana. Grace and graceful. Full of grace. I wonder if Chana's parents were aware of what they were doing."

"Harriet didn't have that information."

The direction the conversation had taken led McGill to a subject far closer to home. "How are *my* kids?" he asked Sweetie.

"Kenny's writing a TV show featuring himself as the youngest Secret Service agent ever; Caitie's still pretty sure the sun rises as her personal spotlight; Abbie ... Abbie could use a visit."

"Yeah," McGill nodded. "Carolyn and the gun?"

"Your peacenik ex is a natural deadeye."

"Could she pull the trigger?"

"To save your kids? No doubt."

"The security's good?"

"Yeah. Some of it's intentionally visible to scare off anybody with a brain. Some of it is very subtle. Everybody's totally committed, playing well with others, and armed to the teeth."

"Good," McGill said.

"You still want to be there, don't you?"

"I will be. Just as soon as I can."

KIRA FAHEY lived in a fifteen-story condo building just off Connecticut Avenue. She'd wanted the penthouse apartment, but her mother had insisted that she live no higher than the fifth floor, she told Welborn with a bit of a pout.

"So the fire department can reach you with their ladders," he said.

"Yes."

He turned back to look out the window at which he was standing.

"You still have a nice view of Rock Creek Park."

She came over to stand next to him.

"Not as nice as it could be."

He looked at her. "Have you always been spoiled?"

She looked back, and said, "Not as much as I'd like to be."

Kira left him to sit on a nearby love seat. A mimosa waited for her on an end table. "My father died in a hotel fire when I was six."

A flute of champagne without the citrus awaited Welborn, should he care to join her. He did. "Can't blame your mother for being worried."

"I can't, but I do anyway. Something you should know about me, I'm not a very nice person at all."

"I saw that right away," Welborn said.

Then he smiled, probably saving himself from getting a mimosa in the kisser.

Kira didn't return the smile, but she kept talking. "Once I understood that my father wasn't coming back, I begged my mother to get me a new daddy. She said not just anyone could take my father's place, and I agreed wholeheartedly. I wanted someone just as good as my old daddy. Better if possible. My mother promised if she ever found anyone that good, she'd bring him right home." She drained her drink. "Mother's never remarried."

Kira got up, went to the kitchen, and made herself another mimosa. She brought the bottle back with her and topped off the millimeter Welborn had sipped from his glass.

"What about you?" she asked. "What's your story?"

Welborn felt sure someone like Kira would have learned of his friends' deaths by then. So what she was asking for, he assumed, was more in the way of an overall biography. Much to his surprise, he found that he didn't mind talking about himself in a way he'd revealed to few others.

"My mother never married," he said.

"You bastard."

"Yeah, I suppose so."

"Is there some lurid Southern Gothic tale behind all this?" Kira asked.

"More of an English mystery. My mother was an early female Rhodes Scholar. Came back from Oxford with a fancy education and me in the oven."

"That's even more delicious." Kira snuggled up against him. "You're the illegitimate heir of some prestigious don."

Welborn sighed. "Think a little higher."

Kira blinked, didn't come up with the answer immediately.

"Blue blood," he hinted.

She slapped his arm. "You're making this up."

"Okay," he said. He drank his champagne and refilled his glass.

"You're not?"

"All my mother will tell me is that my father is a lovely gentleman with other obligations. But my aunt, mother's elder sister, has dropped a hint or two over the years."

Kira studied his face. Shook her head. "I don't see the resemblance."

"Not that crowd around the throne," he said. "A cousin several rungs down the succession ladder is what I've been told."

She stared at him some more. Searching for any sign of deceit.

"Could all be an elaborate joke," he said. "Then again, Mother could have named me Bob."

"And not *Welborn*," Kira said, completing the thought. "You're getting me excited, even if this is all a game."

He kissed her. Chastely on the forehead. Saw she'd clearly expected more.

"We better switch to milk and cookies," he said. "I think Major Seymour has probably grown tired of waiting for me by now."

Welborn gently disengaged himself and stood up.

"Still going to let me borrow your other car?" he asked. Just in case the major was still lurking, Kira had said he could borrow her "work" car, a Jeep Cherokee.

"Are you falling in love with Colonel Linberg?" she asked.

Kira's question came out of the blue. Or maybe out of the misapprehension that she was about to lose out on a bastard Americanized, military-gumshoe royal to another woman. Welborn had the grace to keep a straight face. And to give her a straight answer. "I was infatuated, maybe. Until I started to think better of it. Now I just want to make sure she gets a fair shake."

"But if she's going to resign ..."

"That request hasn't been granted yet."

"Well, how do things look for her?"

Discussing an investigation with unauthorized personnel was taboo; that had been drummed into him time and again at Glynco. On the other hand, the president herself had said Kira was his liaison. And Kira was lending him her car, aiding him in his work.

His classroom training hadn't anticipated such situations.

He told her, "This morning and afternoon, I interviewed eight military officers and two civilians who worked with both Colonel Linberg and Captain Cowan. All ten of them told me they knew the captain was married and separated, not divorced. None of them could specifically remember sharing that information with Colonel Linberg."

Kira said, "But if everyone she worked with knew ..."

"Right. Nobody has to point a finger directly. The weight of their collective testimony is enough. How could Colonel Linberg be ignorant of what was common knowledge?"

"You're still skeptical, though."

"There's a very old expression in the armed forces," Welborn told her. "It's called closing ranks. Today, I could hear footsteps falling into line all over the parade ground."

Kira gave him the keys to her Jeep.

MAJOR SEYMOUR wasn't skulking outside Kira Fahey's building. Maybe he felt he'd seen enough, Welborn thought. He could report to General Altman that Lieutenant Yates had driven with the vice president's niece from a bar in Annapolis to her dwelling in Washington for ... well, most likely, for purposes unbecoming an officer and a gentleman.

Not that they could get him for anything illegal. Like adultery. Neither he nor Kira was married. Nor had they engaged in intercourse. Though it might embarrass Ms. Fahey to admit that a man had visited her lair and left her with nothing more than a peck on the brow.

He'd have to ask Colonel Linberg if there was anything in the UCMJ against forehead kissing. Given her duty of copying all the rules and regs, she ought to know. Then he'd ask her why she wanted to resign.

He was very eager to talk to Carina Linberg about that. And he wanted to watch her carefully as she answered. He'd have done so already if Major Seymour hadn't gotten in the way. Now, he'd have to check out the major, too. Investigate a superior officer who was the personal aide to the Air Force Chief of Staff.

He didn't remember his mother telling him there'd be days like this.

But Galia Mindel had, more or less. Warned him that there'd be people out to screw with him. People who undoubtedly had agendas of their own to advance.

Colonel Linberg had told him her workday ended at 1700 hours. Which meant he'd have to visit her at home. Kira's home computer had access to the colonel's address. She had even printed a map for him so he could find his way.

Made him feel, somewhat uneasily, as if he'd picked up an unofficial partner.

He drove out New York Avenue. The rain had stopped, and traffic was light. He rolled past the National Arboretum and soon came to Route 50 East. It'd take him right back to Annapolis if he wanted. But he was only going to Landover, where Colonel Linberg had a condo, and the Washington Redskins played football at FedEx stadium.

He never got to Landover. Because his fighter pilot's eyes saw a navy blue Dodge Viper parked in the lot of a Courtyard Inn just off the highway, two miles short of the colonel's dwelling. He wondered what the chances were it could it be just a coincidence, somebody else's sports car.

No chance at all after Welborn pulled into the lot and saw the license plate.

He looked at the motel, trying to guess which room Cowan was in.

"So what's the story, Captain?" Welborn asked himself. "Your deal with the brass gives you continuing immunity? You can keep shacking up with the colonel, and she's the only one who has to pay the consequences?"

Welborn parked Kira Fahey's Cherokee in a space directly across the lot from the Viper. He slid down in his seat and adjusted the rearview mirror so he'd be able to see if anyone got in either side of the sports car.

He *hated* the thought that Carina Linberg was in the hotel having sex with Dexter Cowan. Because if she came out of the hotel with him, he'd have to report what he'd seen. Become a witness against her. Damn! Couldn't they have driven to Baltimore? Parked the damn Viper indoors. He almost wished—

Oh, God. They'd really done it to him, he thought. The president and her husband. He was about to wish he'd brought Kira Fahey with him. To insulate him against his feelings of jealousy.

Brought on by his *infatuation* for Carina Linberg.

The president and her henchman had foreseen he might make a fool of himself and a disaster of his investigation, and they'd provided him with Kira as an inoculation against a runaway libido. He wondered if Kira knew what her role was in all this. That thought made him smile. It also reassured him that he had some really smart people in his corner.

He was pretty sure he was going to need them.

CHANA LOCHLAN lay sleeping peacefully in her bed. She was nude. Damon Todd stood next to the bed looking down at her. She'd always been lean and firm. Now, with her increased workouts, her muscle definition was starting to show. She'd hit the weights hard for him, and her appearance excited him greatly. But all he did was gently kiss her shampoo-scented hair and pull the top sheet over her shoulders.

"You're so beautiful, so strong. You've always been my inspiration," he murmured. "I've loved you from the start."

He sat in a chair and watched Chana turn on her side as she slept. Pale light slanted in through the partially open bedroom door. It fell across the right side of her face.

She'd told him about James J. McGill, of course. Going to him for help. Todd blamed himself for that. He'd missed visiting her last year. He'd left her alone for such a long time only once before—and disaster had resulted. She'd gotten married.

But the fact that she'd upped her workout and bought the thong showed that a level deep in her subconscious she still anticipated an annual visit from him. She'd been his first and most successful subject. He'd helped her to become what she had desperately wanted. There shouldn't have been any degradation of that persona.

After all, that was what he was trying to sell to the CIA: a foolproof technique for alternative personality creation. What was he supposed to say now? *Oops.*

Thankfully, he had the opportunity to learn from his mistake and correct it. He was sure that Chana would want it that way, too. They would become partners in a new, exciting round of experimentation. Everyone would be happy.

With the possible exception of James J. McGill. Chana would call him in the morning. She'd told Todd that McGill had the green thong she'd bought to model for him. That gnawed at him. He wanted that thong back. Not one just like it. *That one.*

If McGill hadn't been the president's husband, Todd would have gone after it. After him. He didn't like people who intruded on his plans. But McGill had to have Secret Service protection. And his wife was the ultimate master of the CIA. He didn't want to screw that up.

So, okay, if McGill accepted the news, maybe he could forget the thong. But if McGill didn't …

CIA FIELD Officer Daryl Cheveyo watched from the shadows as Damon Todd departed from Chana Lochlan's town house. He knew who lived there because he'd punched the address into his personal digital assistant. The Company had PDAs like nobody else's. There was no such thing as an unlisted phone number to them; they never had to address a letter to "occupant."

He saw Todd turn the corner of the block and disappear. Cheveyo slipped from the shadows and walked the opposite way. What he'd learned that night had chilled him.

Damon Todd had gotten a senior congressional staffer to ride a horse nude on the Mall. He'd gotten a member of congress to sing opera in the House of Representatives. And now … now he'd visited a reporter who had regular access to the White House. Which begged the question: What did Todd have in mind for Chana Lochlan?

Cheveyo got into his car for the drive to Langley, debating with himself whether Todd would actually try to assassinate the president, using a reporter as his tool, if the CIA didn't hire him.

He wondered if the Company would share his report with the Secret Service.

CHAPTER 15

SATURDAY

ON MOST Saturdays, the president slept in. All the way to 6:00 A.M. McGill's everyday hour to rise. Getting up at the same time, the First Couple swam together in the White House pool. Well, Patti swam. McGill lumbered, stopped for a breath at the end of each length, then pushed off the pool wall, the only time he got the feeling he was moving with any grace.

Patti had worked with him on his stroke, his breathing, and his kicking. Flip turns were out of the question. McGill had made some improvement, but the basic problem was that he never felt relaxed when he knew the water was too deep to touch bottom. His muscles tensed. His heartbeat raced. He became short of breath much sooner than he ever would have running.

He'd told Patti once, "I must've been a drowned cat in a previous life."

When they got out of the pool, McGill joined Patti in doing resistance training. But he used only one station—the chin-up bar. He did one set of as many reps as he could manage without having a stroke. That day he gutted out twenty-four.

Patti looked over from where she was doing leg extensions, and said, "I'm told Lieutenant Yates can do one hundred pull-ups without stopping."

McGill sneered at her.

He moved on to the second stage of Father McNulty's Holy Trinity of Physical Fitness. Sit-ups. McGill could do, and did, one hundred of those. After that, came push-ups. Fifty-seven. Father McNulty had devised the regimen of chin-ups, sit-ups, and push-ups because his parish—and McGill's as a child—had no school gymnasium. Everyone worked out in the lunchroom.

The good father told all his young charges that no matter what cross life gave them to bear, these exercises would give them the muscle to carry it. So break a sweat for Our Lord.

Once a week, on the same day he heard their confessions, Father McNulty also had the children run around the block as many times as they could. Technically, this was a fourth exercise and should have ruined the allusion to the Trinity, but the canny priest had a new name for running: physical penance. No matter how many Our Fathers and Hail Marys the children of St. Andrew's school might have to say after their confessions, their souls weren't cleansed until they finished running.

The one thing Patti had added to McGill's fitness routine was stretching. It was understandable how Father McNulty had missed that. The Church taught dogma not flexibility.

After showering and changing their clothes, Patti and McGill sat down to breakfast in the residence, and the phone rang. Normally, the president wasn't to be disturbed during meals. Unless it was something important. Patti put down her seven- grain toast and picked up the phone.

"Yes." She listened impassively. "No, no, that's all right." She handed the phone to McGill. "For you. Sweetie. Tell her she can call anytime."

McGill told Sweetie she could call anytime, and listened.

"Oh," he said. "Yeah, I'll be there in ten minutes."

He put the phone down and looked at Patti.

"Chana Lochlan called my office. I've been fired."

WELBORN'S EYES fluttered open, and he saw someone staring at him.

Carina Linberg. The *colonel,* he reminded himself. Wearing civvies and leaning over to look in his car. *Kira's* car. He was still groggy and having trouble orienting himself.

But he thought to check his rearview mirror. Cowan's Viper was gone.

A rap on the window brought his attention back to the colonel. It was hard to think of her as military in her sleeveless pink top and khaki shorts. She gestured to him to lower his window, and he followed orders.

"Good morning, ma'am." His voice came out as a croak.

She smiled at him. "They rent rooms here, Lieutenant. You don't need to sleep in your car." She noticed the OSU decal on the rear window. "If this is your car."

"Borrowed it from a friend, ma'am."

"And just happened to park it in the lot of the hotel where I'm staying."

Welborn winced at the colonel's admission that she'd spent the night at the Courtyard Inn.

"You look like you're in pain, Lieutenant. Tell you what. I owe you a breakfast. I'll repay you now." She stepped back from the door.

"Ma'am, I … I …"

"Look like you slept in a car?" She took a keycard out of a pocket and neatly flipped it onto Welborn's lap. "Room 213. Go take a shower, brush your teeth, whatever. There's a diner on the other side of the hotel. I'll be waiting for you there."

She turned and walked away. Having given him permission to enter her room alone. Where he might peek into anything he wanted. Very interesting. But what really intrigued Welborn were her tanned shoulders and the way her backside moved inside those civilian shorts. He picked up the keycard. She'd said she would wait for him in the diner, but if he didn't show up, she'd come back to her room and—

"Kira Fahey," he whispered to himself.

He kept quietly repeating the name as he got out of the car and entered the hotel. Made it a mantra for his self-preservation. Kira, Kira, Kira.

SWEETIE WAS waiting at McGill's office when he and Deke entered the reception area. She extended a business envelope to him. His name was written on it in Palmer cursive. Chana Lochlan's name was embossed in the upper left corner.

"Messenger brought it twenty minutes ago."

McGill told Deke to hold down the fort as he and Sweetie went into his office and closed the door. He took his seat behind his desk and pulled out a letter opener. But before he used it, he held the envelope up to the light.

First the ceiling light, then the window.

"What?" Sweetie asked. "You're thinking letter bomb?"

McGill snorted and slit the envelope open.

"I'm thinking I've never been fired before. Don't know what I'll find in there."

He found a check for $20,000.

He handed it to Sweetie and read the accompanying note aloud. "'Mr. McGill, please accept my apology and the enclosed check for all the trouble I've put you through. The pressure of my job must have left me a bit over-wrought. Right now, I'm truly not sure how much of that harassing phone call was real and how much was a dream. And, as silly as it might sound, I remember now that I bought that thong. I must have been repressing a buying choice I later found embarrassing. I trust you'll keep our dealings confidential and consider this a matter that has resolved itself.'"

McGill looked at Sweetie.

"You remember many self-resolving matters when we were cops?"

"Uh-uh," Sweetie said.

"And the money?"

"Seems to be of the hush variety."

"Or worse." McGill told her about Monty Kipp's wet dream about topless photos, and McGill's own fear that Kipp and Chana were out to embarrass Patti through him.

"How's it going to look if I cash that check?" he asked.

"Like something you wouldn't want to explain on World Wide News."

McGill turned to his computer and booted it up. He clicked on his word-processing program and started to write a response to Chana Lochlan. He didn't get far before he stopped and looked at Sweetie.

"My first case and not only am I fired, I violate the ethics of my new profession."

"Private eyes have ethics?" Sweetie asked. "Like what?"

"Like don't blab about your client's case to anyone else."

He told her about telling Patti the details of Chana's case.

"So what're you going to do?" Sweetie asked.

"I'm going to confession. Then I'll run a couple of miles of penance. After that, I'm flying home to see my kids."

"But you're not giving up on your new line of work."

"I've never been a quitter. And you wouldn't let me anyway, would you?"

"No."

Sweetie nodded at the computer.

"So what are you going to tell, Ms. Lochlan?"

"That she must have misunderstood our fee agreement. A check for the overage will be available to her, and her alone, to pick up at this office anytime during regular business hours."

"You're not going to let her get away without a heart-to-heart."

"Right."

"And if she comes in while you're away?"

"You don't have the combination to the office safe."

"That's true," Sweetie said. "We'll have to change that."

WELBORN'S MANTRA for self-preservation worked. He didn't wait for Colonel Linberg to come back to her room and find him in bed. He spotted her in a corner booth in the diner, a cup of coffee in front of her, reading the *Washington Post*. To his surprise, she had a pair of reading glasses perched on the end of her nose.

That should have made him think of the age difference between them. Instead it made him think that the glasses would be the first things to come off when ... Kira, Kira, Kira, he repeated to himself as he walked over to the booth.

"May I sit down, ma'am?" he asked.

She glanced up. "You'd look rather foolish just standing there."

Welborn took that as a yes and sat.

"So which of us were you following?" she asked, lowering her newspaper.

"Ma'am?" he said, stalling.

She took her glasses off, and Welborn felt his pulse quicken.

The arrival of the waitress provided a welcome interruption. Welborn forsook a cup of coffee in favor of a glass of ice water. He also asked for a large orange juice and a bran muffin. The colonel ordered French toast with strawberries on the side. The waitress smiled and left.

Carina Linberg said, "I made a phone call while I was waiting for you."

"Ma'am?"

"I had a friend run the license plate of that car you slept in."

Welborn stiffened. He hadn't thought military intelligence would have access to civilian databases. Now he knew better. OJT.

"It belongs to Kira Fahey, Vice President Wyman's niece."

"Yes, ma'am, it does."

"The friend who dug up that information also found photos of Ms. Fahey. He sent me one." She brought up a photo of a smiling Kira on the screen of her cell phone and showed it to Welborn. "Attractive young lady."

"Yes, ma'am."

The colonel put her phone away. "And you know her well enough to borrow her car. Unless, of course, you stole it."

"It was a loan."

"All perfectly innocent."

"Yes, ma'am."

"So, who were you following, Lieutenant? Captain Cowan or me?"

"Neither of you. I was on my way to call on you at home when I saw the captain's car in the parking lot. I pulled into the hotel lot to check the plates, make sure it was his vehicle, and I decided to wait."

"To catch us almost in the act."

Before Welborn could say anything, the waitress returned with their orders. She topped off the colonel's coffee and said to let her know if they needed anything else.

"I was hoping I wouldn't, ma'am," Welborn told the colonel.

She looked at him as she chewed her first bite.

"But then I woke you up this morning."

"Yes, ma'am."

"But I wasn't with Captain Cowan."

"No, ma'am."

"Do you know what went on at this hotel last night, Lieutenant?"

When he was slow to answer, she told him. "There was a seminar called Command Careers after the Military. It was put on by a civilian head-hunting firm with offices around the country. I attended and so did Captain Cowan. Separately. We saw each other but never exchanged so much as a hello."

Welborn remained silent.

"You should be able to get a list of the people present. They'll tell you."

"Why did you take a room, ma'am, when you live nearby?"

"I'm having my condo painted. So I can sell it faster. Get a better price."

Welborn asked, "Why are you asking for a RILO, Colonel?"

She put down her fork and sipped her coffee.

"Isn't it obvious, Lieutenant? Somebody's out to get me. Somebody I can never beat. That's who you should be looking for. The person who decided to end my military career. See what his motives are." She smiled and shook her head. "The funny thing is, now that I know my days in the Air Force are coming to an end, I'm relieved. Happy, even. I've served my country for eighteen years, and soon I'll be a free woman again—unless, of course, they lock me up."

She took another sip of coffee.

"You didn't sleep with Captain Cowan last night, ma'am?"

"No. Have you slept with the vice president's niece?"

Welborn started to answer but Carina Linberg held up a hand.

"I don't really want to know. I just wanted to make a point. As a civilian, you'd be free to tell me to fuck off. That's pretty appealing, don't you think?"

The colonel got up and told him she'd pick up the check on her way out.

Welborn ate his bran muffin, washed it down with the orange juice. He hadn't found any incriminating evidence in the colonel's room because he hadn't looked. He'd had two reasons for that. He didn't think he could pull off a search without her noticing, and he hoped she'd trust him more when she saw her stuff hadn't been tossed.

But he had checked the view out the room's window. It looked directly down on the parking space where Captain Cowan's navy blue Viper had been parked last night. So maybe the colonel hadn't *slept* with the captain, but he'd probably been in the room. Ready to jump out the window in case anyone had messed with his precious car.

The waitress came by again. "Can I get you anything else, hon?"

"No, thanks. I have to go see the president."

"Of the United States?"

"That's the one."

The waitress laughed. Asked if she could have a few minutes with her when he was done.

THE PRESIDENT had no time for McGill. That was what her personal secretary, Edwina Byington, told him. The president was in the Situation Room and couldn't be disturbed.

"For how long?" McGill asked.

"I'm sorry, sir, I don't know."

"Foolish question," McGill said.

"Yes, sir."

Edwina's eyes twinkled, and the corners of her mouth turned up. She was laughing with McGill, not at him. During his first week in the White House, McGill had asked Patti how many people in her administration would end up writing books about their experiences. Patti'd said, "Everyone with a word processor and a grudge … and everyone who has too many good stories to keep secret." McGill had come to think he'd enjoy reading Edwina's book the most.

"At the next opportunity," McGill said, "please inform the president that I'm flying home to see my children. I'll be chartering the use of a government plane, so if she needs to see my smiling face for any reason, I can get back here in a hurry."

"Yes, sir, I'll do that."

Edwina's smile turned warm, and he felt maybe he'd earned a nice passage in her book.

"Oh, and if he's available, would you please ask SAC Crogher to meet me in the residence ASAP?"

Edwina said she would and picked up the phone to call the Secret Service boss. On the way out of the West Wing, McGill saw a clean-cut young man on his way in; if he had Patti's description right, this had to be the one and only Lieutenant Welborn Yates. His suspicion was confirmed when the young man snapped to attention, started to salute him, hesitated, and then followed through. Turning bright red as he did.

McGill returned the salute. "It's okay, Welborn. Cops salute, too."

CROGHER BEAT McGill to the residence. They went to the drawing room. McGill gestured to the SAC to have a seat. Normally, this would have been considered common courtesy, and while Crogher complied, McGill could tell he was ill at ease. Sitting wasn't one of his usual activities.

Taking his own chair, McGill asked, "Would you be happier standing?"

Crogher wasn't about to admit any weakness. "I'm fine. Thank you."

"We're never going to get along, Celsus," McGill said, "but we both want the same thing. For nobody to get hurt, especially the president."

"And you. And your children."

McGill didn't think for a minute that Crogher was sucking up. He was just being thorough. Which was all you could ask for from someone doing his job.

He'd called for Crogher because he was being thorough, too.

"There's someone who's come to my attention. I think she might deserve your attention, too. Special attention, in fact."

It would have been impossible for Crogher to sit any straighter, but his spine seemed to elongate. "Regarding Holly G?"

The president's code name was Holly G, after the character Holly Golitely, played by Audrey Hepburn in *Breakfast at Tiffany's*. The president considered the name a compliment.

"Yes."

"A threat? Direct or indirect? Where did you hear or see it?"

"It's not a threat of any kind yet. It's a matter of someone who has regular access to the White House and periodic access to the president. This person has displayed behavior I consider erratic. I'm not saying this is a bad person, certainly not a hostile person. But she could be emotionally ... uncertain right now."

"Who is she?"

"Chana Lochlan."

Crogher's eyes widened a micron, as much surprise as he was capable of showing.

"But you're working for her," he said.

"I was. She fired me. And no, I'm not trying to get even with her. Just keep a special eye on her and try not to let her or anybody else know you're doing it."

Crogher wanted to know all the details.

McGill refused to tell him. He'd already compromised his confidentiality agreement with Chana as far as he intended to. He told Crogher that the Secret Service had its secrets and so did he. Crogher didn't like that. Not at all.

They were back where they started. Working toward the same goals. Fighting each other all the way.

ON THE floor of the basketball court at the Political Muscle health club, Senator Roger Michaelson drained a shot from beyond the three-point line—the NBA three-point line, not that chip shot they used in college. Swish. After many years of grueling physical therapy and countless workouts, he felt ... well, almost as good as he used to when he was young.

Problem was he was middle-aged now. He couldn't compete against elite athletes half his age, and unlike golf, pro hoops didn't have a senior's tour. He'd come a long way in life, but he'd never gotten the opportunity he'd wanted most.

More times than he'd care to admit, that still pissed him off.

So he played against guys half his age who were merely good recreational players. He played hard. Threw elbows. But hardly ever had to take any in return. Who was going to mix it up with a U.S. senator? Not the lobbyists, congressional staffers, and rising bureaucrats who played ball on the Political Muscle court.

He told everyone that when he stepped onto the court he was just another guy; he didn't want any special consideration, and he certainly wouldn't give any. But the other players couldn't help themselves. Couldn't trust that he'd keep his word. They had to err on the side of caution. They had their careers to consider.

Still, it was better competition than he'd ever find in the Senate gym. Most of his esteemed colleagues were older than he and none of them had the physical skills to play girls' field hockey. Then, one day, Walter Deschay showed up at the Political Muscle court. Six-six and 210 pounds of shining ebony muscle. He was new to town and probably didn't know any better. He thought anybody who stepped onto the court was fair game. You played ball, you better be ready to take your lumps.

He was out of the University of Arkansas. Played second string for the Razorbacks for three years. Had every move in the book but didn't finish strong. Needed to work on his jumper, too. A booster in the Arkansas delegation of the House had brought him to Washington and gotten him a job in the Department of Agriculture.

Roger Michaelson was going up to tip in a shot that a teammate had missed when Walter slammed into him, grabbed the ball, and left the senator flat on his ass. From his seat on the floor, Michaelson watched Walter rifle a pass to a fast-breaking teammate, grab the rebound of the missed shot for a put-back, and knock another guy on his ass. Michaelson loved Walter as a player from that moment on.

He looked forward to his games against Walter more than he looked forward to tropical vacations with his wife. For nine months they went at it, and he knew Walter loved competing against him, too. They were always the first two to arrive for games.

Michaelson checked into Walter's job performance and was happy to discover that he was a first-rate worker. Went beyond what was asked of him and always had a joke or a good word for everyone in his department. The senator was determined that Walter was going to have an exceptionally successful career in government service.

Then, one winter night, Walter took his dog out for his constitutional. Two street vermin held Walter up at gunpoint. He'd had to take a glove off to get at his wallet. One of the punks thought he wasn't moving fast enough. So he shot Walter's dog. Walter immediately jumped the shooter, actually wrested the gun away and broke the punk's wrist doing it. But the accomplice shot Walter in the head, killing him instantly.

It was only because Walter's killer insisted that he and his injured friend go back to retrieve the friend's gun and Walter's wallet—after they'd originally fled—that the cops caught them.

Roger Michaelson was among the several powerful people in Washington who saw to it that both criminals received life sentences without the possibility of parole, but he was the only political figure the Deschay family asked to be a pallbearer at Walter's funeral.

After Walter died, Roger Michaelson gave up playing recreational games. Now he just came to the gym and shot baskets. Usually alone. Swishing one after another. Hoping that maybe someday a player with Walter's love of the game would step onto the court again.

He hit his last shot as his chief of staff entered the gym.

"Am I interrupting, Senator?"

Michaelson shook his head. "Just finished."

The two of them were the only ones present.

"WHERE ARE we with McGill?" the senator asked.

"Do you remember Lindell Ricker, Senator?"

"The witness against Erna Godfrey."

"Currently doing ten years in Atlanta. Not liking it one bit."

"Prison isn't supposed to be fun," said Michaelson, the former prosecutor.

"Apparently it's not. Anyway, the word among the Evangelicals down I-95 in Virginia and points south is that either McGill, his female storm trooper, Sweeney, or the two of them, beat Ricker's confession out of him."

Michaelson grabbed the towel he'd left on the ball rack. He wiped the sweat off his face. When he lowered the towel, his eyes were gleaming. This might turn out to be *so* sweet. Galia Mindel had taken away three of his biggest convictions. Now, all these years later, he might have a chance to overturn the convictions of the lunatics who'd murdered Andy Grant.

And maybe send McGill to jail in the bargain.

"Where did you get this?" Michaelson asked.

"On the Internet."

The senator shook his head. "Not good enough. Find real people. Get sworn statements that Ricker told them directly about the beating. We can take that to Justice. We'll get that ball rolling, then open congressional investigations."

"You think any Republican chairmen will allow investigations of the president's husband?"

Michaelson laughed. "The conservatives loathe the president. I give them the means to get at Patti Grant, they'll see to it I run unopposed the next time around."

He grabbed a ball off the rack. Turned and fired. Drilled it from forty feet.

"What about the Linberg situation?" he asked.

His chief of staff brought him up to date.

Michaelson thought a moment, and said, "Somebody's trying to fuck with us here."

"Yes, sir."

A cold smile appeared on the senator's face.

"I love it when people try to fuck with me," Michaelson said. "It's like I have to beat the other team and a crooked ref, too. There's nothing more satisfying than doing that."

"Yes, sir," said his chief of staff, Robert Merriman.

CHAPTER 16

THE PRESIDENT had two specially configured Boeing 747-200B aircraft available to her. But when she was aboard *any* Air Force aircraft, the radio call sign was "Air Force One." Likewise, she had several helicopters available to her from Marine Helicopter Squadron One. Any chopper from the squadron that carried the president was known as "Marine One."

The Air Force Gulfstream that McGill had chartered probably had some special designation, but he didn't know what it was. Other than two presidential trips with Patti, and travel during the campaign, it was the first time he hadn't flown commercial. But his guess was every air traffic controller from Andrews Air Force Base to O'Hare International Airport had been informed he was aboard. And he'd bet his bottom dollar the plane didn't have to circle the field before it was allowed to land.

All this came at a cost. He'd have to reimburse the government over $24,000 to use the plane for the Washington–Chicago round-trip. Well, the money would come from one of Patti's trust funds. McGill had two police pensions he was drawing and some investment income, but he didn't have the means to hire private jets.

Patti had told him when they'd married that there were funds—millions of dollars—that were available to him at his request. Nobody would ever question why he wanted the money, especially not her. She'd said she trusted him. He'd kissed her, thanked her, and told her he doubted he'd need any of that money. Now, he did and …

He felt like he was taking it from the ghost of Andy Grant.

Thing was, he didn't see that he had a choice. He felt as if he had to be in two places at once. Abbie needed him at home, and Patti might soon need him back in Washington. For a sympathetic ear if nothing else. Given his situation, he didn't feel he could rely on civilian aviation. As the country had seen on 9/11, all commercial flights could be canceled for days at a time. He didn't want to be stuck at Point A if he needed to get to Point B.

So he dipped into money that he felt wasn't his and resolved to repay it.

The executive jet rose smoothly off the runway, began its climb and a long, gentle turn to the north, then west. There was an Air Force crew of three aboard: pilot, copilot, and steward. There were also three passengers: McGill, Deke, and Leo.

The steward, a first lieutenant who, McGill suspected, was also an emergency backup pilot, served drinks, then went forward. Leo was sipping a Cherry Coke and looking at a car magazine. Deke's cup of water sat untasted as he pondered something without expression. McGill was having a White House ice tea, looking out the window, and speculating on the crisis Patti must be facing. Had to be Cuba, he thought.

He was trying to guess what his wife might do about it when Deke asked him, "Were you serious, back at the firing range? About that Dark Alley stuff. I've checked every martial arts book I could lay my hands on, and I can't find that name anywhere."

Leo joined the conversation. "Can't say I've heard of it, either. Though I do like the name. *Dark Alley.*" He gave the words an eerie warble.

McGill smiled, and said, "You won't find any written reference to it because there isn't any. Dark Alley was the creation of my uncle, Chief Petty Officer E. P. McGill, United States Navy."

"Your uncle created his own martial art?" Deke asked.

McGill nodded. "And I'm the sole surviving practitioner. I haven't decided whether I'll pass it on to any of my kids yet."

"You want to tell us about it?" Deke asked. "Just so we know not to kung when you fu."

Leo nodded. "That would be good."

McGill thought it over. "All right. First you have to understand who Uncle Ed was. He was a Chicago tough guy. Not a criminal. Just someone who expressed himself best with his fists. He got into one of those jail-or-army situations. Only the judge was willing to let him make it the Navy. He told me he spent a lot of time fighting Marines. When it wasn't them, it was Filipino knife fighters. Or Hong Kong brothel bouncers. All sorts of Australians."

"But how did he come to teach you?" Deke asked.

"Uncle Ed liked to play that game where you put your hands palms down on another guy's palms-up hands."

"Your hand gets slapped, you have to keep on taking it," Leo said. "Until you get away without being hit. Then it's the other guy's turn."

"Right. My uncle started playing that game with me when I was ten."

"But you had quick hands even then," Deke said. "He couldn't slap your hand."

"Not often."

"How come you're so quick?" Leo wanted to know.

McGill shrugged. "A lot of fast-twitch fiber, a doctor told me once. Pure luck."

"Your uncle spotted your quickness," Deke said.

"When I was twelve," McGill said, "he asked if I wanted to try a variation on the game. Maybe he'd slap my hand; maybe he'd slap my face. Wouldn't hit me hard if it was the face. I was cocky enough to tell him it could be as hard as he wanted because he wouldn't get me."

"Caught you a good one, didn't he?" Leo asked.

McGill shook his head. "He didn't land a blow. At least not to my face. But he did break my left wrist because at the end he was swinging pretty hard. He felt so bad he paid all my medical bills and I got gifts from every port he hit for the next year."

"By the time he came back, he'd decided he wanted to teach you," Deke said.

McGill nodded. "We started when I was thirteen. Uncle Ed taught me that Dark Alley is divided into two disciplines: Biological Weapons and The Lord Shall Provide."

Deke understood immediately. "Body parts and found objects."

"Exactly. Uncle Ed showed me how to use the back of my head, the top of my head, my forehead, and my chin. He showed me how to use shoulders, upper arms, elbows, forearms, wrists, backhands, heels of hands, cupped palms, stiffened fingers, hooked thumbs, and fists. He showed me how to use hips, thighs, knees, insteps, heels, and balls of feet."

"No teeth?" Deke asked.

"Some things go without saying. There's also a way you can make your tongue firm and poke someone in the eye with it, but that's pretty rare. As for learning to use what comes to hand, that took a whole year in itself."

Both Deke and Leo were nodding.

Then Leo asked, "How's your uncle doing these days?"

"He passed away … struck by lightning."

"No fighting that off," Leo said.

"Stay out of the rain," McGill replied.

The steward stepped up to him and offered him a phone.

"Sorry to interrupt, sir, but the president would like to speak with you."

"SOMEBODY SET off a bomb at an open-air produce market in Havana," the president told McGill. "Current death toll is eighteen, but it's expected to go higher."

"Anybody own up to the blast?" McGill asked.

"No, and that's part of the problem. In Raul Castro's name, the government is claiming it's an act of terror by the Miami exiles. It's even suggested that uniformed antirevolutionary forces may have infiltrated the island, and it says if any are found, it will result in the gravest of all consequences."

"Is there a chance they've got any of it right?"

There was a pause at Patti's end of the conversation.

"The U.S. Special Forces officer in charge of holding the reins on the exile army in Costa Gorda has reported that one squad, a demolition team, is unaccounted for. But the Cuban American commandante has said the squad, which is comprised of four brothers named Obregon, had returned to Miami to be with their dying father."

Didn't pass the smell test for McGill, but he knew all sorts of feds would be swooping down on Miami to verify that explanation. So he tried another tack.

"Could be the Cubans sacrificed a handful of their own people. If they really intend to take the whole country down, to follow Fidel's directive, they're not going to sweat losing a few people buying bananas."

"That's exactly the argument my national security advisor has advanced. Havana is ratcheting up the pressure on us. Trying to get us to disband the exile army and giving us a taste of what horrors might lie ahead."

"Any TV coverage from Cuba yet?" McGill asked.

"CNN started ten minutes ago. Bodies, body parts, and blood everywhere."

"You have any ideas, or should I mind my own business?"

"I'm going to offer to send an FBI team to Havana to investigate. With it goes my promise that the United States will prosecute any U.S. citizens involved in the bombing, should that turn out to be the case."

"Sounds reasonable to me, but how will it sound to the Cubans?"

"If they won't trust us, why should we take their word that our guys did it?"

"Good point. It puts the ball back in their court."

"I think you might be ready to join the National Security Council," the president said.

"And I thought you loved me."

"I do. But we'll talk about that when you get back. I found a few minutes to spare for Lieutenant Yates. He says he thinks Colonel Linberg and Captain Cowan are conspiring."

"Against whom or what?"

"He's not sure." Patti told McGill about the view from Colonel Linberg's hotel room. "He's asked me not to grant the colonel's request to resign. Not until he gets a fuller understanding of the case."

"Good cop," McGill said. "But how's that play politically?"

"Well, it would please the Air Force chief of staff. General Altman has urged me not to let the colonel 'weasel out,' as he so delicately put it."

"Hmmm," McGill responded.

"Hmmm, indeed," Patti echoed. "Any further words of wisdom?"

"I do have one other notion. This Colonel Linberg has been a rising star, right?"

"So I've been told," the president answered.

"Well, why don't you have Welborn look for any great achievements in her service record? If he doesn't find a fistful of them—"

"Then maybe the colonel's been sleeping her way to the top?"

"Yeah ... but there's a problem with that line of thought. You see what it is?"

Patti did. "If you're a colonel, you don't sleep with a captain to get ahead."

"Uh-huh."

The president saw another possibility. "Maybe you do, if you're sleeping with a captain for fun or romance *and* a general for career advancement."

"Whew," McGill said. "Do they teach Machiavelli at Colorado Springs? Of course, our general could be the one who doesn't want to see his two-timing mistress do any weaseling."

"The thought does occur, doesn't it?" The president was silent for a moment, then said, "SAC Crogher also begged a moment of my time."

"Good old Celsus. Came to rat me out, did he?"

"Jim, do you really think Chana Lochlan might—"

"Patti, did *you* ever repress the memory of buying underwear?"

"No ... not that I'm aware of."

"Ha-ha."

"That's what Ms. Lochlan said? She 'repressed.'"

"That's what she wrote. I'm not buying it. Something funny is going on."

"Thank you for thinking of me."

"What's a henchman for?" McGill asked.

GALIA MINDEL browsed top-end dresses at Macy's in New York City. She took one off the rack. Basic navy with subtle pearl piping. Long sleeves, of course. Mid-calf hemline. Modestly cut neckline. She turned to look at a mirror and held the dress in front of her. The line between businesslike and dowdy was a fine one, but she thought this navy number passed muster. She set it aside and continued looking.

Adding to her wardrobe was a secondary purpose that Saturday morning. Galia had gone to New York to meet with one of her spies. *She* had read Niccolo Machiavelli. Lavrenti Beria, too. And like the founder of the former Soviet Union's NKVD, she believed in maintaining several well-placed agents in enemy camps to keep her informed of what the opposition was planning.

On the reasonable assumption that she, too, might merit someone's scrutiny, she never met any of her covert operators in Washington. She always set up her meetings well out of town. In keeping with the clandestine nature of her trip to New York, she'd given herself a legitimate cover: She was to lecture to a political science seminar at her alma mater, Columbia University.

As a further precaution, she picked the locations for her meetings with the character of the opposition in mind. That morning, for example, she would just happen to bump into Merilee Parker, the press secretary for Senator Howard Hurlbert (R-MS), co-sponsor of the failed Support of Motherhood Act—the proposed law that had cost Andy Grant his life.

In the unlikely case that the senator suspected disloyalty from his public spokesperson, Galia felt certain that anybody trailing Merilee would be a male. Most likely a former federal agent. FBI or maybe DIA. Some big guy in a boxy suit sporting a crew cut. In short, somebody who'd stand out like a corned beef sandwich at a vegan picnic should he show up at Macy's better dresses.

As for Galia, she was right at home there. She bought off the rack. It was smart politically, and designers didn't cut dresses for women with her build anyway. Working for Patricia Darden Grant, though, she sometimes wondered what it would be like to be slim, tall, and glamorous. It wasn't envy, just curiosity. And not even much of that. Most of the time she was content being smart, stocky, and powerful.

Merilee stepped into the dress department. Galia was sure Merilee had noticed her, too. But neither of them rushed toward the other; they would *discover* one another. Serendipity. They would shake hands warmly, help each other make selections, and try on their frocks in adjoining dressing rooms at the far end of the corridor. Well out of bounds for snooping males. At some point, they would momentarily step into each other's dressing rooms. Merilee would find an unmarked envelope and place it into her purse. Galia also would find an envelope to take with her.

With some of her people, Galia paid in cash. For Merilee, she made anonymous donations to a battered women's shelter in Merilee's hometown of Atlanta. Her operative had once been married to Senator Hurlbert's campaign manager, Bobby Beckley. The senator, like all good Southern politicians, was a strong family-values man. So was Bobby, supposedly, which had been one of the big attractions for Merilee.

But Bobby's notion of fidelity turned out to be strictly situational. If he was within the length of his wife's shadow or in front of a camera, he was the picture of devotion. If he was anywhere else, he traded on his second-hand Elvis looks and was up for any woman he could attract. It took Merilee three years and two miscarriages to discover that. When she did find out and confronted her husband, he broke her nose with a straight right.

Said there was more where that came from, too, if she started sassing him.

Battered and horrified, Merilee went to the senator, her beloved boss and the man who could fire the no-good bastard she'd been dumb enough to marry. Only Senator Hurlbert hadn't fired Bobby. He'd looked pained she'd even brought her problem to him.

"Merilee, I am truly sorry about your troubles, but Bobby's got me elected twice already, and he's going to do it again next year. I need him. More than anyone."

More than her. But that wasn't all the senator had to say.

"I'd appreciate it if you and Bobby could put on a good appearance until after the election. So you can continue to work here. After the election, y'all can get a quiet divorce if you want."

She stayed on, initially to fuel her fantasy that one day she would kill both her husband and the senator. She even bought a handgun. Imagined the headlines she would make. But she'd been a reporter once, and she couldn't conceive of any murder scenario that didn't end with her own execution. Which just wasn't worth it.

She turned in her weapon to a gun-collection drive and watched it get melted.

She felt pretty much the same way about her life: It was going down the drain. She started looking through the Yellow Pages for a divorce lawyer she hoped wouldn't be frightened by who her husband was or the fact that he had a U.S. senator in his pocket. It didn't look like it was going to be easy.

She also started making discreet inquiries of the bigger newspapers and TV stations back home in Georgia. Maybe if she could get a decent job away from Mississippi, she could make a new start, get a footing to reestablish herself as a person of some value.

That was when Galia Mindel met her, while Merilee was making a trip to Atlanta, ostensibly to visit her mother. Galia, to Merilee's dismay, knew all about her troubles.

"People talk, and Washington's a small town," Galia told her simply. "How'd you like to spy for me and have a chance to screw the two bastards who screwed you over?"

Galia's proposal wasn't what Merilee had expected, but she jumped at the chance. She stayed at her job. Kept up appearances. Divorced the asshole after the election. Got a pot to piss in from him but not much more. And didn't mind a bit. She lived to betray the people who'd betrayed her. In fact, she'd recruited half a dozen more congressional insiders for Galia.

The president's chief of staff had long ago decided that the right wing of the GOP was her boss's biggest enemy. The wing nuts and Roger Michaelson.

Galia and Merilee Parker looked up at the same time and "spotted" each other. Wide smiles lit up their faces. Hellos echoed across the room.

Galia held up the dress she'd taken off the rack. "What do you think?"

Coming over, Merilee said, "I think we're going to have a lot of fun shopping."

"DAD!" ABBIE yelled, a broad smile on her face.

McGill hadn't told any of his kids he was coming home. Leo just drove him up to Carolyn and Lars's house in Evanston—after Deke had alerted the Secret Service and Evanston cops—and he knocked on the front door.

He could have let himself in. Carolyn had given him a key, but that was to be used in emergencies only. So he'd respected her property rights and knocked. But he did it jauntily.

Shave and a haircut.

A moment later, he had his elder daughter in his arms.

Kenny and Caitie, having heard their sister's exclamation, were only seconds behind. He managed to embrace them all at the same time. He didn't know what he was going to do when they got too big to encircle all at once. Out of the corner of his eye, he saw Deke looking around. The street was tree-lined and peaceful enough to be a Norman Rockwell painting, but that wasn't what Deke was thinking.

He was thinking: four-for-one target.

McGill told his children, "Let's step inside and say hello to your mom. Is Lars home?"

He shepherded them into the house and saw Carolyn step out of the kitchen, drying her hands on a dish towel. "Can a guy get a cup of coffee?" he asked.

She laughed. "I'd have a mutiny on my hands if I said no."

"Lars home?" McGill asked again. "I haven't come at a bad time, have I?"

Carolyn told him, "Lars is working. The new store keeps him busy."

McGill thought he heard a strain in his former wife's voice, not that the kids seemed to notice. Somehow he thought he was the cause of Carolyn's trouble rather than Lars's new drugstore. But she kissed his cheek and led him by the hand into the kitchen.

When McGill sat down, Caitie hopped onto his lap.

"Did you bring us anything, Dad?" she asked.

McGill grinned. "Now, I'd be a poor excuse for a father if I didn't."

"Let your father have a minute to rest before you start extorting treasure from him," Carolyn said. She placed a cup of coffee next to McGill. He took a sip. It wasn't up to White House standards, but it was familiar and more comforting.

"All right," McGill said. "Surprises are all well and good, but they do tend to mess up people's schedules. Does anybody here have anything planned for today, or are you free to hang out with the old man?"

Caitie said, "Nobody has anything to do. Except Kenny. He has a baseball game, which is pretty much the same as doing nothing."

McGill looked at his son, expecting a wisecracking rejoinder, but Kenny ignored his sister's insult and told his father. "I went two-for-four last game."

A batting average about .400 higher than normal, but Kenny didn't seem enthused. Just the opposite. Another kiddo in need of a talk. Good thing he'd come home.

"Okay," McGill said. "What I'd like to do then is take everyone to Kenny's game, buy all the hot dogs and soft drinks you can eat and drink without getting sick, and tonight I'll take you out to dinner." He looked at Carolyn. "You and Lars, too, if you're free. Everyone will get dressed up like proper ladies and gentlemen and we'll all have a good time. How's that sound?"

Abbie said, "Good, Dad. But we have to give the guys time to set up."

The guys. McGill knew immediately what she meant. All the gun-toting bodyguards they needed to protect them from the gun-toting crazies who were threatening to kill them. A helluva thing for kids to have to deal with. It made him mad. Very mad.

He looked at Deke, who stood in the kitchen doorway.

"Tell everybody what our plans are." He checked with Kenny and gave Deke the location of the game. Then he suggested a local restaurant to which everyone was agreeable. "I don't want to see the security detail. You, Leo, and I will be the close-in coverage. Everyone else will be perimeter and *invisible*. Everybody's ready to go in fifteen minutes."

For the first time, he felt like he was bossing people around, but he knew it had to be done. McGill set Caitie on her feet, and said, "Okay, who wants presents from the White House?"

KENNY'S GAME was at Dodge Park, a recreational center on the south side of town. Word of McGill's presence preceded his arrival. The Little League people had set up a microphone at home plate and asked him to say a few words. Players and parents looked at him like he was a movie star. Someone of more recent vintage than Rory Calhoun.

He told the gathering, "I'm here today not as anyone special, simply as one more Little League parent. Because I've just come from Washington, where criticizing the next guy is the preferred sport, I promise not to criticize the umpires. And I hope you will join me in cheering for good plays and good sportsmanship by both teams. Thank you."

McGill thought that would take care of his public obligations, but someone asked him to lead the singing of the national anthem. Fortunately for him, and thanks to all the voice lessons his mother had given him, he was able to do a respectable job of it.

The crowd joined in with what he suspected was more-than-usual fervor. Deke allowed a local photographer to take a picture of him at the mike. Everybody cheered their performance, and cheered again when the home plate umpire yelled, "Play ball!"

THEY WERE seated behind the dugout in which Kenny's team, the visitors, sat awaiting their first at-bats. Kenny was shaking, obviously nervous at all the attention his father had commanded and fearing that it would inevitably spill over on to him. McGill wanted to talk to him, tell him to laugh it off, but he thought that would only make matters worse.

Then Deke went over to Kenny, took him aside, spoke to him for all of ten seconds, and went back to looking for assassins in the suburban Little League crowd. Kenny took his seat and immediately every boy in the dugout wanted to know what he'd been told. But Kenny just shook his head. It was his secret. One that apparently had rid him of his anxiety.

McGill and Carolyn looked at their son, then at each other.

They had room to talk quietly because the bleachers had been taped off ten feet to either side of where they sat and three rows up. Abbie and Caitie were sitting with their friends to McGill's right, halfway up the bleachers.

"I thought Abbie was the one who needed to see me."

"She is," Carolyn said. "Now Kenny is, too."

"Caitie's okay?"

"She's irrepressible."

"Great. But I would have said the same about Kenny."

"He was. Until his friends' parents heard about the Secret Service joining the army of bodyguards, and they started getting worried. You can't blame them, but they won't let their boys get near Kenneth McGill. There was even some talk that the baseball team might ask him to leave until the danger had passed. I think this was going to be his last game. I don't know if your being here has changed that or not."

McGill closed his eyes and rubbed his forehead.

He opened them again when Carolyn gave him a nudge. Kenny was up, batting third. That was a change. He'd always batted eighth or ninth. McGill hoped his son hadn't been moved up in the order just to please him. Kenny didn't need the pressure.

Not that he seemed to be feeling any. He was still calm after listening to Deke. In fact, he looked at Deke, then at McGill before he stepped into the batter's box. He gave his father a nod. After which he promptly hit the first pitch right back up the middle, a line drive that made the pitcher duck to save his life.

McGill leaped to his feet, yelled, and shook his fist in the air.

Sitting down again, he said, "That was worth the trip, right there."

Carolyn smiled and nodded.

McGill asked quietly, "Did I cause a problem between you and Lars?"

She looked at him. "I think so. Meeting you back in the sixth grade. Running into you again right after college. Yeah, I think you're the problem. That or me thinking I could ever be successful at being a cop's wife. One of the two."

"Could you boil that down a little?" McGill asked.

The next batter popped out and the side was retired. Kenny took the field, playing first base. The other side of the diamond. McGill nodded to Deke, who went over, ready to sacrifice his life for the younger McGill if necessary.

"I told Lars about the gun, the one I have," Carolyn said.

"He wasn't happy."

"No. He's really been very good about all the other people with guns who've suddenly entered our lives, but he doesn't like me having one."

McGill kept quiet.

"Ironic, isn't it?" Carolyn asked. "Now, I know how you felt all those years. Only I don't want my marriage to Lars to end the way yours and mine did."

"No, I don't want that, either."

"I haven't worked out what I'm going to do, but since you popped in on us, I've been thinking maybe you can take the kids to dinner by yourself, then take them over to your house. Maybe having a night alone, just Lars and me, we can come to an understanding. Would that be okay?"

"That'd be fine," McGill said, and he squeezed Carolyn's hand.

THEY ATE at Wolfgang Puck's on Maple, had Ben & Jerry's carryout ice cream cones while strolling downtown Evanston, and after they couldn't agree on a movie they all wanted to see, went home to McGill's house. The experience of stepping through his front door—after Deke had given the high sign—reminded McGill of tasting Carolyn's coffee. He found the house he'd taken such pride in buying now struck him as incredibly humble—but entirely familiar and welcoming.

Life at the White House was far grander than anything he'd ever experienced, but there was an air of unreality about it. Like winning a stay at a five-star resort in a contest. The glitz was great, but you knew it was only temporary. Real life was comfortable furniture that could use a professional cleaning.

McGill made popcorn in a frying pan, and they watched Tom Petty in a repeat of a *Soundstage* show on Channel 11.

Caitie was the first to fall asleep. His youngest, unlike most children, never fought parental directives telling her to go to bed. She found great comfort, even delight, in her sheets, blankets, and pillows. When McGill and Carolyn had looked in on her when she was little, they frequently found her sleeping with a smile on her face.

She was getting fairly tall, but McGill was pleased to see that he could still carry her upstairs to her bedroom. He laid her down, gave her a kiss, and told her to change into her PJs. She mumbled okay, but by the time he got to the door she'd already pulled her comforter over herself and fallen asleep fully clothed.

He went back and pulled off her sneakers but otherwise left her as she was.

Kenny was waiting for him in the hall outside as he closed Caitie's door. Abbie was downstairs in the kitchen. She'd insisted on washing the popcorn dishes. McGill took Kenny into the boy's bedroom. Kenny sat on his bed; McGill sat on his son's desk chair.

"You want to tell me what Deke said to you, or is that private?"

"No, it's not private, not from you."

Kenny's team had lost the game, 2–1, but he'd had three of their four hits.

Kenny told McGill, "Deke said even Secret Service agents get scared sometimes, but they can't show it, and they *never* let their fear get the better of them."

McGill nodded.

"I'm glad he's the one watching out for you, Dad."

McGill smiled. "Yeah, me, too. Leo's not bad either."

Kenny lit up. "Yeah! I didn't know he was a racecar driver. Maybe that's what I should be. I mean, if Mom won't let me join the Secret Service."

"Or," McGill suggested, "maybe you should get good grades, become a snappy dresser, polish your manners, and see if you can't marry a girl who'll become the president. Then you can have a lot of cool guys working for you."

"Well, if the girl looked like Patti, that wouldn't be too bad."

Hearing his own words, Kenny had the grace to blush. McGill laughed and told his son good night, promising to look for a way he could keep in touch with his friends.

He went to Abbie's room and waited for her, sitting on the edge of her bed. When she came, he was surprised at how mature she seemed at only fifteen. God, but some young man was going to be lucky when he found her. If McGill didn't scare him away with threats of what would happen if he ever made Abbie unhappy.

"What can I do for you, sweetheart?" McGill asked.

She raised her arms and let them drop, stuck for an answer. She sat next to her father.

"I don't know, Dad. At first, I thought there had to be some way you could get rid of those jerks who'd even think of hurting Kenny and Caitie and me. Kill them if you had to."

She looked at her father to let him know she was serious.

"But then I thought if you killed them, that'd only make other people mad. And if you killed them, too, there'd be still more. That's when I realized how many people there must be in the world who do bad things for no reason other than they can't get their own way. Maybe I'm not so great myself, thinking I could kill people."

McGill put his arm around his daughter.

"You're a great kid. Do you know what your name means?"

"Gives joy," Abbie said softly.

"That's right, and that's just what you've done your whole life. To your mother and me and everyone who's ever had the pleasure of knowing you. That's pretty great."

Tears started rolling down Abbie's cheeks.

"Then why would people want to kill me?"

McGill sighed and held his daughter closer. She buried her face in his chest.

"Because there are bad people in the world. That's what you've come to realize. It's a realization that scares everyone sooner or later. But you also have to understand that defending yourself doesn't make you bad ... even if you have to kill someone to do it. Both morally and legally, it's permissible to defend yourself. To whatever extent is necessary."

Abbie looked up at him.

"Is that why Mom has a gun now?" She surprised him with that one; he'd have thought Kenny would be the first to find out.

"I got home from visiting my friend Becky early the other day. I heard Mom arguing with Lars while I was still outside."

McGill told her honestly, "Your mother is afraid she'll be the last line of defense for you and your brother and sister. She wanted something she could fight back with; Lars is having a problem with that."

"Can I have a gun, too?"

McGill winced and shook his head. "Kids with guns is a very *bad* idea."

"What about Dark Alley then?" she asked.

She surprised him with that one, too. Like a good male chauvinist, he'd thought *maybe* he'd teach Kenny someday, but it had never occurred to him that either of his girls would want to learn. Dark Alley was *vicious*. But maybe vicious was exactly what Abbie had in mind.

"Tell you what, kiddo," McGill said. "Let's start with something more traditional: karate, taekwondo, or something like that. You learn the discipline and the technique for a couple of years; then, if you still want to learn Dark Alley, I'll teach you."

"Promise?"

McGill nodded. "Absolutely."

"Thanks, Dad." She leaned in and gave him a peck on the lips. "So how's your case in Washington? That woman with the creepy guy on the phone."

Now he surprised Abbie; he told her he'd been fired.

"*Why?*" she demanded.

He told her that, too. Which made her frown.

"She said it was all a dream? Or you think she's trying to play a trick on Patti?"

"Yes and maybe," McGill answered.

"But you don't know which one."

"No."

"I don't believe it," Abbie said.

"Which part?"

"That it was a dream. Who ever heard of a dream that was so scary you'd go to the police about it?"

McGill was no longer a cop, but obviously his daughter still thought of him that way. He hadn't told Abbie about the green thong, but he suspected she'd be equally skeptical on that point.

"What about the idea that she might try to play a trick on Patti?" he asked.

"Maybe. But has she ever done anything like that before?"

"No, but she works for someone who has."

"But that's not fair."

"What isn't?" McGill asked.

"Thinking she's like someone else. That's ..."

"Guilt by association?"

"Yeah."

"Dad, you know what'd really be bad?"

"What?"

"What if someone made the woman fire you, but she's still in trouble? Who'd help her then?" Abbie gasped as her train of thought stopped at an unpleasant station.

"What is it, honey?"

"I ... I'd rather not say."

"Abbie."

Now she hugged him.

"I was thinking—and I know it wasn't your fault—but this could be like when you had to stop helping Mr. Grant. Look what happened to him."

"Yeah," McGill said, hugging Abbie back. "Just look."

CHANA LOCHLAN sat staring at the video loop playing on the television in her darkened home office. The view never changed. It was an endless stretch of interstate highway seen in the depths of night from behind a steering wheel. Low beams illuminated lane-divider stripes. One after another. After another. After another ...

A soft ceaseless rush of wind blew past.

Chana sat unmoving, eyes glazed.

In a corner of the room, beyond the glow of the TV, Damon Todd watched Chana carefully. Her breathing was shallow but regular. Otherwise, not a muscle in her body moved. He gave her another couple of minutes. He wanted to be absolutely sure she was in a K-hole.

Ketamine hydrochloride had originally been created as a human anesthetic and belonged to a class of drugs known as dissociative anesthetics. Its current legitimate uses were for general anesthesia for children, people in poor health, and animals.

Its street name was Special K. Definitely not endorsed by the Kellogg's people.

In small doses, usually snorted, Special K produced a mild dreamy feeling similar to the effect of inhaling nitrous oxide. Users felt as if they were floating slightly outside their bodies. Numbness in the extremities was also common.

Higher doses often produced hallucinogenic effects and could cause the user to feel very far removed from his or her body. It was known as going into a K-hole and was likened to a near-death experience. It left the user all but paralyzed. Temporarily.

Todd had injected Chana with a large dose. He'd done it after he'd put her into a hypnotic state. The injection site was the lingual surface of the gingiva between her first and second upper left molars. A spot likely to be found only by a dentist. And in a day or two the wound would be healed. Gone.

"My dear," Todd asked, "can you hear me?"

"Yes." Her voice was soft, childlike.

"Are you feeling all right?"

"Sleepy."

"That's fine. I'll let you rest soon. But now I need to know something."

"What?"

"Have you been troubled lately?"

"Yes." Chana's voice became fearful.

"Don't worry, my sweet girl," Todd told her.

"I try to be good. I try to be *perfect*."

Todd wanted to reach out to her, hold and comfort her, but now was not the time.

"And you are, as perfect as any of us can be."

"Not as perfect as you."

Todd had to repress a bitter laugh.

"I'm going to ask you to look at yourself now," he said. "There's a very special mirror in front of you. You look at it and you can see all your troubles. They're stuck on you like the name tags you'd wear to a convention: 'Hi, I'm...' Only these name tags list your problems. Can you see them, my dear?"

"Yes," Chana said.

"Look at the first trouble tag you can see. What does it say?"

"'Too old.' I'm getting too old."

The very idea took Todd by surprise. Chana was beautiful. In the prime of life.

"Too old for what?" he asked.

A snarl entered her voice. "My job. My stupid job."

"What's wrong with your job? Is someone giving you trouble?"

"The *job* is what's wrong. I'm the most fabulous face on TV. What the hell kind of job is that? Who can live up to that? I want to *write*, damnit!"

He hadn't heard her express that ambition before. "Who's stopping you from writing?"

"Everybody. My job is to look great and read what they tell me as if I'm offering my own thoughts. My own words. But that's not what I think. That's not *me*!"

Hadn't taken long to get to the crux of the matter: the question of identity.

"And who are you?" he asked.

"*Nanette* Lochlan."

"Are you sure?"

"Oh, everyone knows me as Chana, but that's not who I really am. I'm Nanette. Nanette's perfect."

"But is Nanette who you want to be?"

Her face twisted in pain. She was unable to answer.

"Do you see any more trouble tags?" Todd asked. "Anyone you can name?"

"You," she snapped.

She might as well have slapped Todd. It was all he could do to maintain control.

"You're going to rest now," he said. "You're falling, falling, falling asleep. As you fall, each of the tags you had on you, all of your troubles, they're falling away, too."

He clicked off the television. The room became completely dark.

"When you wake up," his disembodied voice said, "you will be free from your concerns. You will be rested and refreshed. But your subconscious will continue its debate: Who do you want to be, Nanette, Chana, or someone entirely new? Sleep well, my dear."

Finishing the session with that endearment was the hardest thing he'd ever done. He'd saved this woman's life, recreated her in the image *she'd* wanted, made her famous and affluent. All he'd asked in return was her gratitude. Her love. Occasionally, her body.

Yet she'd said *he* was one of the problems in her life.

How dare she?

He recognized his self-pity and repressed it with contempt.

He would not be weak. *Never* be weak again. He left Chana's house. There was no place he could work out at that hour. No place to shred his muscles against the stubborn resistance of heavy weights. A battle perfectly symbolic of his struggle against a mindless world.

He'd have to run. Run until his legs burned and his lungs were on fire.

Or he found another outlet for his rage.

CHAPTER 17

SUNDAY

SWEETIE ATTENDED 8:00 A.M. Mass at St. Al's on North Capitol at Eye Street near North Capitol. Most parishioners attended the ten o'clock Gospel Choir Mass, but Sweetie preferred to worship more simply. Just her, a priest, and the Lord would have been fine. She received Holy Communion and felt as close to a state of grace as she could imagine.

That was why, after returning home, she didn't pop her land-lord one when he said, "Hey, great legs!"

Sweetie was sitting on Putnam Shady's front steps, tying the laces of her running shoes, getting ready to run the Mall. The lawyer was strolling up the sidewalk carrying a copy of the *Washington Post* and a paper bag from a place called Lox o' Luck. He was dressed in the kind of sweat clothes in which people never worked up a sweat. He wasn't badly out of shape but for a relatively young guy his gut was getting soft. He seated himself next to Sweetie.

"Care for a schmeer?" he asked, opening the bag and tilting it toward Sweetie. "Grab a bagel; there're plastic knives for the cream cheese."

"Not before I run."

"After, then. Just ring the bell." He started to get up.

"What kind of law do you do?" Sweetie asked.

"What kind of law do you need?" Shady asked, sitting down again.

"Not me. A friend."

"Okay, your friend."

"He needs someone who can chew the backside off a senator who might be in the mood to give him some trouble."

Shady recalled the references Sweetie had given him: the president and her husband. He'd thought it was a joke, and not a bad one. After all, what could you do, call the White House and ask for the president? Explain that you wanted to get her take on somebody looking to move into your basement apartment.

But then he remembered Ms. Sweeney's telling him she was a private investigator—and so, famously, was James J. McGill. The inference was easy.

"You really work with the president's husband?"

"Lying is a sin," Sweetie told him.

"Yeah, and we're all sinners."

"Me somewhat less than others."

He looked at her legs again. "Sorry to hear that." When she gave him a frown, he hurried on. "I advocate for the high-tech industry."

"You're a lobbyist."

"Uh-huh. But I know a bulldog litigator or two. Is this for Mr. McGill?"

"No names for now," Sweetie said.

"Okay. I can still refer someone. Like I said, just ring the bell."

Shady got up and took his keys out, started up the steps.

Sweetie finished tying her shoes and got to her feet, ready to start her run. Before she did, she looked up at Shady. He had his key in the front door but hadn't gone in. He was staring at her legs once more. His imagination working overtime. Her state of grace receded.

"Keep it up, you could be in trouble."

The lawyer raised his eyes. "How do you feel about spanking?"

"Some people need it."

Shady grinned. As if that was exactly what he had hoped to hear.

DAMON TODD decided he had to kill James J. McGill.

He hadn't been able to find anyone else to absorb his anger all night long. Not even after he'd offered himself as a target in high-crime areas. It was ridiculous. Washington had a harrowing reputation for inner-city crime, but he hadn't been able to find a jaywalker, much less a felon.

He ascribed the problem to himself. He looked like someone you didn't mess with: obviously strong and visibly pissed off. That fool on the Georgetown campus had to have been blinded by the fact that he'd held a gun. But the more alert predators—they knew. They'd chosen to find easier pickings.

Which left Todd so frustrated he wanted to howl at the moon. Only the sky was overcast that night. That was when it came to him that there was a specific person he *had* to kill. McGill.

That over-privileged prick wasn't going to go away. Perhaps it had been a miscalculation on Todd's part to have Chana offer McGill money. A former cop, McGill had to see the $20,000 as a bribe. Whether the bribe was too big or too small, Todd couldn't say.

Maybe the amount was irrelevant. The son of a bitch might be a do-gooder. An *honest* former cop. What were the odds? With his rotten luck, too damn good. If Chana didn't go to see McGill, he'd come to her. And Todd wouldn't be able to give Chana the intense therapy she needed if he had to keep looking over his shoulder for the meddlesome McGill.

Todd had spent most of the night jogging around. Not nearly enough exertion for him. So he decided to run the Mall until he was exhausted. He entered the area from New Jersey Avenue, SE. He skirted the Capitol complex and ran north to Constitution Avenue and turned left. His path would carry him just south of the White House. There'd be no getting at McGill there. But the note McGill had sent to Chana's house gave his business address on P Street. That was a location that would bear looking into ... as would the woman running toward him.

To his eye, she looked exactly like the blonde in that old TV commercial for Apple computers. The takeoff on Orwell's *1984*. The one where the woman in track clothes smashes the giant image of Big Brother with a sledgehammer. Talk about his kind of woman.

He gave her a polite nod as she approached, thinking if she smiled, he'd turn around and run with her. He should have known better. The look she gave him, it made him think she was a cop. If he tried the slightest move ... hell, maybe *she* had a hammer on her.

Well, there were two other women in D.C. besides Chana Lochlan who would take him in. In fact, he was staying with one of them, a publicist for local sports heroes. She'd been happy to see him. Love him. Welcome him into her bed. True, she was one of his subjects. Acting on implanted suggestions to hold him dear. But there was nothing like a sure thing.

It'd been twenty years since Damon Todd had sex with a woman he hadn't hypnotized first.

"SO IS this guy Svengali or what?" the deputy director of the Central Intelligence Agency asked Daryl Cheveyo.

The field officer had shepherded Damon Todd's proposal through several layers of bureaucratic review. Now he was speaking to the CIA's number two man in the DD's office.

"There's nothing B-movie about this, sir," Cheveyo answered. "It's not legal or even ethical, but from what we've read and seen, it works. And it could have at least one important application for us."

"Run it by me again," the deputy director said.

The man wasn't inattentive; he was bone tired. The Agency was very busy trying to figure out what was going on down in Cuba. Lots of people were sleeping in their offices, but not for very long at any one time.

"The medical term is dissociative identity disorder, DID," Cheveyo began. "It used to be called multiple personality disorder."

"Sybil," the deputy director said. "Sorry. Don't mean to be flip. I have a tendency to crack wise when I'm groggy. Please continue."

"Yes, sir. As a mental process, dissociation spans a broad spectrum. Most of us experience it in a mild way every day. We daydream; we lose ourselves in a movie; we get absorbed by a book. In doing these things we become detached from the world around us. The reasons for such commonplace dissociation are mundane."

"You're bored listening to some numb nuts give a windy speech, you space out," the deputy director said.

Cheveyo smiled. "Exactly. At the serious end of the continuum, if you're a small child being abused in some horrific way, your mind might find a more dramatic way to ease the pain. Repeated dissociation can lead to the creation of one or more alternate personalities to carry the load. Someone tougher. Or indifferent. Or even *deserving* of suffering."

"That's predominantly where this problem originates, abused kids?"

The deputy director had pictures of three grandchildren on his credenza.

"Yes, sir. Current estimates are that 99 percent of all people with DID suffered repeated severe abuse—physical, sexual, or emotional—before the age of nine. When it is physically impossible to escape such torture, a child often turns to the last avenue of retreat: He goes away in his mind. He hides from reality in order to endure it."

"Miserable bastards," the deputy director muttered.

The abusive adults, Cheveyo understood him to mean. Most of whom had been abused themselves. But there was no time to get into that.

"As a means of defense," Cheveyo went on, "dissociation is highly effective. So much so that dissociative escape can become a conditioned reflex. A practiced child may use it automatically anytime he feels threatened, whether the threat is real or not."

The deputy director sighed and rubbed his tired face.

"Please tell me we're not dealing with someone who has abused children."

"No, sir. My concern is that Dr. Todd may have suffered emotional trauma himself. His personality doesn't seem entirely integrated and cohesive, at least from casual observation."

"But he still has something to offer that may interest us?"

"Yes, sir. Standard practice in treating DID sufferers is to use therapeutic counseling, medication, hypnotherapy, and other adjunctive therapies to bring the patient back to his root, or true, personality. This regimen has a good success rate."

"But that's not what Todd does?"

"No, sir. Dr. Todd has reasoned that the root personality had to be essentially flawed, weak if nothing else, not to have physically escaped the untenable living conditions. So he has created a program of what he calls 'crafted personalities.'"

"He's playing God? Deciding who or what people should be?"

"No, sir. He endeavors to elicit from his subjects the kind of person each of *them* would most like to be ... Then he helps them become those people."

The deputy director raised his eyebrows. "And he's succeeded in doing that?"

"So he claims. He says a number of his unidentified subjects have reached positions of some significance."

"If they're unidentified, they could also be fictional. He could claim to have created half the Mormon Tabernacle Choir, couldn't he?"

Funny that the deputy director's should mention singing, Cheveyo thought.

"Sir, with the press of business, you may not have noticed the erratic public behavior of two prominent persons in town the past few days." Cheveyo recounted "Lady Godiva's" ride on the Mall and Congressman Fleming's fatal aria in the House of Representatives.

"That was this man Todd's work?"

"He won't admit to it, given Congressman Papandreou's fatal heart attack, but the two people behaving strangely match the profiles of two of Dr. Todd's anonymous patients."

The deputy director took a moment to absorb this information.

"And what does he propose to offer us?"

"His technique for crafting new personalities."

"Which he hasn't told you so far."

"No, sir. But he claims he could work with covert operatives. Contrive new personalities for them that they could enter at will, the way an abused child can automatically shift personalities to escape pain."

The deputy director finally saw where things were going.

"An agent who could do that could shift to a personality who didn't know what his primary personality's assignment was. He could never give himself away. The information he carried would stay locked up in his head."

Cheveyo said, "It would likely be safe from physical torture. Whether it could withstand psychological assaults and the use of drugs is an open question."

"Still, it'd give us quite a leg up on where we are now. So what's your reservation?"

"As I've said, sir, it's mostly the man himself. I don't trust him. But there's also the question of using research that has no legitimate foundation. Dr. Todd has done his work under the radar for the very good reason that no reputable institution would ever have approved it. Using only Congressman Fleming as an example. He sang light opera in college, but he wasn't going to make anyone forget Pavarotti. To get him to go from good to great, and not have any awareness of it, Todd must have ..." That was when it truly hit Cheveyo. "Todd must have led Fleming in a direction of Fleming's choosing but crafted the personality so that it was completely hidden from his consciousness. It's clear that Dr. Todd has manipulated his subjects in ways of which they are unaware and to which they could not have given their consent. If it got out that we used such research, it would look very bad for us."

The deputy director said, "The sonofabitch is proving himself to us. He didn't kidnap any of his subjects, did he? Didn't do anything that would remind people of Josef Mengele?"

"Not so far as I know." The hesitation was clear in Cheveyo's voice.

"And if he worked for us, it would be under conditions we would control. There'd be no chance of Todd's playing practical jokes on people. And if he doesn't go public with what he's done, and we don't tell, nobody should be embarrassed by anything."

"Yes, sir," Cheveyo said flatly.

"I'm interested, at least at this stage. Learn more about the man. Once we get past this damn mess with Cuba, I want to know whether we should forward your report to the president." The deputy director smiled. "I'd be curious to see what she'd have to say about it."

THE PRESIDENT summoned the White House reporters from the big broadcast and cable networks. All the newsies knew something had to be up. You didn't get called in on Sunday afternoon for high tea. The reporters got to their feet when the president entered the room.

"Please be seated," the president said. "I'm sorry to intrude on your weekends. But I need to ask you a favor, and I must also ask that you keep my request confidential."

She had their complete attention.

"I'd like you to get in touch with your network presidents when you leave here and advise them that the White House might request all of your organizations to carry a statement from me on very short notice. Possibly not more than a few minutes."

"Does this regard an imminent threat to the nation, Madam President?" David Gregory asked.

"Is it Cuba?" Suzanne Malveaux followed up.

"Islamic terrorists?" Chana Lochlan asked.

The president said, "I can't go into it right now. All I can say is it could be a matter of great consequence. Try not to get ahead of the story on this one."

"That could be difficult to honor," Gregory told her.

The NBC man sat next to Chana Lochlan. The president could take her in without being obvious about it. Could Jim be right, she wondered. Was this woman a threat to her? Her face did look a bit gaunt, but otherwise she looked ... strong. *Really strong.*

"Difficult but not impossible," she replied. "There will be many good stories from this administration ... for those who respect the national interest. Thank you all," she said, dismissing them.

They rose from their chairs and chorused, "Thank you, Madam President."

Patti stole one more glance at Chana.

If the president hadn't wanted to check out Ms. Lochlan personally, Aggie Wu would have been the one talking to the reporters.

"HAVE YOU ever heard of *anorexia athletica,* Jim?" Patti asked.

Her phone call had found McGill at his house in Evanston. He'd told her it was raining to beat the band there. The McGill clan had spent a lazy day reading the Sunday papers and eating too much rich food. He'd even gotten the kids to play a little gotcha karaoke with him. They all picked songs they thought someone else would sound funny singing. They'd only just finished when the call from the White House came.

She'd told him about calling in the White House reporters.

"No, that's a new one on me," he said. "Are we talking about Chana here?"

"Yes. Given your concerns, I wanted to get a look at her without showing my hand."

It had occurred to McGill that Patti wouldn't have called the newsies in for small talk. He said, "I'm sure they thought you had other things on your mind."

"They did. We'll get to that in a minute. But what I noticed about Ms. Lochlan was that she seemed both leaner and more muscular than when we first met. I tried to recall if this was a steady, ongoing process. But the way I reconstruct things it's a more distinct, more recent development. As if she's drastically increased her physical routine in, say, the last month."

McGill had no doubt Patti's assessment was accurate.

"So this *anorexia athletica* is …"

"It's also known as compulsive or obligatory exercise. It's an addiction. You see it not infrequently in people who have to appear in the public eye."

"Models and actors," McGill said.

"And the occasional politician, too. I know how to pick my careers, don't I?"

"You ever have any problems in that direction?"

The question was voiced softly, and the answer came after a short pause.

"No, but there were times when I could see I might be heading that way. That's probably why I recognized it in Ms. Lochlan, once I took the trouble to look."

"What's the motivation for this obsession? Can't be for fun."

"The reason is to become or remain attractive forever."

"To stay the most fabulous face on TV."

"Exactly."

"But Chana Lochlan's no fool. She has to know the futility of what she's doing."

"Knowing and accepting can be two different things. People who fall into this compulsion are often high achievers who are unhappy with their achievements. Makes me wonder if Ms. Lochlan is angry or depressed."

"Neither of which is good in somebody who gets to see the president regularly."

"No, it isn't. Jim, I know Ms. Lochlan fired you, but I'd like you to keep looking into her situation for me. Discreetly. Can you do that?"

McGill thought about Abbie's saying how horrible it would be if someone had made Chana fire him; the situation could turn out like what had happened to Andy Grant. Now, Patti was giving him the opportunity to get back on the case.

"Sure," he said. "I don't have any other clients at the moment. So how are things with my president?"

"Difficult. Raul Castro died this morning."

CHAPTER 18

WELBORN WAS about to knock on the doorframe of Colonel Linberg's Pentagon cubbyhole when he stopped to take note that, unlike the last time he visited, her door was open. As for the colonel herself, she wasn't busy copying the UCMJ. She had her chair turned sideways to her desk. Her legs were extended. Her hands rested on her midsection. She stared at a blank wall as if it were a window on her future.

Was she seeing herself as a civilian already?

Carina Linberg turned to look at Welborn before he ever got around to knocking.

She knew what he had to say before he opened his mouth. "No RILO."

"No, ma'am," Welborn answered. "The president's decision."

"Has a date been set for my court-martial?"

Her tone was flat. Not fearful or angry. Whatever happened to her, the colonel wasn't about to show weakness to him or anyone else. It only reinforced Welborn's admiration for her. He wasn't as smitten as he'd been the first time he'd seen her; he knew that something was going on between her and Captain Cowan. He couldn't help but recall Kira Fahey's notion that maybe both the colonel and the captain were lying to him.

And when he'd met with the president, she had rocked his world. Suggested to him that Colonel Linberg might also have slept with General Altman. So be ready—God help him—to investigate the Air Force chief of staff should she so direct.

At the moment, though, he simply wondered how a woman as beautiful and intelligent as Carina Linberg had gotten herself into such a mess. What was it that made people screw up so badly? It had to be more than just sex.

"Lieutenant, are you going to answer my question?"

"I'm sorry, ma'am. No, a date has not been set for your court-martial. It hasn't been determined yet if there will even be one."

She nodded, still impassive. "So I'm to be left here indefinitely. Better get back to my *duty* then." She picked up her pen, ready to resume her copying. "Please close the door before you leave, Lieutenant."

Welborn said, "You can put your pen down, ma'am."

She looked up at him, finally showing emotion. Surprise.

"Per the president's orders" he told her, "you are relieved of this and all other duties. With pay, of course. Your time will be your own until otherwise notified. You are, however, ordered not to leave the metropolitan D.C. area without permission."

"The president's permission?"

"Yes, ma'am."

"I'll be AWOL if I do?" she asked.

"You will."

She gave Welborn a long look. It made him uneasy.

"Well, Lieutenant, if you had anything to do with liberating me, thank you."

"Yes, ma'am."

"Too bad we had to meet under these circumstances."

"It's the nature of my job."

Welborn saluted and left. He *had* asked the president to free Colonel Linberg from both her tedious chore and the Pentagon's dungeon. He wasn't trying to help her, though; he was hoping to help himself. Captain Cowan wasn't about to go near the colonel in the Pentagon. But if she was out and about, and they thought they could arrange a secret rendezvous …

He would catch them. Only the way the colonel had looked at him now, he had the uneasy feeling she'd seen right through his ploy. He could only hope nobody would guess his next move.

WELBORN WAS driving Kira's Audi TT. She'd taken him back to Annapolis the previous day to pick up his Civic only to find that it had, indeed, been stolen. Not towed; they checked. Kira had been abashed by the accuracy of her gibe.

"Who'd want to take that plain old car?" she asked plaintively.

Welborn knew why if not who. Car thieves stole old Hondas and Toyotas for the value of their parts. Older models got stolen more frequently than new ones. His car had to be cut up and shipped to the four corners of the earth. He felt bad. The little vehicle might have been homely, without an ounce of sex appeal, but it had never failed him.

He filed a police report. Kira felt so bad by then that she not only insisted he use her Audi, she also took on the chore of dealing with his insurance company for him. Calling from the White House would make things easier, she assured him.

He pulled his borrowed sports car to the curb in front of a well-kept Colonial in Falls Church, Virginia. As he approached the front door, he saw that all the curtains were drawn.

Nobody home?

His records showed that Arlene Cowan, the captain's wife, didn't work. But maybe that was before she'd learned about her husband and the colonel. A revelation of that sort could incline a woman to secure an independent source of income.

Welborn pressed the doorbell. He heard a *bing-bong* from within the house. Then footsteps. Someone looked at him through the peephole in the front door. He was in uniform. Looking as clean-cut and trustworthy as possible, he hoped. Someone you'd need not fear.

"Who're you?" a female voice asked from the other side of the door.

"Lieutenant Welborn Yates, ma'am. United States Air Force."

"Air Force?"

"Office of Special Investigations." He held up his ID. "I'm a federal agent."

She opened the door. Welborn hadn't known what to expect of Mrs. Cowan, but he'd assumed she wouldn't be nearly as attractive as Colonel Linberg. Then he saw her. And maybe she wasn't quite as good-looking, but it was a close call. Made him wonder if there wasn't a whole generation of good-looking women ten to twenty years older than he.

Mrs. Cowan had chestnut brown hair, dark brown eyes, a pert nose, a playful turn to her lip. She was more finely boned than the colonel but looked just as fit. Maybe more the sophisticate, in her dark blue suit and pearls, to the colonel's sportswoman.

"You realize you're staring?" Arlene Cowan asked.

He noticed her accent now. Southern but not quite like his own. A little farther to the west he thought. "I'm sorry, ma'am. I didn't mean to be impolite."

She smiled at him, revealing perfect white teeth.

"The Air Force uniform threw me at first. Then I remembered *she's* Air Force."

There was no question who *she* was. Mrs. Cowan looked up the street as if expecting someone's arrival. Then she noticed the Audi parked in front of her house.

"Is that little ego-stroker yours?" There was a hint of contempt in her voice.

"No, ma'am. I drive … I drove a Honda Civic, but it was stolen recently. A friend let me borrow that car for the time being."

She relaxed a bit, smiled. "I drive an Accord. Love every dependable, vanilla inch of it."

A kindred spirit. "Yes, ma'am."

"I suppose you want to ask me all sorts of questions."

"Only the pertinent sort."

She smiled again. "You're a nice young man. I wish I could help you."

"You can't?"

"My lawyer and I are in negotiations that require confidentiality."

She looked at her watch.

"Do you need to be somewhere, ma'am?"

"National Airport. The cab that was supposed to be here thirty minutes ago is going to make me miss my plane." She opened the door wider and Welborn saw two suitcases.

"If you'd like, ma'am, I'd be happy to give you a ride to the airport."

"You have lovely manners, Lieutenant," she said. "Call me Arlene."

Welborn grabbed her bags. Mrs. Cowan locked the front door.

On the way to the Audi, she told him, "I can't speak of my personal situation, you understand, but perhaps on the drive to the airport I can tell you about a friend of mine."

Welborn stashed the suitcases and opened the car door for her.

"I'd like that, Arlene," he said.

ARLENE WAS off to her home state of Tennessee to interview for a very nice job with a Japanese automobile manufacturer that had a plant there. While she hadn't been employed during her marriage to Captain Cowan, she'd advanced her education greatly, acquiring master's degrees in both business administration and the Japanese language.

She'd conquered French and German as an undergrad and Spanish in high school.

He asked Arlene, "If you get the job, will you and the captain maintain two homes?"

She favored him with another smile, this one humorless.

"Let me tell you about my friend, Lieutenant."

Arlene's friend was quite a lot like her. A well-brought-up Southern girl. Educated but firmly encouraged to find a good man and help him become even better. Her role was to buttress her husband's ambitions and be a catalyst should his ambition ever start to lag.

She'd filled that role admirably. Even at the cost of not having the family she wanted. But not at expense of letting her mind wither. She yearned for learning the way some people grasped for money. Or others hungered for sex. Problem was, the more she furthered her education, the less her husband liked it. He longed for the sweet *simple* girl he'd married. He'd come right out and told her so.

Well, what was she supposed to do? Unlearn all her coursework. Renounce her degrees. A friend had once told her friend, "He wants you as unlettered, unskilled, and unemployable as possible, so you'll have nowhere to turn but him."

For a number of years Arlene's friend had wanted to turn nowhere else. Her husband was ruggedly handsome and not without charm. But over time his carping got to be tedious. How in the world had he *ever* thought of her as simple? She flirted with the idea of divorce, but she wasn't a quitter.

So wasn't it a kick in the head when he started littering her life with unmistakable signs that he had a lover? Her friend's husband was often away for long periods of time on business. She'd sometimes thought he might have had an affair or two when he was far from home. But if so, he'd always been discreet about it, and it hadn't distracted him from providing her with marital attention.

Her friend's husband had always liked his sex. The more the better.

Welborn kept his eyes on the road. He didn't want to look at Arlene just then.

"Anyway," she continued, "my friend ignored the signs at first, but then she realized he *wanted* her to notice. More than that, he wanted her to ... what, throw the first punch?"

"Did she?"

"She did, but she crossed him up. She went straight to a divorce lawyer."

Now Welborn glanced at Arlene. "As opposed to?"

"A marriage counselor. He thought that was what she'd do. But then he hadn't realized that she'd already considered leaving him *before* she found out about the cheating."

"So your friend wasn't interested in reconciling. Never went to counseling."

Arlene shook her head. "Uh-uh. Not interested at all."

"Did your friend ever complain to her husband's coworkers? Or his superiors?"

"Never. She'd lost her taste for that crowd. Just went out and got a lawyer."

"How did her husband react?"

"He begged her to hold off. If only for a while. If she did that, he said he'd make it well worth her while."

Welborn looked right at Arlene.

"How did she take that, your friend?"

"She was disinclined ... until he mentioned an amount."

"A large amount?"

"Not enormous, but big enough to make her feel she'd been earning a pension for all the years she'd spent with him."

Welborn put his eyes back on the road. They were close to the airport now. "Does your friend think her husband's good for it? The money."

"That's what she and her lawyer are waiting to see ... but he's come up with enough cash to buy himself a very fancy sports car. So she has her hopes."

Welborn stopped the Audi in front of the American Airlines terminal. He opened the trunk and handed Arlene's bags to a skycap.

"Did you enjoy my little story, Lieutenant?" she asked.

"One of the best I've heard in a long time," he told her.

So good, in fact, that he hadn't noticed until that very moment that Major Clarence Seymour, General Altman's aide, had been following him once again.

CHAPTER 19

MCGILL HAD a government limo to take him to O'Hare. As a treat, he brought his kids back to their mother's house in it. Carolyn was out front talking with a neighbor when the stretch Cadillac pulled up. The kids piled out, giggling, as Caitie pretended to be a movie star arriving at her premiere. They gave McGill hugs and kisses and ran into the house. He waved to his ex.

"Things getting any better?" he asked.

"I showed Lars what I could do," Carolyn answered. "How good I am."

At her marksmanship, McGill presumed.

"Was he impressed?"

She nodded, smiling.

"You'll have to show me, too," McGill said.

"Next time you're in town."

The neighbor gave both of them strange looks, and McGill departed.

He had Deke sitting up front with Leo. The privacy screen was raised. He picked up the phone and called Sweetie at the P Street office of McGill Investigations, Inc.

"We're back on the Chana Lochlan case," he told her.

That took Sweetie by surprise. "She changed her mind?"

"Patti asked me to keep on it. She wants to know more about Ms.

Lochlan. She thinks our former client might exercise too much for her own good."

"Is that possible?" Sweetie asked.

"It is if you're doing it for vanity."

"Well, sure, that'd make it sinful."

"Not like you or me, doing it for fitness or to mortify the flesh."

"The sin is in the thought not the deed," Sweetie instructed.

"So how full of shit are we?"

"Saint Peter's sure to let us know," Sweetie said with a laugh.

"Anyway, it's time for us to talk with as many of Chana's old boyfriends as possible. I'm going to start with number one, her old college sweetheart out in California. Why don't you speak with the ones who are still around D.C.? We'll compare notes when I get back."

"Okay," Sweetie said. "You think maybe it'd be worth a stop in Ohio on the way back, see if you can catch up with her father?"

McGill considered the idea.

"Patti wants us to keep all this quiet. Talking to her dad, that'd likely get back to her."

"Yeah, but he'd probably know things nobody else would."

"Let me see how I feel after I talk to the boyfriend. I'll take it from there."

Sweetie was pleased when McGill told her he'd had a good weekend with his kids.

"I think I've got a big kid of my own on my hands," she said, telling him about Putnam Shady and his crack about spankings. "Just what I need living upstairs, a kinky lawyer."

"Move if the guy's creeping you out."

Not that Sweetie creeped out easily. She said, "I can handle him. If he wants some dominatrix action, I'll make him reenact the Stations of the Cross."

McGill laughed. He asked Sweetie to fax the list of Chana's lovers to the Air Force jet he'd be using. "After my limo drops me off. And my bodyguard makes sure all is well."

Sweetie said, "You're doing okay for an old Chicago copper, aren't you?"

"Yeah," McGill said. "Now if we only had a paying client or two."

MCGILL'S JET took off without having to wait in line for other departing traffic. The steward, who McGill had just learned was named Lieutenant Bartholomew Burley, brought McGill his requested White House ice tea as the Gulfstream leveled out at cruising altitude, heading for San Jose.

"Thank you," McGill told him.

"You're welcome, sir."

"You and the guys in the cockpit don't mind chauffeuring a civilian around?"

"We're all combat veterans, sir. A little light duty is fine with us."

The lieutenant wore the grin of someone with a secret as he went forward. McGill waved Deke over, recounted the exchange, and asked what Burley was keeping from him.

"He was joking about light duty," Deke said in a quiet voice.

"So what's the joke?"

"The crew has been trained in light arms, hand-to-hand, and first aid."

"Just in case we run into any trouble you and Leo and I can't handle."

"Always good to have strength in numbers," Deke responded. "Also, they all know how to make parachute jumps—with you harnessed to any one of them."

"Huh," McGill said.

The surprises just kept on coming.

MCGILL THOUGHT Graham Keough looked like a poet. All he needed was a big floppy hat with a feather. He had long dark hair and sensitive gray eyes. He worked in a green-glass tower in Silicon Valley, the Manager of All Things Creative for a computer gaming company called MindGames.

McGill had called him during the flight to California. When Graham heard what McGill wanted, he'd told him he'd clear his schedule to talk with him. McGill's impression, though, was that Graham wanted to *hear* from him. About Chana. The old flame still burned. Graham was waiting for him and Deke in the company's reception area. Pacing. He wasn't going to waste time having his guests escorted back to his office.

Only the Manager of All Things Creative didn't have an office. Nobody at MindGames did. The entire work force, thirty or so people mostly under thirty years old, all too cool to be impressed by McGill, worked in an open floor plan. There were no cubicles either, at least in a formal sense. Desks were separated from one another by groups of plantings, abstract sculptures, life-size cutouts of comic-book characters. Some of the spaces were bigger, some smaller, some tiny.

Graham saw McGill and Deke looking around. "We allot space for working areas according to the point standings in a new game we're beta testing. We move things around every Friday afternoon."

"Anybody ever lose all his space?" McGill wanted to know.

"One guy."

"He get fired?" Deke asked.

"No, he's the CEO. He has to telecommute until he can displace someone else."

Graham opened a door to a large room.

"Conference room," he said. "Only place besides the john that has a door."

Deke stepped inside, checked it out.

After the room had been given the Secret Service stamp of approval, Deke went to wait outside, closing the door behind him. Graham gestured McGill to the seat at the head of the conference table. He took the one to the right of it instead. Graham sat opposite him.

"How can I be of help?" he asked.

MCGILL TOLD him the whole thing. Chana coming to him, the phone call, the thong, and getting fired. Graham Keough's frown got progressively deeper.

"If you've been fired," he asked, "what are you doing here, talking to me?"

"Ms. Lochlan finds herself in regular proximity to the president."

All the color drained from Graham's face.

"No, no, no," he said. "Chana would never—"

"The president is also my wife," McGill reminded him. "Would you take a chance?"

McGill's question started Graham Keough thinking.

"I've read about you, Mr. McGill. You're a *private* investigator. Which I think is pretty cool for the president's husband. But that means you're doing this, what, off the books?"

"Discreetly. Which is all to Ms. Lochlan's advantage. So I hope you'll treat this as a confidential meeting. Have you had any contact with Chana lately?"

Graham shook his head. "Only when I watch TV. Only in my dreams."

"She was hard to get over?"

"Try impossible." Graham was quiet for a moment, trying to decide how much to reveal. McGill, the ex-cop, had seen such calculations many times before. "After I left Chana—"

"You left her?" McGill interrupted.

"I had to. I'll get to that. After I left her, I became a real grind. Focused on nothing but schoolwork. Graduated second in my undergraduate class, first in grad school. When I finally came up for air, I dated every girl I could, tried to drown myself in female attention. That left me feeling like a shit, so I started being very selective about whom I'd date. That made me feel like an elitist jerk, and it was futile because I knew what I was doing. I was measuring the women I dated against Chana, and since none of them was her, none of them could ever measure up."

Graham Keough sighed deeply, lapsed into silence.

After a moment, McGill asked, "And what's the plan now?"

The tech wizard shrugged. "Now, I leave it to fate. If there's a woman who'll make me forget Chana, we'll meet. She'll find me. I hope."

"So you've never tried to get back in touch with Chana?"

"No. I've thought about it, of course. But it just seemed too creepy. A desperate-guy thing. I've managed to hold myself above that."

McGill nodded. He believed the younger man.

"So why did you break up with Chana?"

"Do you know anything about her mother?" Graham asked.

McGill shook his head.

"Marianne Westerly was the mother from hell," Graham Keough said. "I'm a peaceful guy, but there were times I wanted to fly across the country and do terrible things to her." He laughed. "There are *still* times I feel like that."

"What was so bad about her?" McGill asked.

"Well, let's see. She was a professor, you know that?"

McGill nodded. "That much I've heard. Women's studies."

"Right. *Crazy* women's studies. I'm all for individual liberation. But some of Professor Westerly's ideas went way beyond that."

McGill nodded empathetically and kept listening closely.

"While Chana was in her freshman year at Westwood, finding out who she was and making me happier than I'd ever been, good old Mom came up with a fascinating topic for her class to sink their teeth into: Should Professor Westerly divorce her husband of twenty-some years?"

McGill frowned. "Hypothetically, you mean."

Graham shook his head. "Dead serious. The class studied the history of marriage, looked at how women traditionally got the subservient role, discussed whether any legal union between a man and woman could be equitable, and applied their findings specifically to Chana's parents. In the end, it was unanimously decided that Ms. Westerly had no choice but to divorce her
husband."

McGill was at a loss for words.

"Yeah. It boggles the mind," Graham continued. "But the real kicker is that Chana didn't know anything about it until she got home after her freshman year. Mom had made her divorce a class project but hadn't said a word about it to her own daughter."

"And how did Chana take the news?" McGill asked.

"Not well. You want something to drink? This could take a while."

MCGILL SIPPED a chilled green-tea-and-honey concoction that was good enough for him to decide to add to the White House menu.

"She adored her dad," Graham told McGill. "Still does, I imagine. Funny thing was, Professor Lochlan was cool about his wife divorcing him. They still intended to live together; they just wouldn't be married anymore. Pretty '60s idea, if you ask me. But when Chana came home and didn't get with the program, Mom started in on her. Called Chana a *traditionalist*. A *baseball
player*. Said that might have been acceptable if Chana was butch but, no, she had to be straight, too. Probably hoped to make some empty-headed surfer a good little Valley Girl wife."

"Her parents didn't know about you?" McGill asked.

"No."

An omission that still hurt, McGill could see. "So what happened?"

"Didn't take long for Professor Lochlan to see he'd have to make a choice. Going along with his wife's lunacy was one thing, but losing his only daughter was another. And since he and Mom were already divorced anyway, he told her to hit the bricks."

For the first time since he started telling the story, Graham cracked a smile.

"What's funny?" McGill asked.

"Well, being a liberated woman, Mom had refused to take any alimony in the divorce. I think that point got decided in class, too. So when Professor Lochlan kicked her out—the house was in his name—she was left with her clothes and about a buck ninety-eight in the bank, I heard. She could have gone back to court, of course, but then what would she tell her students?"

McGill enjoyed the irony but wanted to pick up on another point.

"Do you know about Nanette?" he asked.

"Chana's sister. She died before Chana was born."

McGill nodded. "So Professor Lochlan had already lost a daughter; it was understandable he didn't want to lose another. But why didn't Professor Westerly feel the same way?"

"Maybe Mom felt Chana didn't measure up to Nan. Or what she fantasized Nan would have become since the poor kid died so young."

Graham excused himself for a moment. Nature calling.

McGill thought it was the younger man's heart that was demanding a respite.

BUT GRAHAM came back and continued. "Chana came back West early for her sophomore year. She had to get away from home. She called and asked if she could stay with me." Graham smiled wistfully. "Easiest question I've ever had to answer. My mom and dad were cool with it. *They* knew about Chana and me. I had her picture in my room. They knew we'd be sleeping together, too, even though Chana was officially staying in the guest room. As long as we didn't flaunt it, they didn't say anything."

"Were you able to help Chana get over the hurt?" McGill asked.

Graham looked like a tragic poet now. He shook his head.

"Chana was always one of those people who strived for perfection, and her mother's criticism had really knocked the stuffing out of her. So she had to rebuild her self-image. I tried to be as positive as I could. Offered the best advice a nineteen- year-old had at his command. But she never needed me for that; she always had some inner voice she followed."

"What did it say?"

"It said become the best female jock UCLA had ever seen. No small challenge if you know the school's history."

"She worked out a lot?" McGill asked evenly, wondering if Graham Keough had ever heard about *anorexia athletica* .

"She almost killed herself. That's why I left her. At first, fool that I was, I thought losing me would shock her back into her senses. When it quickly became apparent that wasn't the case, I consoled myself that at least I wouldn't have to see her die."

"You're exaggerating, aren't you?"

Anger flashed in Graham's eyes. "I was at my apartment studying. February 12. Eight thirty-four in the evening. The phone rang. Julie Simpson, who shared an apartment with Chana, was on the line. Hysterical. She begged me to come over right away. Chana had come home after a long run and passed out. Her breathing was labored. She was white as a sheet. I called 911, and the paramedics got there before I did. But I was in time to see them load Chana into the ambulance. She didn't look bad; she looked *dead*."

It was a minute before Graham could continue.

"I lost it myself, because the next thing I know I'm lying on the ground, and an EMT is reviving me. What I heard was that Chana had washed all the electrolytes out of her body. It'd been unusually hot, but she'd kept running and drinking water. Too much water. She should have been using a sports drink, the paramedic told me, to replace the trace minerals that conduct electrical impulses in the body. Once those nutrients fell below critical mass, all of her brain functions just shut down."

He shook his head as if he still couldn't believe it.

"You saved her life," McGill said.

"Yeah, I was smart enough to dial 911, not freak out like Julie. But that doesn't change the fact that it was the last time I ever saw her."

"You didn't visit her at the hospital?"

"She was in intensive care. No visitors. Once her condition improved, her father took her back East."

"She didn't call or write?" Graham shook his head. "And you don't know why?" McGill said.

"Sure, I do. See, when I left Chana, I told her I never wanted to hear from her again. She was just doing what I'd asked. Being a good friend. Striving for perfection as always."

McGill didn't know what to say.

Graham said, "So you're going to help her, right? Even though you've been fired, you're not going to let anything bad happen to her."

All sorts of people, it seemed to McGill, wanted him to stay on the case.

"Do my best," he said.

Graham nodded his approval. "Come back to my desk with me, okay? I'll give you a card with my home phone and private cell numbers. In case I can do anything more to help."

With Deke in tow, they walked over to Graham's workspace. It was set off by a cutout of Albert Einstein doing a high kick between two Rockettes. He gave McGill his card.

"I'll keep this confidential," he said. "But if you find the right time, tell Chana I said hello."

McGill said he would.

CHAPTER 20

MAJOR CLARENCE Seymour caught General Warren Altman at his Pentagon office ten minutes before the Air Force chief of staff had to leave for the White House. The Joint Chiefs were meeting with the president yet again on the situation in Cuba. The president was demanding intelligence: She wanted to know the situation on the ground. But nobody had anything to tell her. A CIA resource had provided the news of Raul Castro's death but hadn't been heard from since.

The Pentagon's top brass were one hundred percent sure they could stop any Cuban attack on the U.S. if it came to that. But they were at a loss as to what they could do if Havana decided to annihilate its own people. The Armed Forces weren't set up to prevent such acts.

After returning Major Seymour's salute, General Altman asked, "Well?"

"Lieutenant Yates talked with Captain Cowan's wife. He drove her to National Airport in Kira Fahey's car. When he dropped Mrs. Cowan off, things looked very friendly between them."

"Lieutenant Yates has been busy. He got Linberg released from her punishment duty this morning, too. This situation is getting away from us."

Major Seymour nodded, having reached the same conclusion earlier.

"You could deescalate, sir. Handle the situation administratively. Slap Colonel Linberg's wrist, give her a general discharge, and get rid of her."

The major saw the general's face redden at the idea. Still, he took the risk of pushing his line of reasoning. "It might not be what you wanted, sir, but it's quick and clean. And it'll take Yates out of play."

The general shook his head. "No, goddamnit. I won't do it." General Altman turned to stare at an aerial photo of the B-2 bomber he'd once flown. He liked to tell people that bomber pilots came closer than anyone else to knowing what if felt like to be God, because only they and the Almighty knew what it was to rain destruction from on high. "I haven't played fair with you, Clarence. You know I'm digging a grave for Colonel Linberg, but you don't know why."

Major Seymour had his suspicions.

"How far up the chain of command do you hope to rise, Clarence? Surely, you want at least one star on your shoulder."

"Yes, sir."

"How about four stars? Would you want my job?"

"I try not to put any limits on my ambition, General."

Altman nodded. "No reason why a strong man should. If he's willing to take the risks. I know you're strong, Clarence. Smart, too. But I'm not sure you're much of a risk taker."

Major Seymour was tempted to clock the general ... but he *wasn't* that big a risk taker.

"All right, Clarence. Time to decide. How far are you willing to lean out over the void to grab the brass ring?"

Up until that moment, the major had always thought that making a deal with the devil was just a figure of speech. Now maybe he wasn't so sure. But he wasn't going to back down.

"I'll do what I have to, sir. Long as it's not something that'll stick only to me."

Altman laughed. Sounded just like the devil.

GALIA MINDEL, by prearrangement with the president, didn't sit in on the meeting with the Joint Chiefs of Staff. The two most powerful women in the world had sorted out the issue before the inauguration. Whereas a male chief executive could have his male chief of staff at every important meeting and draw no comment on it, having Galia at the president's side might look as if the ladies needed each other's support to stand up to all those brutes with their Y-chromosomes.

The president insisted she would command respect on her own.

That was as Galia thought it should be; there were plenty of meetings *she* chaired alone, and woe betide the man who questioned her authority. Except McGill, of course.

He wasn't a knuckle dragger in his relations with women. Far from it. But neither was he subject to Galia's authority. He'd painfully proven that point. The memory still stung. Which made it hard for her to follow through on the plan that was taking shape in her head.

The meeting she'd had with her spy, Merilee Parker, at Macy's in New York had provided Galia with information on which she would have to act soon. If she didn't, that bastard Roger Michaelson was going to drop a political bombshell on the administration. Worse than that, Michaelson's plan might well wound the president personally. Leave her unable to rise to the demands of contending with whatever crises were sure to follow the mess in Cuba.

Galia wasn't about to let that happen. She was determined to turn things around on Michaelson. Put the SOB back in his place. The problem was, Galia needed a man for her plan. She needed someone smart, tough, and ruthless. Someone who could *scare* Michaelson. Without actually killing him. Damnit, she needed the president's henchman.

Galia cringed at the idea of asking for his help. But she saw no alternative. She buzzed her secretary.

"Yes, Ms. Mindel?" her secretary answered.

"Please locate the president's husband for me."

WELBORN SOON found out it was impossible for one person to stake out the Pentagon. The place was too damn big. There were too many ways in and out. He sat in Kira's Audi in a corner of the parking area where Carina Linberg should have left her car.

If she'd driven to work that day.

If she hadn't already left, after he'd cut her shackles.

If she wasn't running rings around all his schemes.

Welborn thought he had many a mountain to climb to learn all the things he'd need to know to do his job well. Mount Linberg was but the first. Before he could become too self-absorbed, his cell phone chirped.

Actually, it was the White House cell phone. The one Kira had insisted he carry with him. She said it was her job to get in touch with him if necessary, and she wasn't going to race off to Annapolis again to do it.

"Lieutenant Yates," he answered in a polite voice.

Never could tell if the president might be calling.

"Welborn, sweetie, are you taking good care of my little baby?"

Kira. Inquiring about the Audi.

"Not a scratch," he said, keeping an eye out for Colonel Linberg. He could see great distances with amazing clarity, but to his disappointment he could not see around corners. He didn't need Kira's distractions. "I'll return it in like condition. Full gas tank even."

"Wait," Kira told him, correctly sensing his intention to break the connection.

"What is it?" he asked, getting testy.

"You don't need to take that tone. I'm calling because I fielded a phone call for you. I think it could be important."

"Well, why didn't you say so?"

Now there was *frost* in Kira's voice. "I was trying to be friendly. I thought we might be heading in that direction. I won't make that mistake again."

Women, Welborn thought.

"I'm truly sorry, Ms. Fahey. The stress of doing a new job must have made me forget my manners." That was as thick as he was going to lay it on.

"Apology accepted."

"Would you care to tell about the call now, the one you took for me."

"Yes. It was from Cheryl Altman. Do you know who she is?"

Welborn could guess, and his stomach did a flip-flop.

"General Altman's wife?"

"How clever you are. For a boy of uncertain parentage."

Well, she'd warned him she wasn't Little Mary Sunshine.

"Did Mrs. Altman leave a message?"

"She'd like to speak with you at your earliest convenience."

Oh no, Welborn thought, the president hadn't—

"Is the president available?" he asked.

"Meeting with the Joint Chiefs," Kira answered.

One of whom was the husband of the woman who wanted to see him.

"Kira," he asked, "how would you like to get out of the office?"

The reply was slow in coming. "Do you promise to be nice?"

"To you or your car?" he asked.

And thought he might have pushed it too far. Expected to hear a dial tone any second. But Kira said, "I'm trying to decide if you're worth all the aggravation."

"I really can't say. But there might be a bit of adventure here, if that appeals."

That was what might be in it for her. For him, he wanted to have the vice president's niece as a witness should anyone have some skullduggery planned for him.

"Okay, flyboy," Kira told him, "swing by the White House and pick me up."

MCGILL WAS on his way to the San Jose airport. He had a question for Deke, who was seated next to him. "Can our plane fly to Hawaii? You know, without having to refuel at Catalina or something."

Deke gave McGill a forbearing smile.

"Our bird can refuel in midair. It can fly around the world without landing."

McGill wasn't sure he could. "And, of course, the crew knows how to do that refueling."

Deke nodded. He said, "It's not necessary to refuel for a trip to Hawaii, though. Any of the islands is well within range. Which one are you thinking of?"

"Oahu."

McGill was sure he was running up quite a tab on the Air Force executive jet, but now he was doing it at Patti's request and didn't feel bad about spending the money. The bill wouldn't amount to an hour's interest on the fortune poor Andy had left her.

Having talked to Graham Keough, McGill had become interested in Michael Raleigh, Chana's former and late husband. The one who had died in the hang gliding accident in Hawaii. McGill had the urge to get the details of the fatal mishap from the Honolulu cops. It might not come to anything, but he'd long ago learned to trust his instincts.

To his credit, Deke refrained from asking why McGill wanted to head west rather than east.

Leo pulled up at a rear gate to the airport and showed his White House credentials to a guard. McGill's car was admitted, and a utility truck led them to where the Air Force Gulfstream was parked. A pair of guards with machine guns stood watch outside the plane. Took the worry out of flying, McGill thought.

He got on board, intending to have a word with the pilot about their next destination, but the steward, Bart Burley, extended a phone to him before he could say a word.

"The White House chief of staff, sir," he told McGill.

McGill carried the instrument to his preferred seat and clicked it on.

Galia wasn't on the phone; it was her secretary. He had to hold. A thumb of Galia's nose to him. That was okay, he had plenty of time to get even. But McGill forgot his annoyance when he heard what Galia had to say.

"Roger Michaelson is out to get the president. He intends to do it soon. And he's going to use you as his means of attack."

"How?"

Galia told him. "He's going to claim you and Sergeant Sweeney beat a false confession out of Lindell Ricker. I'm sure you understand the implications."

McGill did and recounted them aloud. "It would call Erna Godfrey's conviction into question, hers and the others. There could be a retrial. That would put Patti through the hell of reliving Andy's death all over again."

"Yes it would. It would also wound the president politically."

Already angry, McGill was on his way to furious. "How?" he demanded.

"If Michaelson can make the charge look plausible, it will be widely, maybe even universally, assumed that you must have told the president what you had done. To give her the satisfaction of knowing that you'd go to any length to get justice and/or vengeance for her."

Which wasn't far from the truth, even if it wasn't the case with Ricker. "A husband and wife can't be made to testify against each other," McGill said.

"True, but that won't matter. How will it *look* if the two of you refuse to talk?"

Like they were hiding something, McGill knew. "But none of this is true. Nobody laid a finger on Ricker. All of his rights were scrupulously observed. His confession was videotaped. You can *see* he wasn't beaten."

"Did Mr. Ricker confess in the nude? Did the camera shoot him from the front and the rear? Were there no signs of trauma anywhere on his body?"

Galia's questions made McGill, the ex-cop, wonder if that was what it would come to when cops questioned prisoners. Nude videos. He said, "Ricker had to strip when he was processed into the federal lockup in downtown Chicago. He was given a physical at that time."

"And we all know that physicians and jailers on the federal payroll would *never* do anything unethical. Like falsify their reports or tell fibs to the public and its servants in Congress."

Exercising as much patience as he could summon, McGill said, "Look, Galia, you can twist anything."

"My point exactly. The other thing you have to keep in mind is that once the circus comes to town, it can stay for a very long time, and unveil one new exciting act after another. With Roger Michaelson as your leering ringmaster."

"So he has to be stopped before he can pitch his tent."

"Just so."

"And you called me because?"

"You love the president more than anyone. You're also uniquely suited, in my view, to confront Roger Michaelson. And because your ass is also on the line."

All of which McGill agreed with, but Galia had left one thing unsaid.

"It had to kill you to ask me for help, didn't it?" McGill asked.

"At first, but I've gotten over it."

"A true professional. So what's your plan, Galia? What do you want me to do?"

She told him.

McGill said no.

"But—" Galia began.

"No," McGill repeated. Then he came up with his own idea. "You got the part about taking the fight to him right. But no cameras. Any publicity at all could bring the circus to town. What I know about the guy, what I remember, is that he was a college basketball star."

"What's *that* got to do with anything?" Galia asked.

Her plan had been to have McGill confront the senator in a public forum where there were TV cameras. That would focus attention on McGill and Michaelson. But McGill was right, Galia could see now, damn him. The story would get too big to be limited to the two of them. The flood tide of media attention would inundate the Oval Office, too.

"I'll bet he still plays ball," McGill told her. "Find out where. See if you can learn anything about his game."

This macho nonsense was almost more than Galia could stand, but she lacked a better idea.

"If you're not up to getting this information, Galia, I'll put Sweetie on it. Her reputation is at stake here, too."

"I can do it," the chief of staff asserted. "Better and with less notice than anyone else."

"Good. Then do it," McGill said. "And, Galia?"

"What?"

"I appreciate how well you look after the president. I'm sorry about the donuts."

"Too late for that," she snapped, and broke the connection.

DEKE AND Leo stood at a respectful distance, looking at McGill. The three Air Force officers watched him from the doorway to the cockpit. None of them said a word. Just waited to hear what his pleasure might be.

"Tower needs a flight plan?" McGill asked the pilot.

"It helps traffic move smoothly, sir."

McGill grinned. "Tell them we're bound for Andrews AFB. With a stop on the way at Gambier, Ohio."

The pilot saluted. "Yes, sir."

He and the copilot strapped into their seats and began chattering with control tower and each other. Unsolicited, Bart Burley brought him a

White House ice tea. Leo took his seat and began writing in a notebook; his memoirs would be worth reading, too, McGill thought.

He waved Deke over to sit next to him. "I suppose you can talk to anyone in the world—or on Mars, for that matter—from this plane."

"On earth, yes. On Mars, I'd have to check."

"Good. What I'd like you to do is find the name and the phone number of the Honolulu chief of police for me. When you have that information, let me know, and I'll call the man."

"I'll call him for you."

McGill shrugged.

Deke went to work. Getting the name and phone number took less than a minute. Calling him and having him pick up, maybe thirty seconds.

"Chief Patrick Manuala?" Deke asked. "This is Secret Service Special Agent Donald Ky calling from Air Force 1-A ..."

So that's what they call my plane, McGill thought.

"... Please hold for retired Chief of Police James J. McGill."

Sounded better than Gumshoe McGill, McGill thought. Established professional bonds. He nodded his approval to Deke as he took the phone.

"Hello, Chief," McGill said. "How are you?"

A round of pleasantries followed before McGill got down to business. He asked for copies of any reports and photos the HPD might have concerning the accidental hang gliding death of tourist Michael Raleigh. He gave Chief Manuala the date Chana's ex had lost his life.

The Hawaiian cop was only too happy to comply. Said he'd have the file FedExed out that night. With a laugh, he added it would be the first time he'd ever sent anything to the White House. McGill didn't spoil his fun by asking that the material be sent to his P Street office.

Chief Manuala invited him and, of course, the president to come visit his beautiful island as soon as they could. McGill said he'd speak with the president about it.

Then the chief asked if it would be all right to ask a favor.

"Sure," McGill told him.

"I'm a big fan of the president. Voted for her, you know. I was wondering, you think I could get an autographed picture?"

McGill smiled. "That I can promise. Made out to you?"

"The Manuala family. I want it for home, not an office trophy photo."

That made McGill feel even better.

"I'll make a call," he said. "If the president has a spare moment, it'll go out tonight."

"Mahalo and aloha," the chief said.

McGill broke the connection just as the Gulfstream surged into the air.

He wasn't surprised that he could use the phone during a takeoff.

He started making calls to the other boyfriends on Chana Lochlan's list. All of them were willing to talk. Eager even, as Graham Keough had been. All of them had nicknames for Chana, too—*Gorgeous* being the most common. But none of them admitted to calling her Gracie.

CHAPTER 21

CHANA LOCHLAN lay naked on her bed, sleeping peacefully. Damon Todd sat naked on a chair next to the bed, staring at her, fully aroused. He could take her anytime he wanted. All he needed to do was utter a post-hypnotic prompt, and she would welcome him, wrap her arms and legs around him, kiss him as deeply as if he were her personal Prince Charming. But he just couldn't say the words.

Because he loved her. Because she'd helped define him as much as he'd helped define her. But she was changing, quite independently of his ministrations.

He stood and walked over to a full-length, three-panel mirror set in a corner of the room. The looking glass was normally kept in Chana's dressing area, but he'd brought it into the bedroom for that night's session. By the soft radiance of a night-light that still glowed on the reflective surfaces, he'd had Chana stand before the mirror and tell him who she saw.

He'd expected her to say "Nan."

She'd said, "I don't know."

Chana had always wanted to be the older sister she'd never known in life. She'd projected an image of perfection on Nan—aided by her mother, who'd always done the same. It had never occurred to Chana that although Nan had been beautiful, she'd been fatally flawed. Else, why had her cruel disease carried her off at such a young age? But people tended to overlook even obvious facts when they contradicted their preconceptions.

But Chana was changing.

When Chana had been brought to him for help after she'd nearly died in California, it had taken only two therapy sessions for her to admit she wanted to be like Nan. Given all the execrable role models a young person could have emulated, Todd found Chana's choice touching. Pure. He'd been conducting his experiments in crafting personalities for five years by then, but only in piecemeal ways. Improving one subject's punctuality. Getting another over socially debilitating shyness. Smoothing out a stutter that speech therapists had been unable to correct.

He'd provided such help at the college health-services facility *pro bono*. His only compensation had been sexual access to the females he'd found attractive. A fee he'd kept entirely to himself.

Chana had fallen in love him when he'd told her, several sessions into her therapy, that she could not only be like Nan, but he could help her *become* Nan. The prospect had been so thrilling to her that she'd embraced him fiercely. She was regaining a good deal of her strength by then, and he … he was nowhere near the man he was now.

In fact, it had been the sheer physical might he felt flow from her that had inspired him to change. He'd always been slight of build, but at that moment he wanted to be strong. Very strong. Worthy of the woman he was sure would become his greatest creation.

It would be years before the term *anorexia athletica* came to be coined, but he knew from his workup and sessions with Chana that she was seriously addicted to exercise. So he foresaw that in patterning himself after his patient, he would be taking the risk of falling into the same trap. He wasn't worried, though. He was a professional. He could walk up to the edge and not fall into the abyss. The element of danger only added to the appeal of his new plan.

In the end, however, he did fall. Indeed, he had *wanted* to fall.

The most common body dysmorphia that seized males was called *bigorexia*. It was the polar opposite of *anorexia nervosa*. The sufferers of *bigorexia* obsessed about being small and underdeveloped. Even if they had good muscular development, they saw themselves as ninety-seven-pound weaklings. In pursuit of ever larger and more muscular physiques, they could not and would not stop their compulsive exercising and their abuse of steroids. Not even when they understood the destructive consequences of their actions.

Todd's obsession skewed from that pattern. His self-diagnosis was *riporexia*. He strived not for size but the complete definition of every muscle fiber in his body. He wanted to see every strand of protein when he stood nude in front of a mirror. He wanted to be ripped as no one had ever been ripped. That meant his body had to be stripped of all fat above the bare minimum necessary to sustain life.

He had realized that his body was simply the metaphor for his identity. But as long as there was any ambiguity in his psyche—and there was more than he'd ever admit—he thought that the continuing act of defining himself physically would lead him to a complete understanding of who he truly was.

But having become a physical specimen unlike any other, he had cause to doubt his entire hypothesis. Just as he had to doubt that Chana, of her own volition, had ever really cared for him. He returned to the chair next to the bed and resumed looking at her. Dispassionately.

She had been the first subject whose personality he'd remade entirely. With her eager assistance, of course. She'd been the first one he'd given Special K. He'd read about the drug's effects before he'd ever used it on any of his patients. He'd even done first-person observations of users, sometimes going so far as to provide the money that the recreational druggies used to buy their ketamine hydrochloride.

The fieldwork confirmed the findings reported in the literature. Users of a certain quantity and concentration of the drug all but unanimously reported near-death experiences: going into the K-hole. He had reasoned that his subjects could go into the K-hole as one personality and come out reborn as another.

The preparation for such a drastic change had to be painstaking and willingly entered into by the subject, but he was certain it would work.

And it had. Chana had become Nan. Nan was reborn twenty years after she had died. Nan knew that to keep up appearances she had to masquerade as Chana. But that was a small price to pay for being given a second chance at life.

Similarly, a large number of his other subjects became new, if covert, personalities. Crafted personalities. College towns had been fertile recruiting grounds for his work. Early on, he'd thought about going public with his work, but anytime he'd even hinted to colleagues about an interesting new *theory* he was thinking about, he'd been uniformly rebuked.

Unethical. Immoral. Playing God.

So he'd kept his work secret. But privately, he had been quite proud of what he was doing. It was amazing really. He took young people of promising but conflicted natures and helped them to find their most productive selves. The percentage of his subjects who'd gone on to lead lives of substantive achievement was nothing short of astounding. His subjects had become important figures in business, government, and the arts.

And all he'd asked in return was that they welcome him whenever he dropped in to see them. The nature of that welcome varied with the individual. Women provided him with their warmth. Men provided him with financial help. Everyone greeted him with a smile.

Except that when he'd phoned Chana not long ago, she hadn't even known who he was. Chana, whom he loved.

He put his clothes on—sweats and sneakers—as he continued to look at her. Was Chana starting to assert her own identity, he wondered, and was Nan beginning to recede? In their original therapy sessions, Chana had told him that her mother, Marianne Westerly, was the one who had originally insisted her second daughter be just like her first, or as she imagined Nan would have become had she lived. Parents were, after all, the original craftsmen of their children's lives.

The pity of it was that so many of them did the job so badly.

Chana's father, Eamon Lochlan, had loved her unconditionally for who she was—or so Chana had reported to him—and he had no reason to doubt her. Her only complaint about her father had been that he too readily deferred to her mother. Which made it understandable that Chana's desire to become her sister, inspired by her mother's urging, had come to the fore. Todd knew that Chana/Nan's parents had divorced long ago, but had some new dynamic been introduced to draw Chana closer to her father of late? If so, that might be the reason for this confusion of identity.

He thought it would be a good idea to investigate. Pay a visit to Professor Lochlan in Ohio. While the CIA continued its endless dithering about his work.

He pulled the covers up around his beloved. If she wanted to go back to being Chana, he would help restore her to that identity. He would do so and depart from her life. Maybe forgetting all about his current plans and looking for something new to make of himself.

"Sleep well, my dear," he told her. "When you awaken, you will be refreshed. If you don't know exactly who you want to be, you will at least see the first steps you should take."

He turned and started for the front door.

CELSUS CROGHER grabbed the guy outside of Chana Lochlan's town house.

He said, "Secret Service, put up a fight, and I'll break your neck."

Daryl Cheveyo grunted, "CIA, and I'd like my neck intact, if you don't mind."

"CIA?" Crogher repeated, not letting go of his neck lock. "My ass."

Doing his best to stay calm, Cheveyo said, "I can show you my ID … or we can exchange secret code words."

Crogher didn't like wise guys. He was out there on his own, eyeballing a reporter's residence because that dickwad McGill had sicced him on her. Without telling him the nature of the threat. Thereby creating the possibility of failing at his job, a job in which failure was unacceptable. If possible, the situation had rendered his disposition more grim than usual.

Then this joker had come along and taken up a perch in a shadow between two buildings, directly opposite the Lochlan address and mere feet from the stairway with the wrought-iron risers under which Crogher had lodged himself an hour earlier.

At first, Crogher thought maybe the guy was a well-dressed street criminal. A mugger or a burglar in a nice suit, looking for an unwary late-night pedestrian or a vulnerable house to enter. But then a dog of some size had come charging up on the other side of the metal lattice work gate that stood between the two buildings.

The dog started to act territorial, giving the guy a low menacing growl. Before it could open its yap and bark out loud, the guy turned, not a feather ruffled, and gave it a blast of spray. Not pepper. That would have sent the animal running off yowling and howling. Whatever he used had put it right down. Good night, pooch.

Crogher didn't know if the canine was dead or just unconscious. Either way, he wasn't happy. He liked dogs. Especially guard dogs. He identified with them. So when the guy saw that the dog was down for the count and turned to look back at the Lochlan house, Crogher duck walked out of his hiding place and jumped him.

"Did you kill that dog?" he asked.

"Don't think so," Cheveyo said. "Unless, of course, he had a bad heart. Look, my neck's starting to hurt. I'm here at the direction of the Deputy Director of Central Intelligence. Do I really need to threaten you with the consequences you'll face if you keep this up?"

"Your boss can beat up my boss? I don't think so. I work for the president."

Made Crogher feel good to say that.

"You're in the White House detail?"

"I *run* the White House detail. I'm the SAC."

"And the president sent you to watch that house across the street?"

"Her husband did," Crogher grumbled.

That didn't make him feel good at all.

"James J. McGill sent you to watch Damon Todd?"

"Who?" Crogher asked.

Cheveyo stiffened, then whispered, "Him."

Crogher saw a truly strange-looking man come out of Chana Lochlan's town house.

"Step back," Cheveyo murmured. "Don't let him see us."

Without letting go, Crogher moved them back into deeper shadow.

The figure moved off down the street at a lope, apparently unaware he had been observed. Crogher watched him go, and asked, "What's up with that guy?"

"He likes to work out."

"So do I, but Jesus."

"He also wants to go to work for the Company. You think you can let me go now?"

Reluctantly, Crogher did. Cheveyo rubbed his sore neck. "I'm going to show you who I am, so don't go crazy on me." He brought out his photo ID.

Professional etiquette required Crogher to respond in kind.

"Can't be a coincidence we're both looking at the same house," he told Cheveyo, "even if we're looking at different people. What's this muscle head who wants to work for you do?"

Cheveyo smiled sourly.

"You know, I'd really like to tell you, even if you did almost break my neck."

"But you're not going to."

"That'd make things too easy for government work. If it's any consolation, I've already recommended that my boss pass along the information to your people."

"It's no consolation at all," Crogher snapped.

"Yeah, well. Let's leave it at this then. You see that funny- looking guy anywhere near the president, you jump on him just like you did on me."

Then Cheveyo told Crogher he had to go. He had to try to catch up with Todd.

DARYL CHEVEYO managed to pick up Damon Todd's trail. Not on foot. In his car. Foot tracking was beyond him just then. Not only was his neck killing him, he had a pounding headache, too. Damn blockhead Secret Service agent. Then the CIA man pushed hostile thoughts about Celsus Crogher out of his mind. He couldn't afford any distractions.

He'd spotted Todd jogging up Wisconsin Avenue, heading north. The hour was late, and the traffic, both pedestrian and vehicular, on the trendy commercial street had thinned considerably from its earlier crush. The few remaining strollers quickly gave way when they saw Todd approach. One or two dared a brief glance over their shoulders after he'd passed.

A *Did-you-see-that?* look on their faces.

Cheveyo had to linger a block behind his quarry. Todd knew his car. One look over his shoulder, and the game would be up. Hanging back, though, Cheveyo could simply turn off into a side street if Todd looked behind him, leaving the guy to wonder if he'd seen Cheveyo's car or one of many just like it.

As it was, Todd was the one who turned off, hung a right at P Street. Cheveyo didn't think he'd been spotted, hadn't seen Todd look back. But he couldn't take the chance that Todd had set a trap for him. He'd look like a real *putz* if he let a looney-tunes civilian catch him off guard.

Especially after he'd allowed a Secret Service caveman to ambush him.

He turned left on O Street. He drove west a couple of blocks, then came back east on P Street, lights off, a good, long straightaway of street ahead to look for Todd. Of course, if the crazed doctor had merely wanted to give him the slip, he could have cut over to Massachusetts Avenue, hailed a cab—if one would stop for a freak like him—and been long gone.

If that'd been the case, he'd pick Todd up in the morning. If he could find him.

But he didn't have to worry. He saw Todd stopped in front of a pale three-story brick building in the block ahead, where P Street curved and overlooked Rock Creek Parkway. The building had been gentrified in keeping with the rest of the neighborhood. A café table sat on the sidewalk outside. He pulled into a parking space and watched.

Todd looked at what Cheveyo guessed was the building's directory. Then he looked up. Aside from a security light in the entryway, the building was dark. Todd lowered his gaze to street level and looked around. Nobody was on the sidewalks. No cars were moving on the street. Cheveyo's car was dark, the motor shut down, just another parked vehicle.

Todd slipped around to the back of the building he was checking. What the hell was he up to, the CIA man wondered, a B-and-E? What sense did that make?

When Todd didn't reappear in ten minutes, Cheveyo thought maybe Todd had spotted him after all. He was lurking at the back of a building he'd picked at random, or because it offered a nice quiet place to dispose of a body. With a guy like Todd, you couldn't be too careful. It was Cheveyo's considered opinion that Todd could take it into his head that he was never going to hook on with the CIA, so why get not even and kill the Company's point man? Him.

The field officer flicked the switch on his car's dome light so it wouldn't go on when he opened the door. He silently slipped out of the vehicle, closed the door, and drew his handgun. By law, the CIA wasn't supposed to operate inside the United States. That statute had been broken often enough in the past, and after 9/11, it was pretty much a dead letter. But it would still be highly embarrassing to him personally if he had to shoot somebody in Washington, D.C.

Be even worse if he left any clues behind.

And much worse if his dead body were found at the scene.

He softly recited prayers in both Hopi and Navajo, asking that his ancestors guide him in both stealth and cunning. The ancient ones must have enjoyed a good laugh because when he slunk around the rear corner of the building the only creature to greet him was a one-eyed alley cat. It took one look at him, yawned, and sauntered off into the darkness.

Of Todd, there was no sign.

Cheveyo went back out front. He checked the building's directory, to see if he could divine why Todd had stopped there.

It was hardly a challenge. The mad doctor certainly hadn't been looking for a place to record a CD or have his taxes done. No, he'd come to check out the office of McGill Investigations, Inc. The CIA man, like everyone in town, had heard about the president's henchman going into the private investigation business.

Until that moment, though, he hadn't known the location of McGill's office.

So now Todd had a relationship with a reporter who covered the president and had acquainted himself with the workplace of the president's husband, pulling both halves of the First Couple into his orbit. Ominous didn't begin to cover the feelings that gave Cheveyo.

A reasonable man, he thought of taking his discovery directly to the Secret Service. Except his neck hurt so bad. His head, too. He thought he'd better return to Langley while he could still drive. Get himself checked out. Report to his bosses.

Then see to it the Secret Service got notified.

CHERYL ALTMAN never showed up at *Le Petit Voleur*—The Little Thief—the nouvelle cuisine restaurant on M Street she'd chosen as a meeting place. After checking in at the White House and finding no message from the general's wife, Kira had Welborn's calls forwarded to her condo. They waited until far into the night to hear from Mrs. Altman. They listened to music, shared a sofa, and didn't say much to each other. No call ever came.

"Cold feet?" Kira finally asked at ten that night.

Welborn shrugged.

"She had to have some reason to call you."

"Maybe she liked that picture of me in the *Post*. The one you found so unflattering."

He didn't know why he said that. Maybe after all the quiet time, he felt like a little verbal sparring. Or maybe he was just frustrated. Kira responded but not quite in the way he expected.

"You're not going to sleep with me until this is over, are you?" she asked.

"What?"

"You're not going to sleep with me until Colonel Linberg meets her fate, whatever that might be." There was more certainty in her voice this time.

"I didn't know you were interested."

"You know. You knew I wanted you the last time you were here. Maybe you only like older women. A mother thing."

"No mothers," he said, using the playground admonition.

"What then? You think I'm ugly?"

Welborn grinned. "Nobody has ever called you ugly. I'd bet on that. If some misguided fool actually thought so, he'd be too afraid to tell you."

"I hate you."

"I know. I feel the same way."

"You do?"

He kissed her on the lips this time, but didn't make too much of it.

"I do. I'd better be going. May I borrow your car again?"

"Where are you going?"

"To see if I can find an older woman."

Kira drew back from him.

"Mrs. Altman. Maybe there's an unfortunate reason she didn't keep her appointment. I think I'd better check with the Metro cops, the hospitals … the morgue."

"You think she could be dead?"

"I was thinking of another kind of cold feet, the kind that come with toe tags, when you mentioned it just now. So may I borrow your car? Please."

"Not the Audi for that kind of stuff," Kira said. "Take the Jeep."

ALBERTA CARTWRIGHT was sixty-eight years old. She'd driven up to Lafayette Square in Washington that day from Manassas, Virginia. The ladies of her church were going to take their turn marching in protest outside the White House. The very thought that a great woman like Erna

Godfrey could be put to death for trying to end the scourge of abortion made Alberta sick to her heart. The idea that she might help avert such a tragedy gave her the energy to keep marching, round and round, after some of her weaker-limbed sisters had to hand over their protest signs to younger members of the movement.

Truth be told, however, even Alberta's step was beginning to falter. She'd been at it for hours. Hadn't had anything to eat in even longer than that. Then she felt a gentle hand fall on her shoulder.

"Allow me to afford you a well-deserved rest, mother," a deep and instantly recognizable voice said to her.

Alberta turned to look, a smile already formed on her lips, and there he was.

Reverend Burke Godfrey, pastor of the Salvation's Path Church. Erna's husband. Walking at her side. Only seeing the Lord Himself would have made Alberta happier.

Reverend Godfrey took the sign from her, took her spot marching in the circle. Alberta kept pace to his right and saw that everyone was smiling. As far as she knew, that was the first time Reverend Godfrey had joined in the protest march to free his wife. Alberta thought it must certainly portend something momentous.

Godfrey recognized the unspoken question in her eyes.

"God has called me here at this moment," he said.

Shivers rippled through all those lucky enough to be present.

"It's time to increase the pressure on those who would persecute us," he added.

"God bless you, Reverend," Alberta said.

Her words were echoed by those assembled there.

"And may God curse and condemn the evil woman and her wicked consort who live in that fine house." Alberta thrust a rigid arm at the brightly lit White House.

"Amen," said Reverend Godfrey.

"Amen," chorused his followers.

CHAPTER 22

TUESDAY

THE PHONE rang in Room 121 of the Traveler's Rest Motel in Gambier, Ohio, at 3:30 A.M. McGill opened one eye and looked at the digital clock next to the bed where he lay. He knew there was only one person who would call him at that hour.

He picked up the receiver, and said, "The mattress is firm, the pillows are goose down, the bed is altogether snug and comfy. I wish I had you here beside me."

"Why don't we keep that between the two of us?" Edwina Byington said with a laugh. Then she added, "Please hold for the president of the United States."

A few seconds later Patti came on the line, and McGill asked, "You have your personal secretary place your calls at three thirty in the morning?"

"We're pretty busy around here. Edwina was only saving me a minute in case you were out partying."

McGill snorted.

"I do appreciate the way you answered the phone," Patti said.

"That blabbermouth; she said she'd keep it between us. Bet it winds up in her memoirs."

Patti laughed. "Not that I have any time for you, my love, but I do miss you. It would do me good to know you were near. Do I sound like Abbie?"

"Another sensitive, intelligent woman, yes."

"I'm sorry about the time, but soon the world will be upon me."

"Are you up even earlier than usual, or—"

"Or. No rest for the wicked. Well, I might have had a few hours' sleep, but I chose to stay up and read how John Kennedy handled his Cuban crisis."

"He probably slept a little here and there."

"I'll nap later. If they let me."

"You're no good to anyone if you're too tired to think straight."

"Another reason to have you come home. You're the only one everybody around here is afraid of."

"I should be back this afternoon," McGill said. "Mr. Meanie, himself."

Patti said, "Jim, there's a reason I called besides wanting to hear your voice. Celsus Crogher insisted on seeing me not long ago. He was watching Chana Lochlan's house last night."

"Personally?" McGill asked, surprised.

"Yes. It turns out that not long after Celsus took up his observation post he was joined by a field officer from the CIA by the name of Daryl Cheveyo. Have you ever heard of him?"

"No, why was he there?"

"He was assigned to watch a man named Damon Todd, who would like to join the CIA. Mr. Todd was seen leaving Ms. Lochlan's residence last night. Celsus said he was quote, 'scary-looking,' unquote."

"*Celsus* thought someone was scary-looking?" Talk about the pot calling the kettle black.

"He's asked me to have World Wide News reassign Ms. Lochlan. Pull her White House credentials. I thought I'd talk to you before deciding."

McGill wondered if this Todd character was the guy who'd called Chana. But would she really have had a lover who the Secret Service thought looked frightening? He couldn't see that. And the name Damon Todd hadn't appeared on Chana's list of paramours.

"Did this CIA guy say why he was watching Todd?" McGill asked.

"He didn't feel free to share with Celsus."

"Jesus."

"I have it on my to-do list to chat with the director when I see him a few hours from now."

"Do you have a press conference scheduled soon?"

"No, but the situation is very fluid. I might call one at any time."

Damn, McGill thought. "I'd like to speak with Chana Lochlan before she gets bounced. I'm going to talk with her father this morning. He couldn't see me yesterday."

Patti said, "I'll give her one more day."

"But have Celsus keep a special eye on her."

"If I call a press conference, he'll probably make Ms. Lochlan sit on his lap."

McGill laughed.

Before he said good-bye he asked Patti to sign a picture of herself for Chief Manuala's family in Honolulu, and do a favor for Kenny he'd thought of last night.

She told him Edwina would have the picture sent to FedEx for the first pickup. The White House Communications Agency should know of a private retailer who could help with the favor for McGill's son. She'd see that it was taken care of that day, too.

"You have to keep the world from falling apart, and you still find time to take care of the little people," McGill said.

"See what you get with a woman in the Oval Office," Patti told him.

MCGILL'S PLANE had landed at Port Columbus International Airport the day before. The pilot and the crew stayed with the aircraft while Leo and Deke requisitioned a car from the local Treasury Department office. After leaving Ohio's largest city, they drove for an hour down state roads to reach Gambier. Not wanting to take Chana's father by surprise, McGill called ahead. Professor Lochlan was at home, but not for long. Two minutes later, he said, and he'd have been out. He was quite surprised that the president's husband was calling; he hadn't known of McGill's current line of work until he was directly informed.

"Why in the world would a private eye want to see me?" he asked. Then he followed up with another question, asked uneasily. "You're not working for Marianne, are you?"

"No, Professor, this has nothing to do with your ex-wife."

"Well, that's good. How about I make you breakfast at my place tomorrow?"

"That'd be fine."

"Eight?"

"I'll be there."

"You don't travel with a great big retinue, do you? I don't have enough to feed an army."

"I have only two men with me, and I don't feed them at all. Just let them scavenge. Keeps them on their toes."

Deke shook his head; Leo rolled his eyes.

But the professor laughed, and McGill was pleased both by his sense of humor and Professor Lochlan's sense of independence. McGill put up for the night at the motel just outside of town. He didn't want any attention. Didn't want Gambier's mayor to give him the key to the city, organize a parade, or do anything else that required a public appearance on his part.

Deke got him a room as far from the highway as possible. Rented rooms on either side of McGill's as a buffer and firmly instructed the motel manager to keep the situation to himself.

AT 8:00 A.M. Leo pulled up in front of Professor Eamon Lochlan's well-kept, two-story frame house not far from the university. Lochlan stood waiting on his front porch. Thankfully, there was no crowd of neighbors to greet McGill. Just one old lady sitting on a rocking chair on the porch of the house next door. McGill thought she had to be Sweetie's watchful senior songbird, Harriet Greenlea.

Getting out of the car and approaching the Lochlan house, McGill waved to her, and said, "Good morning, Mrs. Greenlea."

The old woman's eyes widened in surprise at a stranger knowing her name, but she nodded to him.

McGill climbed the stair of the Lochlan house and extended his hand. "Professor Lochlan, I'm James J. McGill. I know this is unusual, but would you mind if my Secret Service agent takes a quick look inside before I enter?"

McGill could see where Chana got a good deal of her fabulous face. Eamon Lochlan had striking features and a shock of wavy silver hair. Tall and lean, he wore khaki slacks and a denim shirt. The smell of frying bacon drifted through the open doorway behind him.

Eamon Lochlan shook McGill's hand, stepped aside, and let Deke enter his house.

Then he said to McGill, "If this isn't about Marianne, it's about Chana, isn't it?"

McGill said, "Deke won't be long, then we can talk inside."

"She's all right, isn't she?"

McGill heard Harriet Greenlea stop rocking, not wanting to miss a word.

"It'll be just a minute," McGill repeated.

PROFESSOR LOCHLAN served McGill two eggs over easy, crisp bacon, sourdough toast, and coffee. He had the same and sat directly across the kitchen table from his guest.

"Worked as a short-order cook when I was an undergrad," he said. "Came in handy after I married a woman who saw a kitchen as a place of female subjugation. Now, sir, would you care to tell me why the hell you're here?"

Only the two of them were in the room. Deke had the back door; Leo the front.

McGill went with the truth. He'd thought last night of trying to con the man, imagining that was what a practiced P.I. would do. Cops lied at times, too. Some of them more often than not. But McGill usually opted to be honest. He had daughters himself; he'd want to hear straight talk if their welfare was in question.

"Your daughter hired me to investigate a harassing phone call," he told the professor. He summarized what had happened after that, including talking to Graham Keough, and the fact that the Secret Service wanted to boot Chana out of the White House.

And how he had delayed that action.

Professor Lochlan hadn't touched his breakfast, and he no longer looked hungry. McGill took the opportunity to eat and give the man time to gather his thoughts. Professor Lochlan had learned his culinary trade well.

"Harriet told me your colleague, Ms. Sweeney, had talked to her," Eamon Lochlan said finally. "She, of course, said that all she told Ms. Sweeney was that I was a highly regarded faculty member at the college." He rolled his eyes. "Despite being a very fine neighbor, Harriet likes to look, listen, and talk. Between her and Graham, I imagine you know a good deal about my family already."

McGill nodded. "Unfortunately, I'd like to know more."

"At this point, you're working for your wife, the president, as I understand you."

"Yes."

"So I take it her interests are paramount to you."

"Always. Though equaled by those of my children. I have two daughters and a son."

"I had another daughter, as I'm sure you know. Would have loved to have had a son."

"Chana was my first client, Professor Lochlan. I'd still like it to work out that I do the right thing by her."

"You're sure she's in trouble?"

McGill had asked himself the same question. He could come up with only one answer. "Yes, Professor, I think she is."

MCGILL'S DIALOGUE with Eamon Lochlan could have ended right there. He'd have understood if the man had thanked him for bringing the matter to his attention, showed him the door, and gotten on the first plane to Washington. Which was why he made his preemptive offer.

McGill said, "I have the use of an aircraft. If you'd like, I can take you to see Chana right away."

Eamon Lochlan leaned forward as if to get to his feet, paused in thought with his hands flat on the kitchen table, and sat back.

"What would I tell her, Mr. McGill, about why I showed up out of the blue? You certainly don't want me to tell her what you're doing. Continuing to work after you've been fired."

"No, I don't. But as a father I can understand if you don't give a rat's backside about what I want."

"Frankly, I don't. What I care about is what's best for Chana." A tremor passed through him. "I don't know if I could survive losing her. Not after what happened with Nan."

McGill stayed quiet, revisited by the fear of how it would kill him to lose one of his children. That fear was swiftly displaced by anger as he recalled that there were people threatening his children's lives. Lost in his own thoughts, he missed what Eamon Lochlan said next.

"I'm sorry," he said, "would you mind repeating that?"

"I said I've been worried about Chana lately."

"Why?" McGill asked.

The professor's face took on a look of guilt.

"After Marianne and I divorced, after I brought Chana home from California so sick, I promised her that I would always be there for her."

"And you weren't?"

"Of course, I was," Eamon Lochlan said self-righteously. But his indignation faded quickly. "What concerns me is that's about to change."

McGill's first thought was, so what? Chana Lochlan was a grown woman, an established professional. Then it hit him for the first time. He, too, would be tied to any promise he made to his children for the rest of his life. Whether they were still young as they were at present or when they were adults like Eamon Lochlan's daughter. If you loved your kids, you wanted them to make their own ways in life, but if all else failed, you were their safety net.

For as long as you lived.

"Change how?" McGill asked.

"I'm going to Eastern Europe to do research and write a book on the literature of newly freed peoples. See if their works of fiction can show where they're heading. Whether they'll succeed in building democratic societies or relapse into authoritarianism. I'll be gone for at least two years. I thought this would be a good time to make a new start, so I'm retiring from my teaching position and selling this house."

Sounded to McGill like a good time for Chana to head in a new direction, too. Accompany her father, be his researcher, edit his rough drafts for him. That was until he heard what Professor Lochlan had to say next.

"I'm also going to remarry. I've met a wonderful woman who will be traveling and working with me."

"Does Chana know about all this?"

"She knows the book project looked promising. And I've talked to her about Imogene. But I haven't told her that either development has had a happy ending. Happy for me, anyway."

Both men could see how a mature child, even one with her feet firmly planted on the ground, might have different feelings. McGill had been very lucky that his kids had fallen in love with Patti. It didn't hurt that their stepmom was soon elected president, either.

"I'd better start packing," Professor Lochlan said. "I'll take you up on that offer of a trip to Washington. It seems I do have a reason to visit. Tell Chana of my plans. See how she feels about them. Ask if there's anything I can do for her."

The two of them got to their feet.

"I won't mention our talk to Chana," Eamon Lochlan said.

"Thank you."

"You will do your best to look out for her?" the professor asked.

"Everything I can," McGill told him.

WELBORN YATES had spent a tense, draining night checking the hospitals in D.C. and the surrounding suburbs in Maryland and Virginia, looking for Cheryl Altman. He didn't find her until, with nowhere else left to go, he tried the city morgue.

From there, he went to the Metro police headquarters and identified himself to the cop working the door. He was asked to have a seat, but it wasn't long before a tall strong-looking black woman in a nicely cut gray business suit came out to see him. Welborn stood as she drew near.

"Lieutenant Yates, I'm Lieutenant Rockelle Bullard. Homicide."

Welborn winced. "Mrs. Altman has been murdered?"

"There's a slight chance her death was an accident, but I don't think so."

"How did she die?"

"She was struck by a hit-and-run driver."

Welborn's head began to spin. He felt Lieutenant Bullard place her hands upon his shoulders to steady him. "You okay?"

He regained his faculties and his balance. "I'm fine. Thank you."

Lieutenant Bullard gave him a look before letting go.

He told her. "I was a victim of a hit-and-run myself. Some friends of mine died. I was laid up quite a while."

She nodded. "My sympathies. Let's go take a look at the crime scene."

CHERYL ALTMAN had died in the parking lot of The Shops at Georgetown Park. She'd just had her hair done. She'd told her stylist that she was going to a very important lunch date. So Lieutenant Bullard informed Welborn as they stood at spot where Mrs. Altman had been struck. She'd landed sixty feet away atop a Lexus SUV.

"Now, more people get hurt and killed in parking lots than you'd ever believe," she told Welborn. "But the offending driver is usually a woman in hysterics who's right there waiting when the uniforms and paramedics roll in. In fact, she's the one who called 911."

"But not this time," Welborn said.

"No. Now, bad guys go shopping, or shoplifting, too. No way they stick around to talk with the cops. But strangely enough, about half of them still call in the accident anonymously."

"That didn't happen either."

"No, it didn't," Lieutenant Bullard agreed.

Welborn looked at the pavement near the spot where Mrs. Altman was struck.

"No sign that the driver attempted to hit the brakes."

"I was getting to that next. No brake marks at all. The medical examiner and the crime-scene team estimate the car that struck Mrs. Altman was doing about fifty miles per hour."

Welborn's eyes widened.

"Yeah, a lot of speed for a parking lot," Rockelle Bullard said. "Now, it's possible we got one blind-drunk sonofabitch behind the wheel here. There are restaurants nearby that serve alcohol, but my people can't find any serving person who remembers someone that inebriated."

Welborn wasn't going to insult Lieutenant Bullard, ask her if her people could spot someone—a bartender or waiter—who was lying to cover his ass about over serving a drunk.

Mostly because he didn't think that was the case.

"Of course, it's possible we have someone who sat in his car in this parking lot drinking, then turned his ignition key," Lieutenant Bullard said.

Welborn shook his head; he wasn't buying that either.

"No, I don't think so myself," the Metro homicide cop said. "What this reminds me of is a variation on that killing down in Texas. The one where the woman kept running over her cheating husband. Crimes of passion, this one and that."

"They sure are," Welborn agreed.

"You wouldn't know anything about that lunch Mrs. Altman was going to, would you, Lieutenant Yates?"

"It was with me," he said.

A smile appeared on Rockelle Bullard's face. "Progress. What can you tell me?"

Welborn had to think about that. "I'll help you all I can, Lieutenant Bullard, but I have to talk with my superior first to find out just how far that will be."

Rockelle Bullard said, "I think it's going to be pretty far."

"Why do you say that?"

"I've already talked with a Major Seymour. He identified Mrs. Altman. He told me he was the personal aide to General Warren Altman, the Air Force chief of staff. The general, according to the major, wants his wife's killer caught right away."

Welborn kept a straight face, said nothing.

"Isn't the general about the highest superior you've got, Lieutenant?"

"I work directly for the president," Welborn responded.

"Huh," Rockelle Bullard said. Her expression said: *Why me, Lord?*

"If the president can see me, I'll get back to you today," Welborn said. "That's a promise. Is there anything else you can tell me?"

The Metro cop was more interested in what Welborn could tell her. But in the end she had no choice but to play along. Couldn't strong-arm the president's fair-haired boy, now could she?

"We know what kind of car it was that struck Mrs. Altman. We have three witnesses, and they all agree."

Welborn gestured for the specifics.

"A Honda Civic. Tan. Four doors."

Welborn said, "Sonofabitch."

"Something wrong, Lieutenant Yates?"

"I had a car just like that. It was stolen last Friday. Or Saturday."

Rockelle Bullard took a long look at him.

"Well, *that's* interesting. Our witnesses, they all said the plates on the Honda were splattered with mud. Couldn't make out the tag numbers. But two of them said the plates were from South Carolina. That accent of yours, Lieutenant, you from down there, too?"

"Charleston," he said.

DAMON TODD'S friend and lover, the sports publicist, was only too happy to rent a car for him. She handled all sorts of travel arrangements for her clients. To the people at Hertz, she was a VIP client. They put her into a Cadillac for the price of a midsize. The car was billed to Starburst Publicity, Laurel Rembert, CEO.

Laurel would vouch for Todd in the unlikely event the police questioned his possession of the vehicle; otherwise, she would have no conscious memory of the favor she'd done for him. Her crafted personality was holding up perfectly.

He'd also checked his four other people who lived in D.C., and they were psychologically intact, too. Even Congressman Brun Fleming, who'd unintentionally inflicted a fatal heart attack on his aged colleague from Florida. Todd had had to help poor Brun, but only one session had been necessary to help him sleep peacefully, deal calmly with the investigators, and, most important, repress all conscious memory that he'd ever known anyone named Damon Todd.

So, generally speaking, if his work was valid and productive, what had happened to Chana? Why should the subject closest to his heart be the one to experience deconstruction of her assumed persona? It was a question he had to answer for both personal and professional reasons.

Which was why he was motoring through western Maryland by midmorning. He'd slice through a strip of West Virginia and drive on to Ohio and Gambier. It was an easy, one-day drive from Washington.

When he got to Gambier, he'd visit Professor Lochlan. Chana's father had always been grateful to him, recognizing that he'd been the one who brought Chana back from the brink of death. He'd be surprised if the professor didn't insist Todd spend the night at his house.

They'd talk at length. He'd learn if there were any extraordinary forces at play in Chana's life—and he felt sure there must be. Then armed with the knowledge he needed, he would return to his beloved and create whatever new personality she desired.

As he glided past the town of Cumberland, Maryland, he decided he would leave himself no posthypnotic access to Chana's life. Or her body. From now on, his love for her would be pure, a memory to be cherished.

Crossing into West Virginia minutes later, he wondered if he could really do that.

EAMON LOCHLAN had told McGill everything he'd thought significant about his daughter's life. He'd even brought along two photo albums and pointed out snapshots of Chana before and after her breakdown. The narration had been an ordeal for Professor Lochlan, and McGill offered him the bed in the sleeping compartment at the rear of the Gulfstream. The exhausted man was only too glad to accept.

McGill reclined his seat and mulled over what he'd learned.

He'd thought Damon Todd, M.D., might have been a good choice for the harassing phone caller. Thought Todd had to be the "scary-looking" guy seen leaving Chana's town house. Until Professor Lochlan had shown him a picture of Todd. Granted, the photo was over fourteen years old, but Todd had been a slight guy who wore glasses. A healer and an academic, Todd was someone who was likely to get less physical with age, not more. Besides, Eamon Lochlan had only good things to say about the man. Concerned. Caring. Effective. Wouldn't take a penny for his efforts.

That left McGill wondering who the scary guy was. He sighed and decided to let his subconscious work on it. He had other worries he could address in a more direct way. He picked up the phone and called the White House.

Not to talk with Patti but Artemus Nicolaides, the White House physician.

"Doctor Nicolaides."

"Nick, this is Jim McGill."

"Still pale?"

"Maybe not. I've been out to California."

"Don't get too much sun," the doctor cautioned.

"Nick, I'd like to get my physical this afternoon, if you've got time."

The physician said, "I might be able to squeeze you in. Bring your insurance card."

McGill laughed. He broke the connection. He'd just taken the first step in dealing with Senator Roger Michaelson and his plan to call into question the confession of Lindell Ricker, the conviction of Erna Godfrey, and whether McGill and Sweetie had railroaded an innocent man for the murder of Andy Grant.

Nick was going to help by making sure McGill wouldn't have a heart attack when he swung into action.

THE PRESIDENT sat in the Oval Office with her eyes closed. Galia Mindel, sitting on the sofa next to her, could tell from the regular, softly audible rhythm of her breathing that the president was asleep. The maternal side of Galia, a thin sliver of her personality, wanted to clear the president's calendar for the day. Let her sleep. Disturb her only if there was no other choice.

Possibly, make a tough decision or two in the president's name, if necessary. The ambitious side of Galia's personality was of a far more generous dimension.

Edwina Byington buzzed the intercom on the president's desk. Galia touched Patricia Grant's forearm. "They're here, Madam President."

Patti's eyes opened. A moment later the cobwebs of sleep had been cleared away.

"Show them in, please, Galia."

The chief of staff rose to admit the chairman of the Joint Chiefs, Army General Joseph Fabin, and director of Central Intelligence Thomas Van Owen. In the current scheme of things, the director of national intelligence normally would have been the civilian official to deal with the matter at hand. But Patti's nominee for DNI, Aaron Phelps, had suffered a fatal heart attack before he could be confirmed. While the search for a replacement continued, Patti was relying on the CIA director. By the time the two men had entered the room, the president was on her feet and extending her hand in greeting.

When everyone was seated, she asked simply, "Well?"

Patti'd come up with an idea that morning on how to deal with the situation in Cuba. She thought it would be both simple and effective, balancing both military and political considerations. But she knew she was very tired when the notion occurred to her, and to be sure she wasn't deceiving herself, she'd had Edwina transcribe her thoughts and had them hand-delivered to the Pentagon and Langley.

The general and the director had come to give her their opinions.

"Militarily," General Fabin said, "it's quite simple. The element of risk is low. As low as you can get when shots are fired."

"Fired without casualties, I trust," the president said.

"That I can't guarantee, ma'am," the general answered.

"Minimal casualties?"

"That would be in scale with the action, yes, ma'am."

The president turned to the director. "You have everything you need, Tom?"

"Yes, Madam President. Right off the shelf. It's all in our inventory."

"So we can put all our ducks in a row. How do you think the plan will play?"

The two men looked at each other.

General Fabin said, "Begging your pardon, Madam President, but we hadn't realized you were so devious."

"We wish we'd thought of it ourselves," Van Owen said. "It should play just fine."

The president kept her smile small. Nodded in appreciation.

"Thank you. Let's hope all goes well. You'll start your preparations immediately then. Let me know when you're ready."

The two men stood to leave. Galia gave the president a nudge.

"Oh, Tom, could you stay just a minute?"

"Yes, Madam President," the CIA boss said.

"If I may, Madam President," General Fabin said.

"Yes."

"A personal note. General Altman's wife was killed yesterday. A tragic hit-and-run situation. The general has taken compassionate leave. I'll have the name of his temporary replacement as Air Force chief of staff to you by this afternoon."

"Do the police have any leads?" the president asked, her face grave.

"No, ma'am."

"Please keep me informed and extend my condolences to the family. The White House will be in contact with them once it's appropriate."

"Thank you, ma'am."

The general turned and left. The director remained.

"Tom, do you know a field officer named Daryl Cheveyo?"

"No, Madam President."

"He made the acquaintance of SAC Crogher last night. Crogher thinks he might have information useful in keeping me safe and sound. Your man didn't think he had the authority to share that information."

The director gestured to the phone on the end table next to where he'd sat.

"If I may."

The president nodded. The director made his call. When he hung up, he looked concerned.

He told the president, "Perhaps you should have another talk with SAC Crogher, ma'am. Field Officer Cheveyo is on the operating table right now, undergoing spinal surgery for a ruptured cervical disc. He won't be available to speak to anyone for an indeterminate period. But shortly before he blacked out he said that Crogher was responsible for his injury."

The president's face remained impassive, but Galia and Van Owen saw her fists clench.

"I'm truly sorry to hear that," she said. "Please keep me informed as to Field Officer Cheveyo's condition."

The director said he would and left.

"Perhaps now's the time for a little rest," Galia said.

The president shook her head. "Do you know Lieutenant Yates's whereabouts?"

"He's in his office. Waiting for you."

"Give me five minutes," the president said, "then send him in."

CHAPTER 23

MCGILL RETURNED directly to the White House from Andrews Air Force Base, after arranging to have a car deliver Professor Lochlan to his daughter's residence. Upon arriving at the Executive Mansion, he went to the residence and called the Oval Office to see if his wife was free.

"The president is meeting with Lieutenant Yates," Edwina Byington told him.

"Please let her know that I'm back and I'll be meeting with Dr. Nicolaides this afternoon to have my annual physical exam."

Edwina coughed. McGill was sure he heard her say, "About time," under it.

"Tickle in your throat, Edwina?" he asked.

"The long hours, sir. I'd better call for some tea and honey."

He let it go. She had reason to give him a little grief; his recalcitrance on the issue having been a distraction to her boss. And distracting the president could have national, even global, consequences. Something for a good henchman to think about.

There was a knock at the door of McGill's Hideaway and Blessing entered. Unbidden, he'd brought McGill a glass of White House ice tea. "Good to have you home, sir."

McGill took the glass and saw that Blessing's smile was more than his usual happy-to-be-of-service version, and his eyes were misted with emotion.

"Everything okay, Blessing?" McGill asked.

"Wonderful, sir. My sister, Aya, and my brother, Merritt, come home from the hospital today. The transplant was a complete success. They're both doing fine."

McGill beamed. "You're right, that is wonderful. Please give them my best wishes."

"I will, sir. I'll be taking the rest of the day off. But when I heard you'd returned to the residence, I wanted to give you the news in person. And I'd appreciate it if you'd pass it along to Ms. Sweeney."

"I'll do that. I was just about to call her. Before you leave, would you please ask Devin to come by in half an hour?"

Devin Waters was one of two licensed massage therapists employed by the White House. The other was Antoinette Barrie. Both were completely professional, but capital gossip being what it was, McGill always used Devin. Today, McGill wanted to get his blood pressure down before he saw Nick for his physical.

"Yes, sir. Will that be all?"

"I think so."

Blessing left, still smiling. McGill took the news about Blessing's sister as a good sign. It was still possible that sometimes things could go right. Occasionally, you even got on a roll and had several good days in a row. He called Sweetie. Told her Blessing's news.

"Bishop Dempsey says a mean novena, doesn't he?" she said, clearly pleased. "I'm glad you're back. I think I found you a lawyer."

McGill said, "We'll keep him in reserve. I've got my own plan for dealing with Senator Roger Michaelson."

"What is it?"

McGill told her.

Sweetie said with glee in her voice, "I've got to be there for that."

WALKING INTO the Oval Office and saluting, Welborn thought the president looked more tired—less glamorous—than he'd ever seen her. Somehow, though, this hint of mortality made her even more appealing.

Like someone for whom he'd give his life. Not that he wanted it to come to that.

"Please be seated, Lieutenant," the president told him.

Welborn took a chair, glad to be off his feet. He was tired, too.

"You've heard about Mrs. Altman?" the president asked.

"Yes, ma'am." Welborn told his commander in chief of his planned lunch with the late wife of the Air Force chief of staff, his check of the metro area hospitals, and his time spent at the crime scene with Lieutenant Bullard, the Metro homicide detective.

He also raised the president's eyebrows when he told her that his stolen car might have been used to commit the crime.

"Someone's trying to implicate you, Lieutenant?"

Welborn had taken the idea a step farther than that, and the president, tired though she was, was still sharp enough to see the other possibility and give voice to it.

She said, "Maybe it doesn't have to be that drastic. Maybe the mere suggestion that you're involved is sufficient to have me remove you from the investigation."

"Yes, ma'am. That idea occurred to me, too."

He waited to see if the strategy was going to be successful.

The president shook her head. "You're in for the duration, Lieutenant."

"Thank you, ma'am."

"You might want to be sparing in your gratitude. I'm sure we have other thoughts in common. Disturbing ones."

For a moment, Welborn was silent. Then he said, "Such as, would the Air Force chief of staff kill his wife to prevent her from telling me about his adultery with Colonel Linberg?"

"That, and as a warning to the colonel that she had better keep quiet. Or be very careful the next time she steps out into traffic."

Welborn frowned. He hadn't thought of that, but no way could you argue that it was an unreasonable assumption. Not if you liked General Altman for murdering his spouse.

"Were the police able to establish the time of death, Lieutenant."

He told her that the three witnesses placed the time at 11:28 A.M. Give or take a minute.

Without having to consult her schedule, the president said, "General

Altman was here at the White House with the other joint chiefs at that time. They were meeting with me."

"Yes, ma'am."

"But four-stars rarely do their own heavy lifting, do they, Lieutenant?"

"That's not been my experience, ma'am."

"Do you have any ideas as to whom General Altman might turn for such help?"

Welborn named the general's aide, Major Clarence Seymour. "When Ms. Fahey gave me a ride back to Washington from Annapolis, she saw a man fitting Major Seymour's description in her rearview mirror. If he'd been following me earlier, he'd have seen where I left my car."

"Meaning he'd be an auto thief as well as a murderer."

"Yes, ma'am."

The president picked up her phone. "Edwina, will you see if a Major Clarence Seymour accompanied General Warren Altman to the White House yesterday for the meeting I had with the joint chiefs. If so, see if he stayed here the whole time General Altman did."

Every visitor to the West Wing of the White House was logged in and logged out. Edwina had the answer within twenty seconds.

"Thank you, Edwina," the president said and hung up. She turned to Welborn. "Major Seymour was also at the White House at the time Mrs. Altman was killed."

Welborn bit his lip, thinking hard. He'd been all but certain Seymour was the killer. Who else could it have been? Unable to solve the puzzle immediately, he wondered if the cop's wife sitting opposite him would turn to her more seasoned investigator for help.

"How are you getting along with Ms. Fahey?" the president asked, changing the subject.

It was all Welborn could do not to blush, and he was very glad he'd done nothing more than kiss Kira. "Just fine, ma'am. I brought her with me to the lunch we were supposed to have with Mrs. Altman yesterday."

The president saw his stratagem immediately. "Which gave you a prominent witness to the probity of your actions should anyone try to put you in a compromising position."

"Yes, ma'am."

"And if someone had more sinister intentions for you, Lieutenant, would you have shielded Ms. Fahey from harm?"

The thought that he might be placing Kira in harm's way had never occurred to Welborn. Which only made him painfully aware of how wet behind the ears he was. But Welborn Yates was no coward, and he answered honestly, "Yes, ma'am, I would have protected her at all costs."

"Good," the president said, "because I'd hate to have to explain to Vice President Wyman and Mrs. Fahey that I was responsible for losing Kira."

"No, ma'am, I won't let that happen. I ... I'll only liaise with Ms. Fahey from now on. I won't take her into the field with me."

The president nodded her approval.

MCGILL SHOWERED before his massage and after. Yet another joy of living in the White House was that you never had to worry about running out of hot water. He arrived at Dr. Nicolaides's office in his DePaul University sweats and what he assumed— hoped—was radiant good health.

The White House physician ran down the list of what the physical would encompass. If there were any findings in the office that required further study, the examination would take place at Bethesda Naval Hospital. Immediately. So as not to be delayed by McGill's outside obligations.

McGill grumbled but didn't flee. He insisted on only one change in the plan. Nick had to take his blood pressure before he did the DRE—the digital rectal exam to check McGill's prostate gland. There'd be no telling how hard his heart would be beating after he'd been goosed. The doctor laughed and agreed.

All of McGill's vital signs were taken. Blood samples were drawn and would be sent to the laboratory. A treadmill EKG was done. Everything was looking good, then McGill got goosed. He was proud that he didn't yelp. Even though Nick seemed to be making a project of it.

Nick stripped off the surgical glove he'd used to do the job and disposed of it. He told McGill to pull up his pants. They went to Nick's office and the physician settled in behind his desk, took just a minute to finish his notes before turning to his patient.

"I didn't know you'd been shot," he said.

"Back when I was a Chicago copper. Wasn't too bad, but it confirmed my first wife's worst fears."

"A dangerous situation?" Nick asked, fishing for details.

"A ridiculous situation," McGill replied. "A high-society temper tantrum."

The maestro of the Chicago symphony had called the CPD and claimed that his life had been threatened by the orchestra's most generous patron. All because the fat-cat philanthropist thought his largesse should give him the privilege of choosing the music for a few of the orchestra's programs. The maestro, being a maestro, told the fat cat to go choke on his money. The fat cat told the maestro he could be replaced quickly, and he would never lead another orchestra again. The maestro chose to interpret this as a death threat.

The department sent McGill to mediate.

The cop and the two antagonists met on the stage at Orchestra Hall. Where a concert grand piano sat. The fat cat conceded that he'd over-stepped himself. Shouldn't have intruded into the maestro's creative pre-serve, but still thought his generosity deserved some consideration. He had a letter from the orchestra's board of directors seconding this point. It was suggested the maestro give a private performance, then and there, for the fat cat.

"The maestro read the letter," McGill told Nick, "and sat down at the piano."

"The maestro gave in?" Nick asked in disbelief.

"He played 'Chopsticks.' A terrific arrangement, but still 'Chopsticks.' The fat cat was insulted. So he pulled out a little .25 automatic, proving the maestro was on the money with his assumption of a death threat, and tried to shoot the guy."

"But you got in the way."

"I did. Got shot in the ribs, lower right, as you saw."

"Did you shoot the fat cat?"

"I took the gun away and slapped his face. Hard."

"That was all?"

"The maestro laughed. So I gave him the back of my hand."

"Were charges filed?"

"Against big shots like them? In Chicago? Just for shooting a cop?" McGill shook his head. "They threatened to sue me. Only reason they didn't, I told them I'd testify in court that they'd both cried like babies after I'd slapped them."

Nick smiled, having enjoyed the story.

"You going to tell me now that I've got to have something done that won't hurt nearly as bad as getting shot?" McGill asked.

"You need a colonoscopy. I felt a rectal polyp that will have to be removed before it can become a tumor. Not as bad as getting shot, not as simple as a DRE."

"Otherwise?"

"For a pale man, you're very healthy."

"Heart's okay?"

"Very good."

As Nick had said, he wanted to have the work done right away.

McGill told him soon but not quite yet.

MCGILL WAS back in his Hideaway, thinking if he had a polyp maybe he'd better start eating more roughage. Or less smoothage. Something. There was a knock at the door, and Galia entered. She looked at McGill sitting on his sofa, glass in his hand, apparently nothing better to do than stare at a cold fireplace. The way her gaze returned to his glass, McGill could tell she was wondering what he was drinking.

"Ice tea," he said. "Care for a glass?"

"No, thank you."

She handed the manila folder she'd been carrying to McGill.

"Here's the information you requested."

She still didn't think much of his plan; that was clear.

McGill looked at the information she'd provided. Senator Michaelson would be at Political Muscle tomorrow morning at 7:00 A.M. He was scheduled for a workout, nothing more. But McGill didn't worry. He'd get Michaelson where he wanted him. Also included in the folder was a fairly thorough scouting report of Michaelson's game and an unmarked DVD.

"What's this?" McGill asked, holding up the disc.

"Highlights from his college career, transferred from videotape."

McGill smiled. "Galia, this is great."

"I watched some of that disc. He looked pretty good to me."

"Uh-huh. That's what I remember, too."

"How good are you?"

"Want to come and see?" McGill asked.

"No, thanks. I can't remember where I put my pompoms."

McGill grinned. "You can always yell, 'Go, team!'"

"You'd better win, that's all I can say."

AFTER READING the scouting report and watching the DVD, McGill built a fire in the fireplace and fell asleep on the sofa. He was awakened, but not to the point of opening his eyes, by someone caressing his cheek with well-buffed fingernails.

"Is that you, Edwina?" he murmured.

"I can be Edwina, if you want. Just keep your eyes closed."

"That's right, you're an actress," McGill said, playing along. "So how come you never won an Oscar?"

Velvety lips made their way around his face.

"I made only four movies, and every time I worked, Meryl did, too."

"Damned inconsiderate of her."

Fingers played arpeggios along his ribs.

"I've heard she voted for me."

"We won't have her deported then."

Good at spatial relationships, McGill found her face with his hands, never needing to peek, and kissed her deeply.

"There's one problem with this game," he said.

"What?"

"I like to look." He opened his eyes.

In addition to seeing Patti, McGill saw that the fire had been rebuilt, a red fleece blanket had been spread atop the rug, champagne was chilling in an ice bucket, and strawberries and whipped cream nestled in bowls of White House Wedgwood.

"On the floor in front of a fire, with edible goodies, to be consumed in who knows what depraved manner?" McGill asked. "The nation would be scandalized."

"If only they knew," Patti said, tugging him off the sofa.

DAMON TODD couldn't remember the last time he'd been back to Gambier. Not consciously. A little self-hypnosis could bring back the precise date, but he applied his techniques to himself for only the most important of matters.

The place seemed so small. A two-palm island in the midst of an agricultural sea. Old haunts had disappeared; the latest crop of retail chain outlets had taken their places. But the roads, what few of them there were, remained the same. He found his way to Chana's street just as the sun was slipping below the horizon.

From the corner of the block where the Lochlan house stood, he saw the old lady who lived next door just going inside. He remembered her. The neighborhood snoop. Her name was ... Harriet Greenlea. He thought she'd have died years ago. He cruised by the Lochlan and Greenlea houses doing just under the 25 mph speed limit.

Lights were on in both dwellings. It seemed reasonable to assume that an elderly woman would turn in for the night before Professor Lochlan did. He'd wait until Mrs. Busybody went to bed before he rang the doorbell at the house where Chana had grown up. It took willpower to defer the completion of his journey, but discipline was his life.

He rationalized that after spending so many hours in a car, he needed a good brisk run, anyway. He'd do a lap or two of the university campus. Maybe he could sneak into the gymnasium and use the exercise equipment. Keep his sweats on so he wouldn't attract too much attention. Feel strong before he talked to Eamon Lochlan.

Not that he anticipated any trouble.

They were friends. Todd would tell the professor that Chana had contacted him. Asked for his help. He was consulting with her father to make sure his therapeutic approach was correct. Why, the story was at least half true.

DAMON TODD was born and raised in Gambier. His parents had been pillars of the community. Dad had been a doctor, a general practitioner. Mom had taught elementary school math. Older sister, Darcy, had been a registered nurse. All of them had been wonderful people. All of them had been such appalling under-achievers that they'd driven him crazy.

They'd sold themselves *so* short. Dad had done his crossword puzzles orally, calling out one answer after the next; and he tossed off *bon mots* with the wit and quickness of Oscar Wilde. He could have been a great surgeon, a great writer, or both. Instead, he tended to a never-ending procession of kids with runny noses, middle-aged women with female problems, and gray-hairs with hip fractures.

Mom was even more gifted, a true math prodigy. She could have taught at her alma mater, MIT. Instead, she worked in a public school, sometimes with children so young they hadn't learned to hold a pencil properly. Darcy was a success at everything she ever tried. She could have become the first female doctor in the family. But no, Darcy became a nurse, and after she married the Reverend Milton Bidwell, a missionary nurse.

Damon just didn't understand it, how everyone in his family could set their sights so low. And whenever he remonstrated with them, they would only chuckle and pat him on the head. *Little Damon, so small but with such big plans.*

They'd gotten that second part right, anyway.

Trouble was, none of them had lived long enough to see him graduate from college. He was still in high school when his father had his fatal stroke. They'd all been sitting in the living room of their home, reading and listening to a Mozart concerto on the turntable, when they heard Dad make a gagging noise. Everybody looked up and saw Dad with a look of utter surprise on his face. Through a constricted throat, he managed to gasp, "I … I'm sorry." And then he fell out of his chair, never explaining for what or to whom he was penitent. They'd all been grief-stricken, but Mom, as the new head of the family, had been determined to carry on, and for two years she had. Until she'd been on beat-the-bell duty, hurrying kids from the curb into school, and the brakes on a late-arriving big yellow bus had failed. She shoved three kids out of the way but didn't get clear herself. The final blow had come when Damon had been an undergrad at Lehigh University, and the dean of students had called him out of an American history class to inform him that Darcy had perished in Africa: Ebola.

Darcy's death was the one that sent him over the edge. No sooner had he grasped the idea that his sister had died than he felt as if he'd entered a whirlpool. He was slipping, falling, spinning away. He reached up for someone to pull him out, but there was no one left to save him. His whole family was gone.

He woke up in a hospital. He knew his name. But the pieces of his life lay scattered about him like a broken pane of glass. He wasn't sure how to put them together again. Or if he even wanted to. For an unknown number of days all he wanted to do was sleep. Eating and drinking weren't important. Bladder and bowel release could be done right there in bed.

Life was unimportant.

Then his therapist arrived. He probably would have ignored her ... except she reminded him of his mother. No, she made him think of what his mother could have been—a professional woman of significance—had she cared to exert even a small fraction of her potential. Damon came to look on the therapist's visits with great anticipation. Truly, he came to love her.

Until she betrayed him by saying, "We'll get you back to where you belong."

Where he belonged? Another underachieving Todd. He'd *never* settle for that. As long as he was making the immense effort to reclaim his life, he was going to make it a *superior* life. One that would achieve both critical and popular acclaim. Because not only would he do great things, he'd help others to achieve success as well.

He'd craft his life and theirs so that victory was inevitable.

TODD WAS able to get in both the run and the workout he'd wanted. He was still pumped when he pushed the doorbell at the Lochlan house. Every muscle and vein in his neck and face stood out. A light sheen of perspiration still covered him.

A woman he'd never seen before answered the door, switching on the porch light as she did. She jumped backward when she saw him. Her response angered Todd, but he remained outwardly calm.

"I'm sorry if I frightened you," he said. "I'm looking for some old friends. I'm pretty sure I have the right address, but maybe they've moved. By any chance, would you know Professor Eamon Lochlan?"

His civil tone let the woman relax. She was closing in on sixty, Todd estimated, but was still attractive and trim enough to wear a Cleveland Indians jersey and blue jeans without looking foolish. Her smile, when it came, made her look a good five years younger.

"Why, yes, I know Eamon. In fact, I'm his fiancée."

The dynamic change Todd had been expecting. The upset in Chana's life. One of them, anyway. Maybe he'd discover more.

The woman extended her hand to him. "Imogene Lyle."

He took her hand, careful to be gentle.

"Dr. Damon Todd. I treated Chana many years ago. I happened to be in town for the first time since then, and I thought I'd drop in on the professor. See how things are going."

Her face dropped. "I'm sorry, Eamon's not here. He left this morning to go to Washington."

Todd's eyebrows rose.

"That's where Chana lives these days," Imogene explained. "She's a television person, you know."

"I believe I heard something about that," he answered.

"Well, that's more than I knew before I met Eamon. I don't watch much TV." She paused a moment to study him. "When you say you treated Chana, do you mean for her ..."

The woman couldn't bring herself to say it, so Todd did.

"For her breakdown, yes."

She looked at him again. Closely. "Eamon has a picture of you, but you look quite different."

"I was in an automobile accident. Lots of physical therapy afterward. I liked the strength I gained and ..." he shrugged, "I just kept going."

It was a lie, but a plausible one. Still, he could see she was about to call an end to their conversation, before Todd could learn if there was anything else he should know.

So he asked, "Is Chana doing well these days?"

Imogene poked her head out the door and looked at Harriet Greenlea's house. The curtains over there were drawn, but Imogene's expression said they might be parted at any time.

"Why don't you step inside for a moment, Dr. Todd? We'll talk privately."

He did and within the first five minutes he learned of Eamon Lochlan's and Imogene Lyle's plans. Knowledge of which would be of great use in treating Chana. Hearing that Chana's father would soon be distancing himself from her, however, made Todd rethink his own plans.

He didn't see any way he could abandon Chana, too. He could have left quickly and returned to Washington overnight. But he didn't want to leave Imogene with any memory of his visit. So he accepted her offer of coffee, and after an innocuous distraction spiked her cup with the dose of Special K that he'd intended to use on her betrothed. After that, the hypnosis session went smoothly.

In deference to her courtesy to him, and her status as a prospective bride, he didn't take advantage of her sexually. He simply tucked the memory of their meeting away in a corner of her mind she'd been instructed never to visit again.

CHAPTER 24

WEDNESDAY

MCGILL, SWEETIE, and Deke showed up at Political Muscle at 6:30 A.M., thirty minutes before Senator Roger Michaelson's scheduled arrival. The high-end fitness club was members only, but as at its sister gym, Corporate Muscle, the manager was overjoyed to have the president's henchman make an appearance. Engaging in a bit of duplicity, McGill asked if he might purchase guest passes to see how he liked the facility. The manager offered a complimentary visit for McGill and Sweetie.

He told the manager it would look better if he paid for his passes—just in case he was ever called before a Senate committee and asked about taking special favors. Having things his way cost McGill $100, but he paid without flinching.

There was no charge for Deke who, after all, was on duty.

Sweetie was shown to the women's locker room, and McGill was escorted to the men's changing quarters. Many of the lockers in the men's area were reserved, the names of those renting them indicated on small brass plaques. McGill spotted Michaelson's directly opposite the massage room. Nothing like a vigorous rubdown following a hard workout.

The club provided McGill with the use of a basketball, which everyone agreed not even Congress at its most picayune could find fault with, most likely. He bounced the ball off the locker room floor three times. Any gym rat in the world would recognize the sound.

After Deke had made sure the locker room was safe, the Secret Service agent stepped outside with instructions not to let Michaelson spot him. McGill quickly changed into his gym clothes: DePaul T-shirt and shorts, sneakers, and a jock. He draped a towel over his head like a prizefighter, picked up the basketball, and enclosed himself in a toilet stall.

He'd no sooner seated himself than he thought he should have brought a newspaper to read. He didn't have to wait long, though, before he heard Michaelson's voice nearby, talking to a guy who had to be his trainer. They were discussing that day's workout: upper body. The trainer said he thought the senator could get 250 on his bench press if he really went for it.

Galia's background information hadn't included how much weight Michaelson was pushing these days. But if he could do 250, he was pretty strong. McGill did only 225, and that was on a machine. Free weights were harder. But then he hadn't heard that Michaelson was doing free weights either. If he was, McGill could only hope that the trainer was giving Michaelson more than a little help with his lift.

McGill flushed the toilet, pulled up his jock and shorts, picked up the basketball, and exited the stall. He washed his hands at a nearby sink to keep up his cover of having used the toilet. He grabbed a paper towel to dry his hands, crumpled it, and carried it with him a good ten feet. Then he turned and neatly flipped the ball of paper into a wastebasket.

Keeping his head down and his face shadowed inside the towel, he began to dribble the basketball. Even if Michaelson hadn't been paying attention earlier, McGill would bet the sound of the bouncing ball drew his attention. As would the Blue Demon logo on his T-shirt. The only Chicago area university ever to win an NCAA basketball championship was Loyola, but DePaul, back in the heyday of Ray Meyer, Terry Cummings, and Mark Aguirre, had made it to the Final Four.

Which was farther than Michaelson's school, Northwestern, had ever gone.

McGill dribbled the ball easily, not showboating, just moving it back and forth, right hand to left, left hand to right, as he crossed to the locker-room door. But when he pulled the door open, never stopping his dribble, he went back and forth between his legs.

To show Michaelson here was a DePaul guy who could handle the ball. To set the hook.

The door closed behind McGill, Michaelson never getting a good look at him.

MCGILL HAD the gym to himself for five minutes. The club manager had told him the floor was of regulation NBA dimensions. The backboards were Plexiglas, just like the pros used. The rims were bright orange. The lighting was almost overpowering.

Keeping his towel over his head, McGill took shots at the baskets at both ends of the court. He looked for dead spots in the floor where the ball wouldn't get a true bounce. He didn't find any. But the rims were tight. Forget about getting a shooter's bounce in this gym. You swished your shot, banked it cleanly, or you didn't make it.

McGill used free throws to establish his depth perception. His eye was naturally good for being on line. Once he got the feel for how far from the basket he was, he'd be okay. Not that he planned to use his outside game much, but you never could—

"Hey there," Roger Michaelson called, entering the court. "You're new around here, aren't you? A Chicago guy. Care to play a little one-on-one?"

McGill looked at the senator. Pushed the towel back from his face.

"Don't mind if I do."

Michaelson might have been a political enemy, but he was no fool. He knew the moment he recognized McGill that he'd been led down the garden path. Of course, he could have turned around and walked right out. But he'd brought his trainer with him. No doubt to enjoy the spectacle of watching the senator thrash the DePaul guy.

Besides that, Sweetie had just entered the gym.

And Deke was visible through the windows of the gym doors as he took up his position to guarantee that no evildoer or anyone else interrupted the game.

So there were three independent witnesses who could testify that Roger Michaelson had wimped out, should he turn on his heel and leave. That was three times as many witnesses as necessary for the word to be spread all over Washington that the number-one jock in the Senate was all talk and no action.

Even that might not have been enough to influence Michaelson to act against his better judgment. But then McGill calmly swished a shot from the top of the key and grinned.

"I know you were a big college star, but I think I might stay with you."

A direct challenge. If Michaelson walked away from that, he was never going to intimidate any of his colleagues in the Senate again. Wouldn't sound too forceful should he ever try to stand up to the Grant administration either.

"What's your game?" Michaelson asked flatly.

The senator was speaking in the most literal sense.

"Twenty-one by ones," McGill answered. "Make it, take it. Have to win by a deuce."

"You got it."

"Need a minute or two to warm up?" McGill asked.

"No."

Michaelson picked up the ball, dribbled slowly to half-court, making his game plan. He turned to face the basket at which McGill had made his shot from the top of the key, a distance of twenty feet, compared to the forty-seven feet where the senator was standing.

"I make it, I get the ball first. I don't, you get it."

McGill nodded.

Michaelson drained his shot … the ball returning to him on the back-spin.

ROGER MICHAELSON made his move the second the ball touched his hands. He faked right and broke left. McGill was ready and cut him off. He'd seen Michaelson's move on the scouting DVD Galia had provided him. More important, he knew Michaelson wouldn't wait for him to get set before he started to play. Surprised that his path was blocked, Michaelson pulled back. He was even more surprised when McGill attacked his retreat.

Poked the ball right out of the senator's hand. Out of bounds.

Michaelson retrieved the ball and picked up his dribble on the far side of the out-of-bounds line. He approached slowly, looking to see if McGill was leaning one way or the other. As he reached midcourt, he burst to his right, intending to drive past McGill and take the ball straight to the hole.

McGill was with him from the first stride. Seeing there was no way he'd get to the rim without McGill cutting him off, Michaelson stopped on a dime and went up for a fifteen-foot jump shot. Money in the bank for him. His form was perfect—but the ball didn't rise with him. McGill stripped it at waist height.

By the time Michaelson came down, McGill had taken the ball behind the free-throw line and put up a soft jumper of his own—1–0.

"Take the ball behind the free-throw line on change of possession, okay?" he said. "And check the ball after a basket."

An implied rebuke at Michaelson's trying to sneak in the first point.

McGill bounced the ball to Michaelson for the check; the senator fired it back.

McGill caught the ball as if taking a pass from a teammate and immediately drove left. His first step was quicker than Michaelson's, and he got to the basket untouched for a layup, even though the senator tried to trip him as he went past—2–0.

The attempted dirty play was okay with McGill. In fact, he was counting on more of the same. Michaelson doubled the room he gave McGill the next time he checked the ball to him. McGill took advantage of the open space and went up for another jumper. It looked good when it left his hand, but it caught just a little of the back of the rim and shot out like a cork leaving a champagne bottle.

Michaelson grabbed the rebound. The desire to put the ball back right back in was clear on his face. But McGill had established the rule. He had to take it out past the free-throw line. Trying to change that now, while the ball was in play, was something only a … well, a politician would attempt. Or a guy who was already worried.

Michaelson brought the ball out as quickly as he could, hoping to get back to the basket before McGill could cut him off, but as he pivoted, he saw that his opponent already had defensive position on him. Anger flashed in Michaelson's eyes. He went up for another jump shot, but this time he fumbled the ball away all on his own.

As McGill grabbed it, Michaelson, in mid-jump, kicked out with his right leg, catching McGill solidly on his left thigh. The senator yelled, "Foul!"

McGill held the ball, his face expressionless.

"Hit you on the foot with my leg?"

"You ran into me while I was shooting."

McGill let the ball bounce toward half court.

As the senator went to retrieve it, McGill said, "You actually call fouls out there in Oregon, huh?"

Michaelson picked up the ball and turned around, knowing that his masculinity as well as his home state had just been impugned.

"We don't have to call anything if you don't want to."

"Let's not," McGill said. "Just slows down the game."

MICHAELSON CAME at McGill every way he knew how. With his right hand, with his left. He attempted crossover dribbles, trying to get McGill to lean one way while he rushed past the other. But he just couldn't do it. McGill's hands were too quick. He took the ball away every time. Made two layups and one out of three jump shots. Went up 5–0, though Michaelson did catch McGill on the left shoulder with a hard elbow the last time he stole the ball.

Finally, Michaelson got on the board with a reverse 360-spin jumper from eighteen feet out on the left side of the basket. Swished it so cleanly the net barely moved. The shot was unlike anything on the scouting video and one hell of an athletic move for a guy in his late forties—5–1.

But Michaelson was panting when McGill checked the ball back to him. He might have another move or two like that left in him for the game. After that, if he tried anything fancy, he'd screw himself right into the ground. The senator knew it, too.

He decided it was time to back his way to the basket, interposing his body between the ball and McGill's quick hands. He'd use his two-inch height advantage and his strength to get in close. He'd bulldoze McGill and put up a little two-foot jumper or a baby hook shot.

Possibly, this strategy was inspired by the senator's trainer, who yelled, "Muscle him, muscle the sonofa—"

The trainer's exhortation ended in an abrupt squeak; Sweetie didn't approve of profanity in general, and especially not directed at those people close to her heart.

Vulgarity aside, Michaelson got deeply involved in his new tactic. He led with his backside, slamming it hard into McGill's midsection. Knocked him back a step. Checking his spot on the court, Michaelson flexed his knees more deeply. He battered McGill again, going for the groin. Forced his opponent back another step. Two more hard bangs, and he'd be in position to flip a little hook off the board and into the basket.

Michaelson was having fun now. But the next time he thrust his ass out, McGill met it with a knee. A bolt of lightning shot up the senator's anus and traveled the length of his spine to his brain. He fell face forward, getting his hands up to break the fall only at the last second. Saving him from breaking his nose. Not sparing his forehead from hitting the floor with a bang.

Dazed, he looked up in time to see McGill calmly hit a shot from the free-throw line—6–1. This time the ball came back to McGill on the backspin. He dropped it in front of the senator.

"Check ball," McGill said.

His forehead bleeding, Michaelson got to his feet to continue the game.

FROM THAT point on the two men played full-contact basketball. Pat Riley's old New York Knicks teams would have admired the fight. Getting the ball into the basket was only incidental to the exchange of forearms, elbows, shoulders, knees, and kicks. Which was exactly what McGill had wanted. He'd taken Michaelson out of his game, basketball, and gotten him into McGill's game, Dark Alley.

Not that the senator, a true competitor, didn't give the latter his best effort.

As McGill grabbed a rebound, Michaelson's hand shot out. Not to take the ball away, but to jam a finger or two into one of McGill's eyes. Relying on Uncle Ed's training, McGill dipped his head, putting his skull not his eyes in line with Michaelson's jabbing fingers. He heard at least one and maybe two of the senator's metacarpals snap. But that was just McGill's defensive move. Counterattacking, he drove the top of his head into Michaelson's chin.

Knocked him flat on his ass.

Left himself a bit wobbly, too. His scalp was bleeding where Michaelson's fingernails had torn his skin. A rivulet of blood ran between his eyes. McGill blotted the flow with his sleeve as it came off the tip of his nose.

A glance to his right showed McGill that the senator's trainer was leaning forward, wanting to take his man out of the battle. For that matter, Deke had entered the gym, and he, too, was on the verge of interceding. Only Sweetie was having a good time. She wanted more.

So, apparently, did Michaelson. He waved the trainer back. Getting to his feet, taking a moment to reestablish his balance, he said, "Check ball."

McGill bounced the ball to him and took it back, another bullet pass, at the free-throw line. Michaelson probably hoped to jam one or more of McGill's fingers with the hard pass, but didn't succeed. McGill drove past the senator, despite taking a knee to his left hip, and laid the ball in—10–4.

Michaelson fired yet another hard check pass at McGill. He sidestepped that one. Let it go to the far wall and roll most of the way back. When he bent over to pick the ball up, he thought his head was going to fall off. It remained attached to his body, but he wasn't sure that was such a good thing. The worst headache of his life had arrived like a thunderclap. The consequence of hitting Michaelson's chin with his head was just making itself known.

Well, Dark Alley wasn't for sissies.

He'd have to remind Abbie of that.

Assuming he wasn't brain-dead when he finished this game.

McGill shifted into high gear the moment he crossed half-court. It looked like he was driving right for another layup, but as Michaelson got close, McGill lowered a shoulder and cut hard left. He slammed straight into his startled opponent's sternum and knocked Michaelson off his feet again.

McGill made his shot from the point of the collision. It went in off the backboard. He'd been trying for straight in—11–4.

Michaelson got to his feet, still refusing to quit. He couldn't fire the checked ball at McGill. Didn't have the juice. Just let it go on a bounce. McGill caught it with his knees bent so he wouldn't have to lean over. He took a set shot from where he stood. The ball actually circled the rim a couple of times before rolling out. Michaelson hobbled over and got the rebound.

From that point on, the senator began dropping bombs from deep in NBA three-point land. More impressively, he was making them with his left hand. The ring and pinkie fingers on his right hand had swollen to the size and color of blood sausages. He made five in a row, McGill lying back, giving the *Anvil Chorus* playing in his head a chance to sound its last note.

The score was 11–9 when Michaelson finally missed a shot, and McGill got the ball back.

The contest became a series of streaks. McGill made four layups, Michaelson, now wary of having his breastbone split in two, didn't get close enough to take another hard shoulder—15–9. Michaelson hit six more outside bombs while McGill was still trying to gather a plurality of his resources. Fifteen all.

McGill made five more layups with Michaelson now daring to inch closer on defense. With the score 20–15, and only one more point needed to win, McGill tried to go to the hole one last time. Having nothing to lose, Michaelson stuck his leg out once more, trying to trip him, and succeeded. McGill sprawled onto the court with a thud, skinning his knees, elbows, and chin.

More important, the ball got away from him and rolled out of bounds.

Michaelson's possession, as they weren't calling fouls.

The senator rattled off another six long-range shots in a row, the last three with McGill's hand in his face. For the first time, Michaelson was ahead—21–20. But it took a deuce—two buckets— to win.

McGill rolled the checked ball to him, intending to take it away the second Michaelson picked it up. But the senator let the ball roll between his legs as if they were a croquet wicket. He picked up the ball behind his legs. He palmed the ball with his left hand, brought it around his own body and behind McGill's back.

To the onlookers it seemed as if the senator was embracing his opponent. He whispered into McGill's ear, "You really thought you were going to win, didn't you?"

Then he kneed McGill in the crotch.

Things didn't work out quite the way he intended. His forty-eight-year-old kneecap hit not McGill's genitals but the hardened plastic cup McGill had presciently inserted in his jockstrap. The jolt hurt McGill, but not badly, and the family jewels remained intact. Michaelson's patella, on the other hand, suffered extreme pain and three hairline fractures. He had to let go of the ball to cover his injured kneecap with both hands.

McGill spun around and retrieved the ball, his right elbow slamming into Michaelson's jaw, knocking him down for the third time. He laid the ball in to tie the game—21–21.

This time, however, the senator was unable to get back to his feet. His knee injury, the bane of the older athlete, had put him out of the game. The senator's trainer started forward, but when McGill shook his head, both Deke and Sweetie pulled him back.

McGill lowered himself to one knee next to Michaelson.

"Game ends in a draw," he said in a quiet voice.

Michaelson had no reply, content to fix McGill with a hate-filled stare.

"Maybe we'll have to do it again," McGill said. "But if you decide to hold hearings to question whether Lindell Ricker confessed freely, whether Erna Godfrey deserves to be on death row for killing Andy Grant … well, then I'm going to dedicate my life to investigating your life. And I'm much better at police work than I am at basketball. I'll look into every minute of every day you've been in politics. You think you can give the president and me a hard time? Try it, and I'll make the last half hour seem like Sunday brunch."

To emphasize his point, McGill stepped on Michaelson's broken fingers as he limped off the court.

PATTI FOUND McGill in his bathtub, the whirlpool jets on high. Doctor Artemus Nicolaides had been by to check him for, and clear him of, a concussion. Both White House massage therapists had worked on him simultaneously for ninety minutes. Blessing had brought him a pitcher of White House ice tea and drawn his bath for him. Sweetie was probably saying a rosary for him somewhere. And now Patti had stopped by. In the middle of the morning.

"I thought your job kept you pretty busy," McGill said.

Patti ignored the joke. She asked, "What did you do?"

"You haven't heard?"

"Tell me in your own words."

"I beat up Roger Michaelson for you."

"You assaulted a United States senator?"

"In the guise of a basketball game. He won't complain."

"Why did you do it?"

"To save you some pain."

"I can take all the political heat Roger Michaelson can generate."

"Personal pain."

He told her of Michaelson's scheme, which could conceivably have resulted in Erna Godfrey's guilty verdict being overturned. He didn't mention Galia's role in the day's events, but Patti was smart enough to figure out that she had to have one.

"I didn't think you should have to relive *US v. Godfrey,*" McGill said.

Tears welled in Patti's eyes, and she nodded. "Did you hit Michaelson hard?"

"Many times."

"Do you think he'll back off?"

McGill told her of his threat to Michaelson.

"Thank you," Patti said. "I've got to get back to work now."

CHAPTER 25

ABBIE MCGILL went to Saint Viviana's High School that morning. She was luckier than her brother, Kenny. While Abbie's friends weren't allowed to travel with her, their parents let them pal around with her once they'd all reached a safe place. Safe being a site the Secret Service had already inspected for and cleared of all imaginable threats, a location that was then protected by Abbie's contingent of Evanston PD coppers.

St. Viv's made the grade by those criteria. Abbie's best friends, Clare Daniels and Lissa Mulvay, met her inside the main entrance. All three girls would be starting their junior year at the school in September.

The junior class had the responsibility of welcoming the student body back for the new school year. Abbie, Clare, and Lissa were the co-heads of the Welcoming Committee. Each of them had two years invested in St. Viv's, and two more to go. The way the administration saw it, that was the right combination of experience and continuing interest.

Their responsibilities went beyond hanging banners and bunting, and picking a band for the annual Are You Getting Smart with Me? Dance. There were also substantive matters to consider. Past welcoming committees had addressed everything from replacing worn-out P.A. speakers to improving hallway traffic flows for class changes and fire drills; from upgrading the cafeteria menu for both nutrition and appetite appeal to refining the dress code in ways that pleased both student and parent aesthetics.

The goal was to create a school that offered no excuses for failing to excel.

That year's committee heads took their work seriously.

Abbie, Clare, and Lissa walked the otherwise deserted halls of St. Viv's. It was a lot easier to see what needed fixing when the building wasn't jammed with kids. The only sound was their sneakers squeaking on recently waxed floors. They covered the three main floors of the building before anyone said anything.

"You know what I'd like to see?" Clare asked.

Abbie and Lissa looked at her.

"A wider selection of magazines in the school library. Maybe get *Vanity Fair*."

"Vanity's one of the seven deadly sins," Abbie said with a grin.

"Boredom's deadly, too. I'd like to read something with a little sass. Show the faculty and our parents we're ready for controversial takes on current events and politics. You know, I bet *Vanity Fair* does a story on your stepmom before too long, Abbie."

Abbie only nodded. Most of the time her friends were pretty good about not making a big deal that her dad was married to the president. But it was getting harder with all cops and Secret Service around. Besides, Clare was probably right. Once the media got over their honeymoon with Patti, they probably would start writing snarky stories about her.

Geez, she thought. Maybe about Dad, too.

"What I'd like to see in the library is more DVDs," Lissa said.

"Undercut NetFlix?" Clare asked. "That'd be great."

"No, I'm serious. Think about this. The school library should have a DVD movie of any book that's on the assigned reading list of any class that's taught here. You know, as long as a movie's been made from that book. You get to watch the movie only after you've done the reading, not before, not instead."

"What's the point?" Abbie asked.

"This is: You know how some teachers always think they understand better than anybody else what an author is really saying in his or her book?"

The girls agreed they all knew such teachers.

"But if you have a movie made from a book that takes another point of view, then you've got a dissenting voice. Another opinion that could be just as valid."

"From somebody who can't be given a failing grade," Abbie said with a smile.

"What about you, Abbie?" Clare asked. "You got any big ideas for the school?"

"Big, yeah ... dramatic, no. The one thing I've never liked about St. Viv's is the lockers."

The girls were in the corridor where they would take most of their classes in the coming year. As a privilege of their position, they'd already been assigned their lockers, ones that were centrally located so they wouldn't have to race from one end of the hall to the other between classes. Abbie stopped at hers. She'd been given the combination but had yet to open it.

"I mean, you get to school the first day, they seem big enough, if a little beat-up. But when your book bag is bulging, and you add your gym bag ..." She started to dial her combination. "And the weather turns cold, and you add your winter coat, these things just get too cramped and smelly. I know it would cost a lot to buy better lockers for the whole school, but maybe we could start a fund so kids five or ten years from now could have something nicer."

"Miss Generosity," said Clare. "Always thinking of others."

"I like the idea," Lissa said. "There've been times I've opened my locker and thought I'd find—"

Abbie opened her locker and shrieked.

Her friends jumped, then crept forward to peek over Abbie's trembling shoulders. There was no dead frog or pile of dog poop or anything disgusting like that in Abbie's locker.

Only a note. But it said: *There's nowhere we can't reach you.*

WELBORN PULLED up to the northwest gate of the White House. The uniformed Secret Service detail knew him and Kira by both sight and name. They checked their security passes anyway. Looked them over closely. Made sure no bad guys were trying to impersonate them.

After they were cleared, Welborn put Kira's sports car in motion, intending to drop her off. He said, "You know, way back when, the White

House gates were open to the public. In the thirties, young people even used the driveway as a lover's lane. That all ended not because of any security problem but because Eleanor Roosevelt thought it was unseemly."

Kira was not amused.

Welborn asked, "If security weren't a problem now, you think Mr. McGill would mind people making out in front of the White House?"

That notion tickled her. The corners of her mouth started to turn up, but she quickly squelched her amusement and went back to frowning.

"I don't think he would," Welborn continued. "Not unless it was his daughters doing the making out."

He got her there; she laughed.

Then she said, "I'm still mad at you, flyboy. Don't think I'm not."

Welborn had told Kira that she could no longer accompany him as he went about his work; she had to stay safely ensconced in the White House. He'd promised the president.

"I could quit my job, you know," she said.

"What are you qualified for besides government work?"

The look she gave him should have stopped his heart.

"Besides," he said, "if you were an everyday civilian, you wouldn't even get to *hear* about what I turn up."

A telling point, and she knew it. Not that she was about to give up.

"I should at least take my car away from you."

"I'm sure the White House could find me another one."

"I hate you."

"I know. I still feel the same way."

Welborn stopped in front of the entrance to the White House. A Marine in dress uniform stepped forward to open the car door for the vice president's niece.

"Really?" Kira asked.

"Really."

A bright smile appeared on her face, but there was mischief in her eyes. She abruptly leaned over, put an arm around Welborn's neck, and planted a good one on him. A kiss deeper than any they had shared before. Right in front of the Marine.

Meaning everyone in the federal government would know about it within twenty-four hours. That was what he got for telling her about people making out in the White House driveway.

Kira sat back, and told him, "You'd better call me. I expect progress reports."

Welborn saluted. "Yes, ma'am."

The Marine closed the door after she got out of the car. The guy was supposed to keep an impassive demeanor while on duty ... but he grinned at Welborn.

THE AUDI TT was growing on Welborn. Despite Arlene Cowan's description of the car as a "little ego-stroker," and his previous devotion to the simplicity of Hondas, he had to admit that it was fun to drive the sports car. Closest he'd come to the exhilaration of flying since his accident. Maybe he ought to look into—

Captain Dexter Cowan's Dodge Viper. The sleek navy blue machine shot past in the westbound lanes of Route 50. Welborn was heading east on the same road. Heading to Landover to see Colonel Linberg. He couldn't help wondering if that was where Captain Cowan had just been.

Of course, a Navy man like Cowan could have had business farther down the road in Annapolis. A new thought tickled Welborn's mind. But he couldn't quite rein it in. Following the advice of his mentors from Glynco, he didn't try to force it. He let the thought go until it was ready to return and make itself known.

IF CARINA Linberg had been entertaining Dexter Cowan, she hadn't dressed up for the occasion. She wore a Denver Broncos jersey and faded jeans. Her feet were bare. She had dark circles under her eyes, and her jaw muscles were tense. When she saw it was Welborn at her front door, she didn't invite him in. Not at first. Then she opened the door wide.

"Care to come in, Lieutenant? You can help me pack up my kitchen."

"Certainly, ma'am. Any way I can be of help."

He stepped inside the condo and saw that most of the furniture had been removed. He did spot an unmade bed through an open doorway. The walls were bare and freshly painted, as she'd told him earlier. The carpeting looked as if it had been professionally cleaned. Welborn followed Carina Linberg into her kitchen, where there were still two chairs and a table.

She turned and saw the look on his face. "I sold the place, Lieutenant. Turned a nice profit, too. But don't worry, it's not enough to start over in Rio."

She smiled, which made her look both prettier and more forlorn.

"Come to tell me a date for my court-martial has been set?"

"No, ma'am. Would you like to start packing, or would you rather sit down?"

Carina Linberg sat. As did Welborn.

"I came here to talk with you, ma'am."

"About?"

"I spoke with Arlene Cowan—Mrs. Dexter Cowan—the other day."

"The injured party. The betrayed wife. Did she tell you how evil I was?"

"How would you feel in her place?"

The colonel's eyes drifted to the ceiling as she thought. Returning them to Welborn, she said, "Relieved, I think."

Welborn found that interesting. He remembered what Arlene Cowan had told him.

"Mrs. Cowan said her husband had once wondered, in thinking of her, where his sweet, simple girl had gone. Mrs. Cowan is multilingual and has two master's degrees. She may have been sweet, but I doubt she was ever simple."

"Your point, Lieutenant?"

"I don't think you're simple either, Colonel."

Carina looked like she had a response to that, but she thought better of it and kept quiet.

"Mrs. Cowan also told me that her husband had taken pains to make his infidelity clear to her, not exactly common behavior for a cheating husband."

"Not that you'd know."

"Not from experience; I've never been married."

"And probably never even cheated on a girlfriend."

"No, ma'am."

This time Carina wasn't able to repress her thoughts.

"A real officer and a gentleman. Just what every girl who loves a warrior wants to marry." The colonel's sour tone was at odds with her words. "I had a friend at the Academy who thought that way. Until four guys from our class grabbed her one night and raped her. Told her that was all that women in the military were good for. She told me what happened, but wouldn't say a word to anyone else. She said the school administration would just cover it up. Said men were too valuable to expel much less prosecute. So she left school."

Welborn grimaced. The rape scandals at Colorado Springs tortured the souls of every decent male cadet who'd been to the Academy.

"My roommate's father called me," Carina went on. "He knew something terribly wrong had happened to his daughter, but she wouldn't tell him what it was. I pleaded ignorance to this poor man. How could *I* tell him his daughter had been gang-raped? I was too busy watching out for my own pink ass. But then my friend committed suicide, and at her funeral I told her father what she'd told me."

Welborn said, "I'm very sorry, ma'am. I hope you believe that."

"I do, Lieutenant. But you're not as sorry as I was. My roommate's father killed two of the cadets who raped his daughter. Shot them right through the head with his hunting rifle. Would have gotten the other two as well if they hadn't been too sick to go out drinking with their friends that night. The poor man then turned his weapon on himself. The school and the local D.A. did their best to keep the whole thing quiet. Why not? The killer was already dead. So if you haven't heard about it, I'm not surprised."

Welborn felt there was more to the story.

"It didn't end there, did it, ma'am?"

"No. Somehow the two survivors learned I was the one who gave them away. They blamed me for their friends' deaths. The administration had the school under close watch after the killings; they knew that vengeance for a rape lay behind them. So my two new worst enemies couldn't exact their own vengeance. But they warned me I'd better either get out of the military or make damn sure I rose in rank faster than they did. Because if I didn't, they would see to it that I suffered. Suffered greatly."

Welborn was sure he could track down the names of the cadets who'd been killed, and the names of their two friends. See if the living and the vengeful had gone on to serve at the Pentagon and renewed their enmity with Colonel Linberg.

"I'm sure you know that Mrs. Altman, General Altman's wife, was killed, ma'am."

The colonel nodded, her face a mask. No reason not to admit that knowledge. Cheryl Altman's hit-and-run death was a matter of public record by then.

"But what hasn't been made known is that Captain Cowan has somehow come into a good deal of money recently. He's bought a very expensive sports car, and his wife and her lawyer expect him to make a large settlement in the matter of their divorce."

Carina Linberg remained silent. Welborn stood, ready to depart.

"You're in the middle of another terrible situation, ma'am. I truly hope that you'll find the strength to tell me what's going on before ... well, before anyone else dies."

The colonel saw him out, the two of them passing her open bedroom door.

Welborn was glad for any number of reasons she didn't try to lead him that way.

MCGILL WAS still in the bath, getting pruny, but feeling *so* much better for his soak and the insistent pressure of the water jets. When Galia entered the room, he did a double take and thought to cover his crotch. Then he realized the whirling water in which he was immersed was effectively opaque. It was only then that he realized Galia had a portable phone in her hand and was extending it to him.

"Blessing was about to bring you the phone," she said. "I told him I'd do it."

"How kind of you," McGill said dryly.

"Your son," Galia told him.

McGill's heart jumped into his throat ... until he remembered the likely reason Kenny would be calling him. He took the phone and clicked it on.

"Hi, Kenny, how are you?"

"Dad, they're great! They're so cool. None of my friends have anything like them."

"So you like your new phones?"

"I *love* them. I thought things like this were only for secret agents."

"Well, take good care of them. They cost enough to buy you your first used car."

Kenny said, "Really?"

"And truly," said McGill. "Who'd you give the other receiver to? Somebody you can trust, I hope."

"Billy Tuttle's mom. They've got a big house so the guys are always going over there. But Mrs. Tuttle is real careful about things, so I figure she'll take good care of it. I still can't believe two phones can cost as much as a car, even if they are spy phones."

"Secure phones with scramble/descramble features. And I'll show you the receipt the next time I see you."

"Okay. Maybe I can trade them in on car when I'm old enough to drive, but right now the phones are really cool. My friends and I have been talking all morning, and all our secrets are safe. Nobody can listen in, or understand us if they do. You're the best, Dad."

Kenny's praise did more for McGill's sense of well-being than his whirlpool bath, his ninety-minute massage, or even his pitcher of White House ice tea. He'd thought that if Kenny's friends weren't being allowed to see him, they should be encouraged to talk to him. The secure phones were gizmos whose novelty would wear off even for adolescent boys—as his son with thoughts of a future car already understood—but he hoped to end the threat to his children before then.

"Glad you like your gift," McGill said, "but do me a favor."

"What?"

"Don't share any *family* secrets with your friends, ones that'll get me into trouble with your mom. Or your sisters. Or the president of the United States. Okay?"

There was a guilty silence before Kenny said, "Uh, okay." And a quick, "Bye, Dad."

McGill handed the phone back to Galia and looked at her for a minute.

"Not that I have it in mind," he said, "but does this mean I get to drop in on *your* bath?"

To his surprise, Galia gave the question some thought.

"Yes, if your reason is important enough."

"And you have news of great moment?"

"You've put Roger Michaelson into the hospital."

"Outpatient?"

"Being held overnight for observation of a concussion. Also for treatment of various and sundry traumas. The ER doctor, I'm told, said he looked like a truck hit him."

"It was a spirited game," McGill said.

"Which is pretty much what the senator had to say ... publicly."

"And behind the scenes?"

"I'm working on that. But you've got Congress in an uproar. They don't like the idea of *anyone* getting away with pummeling one of their own. Then there's the story that you had a few private words to share with Michaelson after you thumped him. No one knows what they were yet, but the consensus is you weren't telling him to get well soon."

Clearly, Galia wanted to know what McGill had said.

He didn't tell her. He said, "So, I'll probably have a hard time getting a game with any of our friends from Capitol Hill?"

Galia snorted. "You've got them scared now. Handled properly, that can be a good thing. Michaelson will certainly think twice before he goes ahead with his plan. But if you frighten them too badly, they'll do everything they can to destroy you."

"So your advice is?"

"Try not to beat up anyone else anytime soon. At least not anyone prominent. Even if there's a basketball involved."

McGill nodded. Then he said, "Be honest, Galia. Don't you think I did more than make Michaelson think twice?"

She hated to do it, but she gave him his due. "I don't think he'll ever go through with his plan. At least not this one. But he'll think of another. As long as the president is in office, he'll be her number one enemy."

McGill shrugged.

A rueful smile formed on the chief of staff's face. "You know, now that I know the outcome, I'm sorry I didn't accept your invitation. I wish I'd seen you bash that bastard."

Galia was enjoying that thought when the phone in her hand rang. She handed it to McGill and left the room. Didn't even sneak a backward peek.

"Hello," McGill said.

"Mr. McGill? This is Eamon Lochlan. Would it be possible for you to come by my daughter's residence within the hour? We have something important to tell you."

Lochlan's voice was very shaky. McGill said he'd be there in thirty minutes, or less.

He was already gone the next time his phone rang. Barbara Sullivan of the Evanston Police Department was calling. She wanted to advise him of the threat to his daughter Abbie.

AFTER VISITING McGill in his bath, the president returned to the Oval Office and her meeting with the chairman of the Joint Chiefs, General Fabin, and the director of Central Intelligence, Thomas Van Owen. They'd come to inform her of their progress in putting into effect her idea for dealing with the Cuban crisis.

The two men stood as she reentered the room. Edwina closed the door behind her.

"Please, gentlemen, be seated."

She took her customary easy chair while the two men shared a sofa.

The president was having a hard time focusing on the first major test of her abilities to deal successfully with foreign affairs. She couldn't let go of the fact that her husband had physically brutalized a member of the Senate. If anyone else had done that, he'd be looking at a long sentence in a federal penitentiary. But the way Jim had done it … she had to think he was right. Michaelson wouldn't complain.

The junior senator from Oregon would only work ceaselessly for her political destruction. But he was doing that anyway. Only now he wouldn't do it in a way that involved Andy's memory. Jim had spared her that. God love him.

She loved James J. McGill with all her heart. He'd restored her fully to life after Andy's murder. Jim and his wonderful children, their warm and total acceptance of her, had made her feel something she thought she'd never experience: being a mother.

She was respectful of, and always deferential to, Carolyn when it came to Abbie, Kenny, and Caitie, but when the McGill children hugged her, gave her a peck on the cheek, or shared a whispered confidence, it gave her a sense of joy she hadn't dared to hope for most of her adult life.

And yet there wasn't a day that passed when she didn't think of Andy. When she didn't miss him. When she wouldn't love to have his wise counsel.

It was thinking of what Andy would tell her that had stayed her own hand when it came to Erna Godfrey. Once she was elected president and sworn into office, she could have had the attorney general fast-track that evil woman's appeals of her sentence, expedited her execution. But that wasn't what Andy would have done. He wouldn't have let Patti expose herself to the political criticism that would have come with taking such a course. He wouldn't have risked following a strategy that might allow one of Erna Godfrey's appeals to succeed.

So Patti sat back, refusing all comment on the matter, and let things proceed along their normal course at their normal pace.

A course that Roger Michaelson might have wrecked completely had his plan been allowed to go into effect. So, really, what Jim had done was to maintain the course of events that she and Andy preferred. Ergo, Andy would approve of what Jim had done.

There were moments when she wished she could have both of her husbands holding her and loving her at the same time.

You old Hollywood hedonist, she thought, allowing herself an inward smile.

"Thank you for bearing with me while I gathered my thoughts, gentlemen," the president said. "Please resume. You were about to tell me where we stand."

"The boat's in the water, Madam President," Director Van Owen said.

"A Navy crew is aboard. Army Special Ops teams have joined the exile forces in Central America, ostensibly to upgrade their training," General Fabin said.

"A crew from PBS's *Frontline* will be on hand in the exile camp to do a story on the never-say-die Miami Cubans. If their camera operators don't catch the action, ours will."

The president nodded. "So we'll have our Navy people, in disguise, shooting at our Army people, and our Army people will be shooting back, and everybody will be missing, of course."

"Yes, Madam President," General Fabin said. "But please remember, these will be live rounds being fired, and there will be plenty of them. Mistakes often happen in such situations. People might die."

"All right. I'll have to accept that."

The two men looked at each other, passing a silent message.

Director Van Owen spoke. "We've considered whether a few people *should* die."

"For effect, you mean?" the president asked. "To make things look more real."

"There is that, Madam President," Van Owen said, "and there's another consideration. The four Obregon brothers who blew up the produce market in Havana have returned to Costa Gorda. The FBI informs me they're sure these men are guilty, but they don't think the government will ever be able to make a case against them. National security considerations would prevent the Obregons from being able to question witnesses against them. A judge would have to throw the case out."

"So we should just kill them?" the president wanted to know.

"It's a thought. To discourage freelance terrorism on our dollar ... and to add realism, as you say."

The president's decision came swiftly.

"No. I don't want anyone killed. If an accident happens, that will be regrettable, but nobody is to be executed extra-legally. You're right that these men and others must know that we're not going to let them commit murder while they function under our protection. We'll find some way to make examples of them. A little government intrusion into a private citizen's life goes a long way. With these four, we'll lay it on thick. Make their lives a procession of misery."

The director mused, "Maybe if we make them miserable enough, they'll commit suicide."

Which would be perfectly acceptable, the president thought, but she'd save that line for her own memoirs. "When do we go?" she asked.

"Normally, we like to do such things in the dark," General Fabin answered. "But this time, since we'll have cameras rolling to capture the action, we want as much light as possible. A clear sky and a full moon. That will be in two days, Madam President."

"Very well. I'll give the final go-ahead at that time."

Dismissed, the two men got up to leave. Before he left, though, Director Van Owen told the president that Field Officer Cheveyo's spinal surgery had been successful.

"I'm glad to hear that. Please let me know what he has to say."

Which reminded the president she had yet to talk with SAC Crogher about the incident.

CHAPTER 26

LEO HAD just pulled McGill's car to the curb in front of Chana Lochlan's Georgetown address when Deke turned to McGill, and told him, "SAC Crogher's on the phone for you."

McGill didn't want to wrangle with Celsus at the moment.

"Take a message," he said.

"It's about your family."

McGill grabbed his phone. "What is it?"

"Captain Sullivan of the Evanston PD tried to reach you at the residence. When she learned you were out, she talked to me. Your daughter, Abigail, has been threatened."

Those last six words were filled with a compassion McGill had never suspected Crogher could possess. Still, they chilled him. As did the SAC's terse summary of the threat.

There's nowhere we can't reach you.

But McGill thought: Oh, yes there is.

He instructed Crogher where his children were to be taken immediately.

"That was my idea, too," Crogher told him.

Great, McGill thought, he and Celsus were starting to think alike.

"And their mother?" Crogher asked.

"Her, too. The kids will need her."

McGill didn't think Carolyn would balk.

"And Mr. Enquist?"

Lars. Carolyn's new mate. The gentle man who hadn't liked his wife having a gun. He had a business to run. Responsibilities to the people whose prescriptions he filled. To the people he employed. It wouldn't be easy for him to drop everything, close his doors, and go into hiding.

For that matter, maybe Carolyn would balk. How could she leave Lars? How did she choose between her children and her husband?

In a quieter voice, McGill continued, "The threat is against my children. Their safety comes first. Please *ask* their mother and Mr. Enquist if they would like to accompany Abbie, Kenny, and Caitie. If one or both choose to remain behind, please let them know they will be protected with all the resources we can muster. If they both choose to leave Evanston, reassure Mr. Enquist that we will find the personnel needed to keep his business open."

"Yes, sir."

EAMON LOCHLAN answered the door to his daughter's town house. His face was drained of color except for the large dark circles under his eyes. He was unsteady on his feet, as if he hadn't eaten in too long a time. Perhaps worst of all, an air of guilt hung about him as if he'd committed some misdeed for which there was no redemption.

McGill put a hand around Professor Lochlan's left arm to give him support. Per his custom, Deke was ready to enter the premises first for McGill's safety. But McGill asked Eamon if there was anyone in the house besides him and Chana.

"No," the man answered. Then he added, "Not physically."

The response was suspicious enough that Deke started to slip past McGill. But McGill shook his head, and asked Eamon again, "Just the two of you, you're the only ones here?"

The professor nodded.

McGill told Deke, "You and Leo cover the front and rear entrances. Nobody gets in."

Deke said, "I can't let you—"

"I'm armed, remember?"

Deke did, but he still hated to disregard procedure.

"Sometimes you'll just have to trust me," McGill told him.

He stepped inside with Eamon Lochlan, closing the door behind them. The first thing McGill noted was that Chana Lochlan's immaculate house-keeping had been destroyed. None of the furnishings was damaged, but a rumpled blanket lay across the sofa; glasses filled to different levels with liq-uids of various colors had been left without coasters on tables; used facial tissues were scattered everywhere as if a Kleenex factory had exploded.

"Is Chana in her office?" McGill asked.

"Nan is in the kitchen," Eamon told him.

"*Nan?*"

"That's who she was when I went to answer the door," the professor told him.

MCGILL WAS the first to enter the room. Chana—as far as he could see—was sitting at the kitchen table with a plate of untouched scrambled eggs in front of her. Even from the doorway, the eggs looked cold. Chana, fittingly, looked like she'd never want to eat again.

She sat motionless, her eyes open but giving no sign that she saw him or anything else. He'd seen as much expression in the eyes of murder victims. His first impulse was to call for an ambulance. But Eamon Lochlan squeezed past him and went to his daughter. He dropped to both knees next to where she sat and took her hand. Chana looked down at him.

"Nan," he asked, "is that you?"

"Yes, Daddy."

The voice McGill heard wasn't Chana Lochlan's; it belonged to a very young girl.

"I've brought someone to talk with you."

She looked at McGill, and said, "I don't know him."

McGill moved to the table, sat opposite Chana. He looked right at Chana. Or Nan. He let a small smile form on his face and gestured at the plate of eggs.

"May I," he asked, "if you're not hungry?"

She pushed the plate over to him. McGill picked up the salt and pepper and spiced the food. He wasn't looking at them, but he knew both Loch-lans were watching him. He took his first forkful of eggs. Cold all right but still tasty.

McGill looked up, directed his gaze at Eamon.

"You think I might have a cup of coffee? Maybe a couple pieces of toast."

Eamon Lochlan blinked at the request, as if it had been made in a foreign language. Then he put a hand on the table and got to his feet. He turned a flame on under the coffeepot on the stove and opened a plastic bag of bread.

"Medium on the toasting and butter, okay?" McGill said.

Eamon nodded.

McGill turned to the woman seated opposite him.

"How long have you been Nan?" he asked.

"Always."

"That long? Really?"

She frowned. "Almost. Chana was just saving my place."

Professor Lochlan brought McGill's coffee and toast. Then he retreated.

McGill sipped his coffee, and said, "That's too bad. That you're Nan, I mean."

"Why?" The tone of the little girl voice had turned petulant.

"Because someone asked me to say hello. To Chana."

"Who?"

"Graham Keough."

"I don't know him."

But the look on her face said otherwise.

"He was Chana's first boyfriend."

Nan's denial started to give way.

"Nice guy, Graham," McGill said. "He saved Chana's life."

Remembrance and tears filled the eyes looking at McGill.

"Fact is, he still loves Chana."

She reached across the table and took McGill's hand.

"He does?" Chana asked in her own voice.

"Very much, I'd say. He never found anyone else."

Tears fell from Chana's eyes, and she smiled. Right before she passed out.

MCGILL CARRIED her to the sofa in the living room, put the blanket over her. He checked her pulse. Steady and strong. He lifted her eyelids and shined light from a lamp into her eyes. Her pupils were equal in size and reactive to the light. He was no doctor, but he had one on call.

He phoned Artemus Nicolaides and asked him if he made house calls.

Nick said he'd be there in ten minutes.

McGill went to the front door. Leo was there. He had his gun out, held against the side of his leg. McGill noticed that Leo had the engine of McGill's car running. McGill told him that Dr. Nicolaides would be arriving soon, and he should be let in.

Returning to the living room, he found Professor Lochlan down on his knees again. He was gently stroking his daughter's brow. She was still unconscious. McGill's heart went out to the man.

"She was surprised to see me," Eamon Lochlan told McGill. "Quite happy at first. Less so when I told her my news."

"Is that when all this started?"

Eamon looked up as McGill gestured to the general disarray of the room.

"Not immediately. Chana—at least I think it was Chana—suggested that we go out to dinner to celebrate my good news … and so the two of us could have one last dinner together … just the two of us."

"Where did you go?"

"We didn't. I pleaded fatigue, but that wasn't the real reason. I sensed that Cha—my daughter—was in an emotionally fragile state. I didn't want her to suffer a breakdown in public. Chana being a celebrity of sorts, she shouldn't be exposed to any negative publicity. I know there are photographers lurking everywhere to capture such moments."

McGill, himself, had been warned of that very fact by Press Secretary Aggie Wu.

"So, I suggested that we stay in, and I'd cook for her. I can do more than fix breakfast, and Chana has always enjoyed my cooking. She agreed. Dinner seemed to go well. I thought her spirits were picking up, that she genuinely felt happy for my good fortune."

"What turned things around? Did you ask her about the mysterious phone call?"

"I was just about to when … when Nan appeared."

"Appeared?"

"Made herself known. You heard her voice just now. When I first heard it, I almost fell off my chair. Perhaps it would have been better if I had. Then I could have attributed it to a fall. As it was, I was looking at my daughter and hearing another person's voice come out of her mouth. For one horrible moment, I thought I was going mad."

McGill could understand. If one of his kids started talking in a stranger's voice ...

"It must have been even worse once she identified herself," he said.

Professor Lochlan's voice grew quiet, small. "It was ... Nan. My God, but my heart was an open wound when Nan died. I was torn by grief and rage and a consuming frustration that there was no one upon whom I might take vengeance for my loss."

McGill nodded. "You wanted to see your daughter grow up. Share in her joys, shoulder the burden of her sorrows."

"Yes, yes exactly." Tears coursed from Professor Lochlan's eyes. "And after her death one of my favorite punishments for myself was to imagine in great detail the life Nan would never have."

"Did you share any of those dreams with Chana?"

"No! Of course not."

"Not consciously, you mean. You made no direct comparisons."

"No."

"But you kept Nan's pictures on display because you loved her, and trying to hide the fact of her existence from Chana would only have made things worse."

"Yes."

"And you raised Chana the way you'd started to raise Nan."

"Yes."

McGill sighed. He asked, "Did you and your wife, as educated people, know how similar the meanings of your two daughters' names are?"

Eamon Lochlan's voice was barely a whisper. "Yes."

Undoubtedly, Chana had learned of the similarity. McGill was sure. She knew, probably from a very early age, how much her parents wanted her to be like her sister. Chana had probably imagined the kind of life Nan would have lived, too. Then she took things one step farther. Instead of imitating her deceased sister, she *became* her.

Nan reborn. Chana was only the mask.

She gave her father, the only parent she loved, the greatest gift she could possibly give him. So why, after all this time, was he taking another wife? Wives were treacherous; just look at Mom. Why was her father leaving her?

Eamon Lochlan got to his feet. He took a small vial out of his pocket. The kind with a rubber top used to fill syringes. He handed it to McGill.

McGill read the label aloud: "Ketamine hydrochloride."

He looked to the professor for an explanation.

"I didn't know what it was, either," Lochlan said. "So I Googled it. It's an anesthetic. At least, that's its legitimate use. It's also sold as a street drug called Special K. It's said to produce a dreamy high in small doses; a near-death experience in greater amounts. My daughter has *never* done illegal drugs."

"Then, what?" he asked.

"Nan told me Dr. Todd had been here. Recently. She said he was the one who helped her to *come back.*" A shudder passed through Professor Lochlan. "I want Nan to rest in peace. I want Chana to live with peace of mind. I have to get her away from here. I was going to take her home, but I don't think that's safe. Todd can find us there."

His face, already ashen, twisted in fear. "Oh, God. I've got to get Imogene out of there, too. But where can we go?"

McGill, fortunately, had an answer. He'd send the Lochlan's and Imogene to the same place he was sending his own children.

"I have access to a retreat in the Maryland mountains. Very lovely. Completely secure."

Eamon Lochlan understood exactly where he meant. "You mean—"

"Camp David," McGill said.

CHAPTER 27

SWEETIE HAD in fact said a rosary. She asked not only that McGill's battered body heal quickly, but also implored the Blessed Mother to turn Senator Michaelson's enmity against the president—and now McGill—into tolerance, if not love. She also asked that the joy she'd felt in seeing Michaelson get so badly bruised be turned into compassion for the man.

That was a lot of heavy lifting to ask even for the Mother of God. Especially the last part.

Sweetie had overheard McGill, on any number of occasions, liken her to St. Michael, and she relished the comparison. Nothing pleased her more than doing God's work, but she most enjoyed doing it with muscle. Smiting the ungodly was her thing.

The phone rang. Sweetie was at the office of McGill Investigations, Inc. She thought somebody ought to drop by from time to time. Just in case a would-be client had slipped a message under the door. She answered on the second ring.

"McGill Investigations," she said.

"Is that my favorite tenant?" Putnam Shady asked.

Sweetie rolled her eyes. That was what she got for thinking of herself as angelic. A call from her lawyer-lecher-landlord. God's justice was swift indeed.

"I'm your only tenant, Putnam," she said, "but the rent's not due."

"You wound me, Margaret."

"I'm a terrible person. Something for you to keep in mind."

"Oh, I do. Believe me, I do."

She'd tried to warn him, and all she'd done was stoke his fantasies. Truly, she was being punished for her sins. Still, she liked her apartment.

"There's a reason for this call?" she asked.

"I belong to a gym," he replied.

"Good for you. Try hitting the weights a little harder."

"I have. I'm sore all over. I could use some relief."

"Putnam ..." She was about to say she could really make him hurt, but that would be exactly what he wanted to hear. "Get to the point."

"I was in the locker room after my lunchtime workout and happened to hear the Merriman brothers spewing venom about the senior partner of your firm."

"Wait a minute. Do you work out at Political Muscle?"

"Mmm-hmm."

"And who are the Merriman brothers?"

Her landlord chuckled. "You really need to learn who's who in this town. I'd be happy to teach you."

"Maybe later. Who are they?" Sweetie grabbed a pen to make notes.

"Anson Merriman is a fellow advocate. He's number one on the staff representing the interests of American Aviation to Congress."

"He's a big-shot lobbyist."

"Correct. Much bigger than me."

"And his company does what, make airplanes?"

"Fighter planes, cargo planes, tanker planes, missiles, guidance systems, radar, sundry electronics. Billions of dollars in government contracts. All secured by the efforts of a battalion of lawyers and a like number of retired generals."

Sweetie got all that down in her neat parochial school penmanship.

"Okay, what about the other Merriman?"

"That would be the Big Billy Goat Gruff, Robert Merriman. He's the true source of power in the family. Bob is Senator Roger Michaelson's chief of staff. He's in quite the rage over the beating your friend administered to his boss. He's vowing vengeance."

Then, as if he could read Sweetie's mind, Putnam added, "If you're writing this down, you might want to underline that last point."

WITH HIS boss in the hospital, Robert Merriman received the Reverend Burke Godfrey in Senator Michaelson's office. The better to impress the self-important preacher from down I-95 in Virginia. It didn't keep the televangelist from being snotty, though.

"It rains a lot out there in Oregon, doesn't it?" Godfrey asked.

"Except when there's a drought," Merriman answered.

Godfrey's eyes brightened. "Droughts? I never heard of that, not in the Northwest."

"It happens."

"Maybe that's God telling you people something."

"Or maybe it's part of a naturally recurring weather pattern."

"The weather does what God tells it to do," Godfrey asserted.

"You'd know better than me," Merriman replied.

The preacher pointed a finger at the chief of staff.

"I get enough of my people praying hard enough, maybe we can get God to *flood* that state of yours. Visit it with plagues and torments."

"And that would be your idea of winning friends and influencing people?"

"I don't see any friends! Not around this office. I was told Senator Michaelson is going to lead an effort—a crusade—to free my poor wife from that abomination of a death sentence the government obscenely imposed on her, but wait a minute, brother! The senator gets into a basketball game—*a basketball game!*—with that corrupt former cop who lives in the White House. Senator Michaelson takes a few elbows, and now Erna will just have to suck it up and keep on waitin' to die. That ain't right! Not right at all!"

Robert Merriman prided himself on his ability to deal calmly with whatever jackass stepped into the senator's office. He was sure his equanimity was one of the qualities that would allow him to pluck for himself the next open Senate seat from the great state of Oregon.

"First of all, Reverend," he began, "Senator Michaelson has an abiding love of basketball, starting when he was an all-state player in high school, continuing to when he was an honorable mention all-American in college, and extending to this very day."

Godfrey started to interrupt, but Merriman forestalled him with a raised hand.

"Secondly, if you believe the senator suffered only minor physical insults today, you're seriously mistaken. I won't go into his exact medical condition, but I'd be happy to see if I could arrange a game for *you* and Mr. McGill. See how well you'd fare."

"If that man is doing grievous injury to important people, he ought to be the one in prison, not Erna," Godfrey proclaimed.

"Thirdly," Merriman continued, ignoring the preacher's point, "while Senator Michaelson has reconsidered his view on seeking hearings concerning the confession of Lindell Ricker, he does not intend to forget about the precarious position in which Mrs. Godfrey finds herself."

"He doesn't?" the preacher asked suspiciously. "Well, what's he got in mind?"

"All in good time, Reverend. All in good time."

"Erna doesn't have that much time!"

"She has enough. The president has stayed admirably aloof from the process. Nobody's hurrying things."

"There's nothing admirable about that Hollywood harlot! She's a sinner!"

"And who among us isn't?" If Merriman had to choose whom he'd spend the rest of his life with on a desert island, Godfrey or the president, it would be a no-brainer. "If you're not content to wait for Senator Michaelson to find a productive way to change Mrs. Godfrey's fortunes, you're always free to seek help from your friends, Senator Hurlbert and Representative Langdon. Perhaps *they'd* be willing to take up Lindell Ricker's cause and challenge the legitimacy of his confession. That, or *you* could raise your own voice in protest on the issue."

Godfrey had already been to see both Hurlbert and Langdon. They'd told him that they'd be perfectly willing to support Michaelson's effort, but no way could they lead the charge. The president, after all, was a fellow Republican. They had to have Michaelson to give them the cover of a bipartisan effort. One to which all God-fearing Americans could rally.

As for Godfrey raising the issue himself, people would see that as nothing less than self-interest. But what other choice did he have?

"I guess I'll have to keep raisin' my voice that killin' Erna would be just plain wrong," he said with a bitter taste in his mouth.

"Shout it from the mountaintops," Merriman suggested.

CELSUS CROGHER was on duty, watching Chana Lochlan's house from his car this time, but he was on probation. The president had finally caught up with him and he'd had to admit that he'd choked that CIA dweeb, Cheveyo. He hadn't known, though, that he'd seriously hurt the guy. He hadn't intended that. Geez, did the guy have brittle bones, or what? He remembered reading somewhere that people weren't drinking enough milk, getting enough calcium.

Or maybe he'd gotten a little carried away. Squeezed too hard.

If he'd been capable of admitting to human weakness, maybe he'd have taken advantage of the situation. Used his probationary status to request stress leave. Relax for a while. Except he hated the very idea of relaxation. Taking things easy was one step above being in a vegetative state. Step and a half above being dead.

And there was only one way Celsus Crogher wanted to die: in the line of duty.

So there he was, still on duty, but on a short leash.

He had that asshole McGill to thank for the former. The president, he was pretty sure, had intended to confine his activities to the White House. But McGill wanted him out on the street. Watching for that other son of a bitch, Todd, to come looking for Chana Lochlan.

McGill had considered it a Secret Service job since Todd had been messing with Chana Lochlan's head. And who knew if he hadn't been doing the same thing to someone else who had access to the president. He had to give McGill credit for that. He'd cut right through any potential jurisdictional dispute over who ought to grab this Todd creep.

Problem was, McGill hadn't been sure what the guy looked like. Some pencil-necked academic. Or the muscle head freak that SAC and Cheveyo had seen the other night.

But unless Todd was one helluva cross-dresser, Celsus was pretty sure he didn't look anything like the thirty-something babe with the ash-blonde hair and tight bod who was climbing Chana Lochlan's front steps ... and peeking in her window.

That was suspicious enough for him.

Celsus got out of his car and reached the woman just as she dropped something into the mail slot. When he touched her on the shoulder she jumped and spun around.

"Secret Service, ma'am." He showed her his ID and his best frown. "Please identify yourself and state your business at this domicile."

No cross-dresser, this one, he saw. So not Todd. But who?

The woman swallowed hard and began to speak. Still looking at his ID.

"My name is Laurel Rembert."

She sounded like a kid reciting a line from a school play. He pocketed his ID.

"And the reason you're here?" Crogher said.

"I'm a publicist. I'm the CEO of Starburst Publicity." Still sounded like she was reading from a script. But she mentioned the names of several big-time DC pro jocks as being her clients. Her clothes and jewelry said she had the money to play in that league.

"This is how you solicit clients, Ms. Rembert, going door to door?"

She blinked as if taking a moment to remember her next line.

"A friend told me Ms. Lochlan might want new representation. I ... I dropped by to see if we might chat. I left a business card when no one answered the door."

"You work nearby?" Celsus asked.

"What?"

"You arrived on foot. Do you work nearby?"

"Oh. Yes, I do. Not far at all."

Crogher spoke into the microphone at his wrist. He had four cars of agents within two blocks. One car pulled up seconds later. A special agent got out and opened the door to the backseat. Crogher gestured to Ms. Rembert to descend the stairs and get into the car.

She blinked again.

"Am I under arrest? Did I do something wrong?"

She looked genuinely puzzled.

"Not at all. These agents will take you back to your office. You can tell them about your business. That's all."

"Oh. Well, thank you for the ride."

"You're welcome. Do you have a business card you can spare for me?"

"Why, of course." She fished one out of her purse. Then she frowned. "How can you need publicity if you're in the *Secret* Service?"

"Just a memento, that's all. And sign your name on the back of the card."

Laurel Rembert complied and was driven away by Crogher's agents. When she was gone, and after Crogher scanned the street to make sure nobody else was taking an interest, he let himself into Chana Lochlan's town house with the key McGill had passed on to him. He found the card Ms. Rembert had left for Chana Lochlan.

A note on the back was addressed to someone named Nan. Said: *I'll call.*

And the handwriting wasn't Laurel Rembert's.

CARINA LINBERG had graduated in the top third of her class at the academy. Entirely respectable. Portending a solid military career, barring some personal or political misfortune. But by no means would she have been assured a general's star by the end of her ride. Except she'd been on track to nail one faster than any other woman in Air Force history.

Welborn used his own academic record as a point of comparison. He'd graduated in the top 10 percent of his class, and he knew it was by no means certain that anyone would ever address him as General Yates. Maybe if he'd been able to spend his predesk-jockey years as a fighter pilot, he'd have had a chance. The USAF did love its fighter jocks. But as a gumshoe for the OSI? He didn't see it happening.

Unless the president served two terms and kept him working out of the White House. Then he might conceivably become a general, and a very young one. But he'd be a blatant political beneficiary, and his brother officers would view him with contempt.

He turned his thoughts back to the colonel ... and he couldn't forget the threat Carina had shared with him. She'd better rise in rank faster than the cadets who blamed her for the deaths of their friends, the rapists.

He put that together with the president's speculation that the colonel had been sleeping with General Altman. If that was so, it seemed unlikely he'd have been the first superior officer with whom Carina had traded sexual favors for career advancement. Verifying this notion might be as simple as checking whether anybody else in her intelligence unit at the Pentagon held a similar class rank. If not, how did the powers that be explain her presence in an elite unit?

Not that they'd tell him. Even if the president ordered them to explain themselves, the really bright people, the top one-percenters who belonged there, would concoct some plausible fiction.

The whole situation depressed him. Carina Linberg must have started out as an all-American girl who'd only wanted to serve her country in the Air Force. She couldn't have guessed where that ambition would lead her. Fighting off sexual predators at the academy. Prostituting herself to stay a jump ahead of those same predators. Or maybe just to make a good career move. Go Air Force. Fly high.

There was a knock at his office door. He looked up and saw Kira.

"You want to give me a ride home?" she asked. "Or should I just take my car and leave you to fend for yourself?"

He was at a loss to answer. Kira saw he was not himself and, stepping out of character, took pity on him.

"Come on, let's go," she said. "I'll make dinner for you."

"You can cook?" he asked, surprised.

"Of course, I can. But you're right. We'll order in."

CHAPTER 28

THURSDAY

THEY ATE Thai takeout and went to bed.

Neither one of them would be able to remember later who'd made the first move or if either of them had even said anything about sex. They'd simply eaten their stir-fried chicken with ginger, and their fried dried curry of pork, and drunk their Singha beer, two bottles for her, three for him, and wound up in bed, as if they'd known each other long enough, intimately enough, for such a segue to be automatic.

They went at each other for what seemed like eternity, and was, in fact, hours. Gently, vigorously, manically, flesh was exercised, and demons of longing were exorcised. A final kiss on bruised lips, and they fell asleep in each other's arms.

Waking with the summer sunrise, they looked at each other.

"You haven't been diagnosed with anything terminal, have you?" Kira asked.

"No."

"Or anything contagious?"

"No."

"Good. Then maybe we have a future."

She got up to use the bathroom, pulling the comforter around her

shoulders and striding off like a princess on her way to be
crowned queen. She closed the door, so he didn't have to listen to Her
Highness pee.

Welborn gathered the top sheet around him and snuggled back into the
pillows for more sleep. That idea vanished in the next instant when he
twisted around and sat bolt upright. A series of questions had suddenly
filled his brain.

Who had he seen driving west on Route 50 yesterday?

Captain Dexter Cowan in his unmistakable Dodge Viper.

Had he thought Cowan had been out to visit Carina Linberg?

Yes … but he hadn't gotten the impression of any recent visitors from
the colonel.

What branch of the service was Cowan in?

The Navy.

And if you traveled farther east than Landover on Route 50, you
came to?

Annapolis. And the Naval Academy.

And what crime had happened recently in Annapolis that concerned
him?

The theft of his car.

Had Cowan ever seen Welborn's car before it was stolen?

Yes, when they'd run together at the C & O Canal National
Historic Park.

If Cowan had stolen Welborn's car, what help would he have needed?

Somebody to drive his car while he drove Welborn's.

Where might he find such help?

From a friend, say one who worked at the Naval Academy.

"Welborn, are you all right? Welborn?"

Kira was back. She still had the comforter around her shoulders, but
those were the only points of interest it covered. He pulled her down on
top of him, producing a cry of surprise from Kira. But once the shock of
his impetuosity had passed, she joined in the spirit of the moment. After
they finished, he clasped her to him, their hearts beating fiercely against
each other.

"Do you still hate me?" Kira asked.

"More than ever," Welborn told her. He rolled them over so he could look down into her eyes. "I really want you to believe that."

It took only a second for Kira to accuse him. "You *do* have a terminal disease."

"Well, maybe." He flopped over onto his back so they lay side by side.

Kira levered herself up onto one arm and glared at him. "What's that supposed to mean? Tell me. Tell me right now."

Welborn recounted his visit with Colonel Linberg.

"What's that got to do with us?" Kira asked. She was taking him at his word that he had bypassed Carina Linberg's bedroom.

"I was trying to provoke one of two things: a confession from the colonel or a reaction from ... well, I didn't know who at the time, but I'm pretty sure I do now."

He told her of his suspicions regarding Captain Dexter Cowan.

"He killed Mrs. Altman? Why would he do that?"

"So far it looks like money, and the promise of more."

He told her Cowan was the guy who owned a Viper, and the captain had promised Arlene Cowan a generous divorce settlement.

Kira said, "So if you're right, what kind of reaction do you think you'll get from him?"

Before answering, Welborn fetched and booted up Kira's laptop. He looked up Dexter Cowan's yearbook information from the Naval Academy. The guy had graduated in the *bottom* quartile of his class. Jeez! Who'd *he* have to sleep with—other than Carina Linberg—to get his slot in military intelligence? Was he the guy they sent out for late-night pizza or what?

On the other hand, old Dex had been the captain of the Academy's fencing team, and was further described as a "master of all edged weapons." Great.

Welborn looked at Kira, and said, "I think I might get a pointed reaction. And my terminal disease might be curiosity."

THE SECRET Service hadn't arrested Laurel Rembert the prior afternoon, but with her permission, they'd looked through all her business files. As a result, they learned the value of all the product endorsements of every major sports star in town, as well as what those jocks got paid for each motivational speech they gave. While the numbers were staggering, great fodder for water-cooler conversations, they found absolutely no documentary evidence connecting Ms. Rembert with Damon Todd.

After an hour or so of softening her up by the other agents, SAC Celsus Crogher had joined the investigative effort and come right out and asked Ms. Rembert: "Do you know a man named Damon Todd?"

"Who?" Ms. Rembert replied with doe-eyed innocence.

"Would you be willing to take a lie-detector test?"

"Sure, if that'll help."

The Secret Service men looked at one another. The woman seemed perfectly innocent. Except for a couple of things. When Crogher asked, "Who referred you to Chana Lochlan?" she replied, "I don't remember."

Laurel Rembert had a diploma from Wellesley hanging on her office wall. Her files were in impeccable order. She was a well-educated, well-organized, successful Washington professional woman … and she couldn't remember who'd made a referral?

The gods of networking would not be amused.

"May we look at your BlackBerry?" Crogher asked, seeing it on her desk.

"Absolutely."

She handed it right over and told him her password. No mention of Damon Todd was to be found in the electronic data keeper. No mention of a regular boyfriend either. That didn't seem right to Crogher, either. A relatively young, quite attractive, high-wage-earning, white-collar woman? She should have been planning the merger with, or acquisition of, an equally bankable male. Or female, if her tastes ran that way.

"You're not seeing anyone socially on a regular basis, Ms. Rembert?" Crogher asked.

"I'm far too busy for that," she answered. "Maybe someday."

That was the other big problem, as far as Crogher was concerned. The woman was much too cooperative. Anything they wanted to know was okay with her. Business matters that should have been held as strictly confidential, go right ahead and take a look. A nosy personal question, it didn't ruffle her feathers one little bit.

She should have been telling them to piss off. Come back when you've got a search warrant and a subpoena, buddy. Crogher felt more comfortable when he met resistance.

But she was only too happy to cooperate. So mindlessly sweet she made Crogher's teeth ache. Something just wasn't right, but he couldn't find it.

So he apologized for the intrusion, then sicced Galbreath on her. Galbreath was the best-looking agent who worked for Crogher, a single guy who could talk knowledgably on a wide range of subjects. He possessed a well-rounded personality rare in a man who carried an Uzi to work.

As a gesture of appreciation for her assistance, Crogher told Ms. Rembert, Special Agent Galbreath would be happy to take her to dinner. Instead of telling him to get lost, she didn't need a pity date, she accepted the offer with a smile.

Galbreath took her to dinner, and they went out for drinks afterward. He reported that he couldn't get her to acknowledge knowing a Damon Todd. But she did say she was sure she could get him upwards of a hundred speaking engagements per year once he retired from government service. Corporate executives loved to hear tales of high drama from former federal agents.

DAMON TODD retrieved all this information from Laurel shortly after Galbreath had dropped her at home. The Secret Service agent had been sufficiently decent, or disciplined, not to try to worm his way into Laurel's bed. Debriefing Laurel and reassuring her that she'd handled the situation flawlessly, then bedding her himself, had taken Todd the rest of the night.

He'd sent Laurel to Chana's house after deciding it would be foolish simply to show up at her door himself. He knew for a fact that Professor Lochlan had gone to visit his daughter. Who knew what other parties might be lurking about? The Secret Service, as it turned out.

Reflecting on the situation that morning, he was well pleased with Laurel. He could have implanted in her a combative response to questioning, but that would have dragged things out. Added to the intensity of official inquiry. Todd had decided that sunny cooperation was better; it worked more smoothly with Laurel's naturally friendly disposition as well.

There were, of course, different situations and different personalities where other approaches would produce the optimal results. But he was sure, given the right working environment and a reasonable budget, that he could interrogation-proof any subject who was willing to work with him.

Why couldn't the CIA see that? Where was that blockhead Cheveyo?

Of even greater importance, where was Chana?

Laurel had told him that when she looked through Chana's window she'd gotten the distinct impression that no one was home. Had Eamon Lochlan taken her somewhere?

If so, why? The unsettling answer, of course, was that Daddy had come to his little girl's rescue as he had when she'd suffered her breakdown at UCLA. But that implied that Chana's crafted personality as Nan was continuing its deterioration. Understandable, perhaps, in that she still had questioned her desire to continue her life as Nan during their last session.

Then her damn father had to barge in before Todd and Chana could settle on a new persona. Todd considered whether Eamon Lochlan would take his daughter back to Ohio as he had the last time. He didn't think so. The professor had recently severed all his ties to that part of his life. Professor Lochlan's fiancée had told Todd that they would be married and on their way to Europe within a month. Would he have to look for Chana abroad or—

Or had Professor Lochlan found out that James J. McGill had been mucking around in his daughter's life? Todd doubted that Chana would have told her father about that; it just didn't feel right to him. On the other hand, once you hired a snoop, as Chana had, you had to expect a large circle of snooping to ensue. It was easy for Todd to think that McGill could have injected himself into Chana's family dynamics, learned their history, and even interviewed Eamon Lochlan.

If he'd done the latter in person, gone to Gambier, he could be much too close to learning details about Todd's own life. Before now, Todd had thought he needed to kill McGill. Now, he *wanted* to do it. He remembered the most likely means of access to McGill's office from the night he had cased the building on P Street.

Before he did anything else, though, he had to do a session in the mirror. Self-hypnosis. He didn't want to get caught short. If things went badly, he had to make sure he was interrogation-proof, too.

CHAPTER 29

MCGILL'S KIDS met him at Camp David; Carolyn and Lars stayed home.

"The Secret Service has gone," Carolyn had told him when he'd called her after Abbie, Kenny, and Caitie had arrived safely. "But the FBI is investigating the note that was left in Abbie's school locker. Captain Sullivan's people are still watching us ... and Lars feels a little better about my gun now."

"Helluva situation," McGill told her.

"Yes, it is. Jim, this is all going to be over soon, isn't it? Please tell me it is."

"I'm going to take care of it," he said, "one way or another."

"I'd like to see Camp David, too, under other circumstances."

"We'll work something out. Make it festive."

"The kids will be safe there?"

"Navy people run the place, and Marines guard it. Then there's the Secret Service. And, of course, yours truly, Quick Draw McGill."

"Well, okay. But I'm still going to worry."

MCGILL CALLED Sweetie next. He was pleased to find her at their office. It was nice to know the rent he was paying on that space wasn't entirely going to waste. Sweetie told him about

Putnam Shady overhearing the locker-room threats of the Merriman brothers.

"Yeah, yeah." McGill said. He couldn't get too excited about the idea of *political* retribution at the moment. "What else are they going to say?"

Then it occurred to him that he'd seen the name Merriman before.

"I'm helping Patti out with this Air Force case, did I mention that?"

"The woman colonel accused of adultery? The story that's been in the papers?"

"Yeah."

"No, you didn't tell me."

"Well, I am now. It's all confidential." McGill felt his parish priest would spill the beans on his confessions before Sweetie would ever betray his confidence. "I'm backstopping this junior investigator the Pentagon has assigned to the case. I read the reports he submits to Patti. I remember him mentioning the name Merriman in one of them. It had to do with ... something in connection to the Air Force chief of staff, a guy named Warren Altman, a general of the four-star persuasion.

"Putnam said the Merriman brother who lobbies for American Aviation has a lot of retired generals working with him," Sweetie told him.

"I'll put that word into the kid's ear. But right now you and I have a more urgent problem to handle."

Sweetie knew what it was from the tone of his voice. "Your kids?"

McGill told her about the implicit threat to Abbie and how all three McGill children had been taken to Camp David, how Carolyn and Lars had stayed behind in Evanston.

"If the loonies can't get at the kids," Sweetie said, "they might switch targets. Go after Carolyn and Lars."

"Barbara Sullivan still has her coppers watching them. Carolyn's still armed, and Lars is feeling better about it. Other than that, we can only pray."

"Amen."

"That's only for the moment, however," McGill told her. "We've got to put an end to this horseshit. My kids can't stay holed up in Camp David forever. We've got to do something that will make the other side see there's too high a price to pay here."

"You have any ideas?"

"Other than confronting Burke Godfrey publicly in Lafayette Square? Strangling him with my own two hands? Not at the moment."

"Godfrey's out there marching with the others?" Sweetie asked.

"The Secret Service has pictures." There were more than snipers on the roof of the White House. There were people who shot pictures, too. Hang around outside the Executive Mansion on a regular basis, a file got started on you. Celsus had shown Godfrey's pictures to McGill.

In the silence that followed this tidbit of information, McGill could almost hear Sweetie thinking. He asked, "You got something?"

"Couple of ideas. You don't have to choke Godfrey in the public square. Just give him a little of what Michaelson got. A guy like Godfrey shouldn't be too hard to provoke into throwing the first punch."

"That might satisfy me, but it'd only piss off his toadies worse than they are already. Plus, I've been warned about not beating up anyone else for a while."

"Oh, yeah? Patti tell you that?"

"No, she said thanks for thumping Michaelson. But Galia warned me."

"She's probably right," Sweetie said. "That brings me to my other idea. If you don't mind, *I* could have a little chat with the Reverend Godfrey. Do it in front of his flock. Confront him, and by extension, his whole hypocritical crew on a theological basis."

Sweetie was Abbie's godmother. She loved all of McGill's children, but he knew she felt a special affinity for his eldest. McGill also remembered that things had gone very well indeed when Sweetie debated articles of faith with Lindell Ricker. But that was one-on-one.

Facing off with Godfrey in Lafayette Square, Sweetie might have to confront a mob. She was as formidable a woman as he'd ever known, but he wasn't sure he liked those odds.

"I don't know, Margaret. You couldn't go armed, and if things started to go wrong ..."

"Jim, you've got to have faith. I can do this."

"You can't go alone," he said.

"But you can't come with me."

"No. It'd get out of control fast if we both showed up."

"Maybe I'll bring Putnam for company."

"Your landlord?"

"He's a lawyer: a good witness if I need someone to testify in court."
McGill grunted.

"Jim, do you have a better idea?"

He didn't.

THERE WAS a knock at the door of the room McGill was using in Aspen Lodge—the presidential quarters—and Caitie entered. She had a calculating smile on her face. McGill knew from experience that his youngest was entertaining an idea that appealed to her not-inconsiderable ego. That surmise was confirmed when she came over and sat on his lap.

"This is a pretty cool place, Dad. It's got its own swimming pool."

"Glad you like it."

"Are we gonna be here long?"

"A while. Not too long."

"It's all because of those creeps who scared Abbie, right? Why we're here, I mean."

"Uh-huh." He knew Abbie had shared the note's content with her younger siblings.

"I'd like to go out and get those jerks."

"All by yourself?" McGill asked.

"No. You, me, and Sweetie. We could take 'em."

McGill grinned. This one, he thought, would be a natural for Dark Alley.

"But that's not why you're here right now, is it?"

Caitie shook her head.

"A man on the plane that brought us here was telling us some things about this place. Did you know it wasn't always called Camp David?"

"I seem to have a vague recollection. But I don't remember the earlier name."

"It was called Shangri-La," Caitie told him. "That's what President Franklin D. Roosevelt, who they built this place for, named it."

"Roosevelt being a good Democrat," McGill added.

"The best. He was reelected about a million times. But then President Eisenhower came along and changed the name to Camp David for his grandson."

"Eisenhower being a Republican."

"Yeah! He had a lot of nerve, don't you think?"

"Does seem a bit presumptuous."

"So, I was thinking, if the name can be changed once, why not twice?"

"Let me guess," McGill said. "Camp Caitie?"

His daughter nodded vigorously.

"And you think I might be able to arrange this because I know the president."

"You're *married* to her, Dad."

"So I am, but there's one problem. Just like Eisenhower, Patti is a—"

"Republican."

"And you're a—"

"Democrat!"

"So?"

"So it's *our* turn. The Republicans have had the name long enough."

"I'll talk with the president, Toots, but don't get your hopes up."

Caitie's expression was so hangdog, McGill had to repress a laugh.

"How are your sister and brother settling in?" he asked.

"Abbie's glad to be safe. I peeked at what she's writing in her diary. Kenny's talking to sailors and Marines and Secret Service guys. He's happy."

"And you could go swimming," McGill suggested.

"Yeah." Big whoop, her tone said.

At that moment, McGill had an idea so reckless it sent a shudder through him.

Which scared Caitie enough to make her jump off his lap and stare at him.

"What was *that?*" she asked. "Are you okay, Dad?"

McGill was too wrapped up in his lunatic notion to respond. He only stared at his daughter. No ... no, he couldn't do it. The risk would be too great. Carolyn had a gun; she'd shoot him just for what he was thinking.

And yet ... it might be just the thing that could make the difference.

Really turn things around on the Reverend Burke Godfrey.

Let him and all his zealots see how monstrously evil their plans were.

There had to be a way to do it so Caitie would be safe. Not commit her until the last minute. Not reveal her presence at all if things looked too dangerous.

"Dad, come on, you're getting spooky," Caitie said.

"Honey," he said softly, "how would you like to help Sweetie with something?"

MCGILL TROD Camp David's walking and cycling path alone. It was a perfect summer evening in the Catoctin Mountains. The air was balmy. Birds were chirping. Cicadas were warming up for their evening chorus. Trees of more types than he could name rose all around him. But he had his hands clasped behind his back and his gaze firmly fixed on the ground ahead, noticing none of it.

Caitie had been ecstatic at the idea of going on an adventure with Sweetie, especially when she realized she'd be in Washington while her older brother and sister were stuck in the named-for-an-evil-Republican Camp David. The thought of flying to the capital on a Marine helicopter only made the proposition that much more delicious. Kenny would be *so* jealous.

McGill had firmly warned Caitie not to gloat, or even say a word about the idea to Abbie or Kenny. If she did, the whole thing would be off. That dampened some of Caitie's fun, but she agreed to go along with her father's admonitions. She was gung ho to take part in whatever he and Sweetie had planned.

Only Sweetie didn't know a thing about it yet. Neither did Carolyn or Patti. And McGill was having such serious second thoughts he didn't know if he'd ever tell any of them. Pulling the plug on Caitie would be hard; he'd never intentionally disappointed her in his life. But this time he might have to do it—and risk the wrath his youngest child might direct at him.

Still ... still, he thought it was a good idea. One that could ultimately work to all of his children's benefit if only he could guarantee Caitie's safety.

The sound of a throat being cleared made McGill's head whip around. Celsus was approaching him from behind and soon fell into step with McGill. "Just wanted to check something with you," the SAC said.

"What's that?"

"Do you intend to remain here with your children until the FBI finds whoever it was that left that threatening note?"

"You think they will?"

The FBI was Justice Department; the Secret Service was Treasury Department. The two agencies didn't always play well together. But Celsus nodded.

"They will. Nobody wants to disappoint the president—or you—on this one."

McGill didn't respond to Celsus's original question. He was still mulling things over. The two men continued their trek through the woods.

Celsus filled McGill in on his interrogation of Laurel Rembert. He concluded with, "There's no way she just showed up at Chana Lochlan's house while we were watching."

"No way at all," McGill agreed.

"But there's also no way to dispute what she told us. She agreed to take the lie-detector test without blinking an eye."

"You didn't administer one, however."

"No. You think we should?"

McGill shook his head. "You are watching her residence?"

"Yeah. She's got her own Georgetown town house. Not far from Ms. Lochlan's house. Walking distance. I mean, it's possible she could have gone there for exactly the reason she said."

"But you don't believe that for a minute."

"No." Crogher hesitated a moment as if he had to reprogram the software by which he operated. "The president got the CIA to come through with the information they had about Damon Todd. He's trying to sell them on the idea that he can make their covert agents interrogation-proof."

McGill looked at Crogher. "You think maybe he practiced on people like Laurel Rembert. Tinkered inside her head so she isn't afraid of taking a polygraph test."

"The idea occurred to me. And if Todd had anything to do with Ms. Lochlan ... I don't like to think how many times she got close to Holly G."

"Nor do I. You're checking to see if any other members of the White House press corps might also have known Todd?"

"Very quietly."

McGill nodded. "Don't forget everyone else," he said.

"What do you mean everyone else?"

"Everyone who works in the White House or has regular access to the president."

McGill could see the calculation going on behind Crogher's eyes. Literally hundreds of people worked in the White House every day. From the most famous political appointee—Galia Mindel—to the most obscure custodial engineer—whoever that might be.

All of them had been thoroughly investigated already, but heretofore none of the investigators had known that a connection to a Dr. Damon Todd would be a red flag.

McGill took things one step further. "As long as you'll be looking into political types, check out Nina Barkley, chief legislative aide to the House Minority Leader."

Crogher drew a blank on that name.

McGill told him, "Remember when Lady Godiva galloped on the Mall recently?"

Crogher nodded.

McGill said, "Deke Ky identified her as Nina Barkley. But the very next day Ms. Barkley passed a polygraph test claiming it wasn't her. And that congressman who sang opera, what was his name again?"

The SAC needed a second to plumb his memory. "Brun Fleming."

"Yeah, him. He had no recall of giving the performance that left that old gent dead. That's curious, too, don't you think?"

Crogher did … and he had a new respect for McGill's investigative abilities. Maybe the guy deserved the code name Holmes. Not that he'd ever tell him so. He changed the subject.

"So, are you going to be staying here a while?" Crogher wanted to know.

"No." The Secret Service boss had helped McGill to make up his mind. "I'll be going back to D.C. with my younger daughter, Caitie."

Crogher wasn't happy to hear that.

"I'd asked because Special Agent Ky, being your only protection, doesn't get much time off. He could use some rest."

McGill had never thought of that. He should have. He'd have to find another agent or two he could work with, set up a rotation that wouldn't leave any one agent overly tired. But that would have to wait.

"I need Deke for a very special job," McGill told Crogher.

He was going to entrust him with his daughter's life. If Deke's mother had told him to take a bullet for the President's henchman, he was sure she would want her son to do the same for little Caitlin Rose McGill.

"He can have time off after that," McGill told Crogher.

MCGILL DROPPED in at Rosebud, the guest cabin where the Lochlans and Imogene Lyle were staying. Chana was asleep in one bedroom; Imogene was in the other. Eamon Lochlan was in the sitting room with Artemus Nicolaides, the White House physician. The two men had been talking in quiet voices when McGill made his entrance.

He took a seat, and Nick caught him up on the situation.

"Ms. Lochlan is in good physical health, robust even."

"Her *anorexia athletica* hasn't progressed too far then?" McGill asked.

The physician looked at Eamon Lochlan, who nodded.

"No. I saw no acne, overdevelopment of the jaw, or acquisition of secondary male sex characteristics to indicate the use of steroids or testosterone supplements."

McGill shook his head. "Couldn't have any of that, not when you're billed as the most fabulous face on television. She had to do it the old-fashioned way: gut-busting effort."

Eamon Lochlan sighed deeply.

Nick said, "We were just discussing how this obligatory-exercise compulsion is another manifestation of Chana's need to achieve what she sees as perfection. Another aspect of her quest to become her late sister, Nanette, who, in Chana's mind, embodies perfection."

McGill looked at Eamon. He was on the edge emotionally, but McGill needed to make a point that couldn't be avoided if Chana was to recover. "You're going to tell Chana why Nan wasn't perfect, aren't you, Professor?"

He nodded slowly. "Because she died ... much too young. Her own body betrayed her. Her mother and father couldn't save her." Eamon Lochlan's words were as despairing as the look on his face.

"Yeah, it's too late for Nan." McGill turned back to Nick. "But not for Chana, right?"

"Psychiatry isn't my specialty, but I believe her prognosis is good. Patients with dissociative disorders usually respond well to psychotherapy. Treatment is likely to be lengthy, of course, and many unpleasant memories will inevitably surface, but the eventual outcome should be quite positive."

"With the support of her loved ones, naturally," McGill said.

Eamon looked up.

"Of course," Nick replied. "Family first and foremost. Friends who are significant also."

"And work will help?"

"*Meaningful* work is always therapeutic."

"Did you have something in mind for Chana, Mr. McGill?" Eamon asked. "Other than having her continue with her current job."

"I do. I have to talk to someone first, then I'll let you know. You'll be referring Ms. Lochlan to a specialist, Nick?"

"I've given Professor Lochlan three names. All very good people."

McGill nodded. "I'm sorry for your daughter's troubles, Professor. Your troubles, too."

"Thank you, Mr. McGill. Thank you for everything."

McGill bade the two men good night. His own day was not yet over.

HE LOOKED in on all of his children. Caitie and Kenny were already asleep. He kissed Caitie's cheek and Kenny's forehead. Abbie was reading in bed when he went to see her. *The Secret Life of Bees.* She bookmarked her page as McGill sat on the edge of the bed.

"Good book?" he asked.

"I like it so far. Mom gave it to me."

"Your mother has always had good taste in reading material."

"Mom's going to be safe, isn't she? Lars, too."

McGill nodded. "A lot of Evanston coppers are watching out for them."

"I wish they were here. I feel safe here."

"We're going to take care of things, Abbie. Make it safe everywhere for you guys."

"You mean as safe as anyone can be. The world's still dangerous for normal people."

"Yeah. I'm reconsidering about Dark Alley lessons."

"It'd be a good idea to teach us, Dad."

"But I don't want you to beat up people who only annoy you."

"As if."

McGill grinned and so did Abbie.

"Do you ever miss Mom?" his daughter asked McGill.

He sighed. "I did a lot, at first. I still regret that the two of us couldn't make it work for you, your brother, and your sister."

"But you don't miss her too much now because you have Patti."

McGill nodded.

"I like Patti; she's great," Abbie said. "But I'm sorry, too, that you and Mom couldn't make it work out."

"We still care about each other. We're happy for each other when something good happens. And nothing makes us feel better than seeing things go right for you guys."

"I know. For two divorced people … well, it seems like you shouldn't be divorced. And I know things can be a lot worse. Pam Donovan's mom and dad are still married, and I'll be surprised if they don't kill each other someday."

McGill raised an eyebrow.

"Believe me," Abbie said, "the police know all about them. Pam knows half the force by name they come to her house so often."

"I'm sorry for her," McGill said.

"Yeah, me, too." Sorry enough to change the subject. "Kenny was out walking around with the some of the security people. He said he saw Chana Lochlan, the TV reporter. Is she really here?"

McGill nodded.

"Is she the one who you told me about before? Your client?"

"Yes, but that's still confidential."

"Did you get the man who was bothering her?"

"We know who he is. We'll get him soon."

Abbie took her father's hand. "It won't be dangerous, will it?"

"Everyone will be careful."

McGill leaned over and gave his daughter a hug.

"Good night, honey. Don't read too late."

"I won't." She paused, then told McGill, "Dad, I think I'm going to be a writer. The way things are going, I'll have a lot of stories to tell."

McGill smiled. "That's great."

In Abbie's memoirs, he was sure he'd get a fair shake.

MCGILL SEATED himself in the living room of Aspen Lodge. The Navy house staff was discreetly absent. The windows were open to the cool night air. Stars filled the sky above the treetops. The cicadas had turned up the volume. The phone on the end table next to McGill rang, and he picked it up. Waited for the caller to announce herself.

"I placed my own call tonight," Patti told him. "I just heard about the note that was found in Abbie's locker. I'm very sorry about all this, Jim. It shouldn't be affecting your children."

"Can't argue with that," McGill said, "but it's certainly not your fault or mine."

"Director Haskins assures me the FBI will find whoever's responsible."

"We're going to be a little more proactive than that."

"What do you mean?"

McGill could hear it in her voice. His wife—the president—was worried he was going to take hostile action against Burke Godfrey. So he told her about Sweetie's plan to engage the reverend in spiritual debate in front of his followers. Patti approved of that. Civil discourse. What could be more American?

In fact, she said, "You have to record it. Video."

McGill hadn't thought of that.

"Create a record, just as you did with Lindell Ricker's confession," Patti said. "That way there won't be competing versions of what happened. No chance of revisionism."

McGill agreed with what Patti had to say; he'd also heard what she hadn't said.

"And if by some chance," he told her, "Sweetie gets Godfrey to blurt out that he was part of the conspiracy that took Andy's life, why we've got his confession on camera."

Patti didn't deny it. "You've said Sweetie is very good at this sort of thing."

"She is."

"Then by all means we'll have people with cameras in the crowd."

Visualizing that gave McGill a measure of comfort when it came to the idea of using Caitie. Maybe one of the videographers should be right out front. Because people were much less likely to act criminally when they saw a camera focused on them. He told his idea to Patti.

"Oh," she said. "Oh, Jim, that can't be my call. Only you and Carolyn can decide that, but I have to tell you the idea scares me. I don't know if I could say yes."

"Deke will be there just for her. He won't let anything bad happen.

And if she's exposed to public view for only a few seconds, then whisked away?" McGill heard what he was saying and grimaced. "The best-laid plans, huh?"

"Exactly." But by then, Patti, with her acting background, had been caught up in the idea. "As a piece of theater, though, the revelation of Caitie's presence in the midst of the crowd would be very powerful. Especially if, as you say, her appearance was almost ephemeral. It would be as if the consciences of those present had conjured her. You'd probably get the effect you hope for if it was done right."

There was a brief silence before Patti added, "But you couldn't do it without Carolyn's approval."

"I know," McGill said.

MCGILL HAD no sooner said goodbye to Patti than the chief petty officer who kept the lodge functioning smoothly at night brought McGill an oversized FedEx envelope. The air bill noted the return address of the Honolulu Police Department, Office of Chief of Police Patrick Manuala.

"The Marines brought it with the change of shift, sir," the chief told McGill. "Somebody at the White House thought you'd want to see it."

"Thanks, Chief," McGill said. "I appreciate it."

"Anything else you'd like, sir?"

"No, Chief, that'll be all. Thanks again."

"You're welcome, sir."

Left alone again, McGill opened the envelope. He removed a copy of the police report on the death of Chana Lochlan's ex-husband, Michael Raleigh. On the date in question, Michael Raleigh had rented a hang glider from a recreational outfitting shop called Diamond Head Danny's. The day was windy with swirling gusts buffeting the slopes of the famous extinct volcano. Conditions were such that no other flier had launched a glider that morning. But the deceased had persuaded the business owner, Daniel Akapa, that he was a very experienced flier who could handle the high winds. It was also the last day of Raleigh's honeymoon; his plane was leaving for the mainland that evening. He insisted he had to get in one ride before he went home.

Raleigh had launched his glider without a hitch but only seconds later he'd fallen halfway out of his harness. The glider went into a spiral and crashed into the ocean from an altitude of approximately four hundred feet. Raleigh's body was washed up on the beach, but his glider was never recovered. The police theory of the event was that in a hurry to get airborne, Raleigh had failed to secure his harness properly. Somehow, he'd survived the fall, but the impact with the water knocked him unconscious and he drowned.

The coroner returned a verdict of death by misadventure.

The police report included photographs of the launch site, an aerial view of the ocean from the approximate height of Raleigh's fall, a superimposed indication of an estimate of where he'd entered the water, and, of course, his body on the beach.

McGill had been to Hawaii on a number of occasions. He knew there was no continental shelf off the Islands. The water off the beaches got very deep very fast. If the tide hadn't been coming in when Raleigh hit the water, his body never would have been found. It would have been consumed by sharks or simply lost to the deep.

In addition to the police report, Chief Manuala had sent a personal note to McGill.

I had a nodding acquaintance with Danny Akapa. He'd been in business locally for over twenty years. Rented every sort of recreational equipment a tourist might want: snorkeling gear, surfboards, sailboards, skateboards, roller blades, bicycles, and hang gliders. He was a good guy with a good reputation. Gave to the Police Benevolent Fund and other charities.

It wasn't lost on McGill that Chief Manuala referred to the man in the past tense.

Danny committed suicide about a year after Mr. Raleigh died. Everyone thought it was because of business problems. Things here go up and down with fluctuations in the tourist trade. The family didn't say any different. They sold the business to a Japanese company for what people tell me was a big loss, even considering business was off.

Nobody ever thought there might be any connection to the death of tourist on a day when anyone should have known better than to jump off a cliff, hang glider or no. But since you asked me to look into it, I went out to talk with

Danny's widow, Loni. It was like she'd been waiting all this time to confess.

The muscles in McGill's neck and shoulders tightened.

She said right after Mr. Raleigh crashed, the first thing Danny did—he'd seen the whole thing—was call 911. But right after that, he checked his remaining gliders and found they'd all been tampered with. Every single one. Didn't matter which one Raleigh would have used, they'd all have led to the same ending.

Danny got right on mending them. Never told anyone but his wife. Said if word got out, they'd be out of business. The way things were, he said, people were blaming that dumb a-hole from the mainland, but if they told the truth, people would blame them—for letting someone screw with their equipment if not being in on the crime themselves.

Turned out Danny's conscience wouldn't give him any peace. Then when the economy got soft, and his business fell off, he took it as a judgment. Decided the only way his family would be free of what he'd done was to end it all. After that, Loni didn't want the business either and sold it cheap just to be rid of it.

She told me neither she nor Danny ever had any idea who would sabotage their gliders. I believe her. Sometimes we're a little naive out here, childlike even, in not wanting to believe people can do bad things. Your business is helping people have fun, like Danny's was, who'd mess with that?

Which is just what I hope to find out. We're investigating. Very quietly. You have any ideas for me, Chief McGill, I'd be happy to hear them.

McGill had a name: Damon Todd.

Could be Todd had feared that Michael Raleigh, even remarried, had a continuing emotional hold on Chana Lochlan. Especially if Chana had filed for the divorce at Todd's instigation.

That would fit with the pattern of Chana's never having an enduring relationship with a man after her marriage had ended. Todd would allow her to have transient relationships. That would work with Chana's image of a successful media figure. It would also allow for a perverse equity. Chana could have her lovers because Todd had other women. Say, Laurel Rembert, Nina Barkley, and who knew how many others?

But Raleigh had somehow latched onto Chana, married her, and kept her for three years. Maybe Todd had something really important going on that kept him away from Chana at the time. Hadn't anticipated such a development. But once he'd found out, he couldn't allow anyone to come between him and Chana. And so the divorce. And Raleigh's subsequent remarriage.

But Todd must have wanted Raleigh permanently out of Chana's life. Or else Todd was being vengeful toward a guy who'd won Chana's heart without first having to administer ketamine hydrochloride.

Maybe anyone who'd come between Todd and Chana in a serious way had to die.

Maybe, McGill thought, he was a target, too.

CHAPTER 30

WELBORN ENTERED his office at the White House that morning and found a clue. It had been left smack in the middle of his desk. An unlined index card. On the card printed in black ink and a font he'd later identify as Times New Roman he saw the following:

Robert Merriman
Chief of Staff to Senator Roger Michaelson (D-OR)
Member Senate Armed Services Committee

Anson Merriman.
Chief Lobbyist
American Aviation Corporation

Relationship: Brothers

As even well-intentioned people weren't allowed to drop by the White House and whisper secrets into Welborn's ear, and he was pretty sure the clue fairy hadn't left this gem for him, he felt the card might have noted one more tidbit of information.

Courtesy of: James J. McGill.

The guy was carrying him, at least part of the time. Not that he was going to complain. He stuck the card in his pocket, sat down, and picked up the phone. He called the Courtyard Inn off Route 50 near Landover, Maryland. An operator told him he wanted to talk with their special-events coordinator, Mary Kay Kinsley. She connected him.

"You recently held a jobs seminar," Welborn said. "I believe it was called Command Careers after the Military."

"Yes, we did," Ms. Kinsley said brightly. "Were you a participant? Did you get a great new job?"

"I'm a lieutenant, ma'am. I don't command anyone, and I'm still on active duty."

"Oh. Well, maybe someday."

"Until then," Welborn resumed, "perhaps you can help me with some information."

"Whatever I can."

Welborn asked if anyone representing American Aviation was in attendance at the seminar. Mary Kay looked to see if that was the case.

"Why, yes, a Mr. Anson Merriman."

"Are you allowed to divulge the names of military personnel who participated in the event?"

"I'm really not supposed to. Some of them might change their minds and stay in service, you know."

"And job-hunting wouldn't look good if their commanding officers found out." Hence Colonel Linberg in her civvies. The others, too, no doubt.

"Exactly."

"Thank you very much, Ms. Kinsley."

She told Welborn to stop by the next time he was in the area. He sounded cute, and she'd like to buy him a drink. Welborn thanked her and said he was all but engaged. He intended that as a polite excuse, but he wondered if there wasn't a kernel of truth to it.

With an inward sigh, he thought it would serve him right if Kira was out shopping for a ring right now. Turning his thoughts to more unpleasant matters, he now had a much better understanding of what motivated Captain Dexter Cowan. Someone had convinced him that his charm and good looks had carried him as high in the military as he would ever rise. So why not take a plum job with a defense contractor that would pay him ever so much more money? The signing bonus alone would be enough to set him up in high style, e.g. his Viper. All he had to do to earn his new position was fornicate with the lovely Colonel Linberg—and later accuse her of adultery.

Hardly gentlemanly behavior, but not exactly tough duty.

Only things had gotten complicated as they so often did. Welborn was sure of that. Otherwise, why had Carina Linberg also attended the Command Career seminar? How could she hold down a fancy civilian job if she was serving a sentence for adultery in Fort Leavenworth?

The explanation, as Welborn saw it, was that Captain Cowan had compromised his mission by falling in love with Colonel Linberg. Welborn had damn near done the same thing, and he was only investigating the woman, not sleeping with her. Cowan would have had to be made of titanium to be Carina's lover and not melt under the heat.

So the two of them had planned a double cross of General Altman.

Carina's other lover, as the president saw it.

The general, who'd been on the phone to one of the Merrimans when Welborn had first met him, was also planning for his post-military employment. But now that Welborn thought about it, someone of his rank wouldn't attend a job fair at a roadside hotel. His sinecure would be arranged in a far more elegant and private setting.

"You're thinking again, aren't you?"

Welborn looked up and saw Kira in the doorway.

"One of my failings," he said. "You'll have to get used to it."

"I thought we could go to the mess and get some coffee."

"I have to make a phone call."

"I'll bring the coffee back here."

He wondered if sex would continue to make her solicitous of him. He didn't want to spoil either the sex or the solicitousness but ... "After the call, I have to go out."

"Oh."

She frowned and started to leave, but Welborn caught her before she got away. He kissed her, only briefly, but long enough to raise the eyebrows of two women from the clerical pool who were passing by.

"People will talk," Kira whispered.

"I'm sure they already do."

That possibility scared Kira. She fled. Welborn kept his laughter to himself so he wouldn't raise her ire. Any more than he already had.

He returned to his desk and made his phone call to the Metro police. When the president had removed him from the working structure of the OSI, she'd effectively eliminated any chance he could ask for backup from his own agency. He couldn't pick and choose when he wanted to be one of the guys. But the way things were playing out, he needed to have someone in his corner.

"Lieutenant Bullard," a voice answered his call.

"Lieutenant Welborn Yates calling from the White House."

"Do tell. I was just about to call you. We found your car."

"You did?"

"Yes, indeed. It's being checked by our forensics people right now."

"I think I know who was behind the wheel," Welborn told her.

"And you called to share. How nice."

"I'd like to get together with you, Lieutenant."

"The feeling's mutual, Lieutenant."

BY THE time Welborn got to Annapolis and entered Ruggers, the place was packed for lunch. Most of the diners were civilians of the yuppie stratum, but many were off-duty naval officers. Their haircuts and erect postures, even while seated, were dead give-aways. So was the fact that they hadn't peeled the labels off their bottles of Aviator Lager. Scanning the room, Welborn didn't see Dexter Cowan among their number. Several of the Navy guys and a handful of civilian ladies were looking back at him. Welborn was wearing his Air Force uniform.

A familiar figure waved to him from behind the bar. Carleen. The friendly barmaid who'd warned him of the impending arrival of the TV crew on his last visit. She pointed out an empty seat at the bar to him. He quickly crossed the room before anyone else could claim it.

"How you doin', honey?" she asked. "Leave that little redhead at home today?"

"She's darning my socks," Welborn said.

Carleen laughed. "Not her. I know the type. Suck your tocs, yeah.

Darn your socks, no."

Carleen asked, "Get you a beer and a burger? Or you want a menu?"

"I'm working today, came here hoping to find you."

He was seated between the station where the waitresses picked up their drink orders and a civilian couple who only had eyes for each other. Meanwhile, Carleen was giving him the eye, trying to determine the nature of his interest before she said the wrong thing.

He helped her out. Put a headshot of Captain Cowan on the bar.

"This guy come in here by any chance?"

"Dex? He's been coming here for years. Anytime he's nearby and off duty."

"Life of the party?"

"As often as not."

"So he has friends who come here, too."

"Sure."

"Any of them here now? I'm interested in anyone who's a close buddy."

Carleen was getting the idea by now that this could be serious and frowned.

"Is Dex in trouble?" She looked at his picture again.

From her tone of her voice and the way she looked at the photo, Welborn knew that Carleen's feelings for Cowan were based on his being more than a good tipper. Neither Arlene Cowan nor Carina Linberg was a sweet, simple girl, but Carleen fit the bill perfectly. He put the picture away.

"I'm afraid he is," Welborn said.

"He's a good guy," Carleen asserted.

"In many ways, I'm sure he is," Welborn agreed.

"Is it *really* bad?"

"I suspect there are people grieving." Assuming Mrs. Altman had family.

"Well, shit." Carleen's chin quivered. "The guy you want is right over there."

She nodded in the direction of a booth against the far wall. Three Navy men, two on one side of the table, single guy on the other. All three had their eyes on Welborn.

"The one by himself," Carleen said. "His name's Tony Sheridan. Dex's best friend."

"Rank?"

"Commander."

"The other two?"

"A pair of lieutenant commanders." Welborn didn't insult Carleen by leaving money for the information. He simply said he was sorry for her pain and thanked her for her help. Then he crossed the room. Sheridan and friends never took their eyes off of him.

Welborn stopped in front of their booth and showed them his ID. "Gentlemen," he said, "I'm Lieutenant Welborn Yates, Air Force OSI. I'm sorry to interrupt your lunch."

"Then make it brief," one of the Navy subordinates told him crisply.

Welborn ignored the tone. "Commander Sheridan, I need you to come with me, sir."

"Why is that, Lieutenant?" Sheridan asked.

"For questioning, sir."

Both of the commander's companions glared at Welborn.

Other diners were starting to look at them as well.

"Regarding what?"

Sheridan was doing a nice job of keeping his voice down, but the volume of conversation in the restaurant was dropping, too. A drama was being acted out, and people were paying attention. There wasn't even any clank-ing of silverware.

"Regarding a homicide, sir, and your possible role in it."

"Just a goddamn minute, buddy!" The lieutenant commander nearest Welborn started to rise. Welborn shoved him back onto his seat.

Looking at the man, taking control of the situation as he'd been taught at Glynco, he told the Navy officer, "Right now, you're not involved in this, sir. But please remember, I'm a sworn federal agent. Try to interfere with me again, and I'll arrest you. Your military career will be over."

As his table companions glared at Welborn, Sheridan got to his feet.

"Put a hand on me, Lieutenant, I'll file charges against *you*. I'll get my attorney, then report to your office with him. I imagine we'll have an in-teresting conversation with your commanding officer. Where do you work, Andrews?"

"No, sir," Welborn told him. "I work at the White House, but I don't know that the president will have time to see you."

Sheridan paled, realizing he was in more trouble than he could have imagined. He muttered an expletive and started for the door. Welborn didn't chase, he followed. Certain that Sheridan's demeanor betrayed an awareness of guilt, his own.

Outside Ruggers's door, Rockelle Bullard was waiting with a pair of Maryland state troopers. They brought Sheridan up short. Welborn took his arm from behind.

"You're in a *world* of hurt, Commander," he said. "Unless, of course, you choose to cooperate with me and with Lieutenant Bullard of Washington Metro Homicide. You think you might like to do that, sir? So I won't have to arrest you here and now?"

The fight had gone out of the man. He rode back to Washington without saying a word, but he heard Rockelle tell Welborn, "You were right about Captain Cowan. We found his fingerprints in your car. He wiped the steering wheel and the door latches but he forgot the rear view mirror."

"IT WAS all a joke," Sheridan said. "That's what Dex told me." Having been Mirandized, he was making his statement in front of a video cam in a Metro PD interrogation room.

"The joke was on me?" Welborn asked. "It was my car."

"Dex didn't give me a name. He just said it was some Air Force twerp."

Welborn didn't bat an eye at the slur.

"That's why I was keeping an eye on you at Ruggers today," Sheridan continued. "Your uniform, I thought you might be the guy, and you didn't look like you thought the joke was funny."

"Grand theft auto's a felony," Rockelle pointed out. "And if you knew Captain Cowan was going to steal a car, didn't matter whose it was. You're an accessory."

The commander's face tightened. "Look, I didn't think Dex was going to *keep* the damn car. It was just a shitty little Honda; he has a Viper, for God's sake. I thought he'd let the guy sweat it for a few days then tell him where could find his car. *That's* a felony?"

"Yes, it is," Rockelle answered. "Some jokes you don't get to play on people."

Welborn asked, "Did Cowan say why he wanted to play this joke?"

Sheridan looked mad at himself. "He said he was out running with you, and you made him look bad. How's that for stupid?"

"You or him?" Rockelle wanted to know.

"Both."

"He never mentioned any other reason?" Welborn asked.

"No."

"You're aware of Captain Cowan's role in the investigation of Colonel Carina Linberg for the possible bringing of a charge of adultery?"

Sheridan folded his arms across his chest. "I know Dex was scr ... having relations with her."

"Did he tell the colonel from the outset that he is a married man?" Welborn asked.

"I don't know," Sheridan said.

"Was Captain Cowan aware that he was sharing Colonel Linberg with another lover, another military officer?"

That one caught Sheridan by surprise. He laughed.

"Dex Cowan share a woman with another man?"

"His wife was sharing him with another woman, albeit unknowingly. At least initially."

"Yeah, well, that'd be the only way Dex would share, too. Unknowingly. If he found out different, he'd break it off."

"Even if he'd come to have feelings for the woman?" Welborn asked.

"Feelings are what you maybe have for your wife, not for your ... you know."

"You boys musta had different wedding vows than I did," Rockelle said dryly.

"Did you know that Captain Cowan was resigning from the Navy?" Welborn asked.

"Yes ... he's going to work for American Aviation. That's how he got the money for the Viper."

"Nice car. You must've enjoyed driving it. Is that why you helped him?"

"Damn right. I thought we were just having a little fun."

"Would you have done it if he'd asked you to drive my car?"

"He did. I told him no. I was going to drive his car or forget it."

"How do you think Captain Cowan got his new civilian job?"

Sheridan smirked. "Same way he gets everything. Somebody did him a favor. Thing is, men are almost as easy as women for Dex. To charm, I mean. People just like him. He's good-looking, he's smooth. You could be Don Juan on his leftovers. I know for a fact he's set up superior officers with some of the best-looking women they ever had. His reputation is service wide. Hell, I'd be surprised if the *Boy Scouts* didn't know about him."

"He's helped you find companionship, too?"

The commander's smile grew smugger. "Yeah, he has."

Welborn looked over at Rockelle and she popped the $64,000 question.

"So, why would he want to kill Cheryl Altman with Lieutenant Yates's car?"

Sheridan's smile vanished, and his face got tight again. "I don't know anything about that. You think I'm going to help somebody commit murder just so I can drive his car?"

"And eat his leftovers," Rockelle said. "Maybe Captain Cowan promised you something else, too. Like your own fancy civilian job."

Sheridan denied it. But while the homicide detective and the commander matched stares, Welborn thought maybe a big-money job was exactly the promise Cowan had made to Carina Linberg. Sure would explain why she was at that Command Careers seminar.

In the same room with Anson Merriman.

WELBORN LEFT Commander Sheridan in Rockelle Bullard's safekeeping for the time being and returned to his office at the White House. He tried to reach Cowan at his Pentagon office and at his home in Virginia. He didn't pick up at either place. Next, Welborn tapped out Carina Linberg's home phone number. He half expected that she wouldn't answer either, and he'd have to make the drive out to—

She answered on the sixth ring. "Hello."

"Colonel Linberg, this is Lieutenant Yates calling from the White House."

"Always a pleasure, Lieutenant," she responded dryly, "wherever you're calling from."

"Yes, ma'am. Have you seen Captain Dexter Cowan recently?"

"No."

"Do you know where I can find him?"

"No."

"And you do remember, ma'am, that it's a crime to lie to a federal officer?"

"Oh, yes. I'm very clear on that."

Welborn frowned, trying to decide to what extent Carina Linberg had been working with Dexter Cowan. To what extent, if any, he should trust her.

"Ma'am, I must advise you to call me promptly should you hear from Captain Cowan or should he approach you. Failure to do so would only add to your troubles."

"Well, I certainly wouldn't want that, would I?"

"No, ma'am."

"Would you care to tell me your interest in finding the captain?"

"No, ma'am."

"Will that be all, Lieutenant?"

"One more thing, ma'am. Please remember you're under orders not to leave the area."

She hung up on him.

CHAPTER 31

KENNY MCGILL was seriously aggrieved that his younger sister was going to get a ride in a Marine helicopter to Washington, and he wasn't. For her part, Abbie McGill told her father that she would feel less comfortable with his leaving her behind at Camp David even though she knew she would continue to be safe from those who wished to do her harm.

McGill had told his two older children a lie.

"Caitie has a toothache."

His youngest was already aboard the helicopter. McGill didn't trust her not to give away the deceit by taunting her brother. Then he'd have to take all his children along.

"And this place doesn't have its own dentist?" Kenny asked.

"An oversight. I'm sure Patti will have it corrected it shortly."

"I still want to go," his son said.

"You can't."

"I won't mind sitting out in the waiting room."

McGill sighed. "Kenny, did you know this place does have a skeet-shooting range?"

"What's that?"

McGill told him. Kenny beamed. "You'd let me shoot a shotgun?"

"At clay pigeons only. I'll tell the range master to expect you after breakfast."

"Thanks, Dad. That's way cooler than going to some old dentist."

But Kenny still wanted to ride on the Marine helicopter sometime.

As for Abbie, he could only give her a hug.

"We'll be back as soon as we can, honey. We'll work it out so all you guys can go home soon and not have to worry."

Abbie's arms tightened around her father. "You know how Mom used to worry about you all the time, Dad?"

Abbie was the only one of his children old enough to know about that.

"Yeah."

"She still does. I do, too."

McGill kissed the top of his daughter's head and told her he had to go.

THE SIKORSKY Sea King, part of Marine Helicopter Squadron One, took off with a roar. Both McGill and Caitie were looking out windows and waving good-bye to Abbie and Kenny. In seconds they were out of sight as the machine rose into the sky, and the sweep of the Catoctin forest hid Camp David.

Reclining in the oversized leather seat that was normally the province of the president of the United States, Caitie asked, "Did they buy it, Dad? The toothache story."

"I think so. They're not used to hearing lies from their father."

That concept didn't seem to bother Caitie—as long as it wasn't used to her disadvantage. She wriggled her bottom on the plush seat and looked around the cabin of the aircraft. McGill could almost see the idea form in his daughter's mind that one day she would have such perquisites of power for her own.

Looking back at him, she asked, "Dad, you're somebody special these days, aren't you?"

"I'm just along for the ride. Patti's the special one."

An honest answer and suitably humble, but he feared he was only cementing his little megalomaniac's ambitions. Caitie's nod confirmed it. He could only hope she'd develop a taste for tattoos and body piercings that would make her unacceptable to the voting public.

"We need to talk, you and me," McGill told her.

"About what?"

"I told you I want you to help Sweetie, but I didn't tell you how."

"I don't care. I'll do anything."

"It could be dangerous."

Caitie grinned, as if he'd sprinkled sugar on her favorite cereal.

"And your mother could still veto the whole thing."

"Daaad … we won't tell her."

"You might want to change your mind, too."

"Uh-uh."

"Listen, then tell me what you think." He held up a hand to wave off another denial of anything but eagerness to participate. "You know the people who've threatened Abbie and Kenny and you? They're the ones Sweetie plans to confront."

"She's gonna *bash* them?" Caitie's eyes grew wide at the prospect.

"She's going to make them see the light of reason."

His bloodthirsty imp's glee disappeared. "What fun is that?"

"Grown-up fun. The kind Patti and I, and maybe your mom, can get behind."

"You mean Sweetie's only going to *talk* to them?"

"She's going to talk to them forcefully. It should be very interesting."

"I don't see how."

McGill considered his words carefully and hoped none of the helicopter's crew had family or friends in Reverend Godfrey's movement. Just to be safe, he leaned forward and dropped his voice. "You remember *The Lion King?*"

"Yeah, of course. But I haven't watched it in a long time." The animated classic had become far too jejune for the sophisticated Ms. McGill.

"There's a scene near the end," McGill said, "where Scar is facing off against all the hyenas? It could be like that. Where Sweetie's the only lion around."

"But Scar was the bad guy, and Sweetie is a good guy," Caitie said, finding the flaw in her father's cinematic analogy.

"Right, Sweetie's the good guy."

"But the hyenas are still the bad guys?"

"Right again. The point I was trying to make was you should remember how that scene in the movie ended for that particular lion."

Caitie did, and her enthusiasm waned. "Oh."

"Now, I'm not saying that's how it'll happen this time, only that there's an element of danger. For you, too, if you decide to join in."

"Well …" His daughter was much more deliberate now. Which he found very reassuring. "… what would I have to do?"

"Just show your face. Only for a few seconds."

"That's it?"

"Yes, and Deke will be right behind you. If anything goes wrong, he'll grab you and get you out of there fast."

"*You* won't be there?"

That was McGill's original plan. Not to give Godfrey and his minions anything more than Sweetie to inflame their passions. But he could see now that like his movie analogy, this, too, was imperfect thinking. No way was he going to let Caitie go out there without him. No disrespect to Deke, but McGill just wouldn't be able to do it.

"Of course, I'll be there. But I'm going to have to hang back a little ways. Keep my presence a secret." As ever in Washington, compromise was a must.

"Then it will be you, me, and Sweetie against the bad guys."

"And Deke, too."

Caitie stuck out her hand for McGill to shake.

"Count me in, Dad."

McGill pulled his daughter onto his lap. Held her close.

"If your mother says okay," he told her.

THE INTERCOM on the president's desk buzzed.

"Mr. McGill and Caitlin have arrived. They're in the residence, Madam President."

"Thank you, Edwina," the president told her secretary. "Would you ask Jim if he can spare a few minutes for me now? Please tell Caitie hello for me and ask Blessing to find something to keep her amused while her father's in the Oval Office."

"Yes, ma'am."

Welborn Yates, who'd just spent the past fifteen minutes briefing the president on his investigation, got to his feet and saluted. The president looked at him with a bemused smile.

"You have pressing business elsewhere, Lieutenant?"

Welborn's cheeks reddened. "Ma'am, I ... I thought I was being dismissed ... as you've sent for Mr. McGill."

The president shook her head. "I thought I'd introduce you. The two of you haven't met, have you?"

"Only informally, in passing one day."

Welborn felt like a complete idiot and was relieved when the president asked him to sit down and turned her attention to the notes she'd made on his briefing until her husband arrived. Whereupon he got smartly to his feet once more and saluted McGill.

Who grinned and returned the salute.

"I think we can dispense with that courtesy from now on," McGill told him.

"Jim, allow me to introduce Lieutenant Welborn Yates, United States Air Force, Office of Special Investigations. Lieutenant, this is my husband, James J. McGill."

The two men shook hands.

"A pleasure, sir," Welborn said.

"Likewise," McGill responded.

They looked each other in the eye, both of them knowing the relationship they had, one helping the other, but neither so much as winked at it.

"Now you may leave, Lieutenant," the president told him.

Welborn snapped off his best salute, did a perfect about-face, and left.

After he closed the door, McGill said, "Nice kid, but a little intense."

"He's young, he's nervous, and I'm the big boss."

McGill sat down opposite his wife. "Sometimes I forget."

"Of course. You've never been in awe of me."

"Oh, there *are* times. If I'm allowed to say that in the Oval Office."

Patti gave him a grin. "It' perfectly all right. No president since Nixon has made recordings in here." Changing the subject, she asked, "So you've decided to let Caitie participate with Sweetie?"

"From my point of view, and Caitie's, yes. I wasn't able to reach Carolyn just now. She and Lars decided to get out of town for a couple days. Barbara Sullivan tells me they've gone up to Wisconsin by themselves. I know where Carolyn likes to stay. I'll try her again in a couple of hours."

"Abbie and Kenny are fine at Camp David?"

"They'd be finer if Carolyn or I was there. They're feeling a bit isolated."

Patti hesitated a moment before asking, "Would it help, do you think, if I went up and spent the night with them?"

McGill beamed … then he thought the question through.

"They'd be thrilled. But why do *you* need to get out of town?"

Patti told him what she had planned for Cuba and that the balloon was about to go up. "For appearances' sake," she continued, "I thought it would look better if I wasn't at the White House when the action commences."

McGill nodded. "I think you're right about that."

"And my plan?" Patti asked.

"Outside my area of expertise, but I'll light a candle."

"When you light one for Caitie and Sweetie?"

"Exactly."

"You're sure the kids will want me at Camp David? I won't be a poor substitute?"

It amazed McGill that the most powerful woman in the world, one of the richest and most beautiful women in the world, could still find something about which she felt insecure. But he kept the thought to himself.

"My children love you," he told her. "So much so that at least in your heart, if nowhere else, you should think of them as your children, too."

The president suddenly had to clear her throat and look away. When she turned back to McGill, there was a smile on her face. "I'll go to Camp David then."

"And if the brats give you any guff, spank the hell out of them."

Patti and McGill both laughed.

"I understand you've also lodged Ms. Lochlan at Camp David. So she's not a threat to my welfare, after all?" McGill told Patti what had happened to Chana. "Poor woman," Patti said.

That matter settled, Patti recounted for McGill the briefing Welborn had given her.

"Wow," McGill said, "talk about your tangled web."

"And how would you sort it out, my dear private detective husband?"

McGill let his eyes lose focus for a moment as he reviewed and sorted the facts. Bringing his attention back to Patti, he said, "Let's start from the beginning."

"A logical place."

"The Air Force is considering bringing a charge of adultery against Colonel Linberg for having sex with Captain Cowan, a married man."

"Correct."

"The colonel admits the sexual relationship but says the captain told her he was divorced."

"Also correct."

"General Altman, the Air Force chief of staff, is pushing for Colonel Linberg's court-martial. We suspect, but don't know, that the general may also have had a sexual relationship with the colonel. That suspicion, however, becomes stronger with the death of Mrs. Altman, allegedly at the hands of Captain Cowan."

"Cowan killed Mrs. Altman before she could spill the beans on her husband to Lieutenant Yates. That's Welborn's thinking."

"It's a natural enough assumption," McGill said. "On the other hand..."

He lapsed back into rumination. Patti waited him out in silence.

"Let's remember what this Commander Sheridan, the friend of Cowan's, said. He said the captain would never knowingly share a woman with another man. Do you think General Altman would knowingly share a lover with Cowan?"

Patti shook her head. "I don't see that."

"Then if Altman had been sleeping with the colonel, the affair was over. And he'd have to be a pretty vengeful guy to push an adultery charge against a *former* lover, don't you think?"

"Yes, he would. But push it he did. So something had to be motivating him." Then Patti saw what McGill was getting at.

He nodded. "What if Colonel Linberg had been sleeping with *Mrs.* Altman to get ahead?"

"Oh, my," the president said. "That certainly would have embarrassed the general once it got out."

"Not to mention the Air Force," McGill added.

"But why would she have done it?"

"Mrs. Altman? Sleep with the colonel?" McGill shrugged. "She found her alluring. Possibly, she was following her husband's example. Sleeping with comely junior officers. Be a heckuva way for a senior military wife to get even with a wandering husband. Especially if Mrs. Altman was also blackmailing the general into advancing the colonel's career."

"All right, but then why would Mrs. Altman want to confess? Why did she set up that lunch date with Welborn?"

McGill had a notion. "The general wants to break up his wife's relationship with the colonel by sending the colonel to prison. So he brings in Captain Cowan. That punishes his wife in two ways. It shows Mrs. Altman just what a tramp Colonel Linberg is, and it sends Mrs. Altman's lover off to languish in durance vile. Mrs. Altman doesn't want her husband to win. So she plans the unthinkable: going public. She'll have to reveal her own sins, but she'll have the pleasure of ruining her husband. Her mistake was letting the general find out what she was about to do."

"And he couldn't let that happen," Patti said.

"No."

"So he turns to Cowan, whom he's sponsoring for a cushy job with American Aviation, to get rid of her—and possibly incriminate the pesky Lieutenant Yates. Or at least get him thrown off the case so he can bring in another investigator who will be under his control."

"Yeah," McGill said.

"But there's a hole in your theory, Jim. Even with Cheryl Altman gone, Colonel Linberg, could still testify against General Altman if she was really his wife's lover. She could still embarrass both him and the Air Force. Why wouldn't the colonel just preempt the possibility of facing a court-martial by saying she'd reveal her affair with Mrs. Altman?"

McGill had considered that. "If she made that threat to General Altman up front, she'd be *confessing* to adultery. Cheryl Altman was, after all, a married woman. Plus she'd be admitting a lesbian relationship, and as far as I know, the military still frowns on homosexuality. She might have relied initially on Mrs. Altman to keep her from anything worse than being discharged from the Air Force. But then for further protection, the alluring Colonel Linberg gets Captain Cowan to fall in love with her. He double-crosses the general. He plans not to testify against the colonel but to take her along with him to enjoy gainful employment in the defense industry. How can the general object without risking that Cowan, too, will turn against him?"

"And I thought I'd seen it all in Hollywood," Patti said. "And the American Aviation connection tells us that Roger Michaelson is also involved in this mess through the Merriman brothers."

"A fine Washington stew, indeed," McGill said. "But to confirm *any* of it, you'll have to get Cowan talking."

"Lieutenant Yates intends to arrest him today," Patti said.

DAMON TODD had a new plan for James J. McGill. Death was no longer enough for the man who'd come between him and Chana. He had a much better idea now. He would send McGill deeper into a K-hole than he'd ever sent anyone. When he pulled him out the other side he would know all of McGill's secrets, understand how the man was put together. With that knowledge in hand he would twist the fundamentals of McGill's personality.

If McGill had moments of temper, they would become fits of maniacal rage. If he had a suspicious nature, he would become an unrelenting paranoiac. If he had restless nights, he would experience debilitating insomnia.

The possibilities were endless. Everyone had weaknesses. Extending those flaws, amplifying them, would be no harder for him than getting a rock to roll downhill. True, he'd never worked in a destructive fashion before, but that's what these people, McGill especially, had driven him to. Maybe he should thank them.

Because messing with people's heads would be a lot more fun than sorting out their conflicts, defining their goals, winding them up, and sending them off down productive paths they never could have found on their own.

That ungrateful bitch Chana.

There was only one problem with his plan. The means he'd found for getting into McGill's P Street office, the place Todd intended to ambush him, had been taken away from him.

On the night he'd first cased the building, he'd gone around to the rear and easily clambered up a sturdy drainpipe to the roof. He found a door there that opened to his touch. A stairway from the roof led to a landing and two doorways. Directly ahead was a door that opened to the hallway outside the office of McGill Investigations, Inc. To the right of the landing was another door to the same suite. That door was locked, but it was also concealed from public view. Todd was sure he could quietly force it open.

Last night, however, he'd gone back to make sure he could still gain access from the roof. But he couldn't. Some cretin had put a sturdy new lock on the roof door.

As he strolled along P Street in the early-morning sunlight, he saw the very man who might have been responsible for creating that problem. He was dark-haired, with a prominent nose and an olive complexion. Fortyish and fairly large but soft. He was placing chairs around the café table in front of McGill's office building. The man had just opened a Cinzano parasol above the table when Todd stopped a few feet away from him.

Todd was wearing a loosely cut long-sleeve white dress shirt and relaxed-fit khaki slacks. A pair of clear-lens glasses rested on the bridge of his nose. The clothing hid his musculature; the specs gave him a professorial air. The dark-haired man smiled when he saw Todd.

"Good morning to you, sir."

"Good morning," Todd replied genially. "Are you the caretaker of this lovely building?"

"No, sir. I am the owner. Dikran Missirian."

"Well, good for you." He'd been right. The prick who'd put the lock on. "I'm new to town. Just found a place to live nearby. Now, I'm looking for office space."

"I am sorry, sir. I have no space here. But may I ask what is your business?"

"I do medical-research grant referrals."

"I am sorry. You are a doctor?"

"Yes, I am. But I don't see patients. When other physicians are seeking money from the government to do research, they call me. I find the most likely source of funding for them, usually from the government but sometimes from the private sector. I guess that's a long way of saying I'm a consultant."

Todd was making it up as he went along, but he wouldn't be surprised if people actually did what he'd just described. It sounded useful enough. Certainly respectable and lucrative enough to appeal to a commercial landlord. And he was right again.

"I have another building," Dikki said. "Quite close, a few blocks away only."

"As nice as this one?" Todd asked, playing out his role.

"Much the same. Right now it's being renovated. Workmen very busy, done soon."

Todd glanced at the list of tenants on the outside of the P Street building.

"I notice you have an accounting firm here."

"Wentworth and Willoughby, yes. Very fine people."

"I'll need new accountants. Do they handle your business?"

Missirian's smile vanished. "I am sorry. I talk about this only with my wife and God."

"A wise practice, I'm sure. Would it be all right if I took a peek inside, since your workmen are busy at your other building?"

"No one is here yet, and I cannot let you into their offices, of course. But if you wish to see the common areas ..." Dikki shrugged.

"That would be fine."

The two men walked up and down the stairs. Dikki didn't comment on having the president's husband as a tenant when they reached the third floor, and neither did Todd. Back on the ground floor, though, Todd asked, "It's just the three firms here then?"

"I have a small office at the back of this floor."

"So, I could contact you there if I decide to look at your other building?"

"Yes, of course. I am here until five thirty." He deftly pulled a card out of his shirt pocket. "If you need to talk to me later than that, please use my cell phone. I write down address of other building so you can see it from outside." He wrote the information on the back of the card.

Todd put it into his own shirt pocket.

"Thank you for your time, Mr. Missirian."

"I am happy to help. And your name please, Doctor?"

"Casey," Todd told him, "Benjamin Casey."

He couldn't imagine that an obvious immigrant like Missirian would know the old TV show. It was one of two names that had popped into his head. He'd always liked Ben Casey better than Dr. Kildare. Ben had more muscle.

DARYL CHEVEYO woke up to find he'd fallen asleep in a sitting position. A baseball game was being played on a television in front of him. Both circumstances were very strange. He never slept in chairs, and he didn't like baseball. Glancing up he saw something silver and shiny encircling his head. He reached for the object with his hands and touched it gently.

He knew what it was as soon as he did: a halo brace. Used to stabilize cervical spine injuries. Which explained why he'd slept in a semi-upright position. Couldn't have weight bearing down on a neck injury.

Had he had surgery? Couldn't remember, but the brace would seem to indic—

The TV blinked off, and he saw the doctor at his bedside.

"Hope the game didn't disturb you," the doctor said.

"No ... I don't think so."

His throat was terribly dry. The doctor heard the raspiness in his voice and gave him water to sip through a straw. He let Cheveyo hold the plastic cup.

"You can move your hands, I see. How about your lower extremities, do you feel your legs, feet, and toes?"

Cheveyo tried to look down, but the halo wouldn't let him.

"Try a few small movements," the doctor said. "You'll know if you succeed. No need to look. Keep your head and neck still."

He wiggled his toes. At least he thought he did.

"Very good," the doctor said. "Can you flex your knees slightly. A little's enough."

Cheveyo managed the feat without difficulty. Tried not to let the relief he felt show. The doctor obviously had concerns that he might be paralyzed.

The doctor took the cup from Cheveyo after waiting for him to take another sip.

"Looks like you're going to be all right. You'll have to take it easy for several weeks, of course, to protect your neck. Then there will be a few months of rehabilitation. All in all, though, you should be able to resume most of your normal activities."

Cheveyo managed to smile.

"You want the ball game back on?" the doctor asked.

"No, no thank you. Some more water, please."

The doctor gave him the cup, moved a bedside tray to where he could reach it.

"You can put the cup down here when you've had enough. There are some people waiting to talk with you. I'll go get them and be back in a couple of minutes. If you need anything, just say, 'Nurse, please.' They'll hear you and be right in."

Which told Cheveyo he was in the Company Clinic. A fully equipped hospital for patients whose unconscious utterances couldn't be shared with the world at large. No deductible or co-pay on the room or the doctor's fees.

Awake and alone with his thoughts, Cheveyo tried to reconstruct how he came to be in his present circumstances. He had only vague memories. The last thing he could recall was being in Georgetown at night. Doing a snoop on somebody's residence there ...

Not alone, though. Somebody'd been with him.

Friend or foe? He couldn't remember, make the distinction.

But he knew he'd learned something important that night.

Something he had to warn someone about. Something really bad. But he couldn't remember what it was or who needed to be warned. Suddenly he was all wet. He could feel water running down his chest. Then he realized his right hand was *fully* functional. He'd just cracked the water cup he was holding.

"Nurse, please," he said.

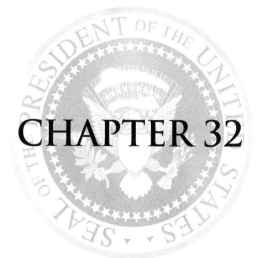

CHAPTER 32

MCGILL SUMMONED Deke and Leo to the residence. Caitie was off with Blessing and two other household staffers learning how to play bridge. A phone call to Camp David had confirmed that Abbie and Kenny would be delighted to have Patti's company that night. They were so pleased, in fact, that they didn't even inquire about their sister's dental visit. McGill had guessed right as to the Wisconsin resort where Carolyn and Lars would be staying, but they hadn't checked in yet.

The hotel phone operator was impressed when McGill asked to have Mrs. Enquist call him at the White House the moment she arrived. It bothered him a little that Carolyn wasn't there already. The trip shouldn't have taken long. He told himself that his ex-wife and her husband had simply stopped for lunch or maybe some antique hunting: Lars's idea of high adventure. They would reach their destination soon enough, and McGill would talk to Carolyn about Caitie's role in that night's drama.

A polite knock sounded at the door to McGill's Hideaway.

"Come in," he said.

Deke and Leo entered.

"Have a seat, guys. Sorry to call you in on your time off."

Neither of them grumbled; the right to complain wasn't a part of their job description.

"Deke, I'm going to need you tonight. You, too, Leo."

McGill described what Sweetie would be doing that night in Lafayette Square, and that Caitie might be taking part, too.

In a carefully neutral tone, Deke asked, "You're going to expose your daughter to danger?"

"You're supposed to see that it's not dangerous," McGill replied.

"Are you going to be there, too?"

"Incognito. To back you up."

"Who's going to back you up?" Deke asked.

"It won't get to that. This whole thing is going to be non-violent."

"Really? But you'll want full-measure protection for your daughter."

Meaning die for her if necessary. Open up with the Uzi if need be.

"It won't come to that, but yeah."

"Okay, let's say it doesn't. Your daughter's exposure time will be minimal. I'll get her out of there safe and sound. Then what? You come with us … or you stay behind to cover Ms. Sweeney until she's done speaking? And I leave you behind?"

McGill, of course, intended to back up Sweetie.

"I don't make things easy for you, do I?" McGill asked Deke.

Deke took the question as rhetorical.

"Leo," McGill said, "you be ready to get Sweetie and me out of there fast, if need be."

"Sure thing, boss. Always wanted to be a getaway driver."

"You'll probably be disappointed about that. Everything's going to be all right."

Neither of his minions said a word.

"Then you can get back to your time off."

They didn't look like they were counting on that either.

MCGILL GOT in touch with Sweetie, told her of his idea to use Caitie that night in Lafayette Square. He suggested meeting her at the office for further discussion, but Caitie, back from her card game, asked if she could see where Sweetie lived.

"Why?" McGill asked.

"I want to see if it's as big as this place."

"It's somewhat smaller than the White House, I'm sure."

"I'd still like to see."

"Why?"

"I might want to sleep over the next time I'm in town."

McGill laughed, but Sweetie said okay. So they convened at Sweetie's apartment on Florida Avenue. It was the first time either of the McGills had seen the place. James J. thought the apartment was suitably modest for Sweetie, who did her best to eschew most of the world's material offerings. Caitie thought it was the coolest clubhouse she'd ever seen.

She was particularly taken by the two pieces of art Sweetie had hung on her walls.

A lithograph of *The Temptation of Jesus* and a black-and-white photo of the Cathedral of Cologne taken shortly after the Allied bombing of World War Two had reduced the center of the city to rubble.

Pointing at the lithograph, Caitie asked, "That's God and the devil, right?"

Sweetie nodded.

"When Jesus got tempted?"

"Yes."

McGill took a seat on one of Sweetie's two kitchen chairs and watched the proceedings.

"I never understood that story," Caitie said, looking at the picture.

"What don't you understand?" Sweetie asked.

Caitie turned her attention to Sweetie. "Well, the devil's offering Jesus all the kingdoms of the world, right?"

"That's right."

"But the kingdoms aren't his to give away, so how can he do that? And what would Jesus want them for, anyway? He could *make* all the kingdoms he wants. He's *God.*"

Sweetie sat on her sleeper sofa; Caitie plopped down next to her.

"The *Son* of God," Sweetie corrected. "Born of a woman as human as you or me."

"Or Dad?" Caitie asked.

"Well, we might not want to go that far. Because of his mother, who was still pretty special, Our Lord was subject to some human weaknesses. You've learned that he had his moment of doubt, haven't you?"

Caitie nodded.

"What these stories tell us is that we're *all* subject to certain weaknesses. There are people who want to trick us. Who want to tempt us. Thing is, sometimes we're ready to let them. Maybe we even *want* to do the wrong thing. You ever feel like that?"

Admitting to imperfection, especially in front of her father, was a challenge for Caitie, but she said quietly, "Sometimes ... maybe."

"Well, that picture is my warning sign. Tells me when to pull back."

Uncomfortable now, Caitie wanted to change the subject.

"What about the photo of the church?" Caitie asked. "What's with that?"

Sweetie told her the abridged story of Cologne's cathedral.

"They started building it in the thirteenth century," she said. "But they didn't get around to putting on the finishing touches until the nineteenth century."

"Wow, they sure worked slow back then."

"They had a lot to do. Anyway, after six centuries of off-and-on work, they had it done. Then one day in May of 1942, England sent a thousand planes to bomb Cologne, and in a few hours undid a lot of those centuries of work, leaving the cathedral looking like it does in that picture."

Caitie looked at the blackened shell.

"That's *awful*," she said.

"Yeah, and the English were on the good guys' side."

"Then why'd they do it?"

"Because the Germans bombed some English cities and cathedrals first."

"Oh." Caitie thought things over. "Guess they had it coming then."

"We'll talk about that when you're older. That picture is up there as a reminder to me. Sometimes I have a pretty bad temper. I get mad at people; they get mad at me. And if you're not careful, well, pretty soon you're bombing each other's churches."

Sweetie took Caitie's hand. "Are you sure you want to help tonight, kiddo? I won't think less of you if you don't."

Caitie sat up straight. "I want to."

"Are you scared at all?"

Ten-year-old Caitie McGill looked at her father, then at Sweetie.

"Yeah, a little. It's like a tickle. It makes me want to run as fast as I can. But I won't run, not if you and Dad are there with me."

McGill and Sweetie looked at each other.

They all went outside and got into the car with Deke and Leo. They drove to St. Matthew's Cathedral on Rhode Island Avenue. It didn't have the gothic spires of Cologne; it had a Romanesque dome and a red-stone-and-brick façade. The church was where the funeral mass for John F. Kennedy had been said, and apropos of Washington, St. Matthew was the patron saint of civil servants. The McGills and Sweetie partook of the sacrament of confession, reasoning that if you were about to enter a potentially dangerous situation, it was best to do so in a state of grace.

McGill lit two candles before they left. One for all the people he loved. One for the best-laid plans of the president of the United States. When he was still unable to reach Carolyn from his car parked at the curb, he went back inside and lit a third candle. For his ex-wife and her new husband.

EVERYONE RETURNED to the White House and went up on the roof to look out at Lafayette Square. The Secret Service was not pleased to have anyone outside of the brotherhood see their rooftop defensive emplacements: the radar arrays, missile batteries, and snipers' stands. Crogher himself had tried to make that point to McGill but to no avail. Unlike Deke and Leo, however, Crogher chose to object, for the record if nothing else.

Looking out across the grounds of the Executive Mansion and the breadth of Pennsylvania Avenue to the park, Caitie said, "This is cool!"

McGill knew that Caitie would boast of the rooftop visit to her brother and Kenny would demand equal treatment, but he'd deal with that when the time came.

Sweetie was studying the FREE ERNA marchers through a pair of binoculars.

"The rev's not there," she said. "You think he went home?"

"Maybe," McGill answered. "Richmond's not that far away."

"Should I walk across the street, let his people know I want to chat with him?"

McGill thought it over. He wanted the matter settled. He didn't know how long his resolve to use Caitie would last, and he didn't want the threat against his children to remain in place for another minute, much less indefinitely.

"Yeah," McGill said, "do that."

Deke offered to go with her, catching Crogher off guard.

Sweetie, however, said no thanks.

"I want all eyes on me," she explained.

All eyes on the White House roof were. McGill used the binoculars Sweetie had handed him. Caitie cadged a pair from someone else. Everybody watched as Sweetie entered Lafayette Square. The effect was immediate and dramatic. Sweetie brought the marchers to a dead halt.

They all knew who she was. Her face had been on television, arriving at and leaving Erna Godfrey's trial. Artists' renderings of Margaret Sweeney testifying at the trial had been published in newspapers and magazines around the country. Here, before the assembled believers, had come the blonde demon who had seduced or coerced Lindell Ricker into falsely confessing, betraying Erna Godfrey and their holy cause. In Reverend Godfrey's hierarchy of evil, she was exceeded only by the president, McGill, and Satan himself.

McGill could see the marchers' expressions, a combination of hostility and fear. For a tense moment it looked like animus might win out, and they would rush her. But Sweetie held up a hand like a traffic cop. Maybe she delivered a few words of wisdom or warning. Whatever the case, she curbed any impetuous feelings the marchers might have had. They went into a huddle like a football team. When they broke from the cluster, one man pointed a finger at Sweetie, then jogged out of the park, heading north, away from the White House.

The others, with impressive discipline, resumed their circular protest route.

Sweetie turned toward the White House and made a gesture with her right hand held tight to her chest. Thumbs-up. The word would be passed to Godfrey. He'd have to show up. How could he fail to do so? He claimed to have God on his side.

"We're going to do it, Dad?" Caitie asked.

McGill put an arm around his daughter's shoulders. He felt the tickle of fear himself.

"Looks like it, honey."

"I hope I can be as brave as Sweetie."

"Me, too."

MCGILL WAS taking Caitie back to the residence when Galia intercepted them.

"Hello, Caitie," she said. "Do you remember me?"

They'd been introduced on Inauguration Day.

"Yes, you're Ms. Mindel." Caitie was good with names and faces. "You're Patti's right-hand man." She was less adept at job titles.

But Galia smiled, and said, "Pretty close. I'm the president's chief of staff."

"Is that a good job?" Caitie wanted to know.

"I like it."

"What do you do?"

"Well, I advise the president, and I do my best to protect her."

"You mean when my dad's not here."

Galia shot McGill a quick look. "Protect her in a different way. Politically. So people will continue to like her."

"You'd have to be crazy not to like Patti," Caitie said, "even if she is a Republican."

McGill intervened, prevailing on a uniformed Secret Service agent to take Caitie back to the residence. Then he turned to Galia.

"The president would like to see me?"

"Yes, I've been looking all over for you."

They started walking to the Oval Office.

"I was up on the roof," McGill said.

"So I've learned. You're not supposed to go up there."

"Yeah, I've heard."

"SAC Crogher just told me he intends to resign."

"What, because of me?"

"Yes."

"Don't let him."

"And how should I stop him?"

McGill knew how. "Ask him how'd he'd feel if he left, and ..."

"And what?" Galia asked.

"He'll be able to fill in the blank. I'm sure you already have."

Galia had, but she wouldn't give voice to that terrible thought either.

MCGILL HAD to hand it to Galia. Celsus, too. They kept trying to manipulate him, to get him to be submissive to their wishes. It wasn't going to happen; it looked like the three of them would be stuck with each other—battling—for a long time. Maybe eight years.

Welborn was standing next to Edwina Byington's desk as McGill and Galia approached the Oval Office. Welborn remembered not to salute McGill, but he straightened his posture. McGill said at ease with a wave of his hand. He stopped and looked at Galia. "Is there anything else, Ms. Mindel?"

Galia inclined her head, and McGill followed her a few feet away from Welborn and Edwina Byington. She spoke in quiet but urgent voice.

"Do you know Monty Kipp?"

"Yes."

"Well, Aggie Wu says he's telling stories that you threatened his life."

"Never did."

"But you talked to him privately. While you were cleaning your gun."

"Yes."

"Now Kipp is looking into your basketball game with Michaelson."

"So?"

"You put Michaelson in the hospital, remember?"

"He's still there?"

"No."

"He say I beat him up?"

"He'd never admit that."

"Then there's nothing for Kipp to find."

"You've never heard of a whispering campaign?"

"I have indeed."

"Then you know how harmful they can be. If it gets out that you're a menace to society, the president's reputation will suffer, too."

McGill said, "Kipp is just trying to get my attention."

"What do you mean?" Galia asked.

"I've got something on him. Maybe I can get him indicted. I certainly can wreck his career. He's letting me know he can hit back." McGill mused on the situation for a moment. "Actually, I'm glad this dummy surfaced again. I can use him to help Chana Lochlan. Don't worry about

Monty Kipp. I've got him covered."

Galia gave him a dubious look.

McGill wanted to say, Hey, I do okay fighting you and Celsus off, don't I? But he resisted. He stepped over to Edwina's desk.

"Is the president ready for me?" he asked.

"It'll be just a moment, sir."

McGill turned to Welborn. "I'll let the president know you're here."

"Actually, sir, I'm here to talk with you."

"Really?"

"I understand you have a special driver, sir. One who used to be a NASCAR racer."

"Yes, I do. Who told you?"

"Ms. Fahey."

McGill wasn't surprised that Kira knew; she was the kind who would gather intelligence about her workplace. Ceaselessly.

"If you don't mind, sir," Welborn continued, "I'd like to ask if I might borrow his services."

Almost like Junior asking Dad if he could borrow the car, McGill thought.

"I need Leo tonight," McGill told Welborn. "After that, I promised him some time off."

Welborn tried to mask his disappointment and almost succeeded.

"Thank you for taking the time to talk with me, sir."

Welborn almost saluted but caught himself. McGill took pity on him.

"Listen, Lieutenant. I'm pretty sure Leo misses the excitement of racing. Driving me around has to be boring for a man with his skills." Witness Leo's comment about wanting to be a getaway driver. "If you have a proposition that'll get his juices flowing, talk to him. He might think it's a good way to spend his free time."

"I have your permission then?"

"Sure. Tell Leo I sent you."

THE PRESIDENT invited her husband into the Oval Office and introduced him to the chairman of the Joint Chiefs and the director of Central Intelligence. Two of the most powerful figures in the government shook

McGill's hand and expressed their pleasure at meeting him. He almost believed them. Thought they'd given a good performance for the boss, anyway.

McGill played nice, too. Didn't tell them how to run the military or the CIA.

A moment later he was alone with his wife again.

"You gave the word?" he asked.

"Yes. Things won't happen until after dark, but I gave them the green light."

"I lit a candle for you."

"Thank you. You remembered to light one for your own plans, of course."

McGill said he had, and mentioned the third candle he'd lit for Carolyn and Lars. He told Patti he was starting to worry about them. More than he was worried about Caitie, Sweetie, or himself.

Patti picked up the phone on her desk.

"Edwina, please get FBI Director Haskins for me immediately."

While they waited, Patti talked to McGill, hoping to distract him. "You know, we're trying to smoke out Fidel with our little gambit."

"You think he's still alive?"

"Ironically, we have to hope so. Every president since Eisenhower has wanted to get rid of him, but right now our experts think he's the one who can stabilize things the fastest."

McGill nodded, trying to pay polite attention.

"There's one theory circulating that he shaved his beard when he went underground."

"Come on," McGill said, "you're pulling my leg."

"No, think about it. Who'd ever recognize a beardless Fidel Castro?"

"Good point."

"Now, the theory has it, he can't show his face and hold power publicly again until he grows his beard back."

The president's phone rang. The FBI director had responded to Patti's summons. She got from McGill the name of the Wisconsin resort where Carolyn and Lars Enquist had their reservations. He was also able to give her descriptions of and license plates numbers for both Carolyn's and Lars's cars. Patti passed all the information along.

"I want to know the whereabouts of Mr. and Mrs. Enquist as soon as possible," the president told the FBI director. "Yes ... Thank you."

She put the phone down and looked at McGill. "The FBI will find them."

"Yeah."

"But if it's not soon, are you still going to use Caitie tonight?"

McGill considered the question anew; he'd been pondering it for a couple of hours.

"I think so ... No, I know so."

Patti Grant came around from behind her desk and embraced her husband. Held him so close he could feel her heartbeat. She kissed him deeply. Passionately.

All but breathless, McGill said, "Right here in the Oval Office?"

"Probably won't be the last time," the president told him. "Come on, walk me out to my helicopter. I have a babysitting job tonight."

DAMON TODD called Dikran Missirian at his P Street office at 5:26 P.M., four minutes before McGill's landlord was scheduled to go home for the day. Todd wasn't worried that Missirian would have left early. Everything he'd seen about the man told Todd that Missirian was a striver: an immigrant who had managed to purchase two commercial properties in Georgetown before enough time had passed for his accent to fade. He hadn't arrived in America with money in hand, either. If he had, he would have hired someone to put out his café table in the morning instead of doing it himself. Mr. Missirian was clearly a hardworking fellow. He wouldn't leave work early.

On the other hand, he wouldn't stay late, either. He'd told Todd that his wife was his financial confidante. A clear sign that he valued her as more than someone to cook his meals and share his bed. So while Missirian would work hard, he would not neglect his wife.

Missirian's mention of God implied that he had certain behavioral values. It was reasonable to assume that they would include a thoughtfulness for others. Todd hoped so anyway.

Missirian picked up on the first ring. "Dikran Missirian."

"Hello, Mr. Missirian. I'm glad I caught you. This is Dr. Casey."

"Yes?"

Todd could hear the expectation in the man's voice. "I looked at your other building today. I was very impressed. I think it might be just what I'm looking for."

"I assure you, Doctor, it will be very nice. Just like P Street. Maybe better. I try to learn new things all the time."

The irony, Todd thought. Here was a man who knew himself, believed in self-improvement, and could make his way in life without the least bit of help from any therapist.

"Since I wasn't actually able to enter your other building," Todd continued, "I was wondering if you might have floor plans of the office suites. So I can see if one of them will meet my needs for space. If you do, I'll come right over ... if I won't be keeping you from some other obligation."

"No, no, Doctor. Please come."

"Very well then. I have to tell you I'm really excited. If I like the floor plans, I'll sign a lease tonight." He'd thought about saying he'd write a check for the first year, but he didn't want to overdo it. It wouldn't pay to underestimate the man's intelligence.

"I will be waiting, Doctor, in my office. When will you make your arrival?"

"I should be there by six, if that's not too late."

"Not late at all," Missirian said. "I call my wife. Let her know not to worry, I am coming home after regular time."

Just what Todd wanted to hear.

CHAPTER 33

PUTNAM SHADY faced a terrible dilemma. Not to mention an incredible temptation. Margaret Sweeney had called him at home—one story up from her apartment—and asked if he'd like to come down and discuss being her escort for the evening. He'd said to give him fifteen minutes, and he'd be happy to talk with her.

He showered, shaved, donned his favorite Armani suit, and arrived with a bouquet of flowers that his housekeeper had bought for his dining-room table that morning. The vision that awaited him was unlike any other he'd ever seen.

"My God, Margaret," he said. "You look just like an—"

"An angel. Yeah, yeah, I know." She grabbed his wrist and pulled him inside.

Sweetie was dressed entirely in white. A summer-weight cotton sweater. Linen slacks. Matte finish, low-heel leather shoes. Not a speck on her anywhere. Her grooming was immaculate, too. Her short blonde hair was brushed back, gleaming, and not a strand out of place. Her blue eyes were clear and full of high purpose. Her complexion was completely without makeup but glowing with radiant good health.

She smiled when she saw that Putnam had brought her flowers.

"Nobody's done that for a long time," she said.

She took the flowers and arranged them in a glass jar. Welch's grape jelly.

Then she said, "I need a lawyer tonight, Putnam."

The look of disappointment on his face was comical, but she didn't laugh.

For his part, Putnam grunted and shifted gears into professional mode.

"Why? What did you do?"

"It's what I'm going to do."

"I can't be part of any criminal conspiracy," he said. But he knew he would, if she asked. At that moment, he couldn't think of anything short of committing suicide or going bankrupt that he wouldn't do for her. She looked so innocent, so pure. So strong and commanding. The combination was almost more than he could bear.

"Relax, Putnam, I don't intend to do anything illegal."

Sweetie told him what she had in mind.

"You're going to confront a mob of religious crazies?" he asked in disbelief.

"Sure, why not? I'm a bit of a zealot myself."

By that time, Putnam Shady had Googled the woman to whom he'd rented his basement apartment. He knew all about Margaret's involvement in the capture and conviction of Erna Godfrey. Now, she wanted to antagonize the woman's husband, a televangelist loon who claimed to have God on speed dial. It wouldn't be just Reverend Godfrey, either. Margaret said she expected the man to have his congregation, choir, and makeup artist with him. Probably carrying torches, the lot of them.

His fevered imagination led him to stare at her. Sweetie took it personally, as he seemed to be concentrating on her chest and navel. "See something you like, Putnam?"

He liked *everything* he saw, but he said, "I'm just trying to figure out where you'd wear a gun with that outfit."

"Oh. Not a problem. I'm going unarmed."

"*What?*" He couldn't believe it. Then he thought he saw. "Oh, okay, you're going to have backup."

"Yes, I am. A ten-year-old girl. But she won't be packing, either."

"That's crazy. You can't go alone, and you certainly can't bring a child."

"It's all set. The only question is, do you want to come, too? To be my witness, able to testify truthfully that I didn't do anything illegal. Didn't incite anyone to riot."

"I'm a *lobbyist,*" Shady whined. "Danger is *not* my middle name."

"Probably won't be any rough stuff … but I thought you liked that sort of thing."

He did. Oh, yes he did. But not to the point of being publicly dismembered. Still, he understood clearly that if he didn't accompany Margaret that night, he'd never stand a chance with her. Wouldn't get to do any of the things he'd fantasized. She might even get so disgusted with his wussy behavior she'd move away. He might never see her again.

And, my God, the way she looked. He wanted her very badly. He'd never been spanked by an angel.

"Okay, Putnam," Sweetie said, "I've got to get going. Thanks for the flowers."

She started to leave. Picked up her keys and wallet at the front door. Waited for him to follow.

"You win," the lawyer said. "I'll bear witness for you." Then he thought to ask, "Can *I* carry your gun?"

"No, Putnam, you can't. Just have a little faith."

"DID YOU hear from Mom?" Caitie asked.

"No," McGill said.

Presumably, legions of FBI agents and state and local cops had been out combing the Wisconsin countryside for Carolyn and Lars since Patti made her call four hours ago, but he hadn't heard a word. Even so, he couldn't burden his daughter with his anxiety.

"But we're still going, right?"

"Do you still want to?" McGill asked.

He could see that Caitie had a few jitters, but she was a stubborn girl.

"Yeah. I can do it."

"Okay, let's go. You remember what you're supposed to do tonight?"

"You've told me a million times."

"So you remember?"

"Yes, Dad. I'll be good."

He believed her, but he couldn't remember the last time he'd been so nervous.

AS THE McGills left the White House, Welborn Yates was in his office and had just placed a call to the Falls Church, Virginia— home of Arlene Cowan. He'd spent all day looking for her husband without success. He fervently hoped she could remedy the situation. After five rings, she picked up. Out of breath. "Are you all right, ma'am?" Welborn asked.

It took her a second to reply, but she said, "I'm fine, thank you. Who is this?"

"Lieutenant Welborn Yates, ma'am. I gave you a ride to the airport the other day."

"Oh, yes."

He thought he heard a smile in her voice. He hoped it stayed there. Long enough to help him, anyway. "I inquired if you were all right because you seemed a bit breathless."

"I was." She laughed. "Still am a touch. The phone rang as I was about to bring a fifty-pound box of books down from the second floor. I started to hurry, slowed down so I wouldn't fall, thought it might be my lawyer, and hurried again."

Welborn drew the obvious inference from someone's hefting a box of books.

"You're moving, ma'am?"

"Tomorrow."

"You got the job in Tennessee?"

"I did." Definitely a smile in her voice now.

"Congratulations, ma'am."

"Thank you, Lieutenant. But we agreed the last time we met you'd call me Arlene. 'Ma'am' makes me feel old."

"Won't make that mistake again, Arlene."

"I'm packing my belongings, Lieutenant, far more carefully than any movers would ever do, and I'm toasting my good fortune with real French champagne. If you're a careful packer, too, why don't you come over and join me?"

He knew her good mood was boosted by the bubbly. And no, he cer-

tainly wasn't going to Falls Church to help her pack. Because Arlene Cowan was still *Mrs.* Dexter Cowan, and he wasn't about to
fall into the trap of committing adultery while investigating an adultery case. Besides which, Kira would kill him.

"I'm all thumbs, Arlene. I have to stay away from anything marked fragile."

She laughed deep in her throat. "I bet there are a few exceptions."

He felt a new sympathy for military personnel who fell prey to human weakness. But he said, "Arlene, you mentioned just now you thought your lawyer might be calling."

Her voice changed, taking on a guarded note. "Yes, I did."

"Pardon me for asking, but would that be about those negotiations you mentioned to me?"

"Yes." She sounded even more cautious.

"I have something to tell you that will have a bearing on that."

He could almost see her bracing herself. She had no answer for him.

"If it's all right, Arlene, I'd like to stop by your house later tonight. Tell you in person."

"I should probably stop drinking, shouldn't I?"

"I think that would be a good idea," Welborn said.

A PAUK II Class corvette flying the ensign of the *Marina de Guerra Revolucionaria,* a.k.a. the Cuban Navy, and emblazoned with the proud name of *José Martí,* weighed anchor and steamed away from the windward side of the Isla de San Andrés, a speck of land in the Caribbean Sea belonging to Colombia on which the United States held a ninety-nine-year lease. A course was laid in that would take the vessel to the territorial waters of Costa Gorda, a mere sixty miles distant.

The vessel had been built in Russia in 1989. The original buyer was supposed to have been Fidel Castro's government in Havana, but the Cubans, as ever, had no hard currency. So the Kremlin decided to sell the craft to a gentleman who had a purchase order from a revolutionary movement in a southern African country and a bank account in Switzerland.

That arms dealer had, in fact, been a CIA agent. Langley thought it might come in handy someday to have a spot-on stand-in for one of Castro's coastal patrol craft. The original *José Martí* had been moved the preceding year from its normal anchorage in Havana Bay to Cienfuegos for refitting. Using parts from '57 Chevys, wags from the U.S. Navy said.

As with the real *Martí*, the impostor displaced 485 tons, was 184 feet long, 33 feet wide, and drew 11 feet of water. It could make a top speed of 32 knots or cruise for 2,400 miles at 14 knots. The ship could knock helicopters out of the sky with its SAM missiles. Other watercraft could be attacked or repelled with either its 76mm gun, capable of firing 120 rounds per minute up to a distance of 8 miles, or for close-in work, its 30mm gun, which fired 3,000 rounds per minute up to a distance of .5 miles.

Best of all, not even the *marineros cubanos* who still sailed for and defended their revolution would have doubted it was one of their ships.

But unlike the twenty-six sailors and six officers who saluted Fidel, or at least his memory, aboard Cuban corvettes, this craft was manned by only a dozen U.S. Navy personnel. Along to provide muscle and firepower was a team of eight SEALs in case things went wrong.

Also, unlike its Cuban counterpart, this iteration of the *Martí* was in continuous encrypted communication with an Air Force AWACS aircraft, a CIA U-2, and an NSA spy satellite.

All this deception and technology was being employed for one reason.

The president of the United States had ordered the faux-*Martí* to attack the military base in Costa Gorda that her predecessor in the Oval Office had bankrolled for the anti-Castro community in Miami. He'd needed the Cuban vote in South Florida.

Patricia Darden Grant didn't.

•

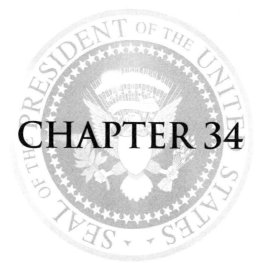

CHAPTER 34

THE REVEREND Burke Godfrey crackled with nervous energy. He was sure that if his hair hadn't been shellacked into place, every last strand would have been standing on end. As it was, he paced the twenty-by-ten-by-two-foot stage his people had brought with them to Lafayette Square from Richmond. Stage right, there stood a lectern draped with a white silk cloth on which a cross sewn with threads of 24K gold shone forth. Atop the lectern was a cordless microphone for the reverend's use. Its output could be amped up by an audio technician working from cues, both scripted and visual, at a soundboard placed front row center, had there been anything but lawn seating.

But nobody was sitting. Everyone stood and swayed. Many listened to podcasts of Reverend Godfrey's favorite gospel music. Others listened to choirs furnished by their own imaginations.

Mirroring Sweetie's wardrobe choice, Godfrey was dressed head to toe in white: suit, shirt, tie, and shoes. He couldn't match her blond hair, though. His was dark brown, cosmetically silvered at the temples. He wasn't as lean as she was either. No disciple of Dr. Atkins, the reverend liked his carbs in large numbers.

The summer sky was darkening not only from the sunset but also the arrival of storm clouds, portending the possibility that divine judgment might soon be loosed upon the land. Anticipating official interference if he brought too many of his followers—and *thousands* had wanted to come—Reverend Godfrey had selected only 250 of his flock to be in attendance. Every one of them was devout. That is, they attended his Sunday services faithfully and gave freely when they did. A canny man, Godfrey hadn't chosen his most affluent believers, but the most zealous. The ones he'd seen from his pulpit whose faces showed the clearest devotion—to him.

All the others who'd wanted to attend would also see what transpired. The reverend had brought three video cams to provide a live webcast, and lighting people to show him in, well, the best possible light. Downloads of the coming clash would soon be on sale for those who had missed it live.

The stage lights were already on, as the sky continued to darken.

All of Reverend Godfrey's stagecraft, ironically, made it far easier for the two less obvious videographers sent by the White House to do their work. The same benefit pertained to the special agent Celsus Crogher had independently assigned to record the event.

Added to the other advantages he'd given himself, Burke Godfrey had made sure he was the first to arrive. That way it would seem as if the cursed woman who'd helped send his Erna to Death Row was entering the reverend's own temple. He and his people would be there waiting for her, to fling the defiler from their holy gathering.

The only problem was, with all the other things he'd had on his mind, he'd forgotten one very important detail. He hadn't gone to the bathroom before taking the stage. Back home, where his routine had been set for years, he always relieved himself right before he started a service. It was just common sense. But tonight he hadn't remembered. And where the day had been warm, the night, with the arrival of the storm front, was turning chilly. The air was getting damp, too. Of course, he was also tense as he awaited a battle he was sure would be a preview of Armageddon. All in all, his bladder already felt uncomfortably stretched.

What was worse, that damnable Margaret Sweeney was late. No telling when she might arrive. If cowardice kept her away completely, all glory would be his. But not if he soiled his beautiful white pants. His pacing before the crowd became more urgent.

Finally, the TV professional in him, if not the preacher, dictated that he momentarily abdicate his stage. He lifted a hand to his congregation, smiled, and said, "I'll be right back, brothers and sisters. Until I return, say a prayer for our sister, my precious wife, Erna."

He hopped off the back of the stage, careful not to slip, and headed for one of the porta-potties his people had brought with them.

A FINE mist began to descend, adding to the chill in the air. Standing at the curb of Pennsylvania Avenue, on the edge of the crowd, McGill gathered Caitie into his arms. He wore a windbreaker, jeans, and sneakers. He had a Chicago White Sox cap pulled low over his face. No one gave him a second glance. Caitie wore a hooded sweatshirt; no one paid attention to her either. On McGill's right was Deke, not saying a word but scanning each face in the gathering, searching for madness in the eyes of anyone who might be looking to make history with a handgun. Parked up the street, Leo had the Chevy's motor running.

McGill surveyed the crowd, too. To his surprise, he spotted Welborn Yates dressed in casual civilian clothes. The lieutenant met McGill's eyes and gave him a tiny nod. As a federal agent, McGill had no doubt that Welborn was armed; but his gut told him Welborn was there of his own accord, not at Patti's direction. McGill turned and whispered into Deke's ear, advising him of Welborn's presence. Deke took note of the young Air Force officer, nodded, and went back to looking for assassins.

McGill dropped to one knee, looked Caitie in the eye, and spoke quietly.

"It's still okay to change your mind," he said.

She shook her head.

"You're sure?" he asked.

"Positive, Dad. I'm going to be all right."

THE COOL air and the mist had turned Caitie's cheeks pink. She looked impossibly pure and beautiful to him. Of his three children, Caitie was the one who most resembled her mother. His

anxiety doubled when he thought of Carolyn. Where in God's name could she be?

His daughter sensed his disquiet. She laid a palm against his cheek as if she were the adult comforting her child. There was an air of serenity about Caitie at that moment. He could see it in her gaze. It only served to unnerve even him more.

"Really, Dad, I'll be fine," Caitie told him. Then she smiled. "Oh, look, there's Sweetie. Isn't she beautiful?"

THE REVEREND Burke Godfrey leaped nimbly back onto the stage, skidded on the now-slick surface, but caught his balance before he did a pratfall. When he looked up, he thought he saw an angel. All white and golden and glowing. There was a halo where the lights hit the mist around her blond hair. He'd have been happy to have such a creature greet him at the gates of heaven.

As long as she wasn't Margaret Sweeney.

The crowd had parted for her like the Red Sea before Moses. She stood maybe thirty feet from the stage. Godfrey had warned his people not to curse this woman, and certainly not take the name of the Lord in vain. Not with his three video cams going. It was clear that this admonition had been superfluous, at least for the moment. The most credulous members of his flock stood in silent awe of the woman they had been taught to denounce.

The reverend couldn't have that. He crossed the stage and seized his microphone.

"You wanted to see me," his voice boomed. "Well, here I am."

SWEETIE LOOKED closely at Godfrey. The anger on his face was easy to see, easy to understand. The man was looking at a sworn enemy. He wasn't of a mind to turn the other cheek. It would have been easy for her to tear into him, too. She'd seen what Erna Godfrey's missile had done to Andy Grant.

But Sweetie brought to mind the picture of the Cathedral of Cologne.

It wouldn't serve anyone's interest to let things get to that point.

"I respect all life," Sweetie said. Unaided, her voice carried through the heavy air, rang clear to all those present. "The measure of our days should be set by God, not man."

GODFREY TOOK note, uneasily, that several members of his congregation were nodding. But why shouldn't they? He might have said those words himself. In other contexts, he *had* said much the same thing. At least about unborn children. But he hadn't come to Washington that night for an ecumenical hootenanny.

"Then I'm sure," the reverend rebutted, "you've used your influence with your good friend Mr. James J. McGill and his wife, the president, to spare the life of my dear wife, Erna."

TV crews from three network affiliates had arrived to join the row of lenses recording the moment, broadcasting it live to the nation. All of them had caught what was an obviously heartfelt plea from Reverend Godfrey for the life of his wife.

THE TELEVISION was on in the game room of the Aspen Lodge at Camp David. Patti, Abbie, and Kenny sat watching. Patti watched impassively; Abbie's face was soft with empathy; Kenny shook his head, feeling no mercy for Erna Godfrey at all. To hell with her.

SWEETIE SAID, "No, I haven't. Not in person. I know how the president has suffered from the death of her first husband. I held her in my arms the morning after he was killed. I felt her tears against my face. I prayed with her for the repose of Andrew Hudson Grant's soul. Just as I include in my prayers the plea that the president will find enough of God's grace to commute Mrs. Godfrey's sentence. Just as I pray that no one in our country will be executed."

Far from placating Burke Godfrey, Sweetie's words enraged him. He pointed his free hand at the heavens, and the soundman took his cue, boosting the reverend's volume.

"*Commute?* I'll hear no talk of commutation. Erna must be *pardoned.* Erna must be *freed!*"

"Free her! Free Erna!" the crowd echoed, louder than Godfrey himself.

After allowing the chant to continue just long enough, the reverend took the vocal baton back from his followers. "How *dare* you compare a woman who was following God's commands to the vile filth that rapes and murders and fills our prisons?"

"How *dare* you? How *dare* you?" echoed the faithful.

The Richmond congregants had found their footing. Established their rhythm. Their enemy stood before them, and they recognized her for who she was.

The chance of violence was escalating quickly.

Sweetie showed no sign she even noticed. She stepped forward, coming to within ten feet of the stage. Her voice was as true and clear as ever. Even though her pitch was now more intimate, her words reached everyone. Without the slightest quaver of fear.

"And how would you know that, Reverend Godfrey? How would you know that your wife received a command from God? Were you present when He spoke to her?"

AT CAMP David, the McGill kids watched with wide eyes; the president leaned forward, intent on not missing a syllable of Godfrey's response.

THE REVEREND almost shouted out his reply. But then his face twisted into a terrible grimace as if he were having a seizure. His expression was so tortured that it brought an audible gasp from his followers. His personal physician, who traveled everywhere with him, started forward. But the televangelist, bracing himself on the lectern, managed to wave him off.

Burke Godfrey realized, his knees still weak, how perilously close he'd come to falling into this evil trap. He was not used to having his word questioned when he preached. Especially not by someone who'd been a cop.

If he'd admitted that, yes, he'd been present when God spoke to Erna, or claim, as he'd intended to do, that God had spoken to her through him, he'd have confessed in front of the world that he'd been part of the conspiracy that had taken Andrew Grant's life. He wouldn't be able to free Erna then. He'd be on Death Row with her.

But he was not a man without cunning.

He pivoted to turn near disaster into triumph.

"What just happened here," he said in a well-amplified whisper, "what each of you has seen with your own two eyes, is that God has spoken to me this very instant."

Sweetie jumped on that before the reverend could expound.

"Is that so? When I feel God's presence in my life, it fills me with an overwhelming joy. You, Reverend, looked like you experienced a grievous pain. We all saw *that* with our own two eyes. Did God ask you to do something that tried your soul?"

"No, damn you, He did not!"

This woman, this *demon,* was an affliction not to be borne. If he'd had her in private, he would have seen to it that she suff—he realized with no small measure of horror that he had spittle on his chin. The lights had to be catching the reflection; the cameras had to be capturing the image. Let it continue, and he'd look deranged. He made as graceful a save as he could. He frequently used a handkerchief to blot his brow when he preached; he did so then, deftly wiping his chin as he brought the cloth down.

Accustomed to reading the mood of his flock, he saw that they were looking at him with unfamiliar doubt. He'd done something wrong, but what? Then he understood. The night was growing colder; they were all but shivering ... and he was burning inside, sweating. He made another pass with his handkerchief.

"What God just told me," Godfrey said in a soft voice, "confirmed what I already knew." He lowered his head briefly. "He said that my Erna is sentenced to die, and millions of unborn children *will* die"—he looked up at the crowd—"and all manner of evil will occur because too many sinners, too many of His enemies, hold the reins of power."

He cast his gaze directly at Sweetie.

Who looked right back at him.

"What are my sins, Reverend Godfrey?" she asked.

"You support the killing of the unborn," he jeered from the stage.

"I don't."

"You support those who do." Once more the preacher jabbed a finger at Sweetie. *"Your guilt is as theirs!"*

Some of the more zealous members of the crowd surged toward Sweetie.

TO HIS great surprise, Putnam Shady grabbed a man and yanked him back.

The man stayed yanked, and the others halted because Godfrey gestured restraint. "Stay thy hands, brothers and sisters. We are not here to do violence."

"I'm glad to hear that, Reverend," Sweetie said. "Not for my own safety. Not because you're wrong. But because your followers are the ones threatening the lives of innocent children."

"No! Never! Lies!" The crowd needed no urging on this point. While they didn't physically confront Sweetie, they leaned forward to shout their denials and shake their fists.

With fine timing, as the crowd wound down, Godfrey added, "Calumny."

"Is it, Reverend?"

"Of course, it is."

"Then you'll allow no violence here tonight?"

"You've heard my words." He smiled condescendingly. "You have no worries from us, only from God."

"I have no worries for myself, Reverend. None at all."

"Then whose safety concerns you? Who are these innocent children?"

Sweetie turned her head and extended a hand to Caitie. Her moment had come.

McGill had never done anything harder than to let his daughter go at that moment. He didn't trust Godfrey any more than he did the devil. For her part, Caitie did not hesitate. Nor did Deke. He followed at her side, right hand under his coat, until they reached Sweetie. Then the special agent faded back, but not far.

Caitie took Sweetie's hand. Together, they turned toward Burke Godfrey. Sweetie nodded, and Caitie pushed back the hood of her sweatshirt. Every camera present pushed in on her face, looking as calm and fearless as that of the woman who stood next to her.

"This is Caitlin Rose McGill, daughter of James J. McGill, the president's husband."

The crowd gawked in surprise at this development.

Sweetie and Caitie turned to face the onlookers.

"What you may not know," she told them, "is that Caitie, and her sister, Abbie, and her brother, Kenny, have *all* had their lives threatened. The Secret Service finds these threats entirely credible. Just two days ago a threatening note was left in Abbie McGill's school locker. It said, '*There's nowhere we can't reach you.*' Because of this note, the McGill children were driven from their mother's home, forced into hiding to protect their young lives."

"I had *nothing* to do with that!" Godfrey boomed.

Sweetie and Caitie turned back to him.

"*Nothing!*" he repeated, shaking a scolding finger at them.

"Reverend Godfrey, this threat is being made at this very moment in the name of your wife. It claims to be a threat of vengeance, but at the moment it's more a means of vile coercion. If you have nothing to do with it, renounce it now. Tell those who make such evil threats that they sin against God and that you just as surely condemn such views. Tell these people that they have no place in your congregation. Tell those who worship in good faith with you that they must reveal to the authorities any knowledge they have of these extortionists. These would-be child-killers."

Burke Godfrey shook his head. "Erna must be freed!" he pronounced.

This time the echo from the crowd was but a few scattered voices. It was clear that a large majority of the congregation had not known that the murder of children was being threatened in the name of their cause. They'd seen Caitie's face, and they could not countenance killing her.

"Free Erna with your prayers, Reverend," Sweetie said. "Write to your congressmen, call your senators, march peacefully in the streets ... *ask* if a majority of your fellow Americans agree that Erna Godfrey should be freed."

"They do. They do, and you all know it." Godfrey's tone was beseeching.

"You don't save one child's life by taking another's. Tell the people acting in your name, tell them now, Reverend Godfrey: *End your threats against the McGill children.*"

At that moment the sky opened. Rain fell in sheets. Lightning flashed. Thunder boomed. More than a few congregants fell to their knees and bowed their heads.

Reverend Burke Godfrey, though, stubbornly repeated, "Erna must be freed."

No one heard him. The downpour had shorted out his soundboard.

CHAPTER 35

THE STORM was intense but brief. And extremely localized. As Welborn Yates and Leo Levy drove down I-66 to Falls Church, Virginia, the roads were dry. The two men were lost in thought. Glancing at Welborn, Leo asked, "You thinking what I'm thinking?"

"I'm thinking my mother told me not to rile Jesus."

Leo laughed. "I'm Old Testament myself, but that's when God was *really* wrathful."

"Heckuva thing that rain and lightning and thunder showing up just when it did."

"Charlton Heston couldn't have done better," Leo agreed.

Welborn had gone to talk with Leo after receiving permission from McGill. The Air Force lieutenant had explained to the former NASCAR driver that he planned to arrest a Navy captain who might try to avoid being taken into custody.

"How's he gonna do that?" Leo asked.

"In his Dodge Viper is what I'm thinking," Welborn replied.

Leo grinned. "This Navy captain have any real driving experience?"

"Not professionally, if that's what you mean."

"That's what I mean. So he's just your average Bubba with a whole lot of horses under the hood and a heavy foot."

"That's how I see it. I can get us the use of an Audi TT, if that'd help."

"Don't bother," Leo said. "My ride's a lot faster."

"Faster than a Viper?"

"I'm really not supposed to say what top end is."

But as McGill had suggested, Leo was interested in helping. After he took care of a little matter at Lafayette Square. Which was how Welborn had come to be present.

Leo took the Route 29 turnoff and dropped down to the Leesburg Pike. A few minutes later, he pulled smoothly to a stop in front of Arlene Cowan's residence. The curtains were drawn, but a light was on downstairs.

"If Captain Cowan should pull up while I'm inside, place him under arrest."

"As a duly sworn driver of the White House Transportation Agency?"

"As a citizen of the United States. Just put your gun on him and call out." Welborn had already ascertained that Leo was licensed to carry. "I'll be right there with my federal warrant."

"And if he rabbits, I'm the hound."

"And call the state police. I'll be along shortly."

Leo looked at a dark house across the street. "I'll be over there in the driveway."

"Thanks, Leo."

"Thank you, brother. I'm hoping to have some fun tonight."

ARLENE COWAN had a spot of dust on her chin when she opened her door. Welborn was tempted to wipe it off, she looked so fetching. Her hair was piled up atop her head, strands poking out here and there. She wore a man's white dress shirt, the sleeves rolled up and the tails out. A pair of denim shorts did little to hide long legs shaped by lean muscle. Her feet were bare; her toenails painted a dusty rose.

Welborn offered her his handkerchief. His mother advised he always carry one.

"Your chin, Arlene. You smudged it a little."

She tidied herself and gave him his hanky back.

"I'm not going to get my money, am I? From Dex, I mean."

"His car's worth about eighty grand; you ought to get that in the divorce. He won't need it where he's going."

"Well, hell," she said. "Come on in. There's some champagne left. But if you don't want any, I'll drink it."

They went inside. Boxes were stacked high and wide. The living-room rug was rolled up against a wall. The only place to sit was a love seat placed to look out a window on the backyard. Arlene plopped down, grabbed an open bottle of champagne from an ice-filled plastic planter.

"You sure you don't want any?" she asked, holding the bottle up.

"I'm on duty," he said. He sat next to Arlene, but not too close.

"Duty being to arrest my husband?"

He nodded.

"What's the charge?"

"Homicide. Washington Metro PD found Captain Cowan's fingerprints in a car used to run down a woman."

"Oh, God." She knocked back some wine.

"I need your help," Welborn told her. He said Dexter Cowan still listed the Falls Church address as his official residence. The Navy had no other known domicile for him. "I'd like you to call your husband, have him come here, if you know how he might be reached."

Doubt etched itself across Arlene Cowan's features. She was ready to divorce her husband, but that was open and aboveboard. Betrayal was underhanded and at odds with her upbringing. There were some things to which a lady just didn't stoop.

Welborn understood her dilemma and sought to help her resolve it.

"Arlene, there could be a question as to whether Captain Cowan came by his newfound money honestly. I mean, the funds he used to buy his new car and other assets of which you may be unaware. It's possible the government might seize his belongings. Possibly some of yours, too, if the title is held jointly. *Or* in appreciation for your help, it might relinquish everything he has to you."

Her upbringing certainly hadn't prepared her for this mess.

"My new job," she said, "the salary's quite good. But I found this really great house back home. It's just wonderful. There's even land to keep a horse. But I was counting on the money from Dex to swing it."

"Disappointment can be a trial," Welborn said.

Arlene nodded and drained her bottle. It was stooping time, after all.

"Dex gave me a new cell phone number a while back. When I thought he wanted me to catch him cheating."

"Have you ever used it?"

"No, but if you promise to tell everyone how cooperative I was, I'll give it a try."

"Why don't you do that, Arlene?"

MCGILL HAD no sooner gotten Caitie back to the White House than the phone rang in the residence. He was relieved to have his daughter safe, but before picking up he prayed: *Please, please, please. Let it be Carolyn.*

It wasn't. Patti was on the phone.

"Sweetie was wonderful," she said. "I wish there was some kind of medal I could give her. She almost got Godfrey to confess."

McGill knew just the moment to which Patti referred, when the reverend looked as if he might swallow his tongue.

"Caitie was a picture of strength, too," Patti added.

"She wants your job," McGill told her.

His youngest was in a guest room on another phone, talking to her friends back home, asking excitedly if they'd seen her on television.

"The next time I campaign, we'll take her along. A month on the rubber-chicken circuit should cure her of that."

McGill could only hope. "You think we accomplished anything tonight?" he asked. "Godfrey didn't exactly call off the dogs."

"I think we'll know about that shortly. But you did what people in my business always threaten to do to each other. Go over each other's heads and speak directly to the people. I don't know what headway we'd have made with Sweetie by herself, as great as she was. But when those people in the park and everyone watching on TV saw Caitie's face, it had to drive the point home: There's no justification for killing this child."

There was no justification for killing Andy Grant either, McGill thought, but that didn't stop the SOBs. He kept that last bit to himself. Instead, he asked, "Is your foreign endeavor set to commence soon?"

"I expect I'll be hearing shortly."

McGill paused, then broached the subject that was uppermost on his mind.

"The FBI knows you're at Camp David, right?"

"Yes."

"And you still haven't—"

"I'm sorry, Jim. Not a word about Carolyn and Lars."

TWO MINUTES after McGill said good-bye to Patti, the phone rang again.

Carolyn! he thought.

It wasn't her. A woman was on the line. McGill didn't recognize her voice. Which was passing strange, because yet another benefit of life at the White House was that you didn't get wrong numbers or telemarketing calls, not even from charities or politicians.

To direct dial the residence, you needed to know not only the root number but also a special suffix code. The chance of hitting the right sequence randomly was nil.

Yet: "Mr. McGill, are you there?"

"Yes, who is this?"

For one stomach-churning moment, he thought it was an unlikely-sounding kidnapper; Carolyn had the code to call the residence.

"I am Siran Missirian. You know my husband, Dikran."

Dikki Missirian. His landlord on P Street. To whom McGill had given his number at the White House in case of dire emergency. Such as his office catching fire.

"Yes, Mrs. Missirian, is everything all right?"

"No, not all right at all."

McGill could hear her anxiety now.

"Dikki not come home tonight," she said.

It was a complaint he'd heard countless times as a cop. Most were of no consequence; others were very serious. He placed Mrs. Missirian's call in the latter category.

"What time were you expecting him?"

"Seven o'clock, Dikki tell me."

McGill looked at his watch. It was nine fifteen.

"You called the Metro police?"

"Yes."

"And they told you it was too soon for them to do anything."

"*Yes.*" She broke down, and the tears came.

McGill gave her a moment. "Did Dikki let you know if he had to stay late? If he had any unusual business."

She did her best to compose herself. "He tells me this, yes. A man is meeting him to sign lease for his new building. He says this take fifteen, thirty minutes most; fifteen more, he be home."

McGill had never met Mrs. Missirian, but Dikki had shown her picture to him. She was young and quite pretty. McGill didn't think for a moment that Dikki was out fooling around.

"Mrs. Missirian, you've tried calling your husband's office?"

"Yes, and mobile phone. Phones only ring and ring."

"Did you go by his office in person?"

"No, Dikki not like me to go out alone at night."

"Did your husband tell you the name of the man he was waiting for?"

"Yes, the man is a doctor."

"Did you get the doctor's name?"

"I have it written. Wait, please … doctor's name is Benjamin Casey."

Benjamin Casey? A doctor? *Dr. Ben Casey?*

McGill not only remembered the show, he recalled the star's name: Vince Edwards. Likened to Rory Calhoun, he was in touch with that era of pop culture.

"Mr. McGill, please. You are detective. You will help me find my husband?"

Deke had already taken off on his well-deserved personal time. McGill had lent Leo out to Welborn. Sweetie had said she was going out to eat with Putnam Shady, but hadn't said where. He was sure he could get Celsus to provide him with someone, but he'd be damned if he'd owe that stiff a favor.

He could simply play it safe and extend his regrets to Mrs. Missirian.

Only he knew just how she felt: the same way he did about Carolyn.

"Mrs. Missirian, I'm leaving for P Street right now. I'll let you know what I find."

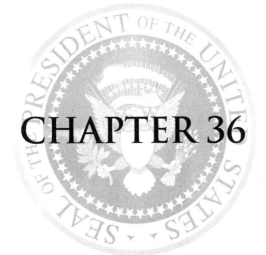

CHAPTER 36

MCGILL CALLED a cab. Had it come to the northwest gate of the White House. It was the only way he could think of getting around. His personal car was back home in Evanston. There were certainly cars in the White House motor pool available to him, but those were government-funded vehicles that were supposed to be used for official business. Not the business of McGill Investigations, Inc. He didn't want to give Patti's political enemies even that small an opening.

Besides, going through channels would alert the Secret Service. He wouldn't wind up with a car, he'd be stuck in a *motorcade*. Not what he wanted at all. It was tough being a regular guy when you were married to the president.

The cabbie had beaten McGill to the gate and, for his promptness, the uniformed agents guarding the White House had him spread-eagle on the hood of his vehicle. Staffers at the Executive Mansion, the ones who didn't rate limos, called for cabs every day. But they let the boys at the drawbridge know they were coming and who had summoned them.

McGill had not. Trying to keep a low profile. Now, his turbaned taxi man was paying the price. Until he stepped forward, and said, "It's okay, guys. He's here for me."

The uniformed agents turned and saw the president's husband.

He shrugged, and said, "Sorry, I forgot to alert you."

"This taxi's for *you,* sir?" the officer in charge of the detail asked. "I don't understand."

"An errand I have to run," McGill explained. "I thought I'd keep things low-key. You want to let that fellow up?"

The driver was released and helped to his feet. He wiped off the front of his shirt and slacks. Resettled his turban to its proper angle. He looked at McGill and bowed.

With great dignity and an English accent, he said, "I tried to explain that I am a Sikh, and as of last week I am an American citizen."

"I'm sorry for your trouble," McGill said. "The fault's all mine."

The uniformed Secret Service agents weren't sure what McGill was up to, having seen no other presidential spouse like him, but they appreciated that he hadn't tried to pass the buck.

"Are you able to drive?" McGill asked the man.

"Yes, of course." He opened the rear door of his taxi for his fare.

"Your tip will be generous," McGill said, entering the cab.

"I'll not take a penny, sir. I know who you are, and I am honored to drive you."

McGill didn't give him their destination until they were out of earshot of the Secret Service.

MCGILL HAD the cab circle the block on P Street and drop him off at the far corner. He gave the driver $50. Not for himself, of course, but for his favorite charity.

He approached his office building from the opposite side of the street. The block was tree-lined, and cars occupied every parking space; he had plenty of cover to duck behind. But there was no one out to spy on him. No other pedestrian walked on either side of the street. No one was peering out a window. The only sounds came from traffic whizzing along nearby Rock Creek Parkway.

He looked across the street at Dikki's building. The café table was still out, but the umbrella and chairs had been taken in. He wondered if Dikki was still inside, too. Unable to answer the phone.

It hadn't taken him long to guess the source of Dikki's troubles. He'd figured it out in the cab on the way over. Who would pick a fictional doctor as an alter ego except another doctor? What doctor could he have ticked off lately? Damon Todd. Could Todd come to express his displeasure to McGill at home? Well, look what had happened when an innocent but unexpected cabbie had come calling at the White House.

So Todd had stopped by his office after hours. The only question was, had he hurt or killed Dikki to get McGill's attention? Actually, there was another question. Could he have known McGill would come alone? No, he couldn't. But if he'd been watching McGill's movements, he would know the level of protection he usually had: one special agent.

If this guy thought he could take care of McGill and Deke, he had quite some opinion of himself. McGill didn't share it, though. Any guy who had to drug and hypnotize women to have sex with them had to be the worst kind of coward.

McGill did a visual sweep of Dikki's building from the top down. There was no one on the roof that he could see. The windows of McGill Investigations, Inc. were dark. As were the windows of Wentworth & Willough by, the accounting firm on the second floor. Down on the ground floor, though, a dim glow showed through the plate-glass window at the front of A-Sharp Sound. Max Lucey could be in one of his recording studios working on a project.

McGill checked again for passersby. He still had that stretch of P Street to himself. He took out his gun and the key to the front door of the building. He crossed the street and slipped the key into the lock. He didn't have to turn the key; the door was unlocked.

That wasn't the way Dikki would have left it. He stepped inside.

To the right was the stairway, leading to the upper floors. To the left, a short hallway led to Dikki's office and the rear exit. McGill flicked the safety off his gun and took a quick peek up the staircase. Didn't see or hear anything.

Dikki's small office was on the right of the hallway, tucked under the stairs. Light painted a yellow ribbon at the bottom of his door. The rear exit door was tightly shut. It could be opened with a push from inside, but an alarm would sound. Dikki had shown him once that the alarm was startlingly loud. Maybe that was the thing to do now. Draw some outside attention.

Of course, if Todd had a gun in Dikki's ear, and the noise made him jump …

Maybe Dikki's office, itself, was the trap. The burning light was the come-on. Open the door and *boom!* A gun or a bomb goes off, and suddenly your future is behind you. Only, as far as McGill knew, Todd had no history of using guns or bombs.

What was more likely for a headshrinker, he'd try to screw with your head. Leave a light on and hope you'd ignore it. Wouldn't take the chance of investigating. You'd consider your own safety first. Then, if you survived, you'd learn that you'd blown the opportunity to save someone else's life; you'd chickened out. Live with that.

McGill looked around once more, saw no one, and turned the doorknob. He flung the door open and flattened himself against the adjacent wall. No lethal engine was triggered, but the door quickly closed again.

It had hit something and bounced back with a bang.

But the noise drew no reaction. No voice called out. No footsteps approached. McGill tried the door to Dikki's office again. Gave it an easy push this time. Halfway through its arc, the door stopped with a soft thump.

McGill took a quick peek and saw Dikki lying on the floor in front of his desk.

WELBORN AND Leo saw the silhouette on the shade in a second-floor window of the Cowan house. A nude woman. Arlene Cowan. Doing her best in a bad situation. Really working for that new house in Tennessee.

The two men watched from Leo's Chevy, parked nose out, in the driveway across the street. It would have been the most natural thing in the world for Welborn and Leo to offer bawdy comments, but neither of them did. They'd both been raised better than that.

Arlene Cowan had reached her husband at the number he'd given her. She'd persuaded him that they had to talk. She had information he needed, but no way was she going to tell him over the phone. Who knew who might be listening in? Person to person, wife to husband, nobody could make them reveal a word of what they said.

After Arlene had clicked off, she'd turned to Welborn with tears in her eyes.

"I actually loved Dex once upon a time. Now, I feel like such a rat."

"Think of your new life," Welborn told her. "Your job, your house, your horse."

"Accentuate the positive." She laughed, but it was a humorless sound.

It had been her idea to do the peep show. Make sure she got Dex into the house. And if Welborn didn't mind, she'd throw him one last good one as it would likely be the last he'd ever have. The law could have him after that.

Welborn didn't like the idea; it conjured images of a hostage situation.

But Arlene looked so forlorn … and the idea of his coming between a man's last conjugal act with his wife was embarrassing … and he thought he could make it work, and …

Welborn was young. It was his first case.

He waited across the street in the car with Leo. For all he knew, a married man could smell another male in his house. If he stayed inside, he was more likely to cause trouble than prevent it. Besides, if Arlene did throw Dex Cowan a good one, he didn't want to be close enough to hear the bedsprings creak.

Intruding on Welborn's thoughts, Leo said, "Lights coming."

Welborn turned his head and saw the approaching car. "It's a Viper."

The car slowed. Captain Dexter Cowan was behind the wheel. He turned the wheels to head into his driveway and … stopped. Seeing Arlene's figure up there could have that effect on a man, Welborn reasoned. Cowan spent several seconds taking in the view. Maybe anticipating the pleasure that would soon be his.

"Enjoy it while you can, buddy," Welborn muttered.

But sex with the missus wasn't what the Navy man had in mind. He suddenly cut his wheels back toward the street, and the Viper took off with a roar. A heartbeat later, Leo had the Chevy rocketing after it.

Welborn had flown fighter jets. Whatever top end either the Viper or the Chevy could manage, it would amount to little more than stall speed for an F-22. Then again, speed was relative, a matter of context. At thirty thousand feet, supercruising at Mach 1.5 could get to feel more like cruising than super. It was only when you flew your bird down on the deck and saw how fast that distant mountain range was coming upon you that you really got to appreciate how fast you were moving.

At street level, being pressed back into his seat by the car's acceleration, Welborn felt like Leo had the Chevy about to break the sound barrier. Stationary objects—houses, trees, light poles—became part of a blurred continuum at the corners of his eyes. The only object that remained in sharp focus lay directly ahead: the navy blue Viper.

Welborn was very glad most of the good people of Falls Church were off that particular thoroughfare just then. God help anyone who got in the way.

"You'll stop for school buses, right?" Welborn asked.

Leo grinned. "Them and people with white canes. But you got a point."

He tapped a button on the steering wheel. The special effects show began immediately. High-intensity lights flashed from the front grille. A howler screamed. Even the engine's growl seemed louder. Seismographs would be picking up their approach.

Welborn only hoped that any other drivers on the road would be equally aware.

Especially after Dex Cowan busted right through a red light. Flew through the intersection and onto the Leesburg Pike entrance ramp to I-66 eastbound. Leo had the Chevy no more than ten feet behind. By great good fortune neither vehicle had threatened any legitimately proceeding cross traffic. But rolling along the highway, approaching the entry point of the on-ramp, was a fifty-three-foot tractor-trailer hauling groceries for the Giant supermarket chain.

Both speeding drivers downshifted. Welborn was thrown forward and caught by his three-point safety belt. He felt it dig hard into his shoulder, chest, and waist. The sensation was so hauntingly familiar it would have flashed him back to the night his friends had died had he not been so focused on his own imminent mortality. The Giant truck filled his entire field of vision; it looked like both the Viper and the Chevy would become decals on the side of the trailer. He closed his eyes, not daring to hope he'd ever open them again.

But the crash never came. There wasn't even a jolt. Only a sideways drifting sensation. Welborn wondered if passing from life to afterlife could be so gentle. He opened his eyes. The truck that had been right in front him was now … where the hell was it? He looked at the right-hand side-view mirror. There it was. The semi had already receded to the point of being tiny. Looking ahead, he saw that Cowan, too, had escaped unscratched.

"Boy's a fair driver for an amateur," Leo allowed.

The Viper and the Chevy were, appropriately, in the fast lane. Traffic on the highway was light at the moment. The cars in the other two lanes might have been stopped to fix flat tires for how quickly they were left behind. Both the Viper and the Chevy weaved around a Porsche that was clogging up the fast lane, doing no more than 95 mph.

Leo made it look effortless. He even started to hum.

Which made Welborn think to ask, "You have a radio? I'll call for help."

"Look out your window," Leo said.

Welborn did, at first seeing only the blur of highway signs. Then he looked up and saw a police helicopter. It was struggling to keep pace.

"We're outrunning an aircraft," Welborn said.

Leo smiled. "Yeah. Who says Detroit can't make a great car?"

"Those cops didn't just happen along, did they?"

"Uh-uh. When I hit the let's-boogie button—the lights and screamer—it started broadcasting an emergency signal. Every police unit in a sixty-mile radius is homing in on us. For all they know the president's husband could be along for the ride."

"That police escort would be comforting … if they can keep up."

"They probably have a few fixed-wing planes that can. Important thing, though, they'll be radioing ahead, clearing the roads for us."

"That *is* good," Welborn agreed.

"But the rest is up to us. Cops tried to set up a roadblock on a vehicle pushing 160 miles per hour, the debris field would cover three counties."

"So your suggestion would be?"

Leo might have been a commuter driving to work with a cup of coffee in one hand for all the concern he showed. "If I had just a bit more confidence in that boy up there, I'd pull alongside and swap a little paint with him. Maybe throw a spark or two. Take the starch out of him."

"Let's not do that," Welborn said.

Leo shot him a look. "You *really* used to fly jets?"

"Yeah. Give me a minute or two to adapt here, will you? There weren't any bridge abutments where I worked."

"Okay, maybe you've got a point. We'll just squat on him then."

Leo narrowed the gap between the Viper and the Chevy. There wasn't room for a stray thought between the two cars. Welborn was able to read Cowan's speedometer.

"The point of tailgating is?" he asked.

"It's my comfort zone," Leo said, "but I doubt it's his."

Or mine, Welborn thought. "You don't want him comfortable?"

"I want him holding on for dear life and running out of gas real soon. Him going dry is our best play now."

"There's something I have to tell you," Welborn said.

"What?"

Cowan goosed the Viper, swerved right, and shot into the lanes for I-495, the Washington Beltway. He gained maybe five feet on Leo for maybe two seconds. Once again, the Chevy drew close enough for Welborn to see Cowan's instrument cluster.

"I was going to say he wasn't running flat out, but he is now."

Leo was having a grand time. "I'm beginning to like that ol' boy."

SAC CELSUS Crogher was right where he belonged, guarding the president of the United States at Camp David, when he got the news.

"Holmes is out."

The bulletin came from Winston Strawn, the officer in charge of the uniformed detail at the northwest gate of the White House.

"What do you mean *out*?" Crogher demanded.

"He left the building in a cab."

"*A cab?*" Crogher would have found it equally credible to hear McGill had been taken away in a flying saucer. "Who's with him?"

"Nobody. Just the cabbie."

"And you let him go?"

"He's free, white, and over twenty-one."

Strawn, being African American and about to retire after thirty years of flawless service, felt free to be politically incorrect and crack wise to his boss.

"Besides," he said, "who's going to tell the president's henchman no?"

Everyone in the Secret Service knew that Crogher hadn't been able to do it.

Damn that James J. McGill, Crogher thought. The SAC *really* wanted to quit. But that bastard McGill had been right. He'd never forgive himself if he left and something bad happened to Holly G. Like everyone else who spent any time with her, except her demented political enemies, Crogher had fallen in love with the president. Platonically, of course.

"Did you hear Holmes's destination?" he asked.

"Negative."

"But you got the cab's number."

"Affirmative."

"Find that cabbie immediately. I'll be touching down in thirty minutes."

MCGILL STEPPED out the front door of his P Street building. He carried Dikki Missirian's unconscious form. He laid the man down on the welcome mat outside of A-Sharp Sound. Dikki was more than heavy enough to activate the pressure plate under the mat. The light at the back of the business, near the recording studios, still glowed. Max Lucey would come out and find Dikki.

He'd see the Post-It note on the landlord's chest: *Call 911. I'll be up in my office. Jim McGill.*

He'd have called for an ambulance and the Metro police if the phone in Dikki's office hadn't been disabled. As for Dikki himself, McGill hadn't been able to rouse him, but his pulse was steady, and he showed no signs of physical distress. He had to be drugged.

Ketamine hydrochloride would be McGill's bet.

He went back into the building. The prudent thing to do, of course, was wait for the Metro cops to come. Let them make the pinch. Lead Damon Todd away in handcuffs. Except he didn't know the response time for the local PD. Should be pretty good for a gilded area like Georgetown, but if the cops already had their hands full on a Friday night with other calls, it could be an hour or more. Todd might slip away.

McGill wasn't going to let that happen.

He drew his gun and started to climb the stairs. Not a single one creaked. The silence was perfect for having second thoughts. Even if the Metro cops were busy, the Secret Service would come on the run. He arrived at the second-floor offices of Wentworth & Willoughby. No light came through the frosted-glass panel in the top half of W&W's door. He tried the door. Locked.

Didn't necessarily mean that Todd wasn't inside. Dikki had keys to every door in the building; he kept them in his office. Where Todd had waylaid the landlord. So you had to figure the psycho-shrink had access to—

Jesus!

It could be Todd, not Max Lucey, who was inside A-Sharp Sound, and he'd left Dikki down there on the welcome mat with a note to call 911. Saying where he could be found, too.

Not a good time to get sloppy, he told himself.

Question was which way did he go: up or down.

Up, he decided. He was the reason Todd was in the building. He was the one who'd been lured there that night. That spoke of a desire for a confrontation. A showdown. Where would a lunatic like Todd most want that to happen? McGill's personal space, of course.

McGill also found the setting apt.

He ascended to the third floor. The landing where lobbyists had once waited to court his favor looked as innocent as at any other time he'd seen it. The door to his suite from the hallway was on the left; the door to the stairs leading to the roof was straight ahead. Both were tightly closed. No light bled through either doorframe.

McGill glanced over his shoulder. No one was climbing the stairs behind him.

He tried both doors; they were locked. He used his left hand to turn the key in the door bearing his name on frosted glass. He pushed it open a couple of inches and waited. If Max Lucey was the one who found Dikki out front, it shouldn't be too long before he heard the sound of an ambulance. On the other hand, if it was Todd downstairs, waiting McGill out, Dikki would be easy pickings for the first street thief to happen by.

McGill couldn't just stay where he was and mark time.

He kicked the door to his office open and burst through the entryway like a sprinter coming out of the blocks. He cut left around the reception desk, skidded to a neat stop, and flicked a light switch with his gun hand. But just as if Thomas Edison had never been born, the lights stayed off.

Behind him, McGill heard a soft laugh mock his efforts.

He whirled, and, in the light from the hallway, he saw a cylindrical object heading straight at him. Not high where he could duck or low where he could jump. But smack-dab in the middle. A rib crusher. A gut buster. A fight ender.

Unless you knew Dark Alley.

"I KNOW where he's going," Welborn said of Cowan. "Where he wanted to go, anyway."

"Where's that?" Leo asked.

They were loafing along at 140 mph. Welborn had grown accustomed to the speed. Liked it actually. He was able to enjoy the velocity without worrying about g-forces messing up his inner ear. The navy blue Viper was a mile or so ahead.

They didn't have to worry about losing Cowan any longer.

"He hoped to take the Beltway to Route 50. From there you go east, and you're in Annapolis. Where Cowan has a lot of Naval Academy buddies. Or go west and you come to Landover. Where Colonel Linberg lives. Unless she's moved out by now."

Welborn had given Leo an overview of his case earlier that night.

"So which is it? The guys or the babe?"

"He's got to know he won't get away. So if I was him—"

"The babe."

"Colonel Linberg, definitely."

"Too bad," Leo said. "He had his only chance for female company earlier tonight."

The fact was, Dexter Cowan was already caught. He just hadn't given up spinning his wheels. His critical mistake had been getting on the Beltway. Acting with admirable speed, the highway cops in Maryland and Virginia had shepherded all other traffic to the shoulder of the road, or off it entirely, as circumstance allowed, and then the cops did what Leo said they wouldn't. They set up roadblocks.

At every exit and entry ramp on the whole of the I-495 loop.

They didn't use valuable police cruisers to do it. Oh, no. They brought in dozens of out-of-service school buses and stacked them four deep across every ramp. They'd learn later that a pragmatic highway patrol officer working on the homeland security problem of how to trap terrorists driving a car bomb on the Beltway had come up with the idea. And it worked like a charm on a naval officer fleeing arrest. If Cowan wanted to end his days by turning his fancy car into a pile of scrap metal, more power to him.

Welborn and Leo followed along to make the bust in case Cowan saw the light of reason.

"I've been thinking about one or two things since all the excitement went out of the evening," Leo said.

"Yeah, what's that?"

"First off, that lady out in Falls Church, the captain's wife."

"Arlene."

"I was wondering if what she did, prancing around up there in the altogether, maybe that was a signal for our boy to take off. Which he surely did."

"Most people would think the opposite. 'Come hither,' you know."

"Well, yeah. But these two were getting a divorce. And what if, even when things were good between them, she'd always liked to do it in the dark? He comes home tonight, sees her all brazen like she was, what's he going to think?"

Welborn thought even a bonehead like Cowan would figure out something was wrong. He'd take off. Which was exactly what he did. And Arlene had expressed to Welborn her regrets at betraying her mate. Damnit! But how the hell could he prove complicity? There was no way. So he was going to write it up that Arlene had cooperated. He owed her that much … he thought.

So much of his job, it turned out, hadn't been covered at Glynco.

"What else are you thinking?" Welborn asked Leo.

"Well, let's say our boy hadn't taken off. He goes inside, has his roll with the wife, she gets emotional as women are apt to do, and she confesses. Now we've got ourselves a hostage situation. What would you have done then?"

Looking at the road ahead, Welborn said, "I think he's slowing down."

"I believe you're right. Out of gas most likely."

"If he'd taken Arlene hostage, I'd have taken his car hostage."

Leo grinned. "You think his car would mean more to him than his wife?"

"The Viper is his *new* love."

"Good point."

"Hey, what the hell's he doing?" Welborn asked.

"That there's called a bootlegger's turn; it was nicely done, too."

Cowan had spun his Viper counterclockwise 180 degrees.

He was headed straight back at the Chevy.

Closing speed between the two vehicles was already over 200 mph, and climbing.

"NURSE, PLEASE."

Daryl Cheveyo had awakened from a nap and remembered everything: who he was supposed to see; who was in danger; who was the threat. Respectively, they were the Deputy Director of Intelligence; James J. McGill, the president's husband; and Dr. Damon Todd, the off-center psychiatrist who wanted to join the CIA and start a program of crafted personalities.

Todd had been casing McGill's office building on P Street.

The DD needed to know about that.

The nurse entered his room, took one look at him, and said, "You're feeling better, aren't you? You look better. Let me get the doctor."

"Yeah, get him. But first get me the deputy director."

The nurse's eyes narrowed. Maybe the patient wasn't fully recovered.

"Please," Cheveyo said in a calm voice. "I'm rational. I know what I'm doing. He'll want to talk with me. A very important person's life might be in danger at this very moment."

DARK ALLEY taught that if someone came at you with a bat, you became a baseball. If you had room, you were a knuckleball, dancing crazily just out of reach while the batter took his cut and missed. If you didn't have room, you were a fastball thrown at the batter's head. That way he had to drop the bat and get the hell out of the way.

McGill didn't have room.

He shot forward and thrust out the heel of his left hand. You didn't want to use a bare fist against somebody's noggin; too easy to break your knuckles. The meaty part of the bottom of the palm was perfect for slamming into someone's forehead. Usually, when that happened, the head snapped back, the brain ricocheted around inside the skull, and as often as not cervical vertebrae lost their structural integrity. Paralysis and death were not uncommon consequences.

In this case, however, things didn't work out quite according to form. The batter's head didn't snap back. He was knocked off his feet, landed on his ass with a thump, and lost his grip on the bat, which rolled away from him. But the blow wasn't the decisive one it should have been.

The assailant's neck had been too strong to allow for a whiplash effect. Chances were that if someone had gone to the trouble of building up his neck muscles to that extent, he'd likely done the same with the rest of his body. It was enough to make McGill glad he still had his gun in his right hand.

"Damon Todd?" he asked.

He got no answer, but the man he'd knocked down got up. Wasn't unsteady on his feet, either. Held his body like he was ready to try McGill again.

"Pay attention," McGill said. "I've got a gun in my hand."

The guy laughed. "The last asshole who pointed a gun at me, I choked to death."

McGill fired a round past the guy's head. Just past it. Close enough to make him jump.

"Thanks for the confession. Try me, and your choking days will be over."

McGill waited. Gave the guy a chance to make a *kamikaze* run if he wanted. Was just as glad when he didn't. Perhaps the gunshot ringing in his ears had dropped his testosterone level a notch or two. For the moment, anyway.

He said, "I'm going to back into my office now, and you're going to follow me. You'll keep the same interval we have now. You'll take a seat in my guest chair. Once you're seated, you'll slide the chair back against the wall behind it. Any of this too complicated for you?"

The guy grunted. Then he asked, "And if I don't?"

McGill fired another round. Just to the other side of the guy's head.

"I've got you bracketed now. Next one's straight up the middle."

He took a step back; the guy took a step forward.

McGill said, "Just so you know, I'm firing steel-jacketed rounds. You try to dive to either side of the doorway, I'll shoot right through the wall. I'll get you. Long before my clip's empty."

There was no dispute on that point. McGill backed around his desk. The guy followed into his office and sat down. The streetlight through McGill's windows was brighter than the hallway light had been in the outer office. McGill could see who he was dealing with.

"You're Todd, all right."

A crazed hypertrophied version of the man he'd seen in the photo with Chana, but Todd nonetheless. A shrink who needed to be shrunk.

"Push your chair back against the wall."

Todd did as he was told. He stared at McGill.

The president's henchman sat in his own chair and picked up his desk phone. He heard no dial tone when he brought it to his ear. Todd smiled as if he'd put one over on him.

"You like music?" McGill asked.

The smile on Todd's face turned into a look of puzzlement. Which was all the answer McGill needed. The SOB hadn't gone into A-Sharp Sound. If he had, he would have understood the question. Had something to say about Max Lucey's recording studio downstairs.

"Well, never mind about that," McGill said. "You've disabled my office phone; I forgot my cell phone when I rushed out of the house. We'll just have to sit here and wait until someone comes along, and I can ask them to call the cops. Might not be until morning, so relax."

McGill hoped help would arrive sooner rather than later. Max should have found Dikki on his doorstep by now. With any luck, Max was calling 911 at that very moment.

But McGill wanted Todd to relax. Think he had all night to get out of his current predicament. Not try to force the issue until it was too late.

It was all a question of whether Todd had bought his lie.

CHAPTER 37

THE OBREGON brothers, Alberto, Bartolo, Ciro, and Darío had just taken their Fountain 38 Lightning, *El Matador,* out to sea from the Cuban exiles' base in Costa Gorda. The boat had twin MerCruiser 500-horsepower engines and a top speed of 88 mph. The fuel tank had been enlarged from 260 gallons to 400 gallons to make the trip to Miami nonstop.

Best of all, *El Matador* had clearance from the Department of Defense to enter U.S. waters without hindrance from the Coast Guard. Those *pendejos* with their cutters and helicopters had been told to keep their hands off the Obregon boys and their boat. And why not? Weren't they fighting to free Cuba from godless communism?

Sí! The president himself had said so. Not the *mujer* who was in the White House now, but the president from before. Even the new one, though, let them continue to do their work.

Part of which, as they saw it, was to take regular shipments of cocaine from Central America to Miami. After all, what was the point of freeing Cuba from Fidel if you couldn't return as a rich man? Selling the load of powder they had aboard that night would allow them to reclaim all the land the Bearded One had stolen from their family so many years ago.

Partly to celebrate that fact and partly to give them energy for the long voyage to Miami, the brothers had partaken of the wares that would make them rich men and aristocrats in their homeland once again. Their futures would be glorious. Any recalcitrant communist peasants who dared to defy them, they would crush like *hormigas.*

Just as they had disposed of the rabble at the produce market they had blown up.

To reach their destination with fuel in reserve, they needed to cruise at no more than twenty knots. But there was no fun in that. No manliness. Push the speed up to forty knots, and they would run out of gas a quarter mile from their slip at the marina ... but their momentum would carry them the rest of the way. Let them jump up onto the dock and tie off their beautiful boat with a flourish. That was what men would do, and it was what they did.

Their machismo, their honor, and the coke racing through their veins demanded it. Nothing could stop them. But then Darío, the youngest, looked ahead, and his eyes widened.

"*Madre de Dios.*"

His brothers followed his gaze, and they saw it, too. The fix might have been in with the U.S. Coast Guard, but the ship that had just come into view flew the Cuban flag.

Apparently, somebody forgot to pay off Fidel's navy.

Then Alberto, the eldest, grasped the true significance of what they were seeing.

"The communists attack our base!" he yelled. "*¡Hermanos, a las armas!*"

Brothers, to arms!

"SKIPPER, THE bogey has changed course," the radarman on the bridge of the faux-*Martí* said. "It's headed straight at us."

"A ramming course?" the captain asked incredulously.

"Yes, sir. Unless it changes course."

"Light him up."

Radar-linked, hundred-thousand-candlepower searchlights cut through the night.

"It's a speedboat for Christ's sake. Fiberglass. Can't be more that forty feet," the captain said. "Damn thing couldn't chip our paint."

The *Marti* had tracked the radar blip from the moment it left port. The captain had been content to let it go on its way. But now that it was on an insane suicide run …

A beadwork of white dots appeared from the onrushing craft.

"Small-arms fire, Skipper."

These dumb shits were starting to annoy the captain. And it occurred to him, times being what they were, that even a light craft could be loaded to the gunwales with high explosives. So he told his weapons systems officer, "Use the 30mm gun. Chew his ass up. Don't let that sonofabitch impact our hull."

"Aye, Captain," the officer replied.

The 30 mm gun began to spit out fifty rounds per second, and the first second undoubtedly would have got the job done. The fiberglass hull of *El Matador* flew apart like a dandelion in a hurricane. Then the fuel tank exploded. A geyser of fire shot skyward as if a volcano had erupted from the surface of the sea. The shock wave from the blast rocked the *Marti*.

The thunderous roar caused a sudden flurry of activity onshore; the exiles' base had been notified it was under attack.

"Cease fire with the thirty," the captain said. "Now that we have everyone's attention, let's open up with the seventy-six."

Using its fire-control radar, and the national technical assets flying overhead, the *Marti* began to shell the base with its big gun. The Navy personnel were skilled at their jobs. Base infrastructure would be destroyed, but no additional casualties would be reported.

Heavy machine-gun fire opened up from the shoreline, but that came exclusively from the American advisors on hand in the camp, and they, too, had been ordered to cause no harm.

It was said no battle plan survived its first contact with the enemy, but the president's hope that no blood be spilled in the Costa Gorda Incident, as it came to be known, was very nearly achieved.

Would have been if not for the assholes in the speedboat.

NAVY GUY, Welborn thought. Just like one to try a ramming maneuver. USAF pilots didn't fly their planes into things. It wasn't the way an airman got things done. The Navy, on the other hand, had its own distinct traditions, seeing whose hulls and skulls were thicker being one of them. The navy blue Viper rushed at them like a bullet in one of those special-effects flicks. Where you could see it coming *inch by inch*. Even though you knew it was moving at incredible speed.

Shit. Welborn could see Dex Cowan's face. Getting closer, closer, closer. Guy looked like he was wearing a death mask. His life was already over, and, as long as he was going, he thought he might as well take Welborn and Leo with him.

A sidelong glance, the most Welborn would dare risk, showed him that Leo was looking mighty grim-faced himself. He had his hands set on the Chevy's steering wheel at ten and two and showed no sign he planned to go anywhere but straight ahead.

Welborn remembered Leo saying how big the debris field would be: three counties. But he didn't think now would be the time to offer a suggestion because you never knew, Leo might have something in mind. Please, Lord!

Which, as it turned out, Leo did. He *accelerated*.

The increase in speed, the sheer lunatic aggressiveness of the move, must have registered in Cowan's brain because, for a split second, his own resolve faltered. He eased up on his headlong charge into oblivion. Not that there would have been any avoiding a crash if the cars had continued to travel a straight line.

But when Leo saw Cowan's hint of hesitation, he flicked his steering wheel just a hair to the right. The two cars streaked past each other without room for a gnat's ass between them. For a second, it seemed to Welborn as if Leo would just keep going, make it impossible for Cowan to make another turn and catch them before he ran out of gas. But then they heard a resounding boom behind them. Leo brought the Chevy to a smooth stop in a shorter distance than Welborn would have thought possible and turned the car perpendicular to its lane.

Looking through Leo's side window, they saw shards of rubber flying a hundred feet into the night sky. The Viper's front-right tire had just exploded. The sports car leaned in the direction of the missing tire, riding on its rim at well over a hundred miles per hour. A curtain of sparks shot into the air where metal carved the road surface. The light show continued for half a mile before the front axle gave way. The car leaned onto its right-front end and abruptly started to flip repeatedly, like a toy discarded by an angry child.

Somewhere in all the horrific somersaulting, Cowan was thrown clear, and he began to cartwheel in the same fashion. As with the Viper, he didn't stay intact either. The only consolation, if there was one to be had, was that he had to be dead before he was dismembered.

Welborn took it all in without blinking.

And thought: No woman was worth that.

Leo's focus was on the car.

He said, "That tire that blew? Somebody messed with it."

CONTRARY TO SAC Crogher's express order, the cabbie who'd departed with Holmes—a.k.a. James J. McGill—in his backseat hadn't been located by the time the Secret Service boss landed at the White House helipad.

"Why the hell not?" Crogher demanded.

Winston Strawn, the head of the uniformed detail at the northwest gate, who'd last seen Holmes, was feeling less flip than he had been earlier. Not that he could have done anything to prevent McGill from leaving ... but he was beginning to worry.

"The cabbie hasn't responded to repeated calls from his dispatcher. So we don't know where he is, or if Holmes is still with him, or if not, where Holmes was dropped off."

"Damnit," Crogher muttered. "Did you ask about this guy? Get his story."

Strawn nodded. "The company owner gave us his name and background. Bharat Singh. From India."

"A Muslim?" Crogher asked.

"Sikh. Described as a good family man. Going to college part-time. Dependable."

"Yeah, dependable. Except we can't find him when we need to. Call Metro PD. Tell them we want this guy if he's on the street. Want him right away. But approach with caution because we don't know if—"

Crogher's cell phone rang. Someone calling to cheer him up, no doubt.

The president.

"Special Agent Crogher? My husband isn't answering his phone."

"No, ma'am. He's not in the White House."

"Do you know where he is?"

"No, ma'am. He left in a taxi approximately forty minutes ago. Destination unknown."

"Try looking for him at his office on P Street."

"Ma'am?"

"I've just heard from the CIA. They're en route."

"I'm leaving right now, ma'am," Crogher said, racing toward his car.

MCGILL LOOKED at Damon Todd, and asked simply, "Want to talk?"

His eyes had adjusted to the low light coming through his office windows. He'd had a good look at the man. His appearance was extraordinary. Capable of frightening small children or intriguing grown women. The man's *eyelid* muscles were clearly defined.

When Todd didn't respond, McGill added, "I mean, as a psychiatrist, you must have had any number of people telling you their problems. But who do you get to open up to?"

Todd laughed. "You mean, would I like to confess?"

McGill shrugged. "If that's what you feel like. You're in no legal jeopardy if you do. There's no one here but you and me. Anything I can assert you can deny."

Todd remained silent.

"Okay, let's start with something safe," McGill said. "I saw a photo of you and Chana when you were younger ..." McGill paused as he saw Todd tense. "You used to wear eyeglasses back then, but you don't now."

Todd relaxed, seeing no threat in this.

"You could be wearing contact lenses, but I don't think so. I'm betting laser surgery. LASIK. Do I have that right?"

Todd nodded.

McGill said, "Sure, because it's obvious you believe people are perfectible. Just look at you." He held up a pacifying hand as it looked like Todd might jump out of his chair. "Hey, I meant that as a compliment. I mean, all my life I've tried to stay in shape, but compared to you I look like a powdered donut."

"I work very hard," Todd said, settling back in his chair. "At everything I do."

"I respect that. So what I'd like to know is how we can talk without you getting upset. Because I'd really rather not shoot you. I've put enough holes in the plaster as it is."

"You want me to incriminate myself," Todd said. "I'm not stupid."

"Of course not. Let's talk about something else. What do you think of the president?"

Todd looked nonplussed. Then he laughed again. "You mean, your wife? I don't pay much attention to politics if you're hustling my vote."

McGill laughed, too.

"No, I was wondering what you think of her as a person. You know, someone who was a model, an actress, a philanthropist, a widow, and a president. What do you make of someone like that?"

Todd took the question seriously.

"She's obviously an exceptional person. High intelligence, formidable willpower, an effective and purposeful self-image ... aided and abetted by a very attractive appearance. Which, for a woman of her age, she must maintain by a vigorous effort."

"She swims and works out daily," McGill said.

"Commendable."

"She's not without flaws, though."

Todd was intrigued. It was always fun to learn people's weaknesses. Especially the flaws of the high-and-mighty. "Such as?" Todd asked.

"Well, there are many people who think the second time she wed, she married beneath herself."

Todd snorted. "Very ingratiating. And equally transparent."

"She's infertile," McGill added.

"A physical deficit beyond her control. Unless the condition was caused by venereal disease."

McGill shook his head.

"Then it's no one's fault, certainly not hers."

"True. But it causes her emotional insecurity."

Todd leaned forward. Not to bolt, but with real interest.

"I could help her, you know."

"I try to fill that role myself. I'm a layman, of course, but I'm devoted to her. There's pretty much nothing I wouldn't do make her feel better. I'm sure you know what I mean."

Todd sat back without offering a response.

"You feel the same way about Chana Lochlan, don't you?"

Once again Todd sat mute. But he clenched his fists.

McGill switched his gun to his left hand and opened a desk drawer with his right. From the drawer he took a stapler, a stopwatch, a box of push-pins, a coffee mug that said WORLD'S BEST DAD, a polished stone paper-weight etched with the words, "Let's rock!," and a silver cigar holder, sans cigar, that he'd been given on the occasion of Caitie's birth. He laid these items out in a row across his desktop. Todd watched carefully.

His interest grew keener when McGill put his gun into the drawer.

"Perhaps you'll feel more comfortable talking now."

Todd smiled wolfishly, a predator presented with a plate of lamb chops.

"I should point out two things," McGill said. "I didn't shoot you earlier even though I could have. And at close quarters I could kill you with any of the objects within my reach."

Todd laughed once more. He didn't believe McGill.

MAX LUCEY came out of his bathroom at A-Sharp Sound after a pro-tracted bout of abdominal spasms and diarrhea. He'd gone to dinner that night with his ex-wife, at her invitation and at her apartment, and they'd eaten Mexican. His ex, María Esperanza Ignacia Ramirez Lucey, knew her way around a Tex-Mex kitchen like nobody's business.

But that night her cooking had hit him like seven courses of ExLax.

Made him wonder if their parting had been as amicable as he'd thought.

He got back to his studio and saw the flashing light. Someone was at the front door. He poked his head out of the studio and took a look. Couldn't see anyone standing there. But the light stubbornly kept on flashing. What the hell was going on?

He went to the front door, opened it, and found Dikki Missirian lying there looking like he was dead. At that moment, Max was glad he didn't have anything left inside to lose. Then he saw McGill's Post-it note. He dragged Dikki inside, found a pulse, called 911.

That accomplished, he went his Post-It note instructions one better.

He got the .45 he kept at the back of the store and went to see if he could help Jim McGill.

MCGILL SAID, "So you think I'm no longer a threat?"

"Not to me," Todd said.

McGill chose not to debate the point at the moment.

"Then you should feel free to answer my questions," he said. "Because you can dispose of me after we talk. Right?"

Todd was still suspicious, but his ego forced him to agree.

"What do you want to know?" he asked.

"Well, the point I was getting at earlier about my wife. She's not perfect, even though she might seem that way to a lot of people. But the imperfections, at least to me, are further endearments. And seeing her overcome life's hurdles and evolve new roles for herself is very rewarding. But you don't view things that way, do you? You want to, what, machine away a person's flaws? *Manufacture* a better self. March your little creations out into a brave new world."

"Most people have a *lot* of room for improvement," Todd said. "Most of them *don't* have the inner resources or the help of a caring companion to make strides on their own. And a brave new world would surely beat the hell out of the one we have now."

McGill shrugged. "You've got a point, up to a point … but you went about proving it the wrong way."

Todd leaned forward, a beautifully defined cheek muscle twitching.

"What's that supposed to mean?"

"I think you would have done better if you'd continued to look like the academic you once were. But you met Chana, saw what she'd done with her body, the *anorexia athletica,* and something in her obsession appealed to you. A physician friend of mine told me the male counterpart is called *bigorexia.* Guys develop bodybuilder physiques and still think they're not big enough. You haven't done that exactly, but you're somewhere in the neighborhood."

Todd began to grind his teeth, and his jaw muscles bulged.

"That's why the CIA had its doubts about you. I've heard they think your work has possibilities. It's you they wonder about. Tell me, were you bullied as a kid?"

Todd leaped to his feet, but no sooner was he upright than the paperweight from McGill's desk whizzed past his head, ticking his left ear. Cracking the plaster wall behind him.

McGill said, "You'd better sit back down."

"MAN WITH a gun coming out of the ground-floor shop," Crogher's driver, Carstairs, said in a low, tense voice.

"I've got him," the SAC responded, jumping out of the car before it had stopped moving. He put his weapon on Max Lucey, who was just turning to face him. "Secret Service. Drop your weapon."

The command hadn't been loud. But it carried the tone of authority Max remembered from his days in the military. He first ceased all movement. Then he slowly placed his .45 on the sidewalk and raised his hands.

Crogher and Carstairs quickly hustled Max back into his shop. There they found Dikki's unconscious form and got Max's story, including the facts that an ambulance should be arriving soon for Dikki and that Max had been on his way upstairs to help.

Crogher quickly reached the 911 dispatch center, identified himself, said there was a possible hostage situation involving the president's husband developing. He ordered that the first ambulance, already on its way, cut its siren and flasher. The paramedics were to park a block away and bring a stretcher on foot to take away an unconscious male.

Additionally, two more ambulances were to be sent and park a block away. They were to be ready to come to McGill's P Street address at a moment's notice.

With that taken care of, Crogher turned to Max for a quick briefing on the approaches to McGill's office. He was just about to decide his next step when Carstairs interrupted.

"Sir," he said, "the CIA is here."

Daryl Cheveyo, wearing his halo brace, had entered the shop. He and Crogher looked at each other.

Both of them said, "You!"

TODD WAS back in his seat. He looked at the remaining objects on the desk in front of McGill. He hadn't even seen McGill pick up the paperweight, much less throw it at him. But the polished rock had been the most obvious weapon to use against him, and now it was out of McGill's reach. The other items available to McGill couldn't possibly be as dangerous.

Could they? He decided to think about that a while. McGill still wanted to talk.

"Aren't psychiatrists supposed to undergo their own analysis?" he asked.

"Yes," Todd answered.

"Did you?"

"Yes."

"You get as mad at your therapist as you did at me just now?"

Todd just smiled. At something only he'd ever think was funny.

When he didn't elaborate, McGill asked, "You tried to advance your ideas to academia?"

"I tried to the point where I would have been ostracized if I'd persisted further." Now, there was more than anger in Todd's voice; there was genuine hatred.

"And you knew, of course, that other men of great vision had been similarly rejected by the pedestrian thinkers of their time."

"Yes!"

"So you took your work underground. That's the part I don't understand."

"What do you mean?" Todd demanded.

McGill leaned forward. "I mean, why didn't you have the balls to say, 'Fuck all you ivy tower pinheads. I've conceived a valuable therapy. I'll prove it not in clinical trials but in the real world!'"

For the first time, Todd seemed uncertain of himself. "I ... I don't know what you mean."

"Look, you're a doctor. You've got an actual M.D. from a reputable school, right?"

"Yes."

"So you have credibility. Legitimate professional standing. Why not set up shop in, say, California? They're receptive to new ideas out there; self-improvement is the local pastime. Let me correct what I said earlier. Looking exactly the way you do right now, you'd be a sensation in Southern California. You could open a clinic in, say, Palm Springs, and you'd have all Hollywood and half of Silicon Valley breaking down your door. You could probably even wangle an exception for a new therapeutic use for ketamine hydrochloride."

McGill had taken Todd to the mountaintop and shown him the kingdoms of the world. The metaphor must have been lingering in his mind after Sweetie had covered the topic with Caitie. Unlike Jesus, though,

Todd didn't command his tempter, "Get thee hence, Satan!"

He looked positively dazzled by the possibility McGill had laid before him.

"You never thought of that?" McGill asked.

"No, I wish I'd talked to you sooner."

Then it occurred to Todd he could still have the glorious future McGill had described. Who the hell needed the CIA? He could be famous. Wealthy. Revered. All he needed to do was kill McGill and go West.

McGill read him like a book. Knew what was coming.

"Just tell me one last thing, okay?" he asked.

Todd was impatient now, but felt he owed McGill that much. "What?"

"When you spoke intimately with Chana, what did you call her?"

Todd hesitated. Revelation would be betrayal. But then Chana had betrayed him. And McGill wouldn't live to talk about Todd's perfidy.

"Gracie," he said. "Just like her father did."

"And her ex-husband, Michael Raleigh, whom you killed in Hawaii. Even after he'd divorced Chana and remarried. What was the problem there? You just couldn't stand him coming between you and her in such a meaningful way? Hell, you were even threatened that I took her on as a client, weren't you?"

Obviously, Todd was. He charged McGill. His mouth was wide in a shout of rage. McGill was ready for him. The open mouth was unexpected, but it provided a wonderful Dark Alley opportunity. He flipped open the top on the box of pushpins and flung them at Todd. Several hit Todd's face, but these were mere pinpricks. Four or five, however, went straight into his mouth. At least one lodged in the back of his throat.

Choking on a pushpin caused Todd's lunge at McGill to come up short. He landed atop McGill's desk, scattering the objects that had been placed there. McGill plucked the stapler out of the air. He hit the stapler's release button and the top half swung back. That feature made it convenient for stapling large stacks of paper. Also for swinging the office tool like a blackjack.

McGill's first blow, a backhand, took Todd squarely in the forehead, a staple lodging in a crease in the bone. Todd started to stagger back onto his feet, and McGill caught him with a forehand winner, stapling his left ear to the side of his head. Todd reeled and fell heavily onto his backside. He was down, and still gagging, but not out. He pulled his ear free from his skull and then, as McGill watched in morbid fascination, he stuck his fingers into his mouth and started pulling out pushpins. Damn guy didn't know the first thing about fighting, but he wouldn't quit.

McGill opened his desk drawer and took out his gun.

"I just went to confession," he told Todd. "You going to make me go back and tell the priest I had to kill someone? How about a little consideration here?"

Todd wasn't interested in McGill's moral dilemma. He dug the last pushpin out of his throat. He pushed himself to his feet. He smiled at McGill, bleeding gums turning his teeth red.

"Shit," McGill said.

Then, like the voice of God, Celsus Crogher commanded, "Freeze! Secret Service."

In a much more reasonable tone, another voice from the outer office added, "CIA, too, Dr. Todd."

Todd looked in the direction of the newcomers. Then back at McGill. After a moment's indecision, he muttered something under his breath. His eyes rolled back in his head, and he blacked out, falling to the floor.

No one was in a hurry to come to his aid. After a minute, Crogher sent Carstairs to fetch a bucket of water. The SAC, himself, did the honors of dousing Todd.

When his eyes opened, Todd was changed. All the fight had left him. So, too, apparently, had the persona of Damon Todd. A young boy's voice asked anxiously, "Who ... who are all of you? Where am I?"

McGill thought if the guy was that good an actor, he *really* belonged in Hollywood.

The CIA in the halo brace stepped forward, and asked, "What's your name?"

"Danny ... Danny Templeton."

"Do you know where Dr. Todd went?"

"Who? Why are all these men pointing guns at me?" Danny started to cry.

Daryl Cheveyo got Danny to lie on his stomach and allow Crogher to cuff his hands behind him. Then the SAC pulled Danny to his feet.

"What ... what are you going to do with me?" Danny asked nervously.

Cheveyo looked inquiringly at Crogher, who looked at McGill.

McGill nodded.

"He's all yours," Crogher told Cheveyo.

The CIA man said to Danny, "We're going to a place called Langley. We'll take very good care of you there."

Carstairs went with Cheveyo. Just in case.

Crogher turned to look at McGill, waiting for an admission that the mighty president's henchman had screwed up.

But all McGill had to say was, "My wife have you checking up on me again, Celsus?"

CHAPTER 38

DAMON TODD had no living relative, close friend, or colleague who could speak on his behalf. So in a closed civil commitment hearing, it was left to Dr. Daryl Cheveyo of the Central Intelligence Agency to tell Todd's story. Cheveyo related how Dr. Todd had sought to enlist in the Agency and initiate a program of crafted personalities that would be of benefit to the nation's human intelligence-gathering capabilities.

James J. McGill testified that Dr. Todd had attacked him in his office with a baseball bat, and that Dr. Todd had told him that he'd strangled the last man who'd pointed a gun at him.

Washington Metro Homicide detective Rockelle Bullard told the judge her unit had an open case in which a victim with a long record of armed robbery, one Royal McKee, recently had been found strangled to death on the campus of Georgetown University. A handgun presumed to be McKee's was found nearby. Lieutenant Bullard said she'd very much like to talk with Dr. Todd if and when he resumed his former identity.

Additionally, the judge was told, Dr. Todd was suspected of the murder of Michael Raleigh in Hawaii and complicity in the death of Congressman Aeneas Papandreou in the House of Representatives. The judge remembered seeing the famous C-SPAN tape of that incident.

A subpoena was issued to Congressman Brun Fleming to testify as to how his impromptu aria had caused Papandreou's death. But he denied knowing or ever meeting a Dr. Damon Todd. He passed a lie-detector test to that effect.

Likewise, congressional aide Nina Barkley and publicist Laurel Rembert denied knowing or ever having sexual relations with Dr. Todd. They, too, passed lie-detector tests.

Only network news reporter Chana Lochlan testified that she knew Todd. That he had hypnotized her. That he had sex with her when she was unable to exercise independent judgment or give her consent. Chana was working with a new therapist, a woman, and many painful memories were surfacing. To her credit, it was her choice to testify at the hearing.

The judge committed Danny Templeton, a.k.a. Damon Todd, to the care of Dr. Daryl Cheveyo. Reports on Todd's condition would be sent to the court quarterly. Should Dr. Todd revert to his base personality, he would be evaluated at that time to see if he should stand trial.

"In the meantime," the judge said, "Dr. Todd will get his wish. He'll join the CIA."

McGill spoke to Cheveyo before they left the courtroom.

"Todd said he'd undergone his own therapy as part of his medical training. Did you check that out? It might offer some insights."

"We thought of that. His analyst was Dr. Evelyn Patanky, the same woman, we recently found out, who helped him recover from a nervous breakdown. Unfortunately, she disappeared one night after teaching a class. Happened just after Michael Raleigh died in Hawaii."

McGill winced. Another murder.

"You think you'll get anything useful from Todd?" he asked.

"Useful to whom?"

"To the court, the CIA, the people who didn't get mentioned at this hearing."

"To the first two, yes. As to the last, who didn't get mentioned?"

"Todd's other *crafted* personalities. The ones we don't know about."

"That's a subject I definitely intend to cover," Cheveyo said.

McGill handed Cheveyo a sealed envelope.

"What's this?" he asked.

"Your instructions from the president of the United States."

The CIA man waited for the other shoe to drop.

"The court isn't the only place you'll be sending your reports. Somewhere in Todd's brain there's a get-even reminder with my name on it. I want all the warning I can get."

"I would, too," Cheveyo said.

MCGILL HAD never played matchmaker in his life. But the way Graham Keough responded—quitting his job, cashing in enough stock to live comfortably through the twenty-first century, and moving East—he thought he might have to try it again someday.

For her part, Chana Lochlan was so happy to see the first love of her life she broke down and cried in Keough's arms.

McGill had cleared the idea of the reunion with Chana's therapist, just as he had the new job he'd finagled for her with World Wide News. Chana would be producing a series of one-hour news specials for the cable network, no fewer than four per year for the next five years. In addition to an appropriate (i.e., substantial) salary, she would also be provided with a budget sufficient to cover offices, a dozen staffers, travel and production expenses. Her shows would air on Tuesday, Wednesday, or Thursday nights at 9:00 P.M. Eastern Time, 8:00 Central.

Her first show would be called *The Literature of Liberty.* Done in conjunction with the book her father Eamon Lochlan was writing.

All this was made possible after McGill had a second brief chat with Monty Kipp, Washington bureau chief for World Wide News. The topic: alleged threats made by McGill against Kipp's life.

"You think I've threatened you, Mr. Kipp? You really do? You must not know what a *real* death threat sounds like. But here's a real threat on another subject. Unless you do the right thing by Chana Lochlan and stop your whispering campaign against me, I'll sue you for slander. Among the other things that will be revealed, I want to remind you, is that you bugged your own reporter's office. How many newsies will be willing to work for your network after that?"

Kipp did the right thing by Chana and decided he wanted no further visits from the president's henchman. He repatriated himself to London.

As to the matter of McGill's fee, still unsettled, Chana insisted that McGill accept the amount that Todd had originally intended as a bribe: $20,000.

This time, McGill agreed. He had expenses to meet.

ANY CHANCE of Colonel Carina Linberg facing a court-martial died with Captain Dexter Cowan, the sole witness against her on the charge of adultery. Colonel Linberg remained steadfast in her determination to leave the military and was honorably discharged. She changed her mind about going to work for American Aviation, though.

She'd been contacted by a major New York publisher. She was going to write her life's story: the modern American woman in today's U.S. military. It would cover her career from her days at the academy to her fall from grace at the Pentagon when she faced the possibility of imprisonment for the "crime" of adultery. It was billed as a tell-all story.

"YEAH, RIGHT," Lieutenant Welborn Yates said, after Kira Fahey had read him the news item from the *Washington Post.*

"She's also going to do a speaking tour in conjunction with the release of the book, according to her publicist, Laurel Rembert," Kira said.

The two of them were in Welborn's White House office. He was packing up the few belongings he'd brought with him, waiting for reassignment to Andrews. Or the Aleutians, for all he knew. After being the president's fair-haired boy, he didn't think either his superiors or brother officers at the OSI would greet his return warmly.

Mostly, though, he was pissed at himself that his first case had gone so badly.

With Cowan dead, there was absolutely no way to determine what had really happened between the Air Force colonel and the Navy captain. Had Carina Linberg been set up on the adultery charge? Had Cowan been the patsy in a larger conspiracy involving infidelity on the part of General Altman and, for all he knew, Mrs. Altman? There were too many possibilities for him to figure out on his own.

There was no evidence as to how the right front tire on Cowan's Viper had blown. No proof of sabotage. Leo had a theory, though. Apply a belt sander to the tread. Just enough to create artificial wear. A weak spot.

Then overinflate the tire by 5-10 PSI. Crank the car up to high speed, and *boom*.

The reason Leo had suspected sabotage in the first place, he said, was that if any tire on the Viper should have blown, it should have been the *left* front tire. Given the counterclockwise motion of the bootlegger turn Cowan had made, that was the tire that took the brunt of the turn's heat and weight. But crime-scene techs from both the military and civilian authorities had been unable to confirm or deny Leo's theory. The destruction of the tire had been too complete. Pieces were still missing and would likely never be found.

Welborn felt the same way about his career.

"Are you feeling sorry for yourself?" Kira asked. "I'd never have guessed. You know, for someone with the blood of kings in his veins."

Welborn snorted. "Have you been paying attention to that crowd?"

"Good point. Well, how do you feel about us?"

"I feel great about us. I'll never stop hating you. But I am concerned about my professional prospects and my future availability. My next assignment might be investigating wing-nut pilferage on Diego Garcia."

Kira handed him an envelope. "The president asked me to give this to you."

Welborn gave her a look and neatly opened the envelope.

Lieutenant Yates,

I hope you won't think me forward but I've invited your mother to the White House next month. We had quite a nice chat today. Your mother offered me several ideas on how I might better run the government. But she thought I had it exactly right when I told her I was promoting her son to captain.

Welborn's face turned red, and he looked at Kira. "I'm being promoted? After the botch I made of things. Did you know about this?"

"If I did, I couldn't betray a confidence."

"Did you have anything to do with it?"

"Don't be silly. I can't tell the president what to do. Only your mother can."

Welborn resumed reading.

I recognize that I've put you in an awkward position with the Air Force. Tainted you politically, so to speak. But I'm sure you have the strength of character to bear up under difficult circumstances. Officially, you'll continue to be attached to the OSI and will maintain your status as a credentialed federal agent. De facto, you'll be a special investigator serving the president.

That is, as long as you are agreeable. Your promotion will be forthcoming regardless, but I do hope you will stay on and be of service to me.

Best Regards,
Patricia Darden Grant
President of the United States of America

Welborn decided he would frame the letter. Put it a place of honor where generations of Yateses yet unborn could come and stare at it. There was no way he could turn down the president's request. His mother wouldn't let him. Kira would kill him. He'd hate himself if he turned down the challenge.

The challenge. It hit him how monumental that might be.

He asked Kira, "How's the president's marriage doing?"

She looked at him incredulously and laughed.

"I haven't been consulted, but I believe it's just fine."

Okay, so he'd have James J. McGill to backstop him. Hell, who was he kidding; McGill was there to *coach* him. He felt much better. He got down on one knee and took Kira's hand.

"Ms. Fahey, if an Air Force captain makes enough to support you in the fashion to which you are accustomed, will you marry me?"

"I'm sorry, but you'll still be in Honda territory. Fortunately, I do have money of my own. And you will be making enough so I won't have to give you an allowance."

"Give me a moment to reconsider my proposal," Welborn said.

Kira yanked him to his feet, put her arms around him, and looked him in the eye.

"So soon?" she asked. "Can't we enjoy our illicit relationship a bit longer?"

"Too unseemly. We work for the president," he reminded her. "More than that, there'll be no fooling my mother once she visits."

"Because your mother knows all about illicit relationships."

"Exactly."

"Very well. I'll marry you." She kissed him. "Shall we invite the queen?"

"Talk to Mother," Welborn replied.

GENERAL WARREN Altman, widower, retired from the Air Force. Things worked out well for him, but not exactly as planned. American Aviation had to withdraw its job offer. No other defense contractor would touch him either. Word from the White House had been passed: Altman is a leper. Take him on, and your defense contracts will go to your biggest competitor.

No CEO was willing to risk that.

Even so, the general wouldn't have to squeak by on his six-figure military pension. Once it became clear that the president was shafting him, her political adversaries rode to his rescue. General Altman was hired as a military analyst by America's favorite right-wing cable network.

It was said he could hardly wait for the first time the president went to war.

MAJOR CLARENCE Seymour, General Altman's former aide, was promoted to colonel the day after Captain Dexter Cowan and his car went to pieces. There was no way to prove it, but Welborn liked him for wielding the belt sander. While that suspicion couldn't be proven before a court-martial, Welborn included his surmise in his final report to the president.

Which effectively ended Colonel Seymour's climb in rank. He would never see stars on his shoulders. A realist, he, too, resigned from the Air Force. He went home to New York City. It was only a matter of a month before he was recruited to run for the seat of a retiring member of the House of Representatives.

The chief sponsor of Seymour's new political career was none other than Senator Roger Michaelson. In Washington, political enemies were harder to kill than vampires. As often as not, they not only survived, they multiplied.

DIKKI MISSIRIAN recovered completely from his run-in with Damon

Todd. His physical injuries had been minor, and the single dose of Special K that Todd had administered to him was not enough to do any lasting damage.

McGill asked his landlord, "Did Todd get the baseball bat from your office?"

Dikki nodded, embarrassed that the madman had tried to use it against McGill.

"Did you buy it for protection?"

"No, I bought it for my son."

As far as McGill knew, Dikki didn't have any children. Then the light dawned, "Your wife is pregnant?"

"Yes. The doctor says a boy. I don't think there are any Armenian big leaguers. So I think, why not my son?"

McGill smiled.

"Siran and I intend to name him after you." Dikki also said McGill's next twelve months rent were on the house.

McGill said it would be okay to use James for the boy's middle name. He would continue to pay his own rent. But he let Dikki cover the cost of repairs for McGill's gunfire and rock throwing.

FIDEL CASTRO resurfaced the morning after the Costa Gorda Incident. He spent five hours vehemently denying that the *Marina de Guerra Revolucionaria* had anything to do with the attack on the *gusanos'* toy-soldier base in the imperialist puppet country of Costa Gorda. He'd rather have seen the worms attack Cuba so they could be smashed as their grandfathers had been at the Bay of Pigs. The whole of the event in Costa Gorda was a lie. A fabrication. A *provocation*!

Rant as he might, the attack was caught on video. The entire world had seen it.

What Castro couldn't deny was that the woman in the White House had smoked him out of hiding. Shown that he was still alive, still in charge, and as defiant as ever. Given that, any notion that Cuba might inflict genocide on itself was quickly discarded.

For her part, President Grant warned Cuba publicly to commit no further acts of war against any of its neighbors. To protect Costa Gorda, she ordered the United States Navy to guard its territorial waters. It would interdict any vessel intending to do harm there.

There were several advantages to this plan. Cuba would never be able to launch another "attack" on Costa Gorda. The Miami Cubans could keep their base, but it would be blockaded as surely as Cuba itself had been in 1963. Thus the exiles would be allowed no independent troublemaking opportunities. But they would be preserved as a threat should Castro ever truly annoy the president in the future. Finally, the Navy presence would end Costa Gorda's role as a transshipment point for drugs destined for the U.S. market, a concern of which the CIA had made the president aware as part of her daily briefing.

While Castro publicly excoriated Patricia Darden Grant, privately he admired her greatly. Forcing him out of the shadows, he had to admit, was a masterstroke. As was destroying those bastard Obregon brothers. Castro was sure that their destruction, the only deaths in the whole charade, was no accident. The president was throwing him a bone, giving him the terrorists who'd attacked his produce mart. The woman had great wiles.

At last, there was an adversary in the White House worthy of him.

MCGILL'S RECTAL polyp turned out to be benign. He promised Artemus Nicolaides he would have semiannual checkups to watch for further developments in the lower forty. He and the president took a four-day weekend on a private island in the Caribbean from which he returned to Washington no longer looking like a pale Irishman.

THE REVEREND Burke Godfrey remained immovable for months. He wouldn't acknowledge that any of his followers had anything to do with threatening the lives of children. Even the offspring of the man responsible for falsely arresting and charging with murder his beloved wife Erna, who with every passing day drew closer to an unspeakable execution.

Godfrey's denials continued even in the face of the arrest of Colm Quigley, a janitor at Saint Viviana, Abbie McGill's high school. Quigley had officially been on vacation the day Abbie found the note, but he had keys to every door in the school, including the master key that opened all the school's lockers. Moreover, Quigley's coworkers on the custodial staff told the Secret Service that the man was fiercely antiabortion, to the point where he said his own church's clerics weren't doing enough to end the abomination.

He told his colleagues that while he wouldn't renounce his own faith, he was a regular viewer of Salvation's Path, Burke Godfrey's Sunday morning television show, and sent a check to the minister every other week.

Once Quigley was brought in for questioning, he not only admitted to leaving the note, he boasted of it. But he either wouldn't or couldn't name anyone else who was threatening the McGill children.

For his part, Burke Godfrey denounced the man. Said he wasn't a member of *his* church. Hadn't been born again. And for Pete's sake, this Quigley fellow didn't even own a computer, so how could he be part of some Internet conspiracy?

As with a certain Cuban dictator, Godfrey found himself protesting in the face of TV pictures. Specifically, the picture of Caitie McGill. The idea of taking vengeance on such an innocent child outraged the American people.

Worse for Godfrey, a poll taken on whether Erna should be executed or spared came down with 72 percent in favor of capital punishment. Nobody read polls more closely than politicians, and those who had long been dear friends to the reverend began to distance themselves. As went the reverend's political support, so too did his financial backing.

The core held true, but less ardent believers tuned out. Viewership of Godfrey's TV show declined. A consultant told the minister he'd made a mistake treating Colm Quigley the way he had. His rejection of the man narrowed the public perception of who was acceptable in his eyes and, by extension, God's eyes.

You shut people out, they'd do the same to you.

Finally, Godfrey had to relent. On a beautiful fall Sunday, he mounted his pulpit, looked into the camera, and asked any misguided souls threatening the lives or the welfare of Abigail, Kenneth, and Caitlin McGill to cease. It wouldn't help Erna. It wouldn't help anyone at all. He never admitted any knowledge of or involvement with any parties who might have threatened those children.

His lawyers had been very clear with him on the need to make that point.

He did announce, that Sunday, the formation of a new group called Innocent Christians. Henceforth it would work to achieve the release of all Christians, including Catholics, from false imprisonment. Capital cases would be given priority, but those incarcerated for lesser crimes of which they were innocent would also be beneficiaries of IC's efforts.

The reverend was putting up the biggest tent he could. When reporters asked him about the falsely convicted of other faiths or no particular belief at all, he had his answer ready.

"Let them find Jesus or look for help somewhere else."

That was good enough for his friends in politics and his fringe audience.

Endorsements and money began to flow again.

AFTER GODFREY'S change of heart, the threats against the McGill children began to diminish and within a couple of weeks the few holdouts calling for blood in chat rooms were being flamed by the overwhelming majority of other cyber-believers. So reported SAC Celsus Crogher.

Which meant Abbie, Kenny, and Caitie could go to school with only their usual complement of bodyguards. Better yet, the relaxation of tension was sufficient to let them play with their friends again. A feat for which Caitie took full credit, much to her brother's annoyance.

McGill thought Sweetie should share in the credit—and even Galia, too.

He walked into her office the day after the confrontation with Godfrey, and said, "You were the one who alerted the TV stations. That's why they had their camera crews in Lafayette Square."

Galia didn't deny it.

"You inspired me," she said. "I know how you feel about your children. I can imagine how I would have felt putting one of my boys out there when he was Caitie's age. So I decided the moment was too good not to put to political use. Put Caitie's face on national TV, and it would not only help the president against her right-wing opponents, it would also get the country behind protecting your children."

"Thank you," McGill said.

Galia nodded.

The two of them passed a moment of uncomfortable silence.

"We should probably continue to keep a professional distance," she said.

"Not like each other, you mean."

"Exactly."

"No worries." McGill flipped a white index card on Galia's desk.

"What's that?"

"My recipe for focaccia," he said.

She gave him a blank look.

"You asked me for a contribution to the *First Ladies Cookbook*, remember?"

She did. The two of them smiled. Knowing their clashes would continue.

MCGILL DIDN'T make focaccia for Thanksgiving dinner, but he and Caitie worked with the White House chef in making the stuffing for the turkey. Kenny sat and watched, eating a bowl of ice cream, making sure no ingredients were left out. Abbie had remained in the residence with her mother, Lars, Sweetie, and Patti.

Carolyn and Lars, despite McGill's high anxiety, had never been in any danger.

"We pulled a fast one," Carolyn told McGill.

She'd gotten in touch with him after seeing Caitie's face on television.

"We made the reservations at the resort, but we purposely didn't keep them."

"Why did you do that?"

"Lars didn't want to travel with the gun, and I didn't know if I could legally. So, we tried to be clever. Drop clues where we were going, then stay at Lars's cousin's condo in Minneapolis. A private residence in another state. The cousin's from his mother's side, so the last name is different. Who was going to find us?"

"Not the FBI," McGill said. "Did you have a good time?"

"Great. Until I saw our daughter on TV in the midst of a hostile crowd."

"It worked out pretty well. And I'd tried to reach you. I worried, too."

They decided all was well that ended well. No harm, no foul.

And now the whole family was together for Thanksgiving at the White House.

Which went splendidly until Blessing appeared at McGill's side.

"I'm sorry to interrupt, sir, but SAC Crogher would like a word. He says it's urgent."

"He wants to see me, not the president?"

Patti, seated at the opposite end of the table, was aware something was up.

The others were engaged in family reminiscing.

"Yes, sir. He asked to speak with you."

"Thank you, Blessing."

When McGill stood up, everyone noticed, and conversations stopped.

"I'll be right back," he said with a smile. "Have to see a man about a dog."

Patti picked up the conversational baton as he left the room. Blessing had left Crogher in McGill's Hideaway. When McGill entered the room, he saw the SAC standing in front of the fireplace, staring reflectively at the flames. Hardly what he'd expect from Crogher.

"Celsus," McGill said.

Crogher looked at him.

"Is it about my children?" McGill said. "More threats?"

"No, sir. We believe the children are safe. This time it's you."

"Me?"

"Started at the beginning of the week. A little chatter on some of the more extreme sites at first. Then it picked up steam, became widespread. Gist is, kids aren't fair game. But you are. You should have been the target in the first place. Just like Andy Grant was."

McGill stared at the flames a moment himself.

Looking back at Crogher, he asked, "How serious do you think it is?"

McGill thought he saw tears in Crogher's eyes, and that scared him.

"We think it's very serious. Tonight, outside his mother's home in suburban Virginia, Special Agent Donald "Deke" Ky was shot by a sniper."

NOW AVAILABLE FROM VARIANCE

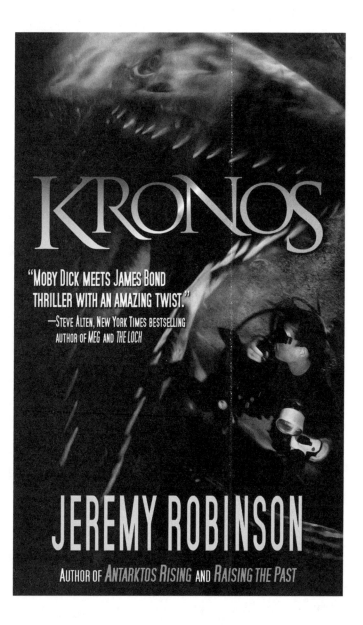

KRONOS is the next amazing thriller from Jeremy Robinson, one of the most fast paced and original thriller authors. Kronos will have readers on the edge of their seat and then knock them out of it with a twist that is impossible to see coming.

"JEREMY ROBINSON IS AN ORIGINAL AND EXCITING VOICE."
-- STEVE BERRY, NEW YORK TIMES BESTSELLING AUTHOR OF THE VENETIAN BETRAYAL AND THE CHARLEMAGNE PURSUIT

NOW AVAILABLE FROM VARIANCE

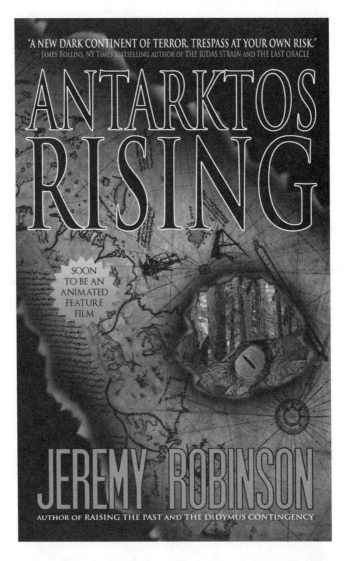

"ROBINSON OPENS A NEW DARK CONTINENT OF TERROR. TRESPASS AT YOUR OWN RISK." —JAMES ROLLINS, NEW YORK TIMES BESTSELLING AUTHOR OF BLACK ORDER AND THE JUDAS STRAIN

"AN AWESOME JOURNEY INTO THE BEATING HEART OF A LEGEND. JULES VERNE WOULD BE PROUD." —STEL PAVLOU, BESTSELLING AUTHOR OF DECIPHER AND GENE

NOW AVAILABLE FROM VARIANCE

"One of my favorite authors, A.J. Tata is the new Tom Clancy. Only someone who has actually operated in the deadly netherworld of international military intrigue could write a book this gripping. Sudden Threat is electrifying."—**BRAD THOR, #1 new york times bestselling author of THE LAST PATRIOT**

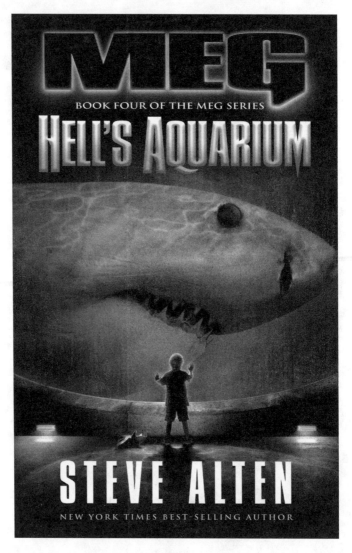